THE KHORASAN RETRIBUTION

JEFFREY JAMES HIGGINS

SEVERN RIVER
PUBLISHING

Severn River Publishing
www.SevernRiverBooks.com

ISBN: 978-1-64875-644-3 (Paperback)

ALSO BY JEFFREY JAMES HIGGINS

The Nathan Burke Thrillers

The Havana Syndrome

The Khorasan Retribution

The China Gambit

To find out more, visit

severnriverbooks.com

For Cynthia, my habibti.

I'd like to dedicate this book to the Coalition members who fought and died in Afghanistan and to the tens of thousands of Afghan allies the United States abandoned during the most disastrous and shameful military withdrawal in American history.

1

2021: Kabul, Afghanistan

Jet engines roared as the C-130 Hercules climbed above Kabul International Airport, and as the aircraft rose into the predawn darkness, my stomach sank—sick with loss, fear, and betrayal. The Americans were gone, and they'd taken my dreams of freedom with them.

I stood in Massoud Circle among a throng of my desperate countrymen and watched the vanishing aircraft. Who was I now that everything I'd hoped to achieve had disappeared along with the Americans who'd sworn to protect me? My dream of a free Afghanistan had melted away in the summer sun. All our work and sacrifice had resulted in . . . nothing.

My daughter, Tara, pulled at the cotton sleeve of my cotton parahan and looked up with deep brown eyes filled with innocence. "What will we do now, Daddy?"

"Do not speak in English outside our home. Not anymore."

"What will happen to us? To momma?"

I should lie to her. I should tell her Afghanistan was back in Afghan hands, though that wasn't really true. Pakistan's Inter-Services Intelligence Directorate pulled the strings and made the Taliban dance like a Buz-Baz marionette. ISIS-K was more stubborn, but they had their foreign masters too. I could say I'd find a new job now that the American Embassy had been abandoned. I wanted to promise her many things, but none of them would be true. The future for those of us who had worked for Americans was dismal, if it existed at all.

I gazed into her trusting eyes and couldn't muster the fortitude to prevaricate tales to placate her fears. Not after all the broken promises, the ambitions and ideals that had just disappeared into the clouds.

"Daddy?"

"We will die, Tara. All of us will die."

2

Terrorists spread like a virus, multiplying in the dark, and when snuffed out, a new strain emerged—but unlike contagion, their novel incarnations were deadlier.

FBI Agent Nathan Burke cradled his cellphone between his cheek and shoulder as he raced out of Washington, DC, and onto the Fourteenth Street Bridge that spanned the Potomac River. His Mustang's 310-horsepower engine growled as he weaved through thickening afternoon traffic. He drove his personal car, because he'd intended to pick up his eight-year-old-daughter, Amelia, from school. That plan had changed.

"How certain are you about this shipment?" he asked.

"Intel is good," Kei Choi said. "This comes from my cousin in Shanghai."

"You call all your Chinese sources *cousins.*"

"He say it coming. It coming."

Kei's information had always been accurate. Over a year ago, he'd agreed to work with Nathan to avoid a gun charge, but he'd trusted Nathan with his life during the Havana Syndrome investigation, and they'd formed a level of trust. Nathan had kept his word and had the charges against Kei dropped. Now, Kei worked for the hope of a big payday from a federal reward for services rendered.

"He's sure it arrives tonight?" Nathan asked.

"Soon."

Shit. Nathan needed to contact Bridget Quinn, his new partner in the FBI's Afghanistan-Pakistan extremism group, and establish surveillance on the Al-Sahaba Mosque, a center of radical Islamic ideology in Arlington, Virginia.

"He explain why Islamists are buying fentanyl?" Nathan asked.

"That's your job to find out, Boss Man. I just give information."

"It's not prohibited in Islam if it furthers jihad, but religious leaders frown on drug trafficking, so why is China selling to the Islamic State?"

"He's not sure they're ISIS, and ISIS buys from cartels, not China."

"And China supplies the Mexican cartels." Nathan crossed the Potomac and entered Virginia. He drove eastbound on the Richmond Highway.

"When do we hunt the Chinese officials behind Havana Syndrome?" Kei asked.

"We don't know who's behind that."

"The Chinese Directorate of Intelligence."

"I thought you were afraid of targeting them," Nathan said.

"That change when I sign as your source. You said it yourself. I'm tied to you now. Chinese proverb say, 'We help each other in the same boat and move forward hand in hand.' I might as well earn big dollars."

"Rewards aren't guaranteed. They depend on results, and even then, I can only request them. I can't promise you'll get anything."

"We catch big target, Uncle Sam will pay. Let's find those bad eggs."

"It's not just China behind Havana Syndrome," Nathan said. "It's the Russians too. They've been attacking Americans with high-energy weapons since the 1970s, and after what happened with the CIA, who knows who else is doing it?"

"I have a cousin in Beijing who can help us."

"Not over the phone. As much as I want to track down people targeting our diplomats, I'm tied up finishing my Islamic terrorism cases."

"Your FBI director love you. You ask for transfer, he give it."

"It doesn't work that way, and that operation of the airport broke loose a lot of chatter and created leads. I need to strike now. Besides, I know more about al-Qaeda and ISIS in DC than anyone in my unit. They need me."

"Whatever, Boss Man. You chase jihadists, and I'll be ready when you are."

"Find out who produced the fentanyl and why it's coming to a mosque, and I'll try to seize it."

"Don't get killed. I need you to earn my moola."

Nathan disconnected and called Bridget at her desk. Bridget had only been his partner for a few weeks and was thus untested. It took time for partners to develop trust, not that the FBI had partners in the traditional sense, like Nathan had when he'd been a detective. Supervisory Special Agent Rahimya Nawaz had assigned Bridget as his co-case agent on the airport missile case and asked Nathan to mentor her, so he'd be working with Bridget on the half dozen other cases he had simmering.

"Where'd you *scampah* off?" Bridget asked in a thick Boston accent.

"I was headed to pick up Amelia from school, and one of our CIs called. Something's going down."

"No shit? When? What's happening?" She fired her words like bullets from a machine gun.

"A large fentanyl shipment arrived in the Port of Baltimore, and it's headed to Arlington."

"Drugs?" Her tone dripped with disappointment.

"Our source's guy thinks it headed to an Islamist cell, maybe ISIS."

"Still, it's not our gig to seize drugs. Why don't we pass this shit off to DEA or the Arlington PD."

Her profanity always shocked him, but she'd grown up the only girl in a house with her widowed father and three brothers, all of them Boston cops, so she'd never modeled refined behavior.

"Radical Islamists purchasing kilos of opioids makes it our business. They might be funding operations. I saw a lot of that in Afghanistan, but even if they're trafficking narcotics to stockpile money, it's an opportunity to lock them up and maybe flip someone. Title 21 attaches heavy minimum mandatory sentences to opioids."

Bridget sighed. "I transferred from fraud to fight jihadist assholes, not chase drug *pushahs*."

"This is how we do that. The shipment's connected to the Al-Sahaba Mosque on Washington Boulevard in Arlington."

"They're slinging kilos out of a mosque?"

"The intel's sketchy, but the buyer's associated with the mosque. They may deliver the fentanyl elsewhere, but the mosque is the only location we've got."

"I'll rally the group and head out."

"Don't sound the alarm until we have more. I tasked our CI to get more, but for now, let's set up surveillance and see what develops."

"Be there in thirty."

"I'm close now. I'll establish the eye and wait for you. Hit me on channel three when you're close."

"I'll step on it."

Nathan drove through the Clarendon-Courthouse neighborhood and passed the intersection where Washington, Clarendon, and Wilson boulevards converged. He continued west on Wilson into the Ballston-Virginia Square neighborhood and slowed in an area between concentrations of restaurants and shops.

The Al-Shaba Mosque sat thirty yards off the boulevard on a grassy lot. A gold dome topped the box-store-sized building, and two minarets rose on either side. Across the street, a six-story building housed residential apartments and commercial space at street level.

Nathan continued past the mosque, then squared the block and parked on North Monroe Street behind a station wagon. He shut off his car and pretended to check his phone while he surreptitiously scanning the area. A mixture of commercial, residential, retail, and college-owned buildings lined the street. A cool wind pelted pedestrians on the sidewalk. Nathan slipped his handheld radio out of his leather messenger bag and clicked it on. He kept the volume low and shoved it between the seat and the center console. He pulled out a manilla folder and covered the radio in case a passerby peeked inside.

The Al-Sahaba Mosque's front door was visible between vehicles that flashed past on Wilson Boulevard. The late November sun hung low, and the mosque's gold dome glowed as if God shined upon it. Only four cars were parked in a dozen spots, and the lot wrapped around the building, offering more parking in back. The building's doors were closed, but certainly not locked. Muslims prayed five times a day, and some mosques offered additional services. The mosque offered *Salat al-'Asr* in the late afternoon.

Nathan checked his watch—3:02 p.m. He had time before the next prayer service began, and it wouldn't be well attended on weekdays.

Amelia's last class ended shortly, but she could take the school bus home. Luckily, she didn't have softball practice until tomorrow. He should call and let her know. Students weren't supposed to have their phones turned on in class, but he dialed anyhow.

"Hi, Dad," she whispered.

"I'm staying late for work," Nathan said. "Something came up."

"An emergency?" A trace of fear seeped into her voice.

"Not an emergency, but it's time sensitive."

"Is it dangerous?"

What concerned her? She never asked questions like that.

"No, honey. Just routine, but I can't pick you up from school. Can you take the bus home?"

"I'll get a ride with Maria. She's been asking me to come over."

Nathan's trapezius muscles relaxed. Maria Hernandez was the daughter of Senator Gabriela Hernandez, a member of the Select Committee on Intelligence. The senator had received numerous death threats after her controversial stands defending the administration's foreign policy, and she used campaign funds for her private security. That meant Amelia would be escorted by security professionals.

"Send me a text to confirm that's okay with her mom, and I'll pick you up at their condo."

"She won't mind."

"Confirm it."

"Okay, Da-ad." She elongated his name, and he pictured her rolling her eyes. Amelia had been asserting herself more, a sign the teenage-rebellion years approached. Arguing with her annoyed him, but his job as a parent was to teach her independence. He repeated that like a mantra when she became stubborn—a trait she'd inherited from him.

"Love you," he said.

"Me too."

"Call me back."

She hung up, and he sighed. Traffic buzzed by, obscuring his view of the mosque's front door. This surveillance had almost no chance of success. Kei's intelligence was always sound, but just because an Islamist affiliated with the mosque planned to receive a shipment of kilos didn't mean he'd take delivery there. That's what Kei's source had said, but it seemed unlikely.

Even if a car pulled up and guys started unloading boxes, it would be hard to take action on private property. And if the packages made it inside, it would be impossible to seize them. Single-sourced intel without corroboration wasn't enough for a search warrant, and even if Nathan had more, reaching the threshold a judge would require to approve the search of a mosque would prove difficult. Violating the sanctity of a religious institution should be hard, but the bad guys knew this too, and some mosques had been used to stage weapons, planning materials, and other illicit goods. If Nathan saw something suspicious, he'd need to do something before it entered the mosque.

Almost on cue, a white-paneled box struck slowed as it approached the mosque. Its brakes squeaked, and it put on its blinker. Why would a cargo truck stop at a mosque? Damn Kei for not asking more questions from his source.

This was it, and Nathan was alone.

3

Nathan dragged his radio into his lap.

"Oh-Nine, Oh-Two," he transmitted. His heart ached every time he said Eddie's old call sign. The poor kid had died because Nathan hadn't trained him well enough. Nathan had filled Eddie with the desire to do whatever was right, but he hadn't imparted the survival skills Eddie needed to go off script. Nathan would never get over his grief.

Or his guilt.

"Oh-Nine," Bridget responded.

"You close?"

"Seven out."

The box truck turned into the mosque's lot. Nathan scanned the street, his eyes moving from vehicles to vehicle, darting to movement. His hypervigilance was justified before an enforcement action, but he never stopped being on guard. Not since the incidents surrounding Havana Syndrome. China had backed off, and Russia too, and there hadn't been another attack, yet Nathan could feel their crosshairs on him. The tension reminded him of being in combat.

"I've got a white cargo truck on the east side of the target location. Maryland tag, Juliet, six, six—"

Traffic blocked his view.

"It's turning into the back lot, out of view."

"I'm frickin' flying."

He should tell her not to rush and risk an accident, but instinct put his senses on alert. Kei's information, even if he hadn't met the sub-source, combined with an unmarked delivery truck arriving at the stated destination was too much to be coincidence.

The truck disappeared around the back.

Nathan watched the mosque. The road to the west may give him a view of the back parking lot but may not provide access. If the truck unloaded, he'd wouldn't have time to react.

"Shit."

Mosques were protected sites, and he possessed little probable cause. The risks far outweighed the potential reward, and if he stepped over the line, they'd lose whatever case they had. He didn't have enough for a warrant, but he could articulate reasonable suspicion. The question was, what should they do?

He started his Mustang and pulled up to the intersection. He waited for traffic to pass, then zipped across the boulevard into the side lot. The mosque offered public access, so technically, he wasn't violating property rights, though things would look bad if he pushed it.

He rolled past the mosque and eased around back into the rear lot, which held another fifty parking spaces, but only four other cars occupied spaces. The truck had stopped beside the mosque's steel back door.

Nathan pulled into the last parking space on the side of the building. Through his rearview mirror, he had a partial view of the truck. Its engine idled, and the driver hadn't had time to exit and enter the mosque.

"Oh-Two, Oh-Nine," Bridget broadcast. "Two minutes out."

"Truck's out back. I can't see the driver, but I think he's inside. Waiting."

"Good copy."

The driver's door swung open, and a heavyset Arabic man lumbered out. He stretched his back, then looked around the lot. His gaze lingered on each car in the back. Why so paranoid?

Anticipation tickled Nathan's core. These guys carried the fentanyl. The information had to be accurate.

The driver walked to the rear of the box truck and unlocked the padlock.

"Oh-Two, Oh-Nine, I'm close. Where you want me?"

He could have her set up on the street to take away the truck when it left. Maybe they could have a local cop stop it on the pretext of a traffic violation and identify the driver. But that would be too late to interdict the drugs.

"Enter the lot and park beside me, but don't go in back. Your Ford looks like a Bu-ride from a mile away."

"'Cause it is. It's the frickin' whip they issued me."

The truck driver rolled up the trailer door. Stacks of cardboard boxes filled the cargo space. The rear door of the mosque flung open, and a thin man wearing wire-framed glasses came out. He had a ring of gray hair beneath his exposed scalp—a cummerbund of male pattern baldness. He glanced around too, forcing Nathan to slouch in his seat.

Wire Glasses spoke with the fat guy, then the truck's passenger door opened, and a muscular guy wearing Ray-Bans and blue jeans jumped out.

Bridget's Chevrolet Malibu entered the lot, and she drove past the mosque and parked two spots away.

They didn't have enough to arrest anyone or search the truck, but nothing would stop him from asking for consent. The lot was open to the public, and intelligence suggested he'd witnessed a felony. He could approach the guys and talk to them. No one at the FBI would fault him for that.

Yeah, right.

Wire Glasses walked back into the mosque, and the two guys who'd arrived in the truck climbed into the back. Nathan had to do something before the contents of that truck disappeared inside.

He had to act.

4

The chunky driver climbed back out of the truck and stood beside the tailgate while the younger, muscular guy retrieved a cardboard box from inside. The box didn't appear heavy, but the guy looked strong. Were Nathan's instincts wrong? The mosque's backdoor remained closed.

Nathan keyed his mike. "Let's talk to them."

Bridget's silhouette showed through her tinted windows across the mosque's parking lot. She made no move to exit. "You want to chat 'em up?" Incredulity dripped from her voice.

"Affirmative."

"And ask if they're pushing dope?"

"Once they move those packages inside, we'll never see them."

"How about we stake out these pricks and snatch them delivering?"

"We'd need to be here twenty-four hours per day, and we don't have the resources. Even if we did, we'd have even less probable cause to stop and search someone coming out."

"We could tail them away and identify their customers."

The young guy moved another package onto the tailgate. Nathan tensed. They were running out of time. "This isn't a gang selling user amounts on the street. They're moving kilos at the wholesale level. If we saw someone leave and we followed them, they'd disappear inside another building."

"Your plan sucks."

"Our strongest reasonable suspicion to talk to them is right now."

"And then what?"

"Ask for consent to search."

"They'll never give it up, and they'll know we're onto them."

"It's our best play."

Nathan cracked open his door and slipped out. He headed toward the truck as the muscular man wearing Ray-Bans lowered a box to Chubby.

A car door slammed behind him, and he turned. Bridget stood outside her car and looked over the roof at him. For all her intelligence and desire to hunt jihadists, her lack of field experience would make confronting bad guys challenging.

He waved her over then turned to the truck.

Both men stopped and watched him. The driver narrowed his eyes, and their frozen bodies told the tale. Innocent people didn't act like that.

Nathan had to prevent them from reaching the mosque. Asking for consent to search now lay within the bounds of legality, but entering the structure would strain their legal authority.

He couldn't wait for Bridget.

Nathan strode toward the fat man. Ray-Bans waited motionless on the tailgate.

"Good afternoon," Nathan said.

No response.

"I need to speak to you," Nathan said. He reached into his blazer and slipped out his credentials case. He flipped it open and displayed his FBI identification card but kept his badge concealed behind its protective cloth. Flashing a gold badge influenced people, and while he should assert his authority, consent was easier to obtain without overt pressure. Most people gave consent when they weren't required to, because they thought refusing would make them look guiltier. If Nathan intimidated them, they'd become defensive, and a court could later determine he'd coerced the search, meaning the fruits of it would be inadmissible in court. He'd achieve more with politeness and let the threat go unstated.

The heavyset guy shifted the weight of the box in his arms and widened his stance—aggressive body language.

Nathan stopped six feet away, just out of reach. "Agent Burke, FBI. Are you employed by the mosque?"

"What do you want?" the driver asked in a Middle Eastern accent Nathan couldn't place.

"Do you work here?"

"No."

"Where are you delivering from?"

"Are we breaking the law?" the driver asked.

"What's in the boxes?"

Ray-Bans laid his hands flat on the tailgate and vaulted onto the pavement. For a guy his size, he moved like a gymnast.

Nathan tensed.

"We are delivering for Imam Kareem Qadir."

"Delivering what?"

"Supplies."

"What kind of supplies?"

Ray-Bans moved beside the driver with clenched hands and a scowl. Both men emitted nonverbal, pre-violence behavior. Would they escalate the contact when he was just asking questions? All they had to do was refuse to cooperate.

Bridget moved into Nathan's peripheral vision, with her pantsuit jacket flapping. He hoped she wouldn't come across too strongly. She stayed silent.

"I haven't seen your truck here before," Nathan said. It wasn't a lie, since he'd never been to a mosque.

"We're doing nothing wrong," the driver said.

"I didn't say you were," Nathan said. "Why won't you tell me what you're delivering?"

The man shifted his feet. "I told you. Supplies."

This wasn't going well. "Want to open the box?" The way he phrased it skirted the line between question and command, but it should hold up in court.

"Why?"

"Why don't you want to show me? Is there something in there you don't want me to see?"

The driver set his jaw, and tension radiated off Ray-Bans like heat.

"You're just delivering boxes, right?" Nathan asked. "Do you even know what's inside?" He gave them an out, a perceived defense. If they hadn't opened the boxes, how responsible would they be for the contents? The answer was "very," but they might not understand that.

Bridget cleared her throat. "Let's see some ID."

Shit. Requesting a consensual search was a verbal dance, and the minute they refused or requested an attorney, the music stopped.

The driver flashed a look at the passenger and nodded at the truck. Ray-Bans headed toward the cab. Letting a suspect out of our sight would be a tactical mistake, especially into an uncleared vehicle, but restricting his movement would nudge us into a custodian detention, which could invalidate consent.

"Neither of you is in trouble," Nathan said. "I'm only interested in the boxes."

The passenger paused then continued to the truck.

Nuts.

"Help him out," Nathan told Bridget.

She cocked her head.

"Let's not hold them up," Nathan said. "Go look at their IDs while this gentleman shows me the cargo." He balanced on a legal tightrope.

Bridget hesitated, then she followed Ray-Bans around the passenger side of the truck and out of sight.

"Will you open it?" I asked.

The driver frowned.

"I only need to confirm what you're delivering."

The driver bent and set the box on the pavement between them. He moved rigidly.

"What are you doing in there?" Bridget said, her voice apprehensive.

Nathan looked from the driver to the box. He was so close to a legal search, but Bridget sounded like she was losing control.

He sidestepped around the box and leaned around the truck. Bridget stood outside, looking into the cab where Ray-Bans had entered.

"Hey, what is that?" Bridget shouted.

Nathan glanced at the driver. Something flashed in the man's eyes. The driver smiled—then bolted.

"He's running," Nathan yelled. He turned to run after him.

"Gun," Bridget shouted.

Nathan stopped and looked back.

Bridget raced toward him as the passenger leaned out of the cab holding an AR-15.

5

2021: Torkham, Afghanistan

I scrunched in the bed of the jingle truck and hugged Farzan and Tara against me as the tractor trailer yawed and pitched along the Jalalabad-Torkham Road. I braced my feet against the driver's seat and prayed the feeling would return to my toes when we disembarked in Torkham. Breaking free of Taliban-controlled Afghanistan by fleeing to Pakistan was our only hope.

Allah had created Afghanistan as a mountain fortress, practically impenetrable from outside, and a prison to those trying to escape. Turkmenistan, Uzbekistan, and Tajikistan lay to the north, separated by mountains, rivers, and armed border police. Iran bordered the west, and Pakistan, the east and south. A sliver of China abutted Afghanistan's Badakhshan Province in the northeast—the most impassable terrain. The only chance for me and my family lay beyond the Nangarhar Province in the east where the Khyber Pass led into Pakistan's Federally Administered Tribal Areas.

"Are we riding this truck all the way to Pakistan?" Tara asked.

I gazed into her young eyes that had filled with wonder. To her, this was an adventure, a break from the smog of Kabul and an excursion to an exciting new land. That was my fault, because I'd minimized the danger and the reasons we couldn't stay in the capital. The poor girl had been terrified by my initial reaction to the American withdrawal, and since then, I'd tried to conceal my fear.

"We must pass customs," I said. "And if they allow us through, we will continue to the capital."

The truck driver looked in the mirror, and I met his eyes. He was a friend of my cousin Ibrahim, and he'd worked for British contractors, which meant he wanted to escape Afghanistan too. Everyone with Western connections feared reprisals.

Islamists controlled the FATA too, but the trip by bus to Islamabad would only take four or five hours. If we made it past the Afghan Border Police, or whatever the Taliban had replaced them with, we'd be forced to deal with the Pakistan Frontier Corps and who knew what Islamists or bandits preyed on the highway through the Khyber Agency and out of the FATA?

But I had no choice. I had to save my wife and daughter.

"What if they stop us?" Farzana asked.

"Then we will get out and take a bus or a taxi."

"They're letting taxis leave?"

"Perhaps."

"We don't have visas," she said.

"I have rupees."

"What if they won't accept—"

"I don't know."

Farzana glanced at Tara and said nothing.

Hills leading to the Spīn Ghar Mountains rose beside the road, and machine-gun nests, once occupied by Afghan Border Police, now sat empty. Hope rose in my chest as we neared the gate.

Then traffic slowed.

We stopped behind a long line of buses, sedans, and trucks. Three men in filthy clothes clung to the rear bumper of another jingle truck, their bodies covered in dust. We weren't the only desperate Afghans aching to escape the Taliban's impending brutality.

Armed men, from the Taliban or ISIS, or some other radical group, lined the sides of the road in groups of two or three. Hard men carrying AK-

47s made their way down the row of vehicles, stopping at each to speak with the drivers and check passports. Those we had—only Farzana's and Tara's weren't stamped with visas.

My heart thumped.

The Bab-e-Khyber gate guarded the entrance to Pakistan's Khyber Pakhtunkhwa Province. And freedom. Or torture and death, depending on what happened once we passed under the brick structure and entered the FATA.

If we made it that far.

Four rough Islamists sporting bushy beards and leather faces stopped at the truck in front of us and interrogated the driver. Two more headed for our truck. Our driver rolled down his window.

Thump, thump, thump.

My breath came faster. I put my hand on Farzana's.

The taller of the two slung his Kalashnikov over his shoulder and climbed onto the truck's running board. He poked his head inside, and the odor of garlic filled the cabin.

Farzana squeezed my hand, and I willed her and Tara to stay quiet.

"Where are you going?" the driver asked in Pashto.

"Islamabad."

"What do you carry?"

"Fruit and melons."

"Who is your father?"

Such an Afghan question. All society rooted in tribal, clan, and familial connections, but that couldn't be a standard customs question. These jihadists had probably been fighting in the mountains before being plucked out to control the border. The surrender of Afghanistan had happened in the blink of an eye.

"Haji Ahmed Zai, from Achin."

"Passport."

The driver handed the man his passport, along with a stack of papers that included the bill of lading, inventory, and consignment papers. Afghanistan's poverty did not lessen its bureaucratic red tape. Quite the opposite.

The man leaned farther inside and glared at me.

"Who are you?"

Our passports were authentic, so I couldn't use an alias. I handed him the three booklets and awaited our fate.

He skimmed through them and then flashed a yellow, toothy sneer. "Where are your visas?"

He knew enough to ask that.

"Here's is mine," I said, pointing to my booklet. The US Embassy had arranged a Pakistan visa for me months ago to courier papers, but the withdrawal had canceled those plans.

He looked at it with disdain. "And for your women?"

"We were told to get them in Pakistan," I lied.

"You are leaving without permission?"

"I've traveled many times. My family's documents are waiting in Islamabad. We just need to go to the embassy and—"

"Liar."

"No, please. It's my family. Let me—"

"Get out of the truck," he said, the hint of civility gone.

"I can pay for our visas now." I dug into my pocket and handed him a stack of twenty thousand rupees. I had most of our money taped to my stomach, but I offered him a yearly salary in Afghanistan. He would either take it and let us pass or he wouldn't.

The moment of truth.

The man peeked at his compatriots, then stuffed the wad of money inside his shirt. I welled with hope. We would escape.

"Out," he said.

"But you took my money. Let us—"

He grabbed the collar of my parahan and yanked me over the seat. Farzana screamed, and Tara cried.

The other door opened, and the man's partner appeared. I climbed over the seat, because struggling with the Taliban never ended well. They pulled me from the vehicle, and I stumbled off the step onto the pavement.

The first kick into my stomach snatched my breath away. They fell on me like jackals, punching and kicking. My vision clouded with a red haze.

Everything went dark.

6

Ray-Bans emerged from the cab as if in slow motion. He raised the black muzzle of his AR-15 and pointed it at Bridget's back like the finger of death.

Electricity fired Nathan's synapses, heightening his senses, and the fight-or-flight response tingled his nerves and threatened to freeze him with panic, but years of training kept him in control. The primal hunter inside him hungered for a kill. This was what he had trained to do.

Nathan brushed his jacked back with a practiced motion, born from hundreds of hours on the range. He jammed his palm onto his Glock's grip as his thumb unsnapped the leather retention in a single motion.

He drew.

The man leaned over the carbine instead of bringing the sights up to his eyes—a sign of an amateur.

Time slowed, as if Nathan had hit a pause button and advanced the action one frame at a time. He punched out this Glock and met it with his support hand. His fingers melded together as he extended the weapon. His elbows locked, and he squeezed his shoulders together to solidify his stance. His body reacted seamlessly with the economy of movement ingrained into muscle memory.

The barrel of the AR-15 tracked Bridget as she fled.

Nathan's finger dropped to the trigger, and he took up the slack. First to shoot would win.

He fired.

The Glock bucked in his hand, but his sights snapped back on target. He double-tapped into the passenger's chest. Center mass.

Ray-Bans twisted and slammed back against the dashboard as he fired. His round went high, shattering the air above Nathan.

Nathan double-tapped again, then raised his sights and took a breath. He fired a single round into the man's face.

Ray-Bans dropped the carbine and collapsed against the door, crouched like a swimmer about to explode out of the blocks, but he didn't move. And he never would.

His brains coated the windshield behind him.

The echoes of the shots deadened Nathan's hearing. He kept his aim on the passenger but glanced at Bridget.

She crouched halfway between him and Ray-Bans. She gawked at the man who'd tried to kill her. She straightened and turned back to Nathan.

"Heads up," Bridget screamed.

She pointed her Glock at Nathan's head, and a flash of adrenaline jolted him. Flame exploded out of her barrel, and the round cracked as it broke the sound barrier.

Nathan ducked and swiveled. The driver stood twenty yards away, pointing a chrome-plate revolver at him. Nathan raised his Glock as Bridget fired again, three times in quick succession. The overpressure from the rounds passing close tingled his cheek.

The driver dropped his gun and grabbed his chest with both hands. He staggered back then collapsed.

The acrid odor of propellant tinged the air, and Nathan's unprotected ears rang from the gunfire.

"Hold fire," he said. "Moving."

He stayed in a crouch, worried Bridget would shoot again, and shuffled across the parking lot. He kept his Glock aimed at the driver, who lay crumpled on the asphalt in a pool of blood.

Nathan kept both eyes open and scanned the lot. No one else was outside except Bridget, who stood near the back door. Her handgun hung at her side, and she stared wide-eyed at Ray-Bans.

"He's dead," Nathan said. "Watch the mosque. There's at least one guy inside."

She looked at him as if she didn't understand English.

"Cover the exit," Nathan shouted.

Bridget nodded and backed against the truck where she could see the door and lot.

Nathan reached the driver, whose hands were trapped under his body. Not seeing a suspect's hands had killed many law enforcement officers over the ages. He should summon Bridget, but the uncleared mosque was a threat. God knew what hornet's nest they'd kicked over.

Nathan moved to the driver's head. He pressed the sole of his shoe against the man's shoulder and pushed.

The driver flopped over with a spray of blood. His eyes remained open and unblinking, and the color had drained from his lifeless face.

Dead.

Nathan should handcuff him, but he only carried one set, and the mosque could be filled with armed bad guys. They needed help, and fast.

"He's dead," Nathan said.

"Passenger's gone too."

"Keep your eyes open. I'm calling it in."

Nathan scanned both lots, then focused on the rear door. No one came out. Traffic whizzed past on Wilson Boulevard. A bird chirped. Leaves rusted in the trees. Life went on, the scene behind the mosque unnoticed, as if two men hadn't just had their lives violently ripped away.

Nathan called 911.

"Nathan Burke, FBI. I have shots fired and two suspects down outside the Al-Sahaba Mosque on Wilson Boulevard."

"Copy shots fired at Al-Sahaba. Are the suspects still shooting?" the operator asked.

"Both are deceased. I need backup to clear the mosque."

"Are you armed?"

"Myself and Agent Quinn. We're in civilian clothes, so tell your officers not to shoot."

"The call is already out, sir. When they arrive, don't have your guns out and follow their commands."

"We're covering the mosque. Please contact the FBI Washington Division and notify Supervisory Special Agent Rahimya Nawaz."

"Yes, sir. Stay on the line until the officers arrive on site."

"No can do. This is an active crime scene."

"Sir, I need—"

Nathan disconnected. He slowly approached Bridget, not wanting to startle her.

"You good?" he asked.

"What the fuck just happened?"

"Take a breath and stay in the game. We don't know what's inside."

Nathan moved around her to the truck's open door. The passenger's body hung out of the cab by his arm, which had caught between the door and the frame. His elbow bent at an unnatural angle. His once-muscular body seemed smaller now that his muscles lost rigidity. Or maybe he'd seemed bigger holding an AR-15.

Something moved in Nathan's peripheral vision, and he turned as the back door to the mosque swung open. The thin, balding man with the wire glasses stepped out.

Nathan pointed his gun at him.

"Hands," Bridget yelled. "Show me your frickin' hands."

The man glanced at her then glared at Nathan. "What have you done?"

"Get on the ground," Nathan said.

"You've violated the sanctity of our mosque."

A siren blared in the distance.

"Down, now," Nathan said.

The man slapped the door closed.

"Get away from the building," Nathan said.

The man sneered. "You have no power here."

"Cover me," Nathan said. He holstered and strode toward the man. He grabbed his arm and twisted it, forcing him to the ground. He cuffed him, keeping an eye on the door.

A cacophony of sirens filled the air, and tires screeched out front.

"Watch the mosque," Nathan yelled to Bridget, "and get your creds out. Keep your muzzle depressed."

"On it."

The man muttered something.

Nathan knelt beside him and leaned close. "What's that?"

The man looked up with his eyeglasses askew. He grinned.

"Your friends are dead," Nathan said. "Think that's funny?"

"They martyred themselves. Glorious deaths."

"Stay still, unless you want to join them."

"I plan to join them . . . in time."

Nathan hoped Bridget could hear their conversation, but arriving police cars made too much noise. The first cruiser squealed into the lot, painting the mosque with colored lights. An Islamic discotheque.

The man said something unintelligible.

"Speak up," Nathan said.

"I said, you'll never stop them."

"Stop who?"

"You're too late."

7

Nathan stared at Ray-Bans's corpse with guilt, relief, and triumph all vying for control. An inch to the left, and Nathan's body could be the one lying on the pavement, not a drug trafficker. His life could have ended just now. Just like that. Gone.

But he'd won the violent confrontation, and that man had lost. It had been a righteous shooting, that was certain. He and Bridget would need to be cleared, but the facts would prove self-defense. The only issue would be their probable cause for being there in the first place, but that was more of a public relations issue than a legal one. Nathan had no choice but to shoot back. The man had tried to kill him with an assault rifle, and use-of-force scenarios didn't get much more black-and-white.

Even though the Office of Professional Responsibility would deem their shooting justified, it wouldn't alleviate the fact that they'd taken two lives. Nathan had done that before, but the act carried moral weight with a gravity of its own. Taking a life wasn't something people did naturally, at least not the most people, and crossing that line had meaning. Whatever good Nathan had done in the past could be erased by one evil act. Killing was the most serious action a person could take. And though the FBI, OPR, and federal prosecutor would review it, he'd ultimately be judged by God.

Bridget walked up beside him. "I can't freakin' believe I . . ." She stared at the ground.

"What?" Nathan asked.

"I . . ." She bit her lip. "When I saw the gun, I ran."

"That was smart."

She looked up with her mouth open.

"You were too close to him with your weapon holstered. You had a choice—either charge him and try to control the carbine or get to cover and return fire. You ran to cover, right?"

She nodded without enthusiasm.

She might have fled out of blind panic, without thought, but characterizing it as a tactical movement would allow her to live with the memory and carry on. Besides, it was a natural reaction from someone uninitiated in a life-or-death contest. She'd get better, but only if she stopped beating herself up and learned a lesson from the incident.

"Listen," Nathan said. "You distracted that asshole long enough for me to draw and take him out. Then you saved me by spotting his partner sneaking up behind me."

She breathed deeply and nodded. Tear glistened in her eyes.

Nathan laid his hand on her shoulder. "I didn't thank you for that yet. I appreciate you saving my ass."

Bridget smiled. "Ditto. Who knows what would've went down if you weren't there . . ."

This was her first shooting, but they needed to save the philosophical rumination for later and manage what came next.

"Don't overthink it," he said. "You faced a violent situation with little warning that required split-second decisions. You acted, and you survived. That's all that matters."

"Solid."

"Now, let's focus on the task before us. Rahimya's getting a warrant signed, so we need to search this truck and find the drugs."

"Should we wait for the paper to arrive?"

"We don't even need it because we're impounding the truck, which gives us a search exemption, but it's better to be safe than lose the case on a technicality. Rahimya said Three Balls is bringing it over."

Special Agent Ron Winslow, a.k.a. Three Balls, and Special Agent Thomas Murphy pulled into the lower lot.

"He's here. Let's get started."

Nathan climbed into the truck, then reached down and lifted her up. At least one hundred unmarked boxes, with crushed corners and peeling tape, had been stacked high in the cargo area. The air reeked of cardboard and mildew.

Bridget opened her penknife and sliced through the wide tape covering the box closest to the entrance. She donned rubber gloves then folded the flaps back and peered inside.

A pile of thick, folded rugs filled the box. Bridget frowned. She reached inside and dug her hands between the rugs. There was nothing else in the box.

"What the fuck?" she said.

She moved to the next box and cut it open. Another rug, this one maroon and beige with hundreds of geometric shapes woven into a symmetrical pattern.

"They're peddling carpets?" Bridget asked. "We just busted a rug *pushah?*"

A familiar worry tightened Nathan's abdomen. What if they found nothing inside?

Their shooting was justified, regardless of the truck's contents. Those assholes had drawn guns and refused to obey commands, so he and Bridget would be cleared, but if they didn't find contraband, the court of public opinion could crucify them. Not to mention how those rear-echelon fuckers would react inside the J. Edgar Hoover Building. The FBI, for all its talent and successes, was a political organization at its core. It was bad enough that government agents had shot and killed Muslims—religious and ethnic minorities—but if they'd killed those men over an unlicensed business or a tax evasion scheme, the fallout would be horrific.

"Why rugs?" Bridget asked. "And what's with these designs?"

Nathan pointed at a green rug in the box next to her. "Look at it from a distance. The little shapes resemble the Dome of the Rock, one of the holiest Islamic sites in Jerusalem. Most of the rugs depict significant Islamic locations or symbols."

"Why put them on carpet where people will walk on them?"

"These aren't decorative carpets, they're prayer mats."

"Prayer rugs aren't illegal." She stepped back and put her hands on her hips, almost accusatory, as if he'd known the truck carried rugs all along.

"These guys didn't strap on guns because they were afraid of someone hijacking carpets. Keep looking, and let's get more agents in here. We're obligated to discover whatever they're hiding."

"We're gonna be in hot water, right?"

"The shoot was righteous."

"Still . . ."

Their boss, Rahimya Nawaz, came around the truck and looked up. She ran the FBI's enforcement group specializing in extremism related to Afghanistan and Pakistan, and any action Nathan and Bridget took reflected on her.

"Nothing yet," Nathan said.

Tension creased her face. "You guys can't be involved in the search. Wait for the shoot team to arrive."

"We won't touch anything," Nathan said, "but I want to know what's in here. I took a life, and I need to make sense of it."

"You've been in shootings before," Rahimya said.

"Those were black-and-white incidents with terrorists trying to kill innocents. This one caught me by surprise. I expected a couple of guys to pull up in a car and offload suitcases from their trunk, not a box truck carrying prayer rugs."

Rahimya nodded. "You can watch until the shoot team starts their investigation. But that's all. I can't let you taint the scene."

"Thanks."

Rahimya called for agents to assist, and two young guys climbed up into the truck. They looked excited. Had they ever been on the scene of a shooting before? The FBI had once recruited heavily from former military and police, but they'd pivoted to hiring accountants and lawyers many years ago—and now they filled their ranks with agents who'd never wrestled a criminal. This new breed of agent was smart with diverse backgrounds, but learning human nature as a cop on the streets was a training ground that Quantico couldn't replicate.

The blond-haired agent photographed the interior while the brunette used a box cutter to open more boxes. He looked inside the first then set it aside.

"You should dig around in them before you give up," Nathan said.

"Nothing's in there."

"Drug dealers know how to hide their product."

"I don't see any drugs."

"And you won't, if that's how you're searching."

"Asshole," the guy muttered under his breath. He opened another box.

More prayer mats. Nothing but rugs. Box after box. Nathan stood close to the tailgate and watched. He tapped his foot to burn off nervous energy as the agents searched.

He'd be fine. They'd be fine. It had been a righteous shoot. The memory of the driver reaching under the seat for his AR-15 played on a loop in Nathan's mind. He'd no choice. Agents trained for shootings from the moment they entered the FBI Academy in Quantico. They regularly qualified on the shooting range in their division offices, all to stay sharp for the time when pulling the trigger became necessary. But it almost never did. Most FBI agents never discharged a weapon on the job. Hell, most of them never fought with the suspect or even handcuffed someone in the field. Shootings were rare across all law enforcement.

And good thing they were.

Complying with agency policies and staying within the confines of the law were serious concerns, but shootings brought death. Life had meaning, and he'd snuffed one out. He'd never been religious, but all human life had value, and God, or nature, or whatever put man on Earth, had created something unique, and Nathan's actions had removed it. Were the laws he enforced morally justified? Was there a greater power that would hold him accountable?

Killing wasn't easy.

It resembled nothing people saw on television or in the movies. It brought esoteric religious and philosophical questions into the material world, coated with blood and smelling of shit. Deadly force had real consequences. Taking a life was a most significant thing a human being could do.

And he'd done it over a truckload of prayer mats.

Bile rose in Nathan's throat. He couldn't vomit. Not on a crime scene, and not in front of other agents. He closed his eyes and braced himself against the wall for support.

"You good?" Bridget asked.

"The waiting is the worst."

She looked at the agents searching the boxes then back at him. "We're screwed, right?"

"Say nothing to the shoot team until you collect your thoughts. Every word you utter can be used against you, either criminally or in a disciplinary hearing."

"Then we're in deep shit. Did I screw the pooch when—"

"Everything you did was perfect. By the book. You'll be fine, but we don't need to commit unforced errors and give them ammunition. Just state the facts and answer their questions."

She nodded.

Assistant Special Agent in Charge Tom Penn drove into the lot and parked behind the truck. As Rahimya's boss, he'd direct the shoot team and bring in the OPR to investigate Bridget and Nathan. A flutter of fear tickled Nathan's stomach.

Penn had never liked Nathan. He considered him a rogue agent after Nathan's intrusion into the Havana Syndrome investigation, and this would be his opportunity to nudge the OPR agents.

If Penn wanted to get rid of Nathan, this was his chance.

8

2021: Surobi, Afghanistan

I slumped on a beaded seat cover in the front seat of our taxi, a Toyota Corolla that must have been fifteen years old. The shag carpeting covering the dashboard looked dirtier than our sixty-year-old driver, a man who emitted the odor of garlic and something else better left unidentified. Tara slept in the backseat with her head in Farzana's lap while my wife glared at me.

Waves of pain pulsed through my temples, and my ribs ached where the border guards had kicked me. I'd curled into a ball on the ground before the Khyber Gate and absorbed their blows until they tired of beating me. Only my lack of resistance had saved my life. The bribe my attacker had taken had helped too.

The guards had allowed my cousin's friend to continue into Pakistan, but they'd forced us to find a ride back to Kabul. Luckily, they hadn't discovered my life savings strapped to my belly—if anything about this failed attempt to escape Afghanistan could be considered luck. It felt like more like fate. Kabul had dragged us back with the gravitational pull of a black hole.

The drive from Torkham to Kabul covered more than 200 kilometers and would take close to five hours, if we were lucky. We'd crossed most of the Nangarhar Province before Tara stopped crying and drifted off. Not long after passing through Jalalabad, we rose into the mountains then crossed into Surobi District on the eastern side of the Kabul Province. The two-lane road serpentined through the Hindu Kush Mountains, the rocky foothills of the Himalayas.

No one spoke as we rolled through the mountains and headed west. Reality and my memory of the attack merged, and I entered a dream state. My pain dulled in my half-sleep state.

"I need to stop for gas," the driver said, pulling me out of my thoughts.

"Where?"

"Near the Surobi Reservoir. Just ahead."

We'd been traveling for almost three hours. I must have slept. I glanced at Farzana and Tara. Both of them slept too. The pain and anxiety of the past days and weeks seemed to melt away in their slumber. They looked at peace.

The driver rounded the corner and pulled into a petrol station. He stopped beside its single pump then ambled out to look for the attendant. Torkham had been overrun with refugees trying to make their escape, but two hours away, the Jalalabad-Torkham Road and surrounding countryside looked deserted.

Farzana jolted awake and sat up, and Tara stirred in her lap.

"I'm calling my friend, Abdul," I said. "His family's from Torkham. Maybe he can help."

Farzana didn't look at me. The hope she'd shown a few hours before had dissipated and taken her energy with it. Tara didn't appear any better.

I dialed, and Abdul picked up.

"As-Salamu Alaikum."

"Wa Alaikum As-Salam," I said. "I need help."

"My brother. I thought you'd left long ago."

"I'm in Surobi trying to get to Pakistan."

"You should flee immediately."

"My family don't have visas. But we won't survive in Kabul. The Taliban will execute everyone who worked at the embassy."

The line was quiet.

"Hello?"

"I know a man," Abdul said. "A smuggler. He may be able to help you."

"What kind of smuggler?" I asked.

"Spin mal."

Spin mal. The white stuff. Heroin. An alarm rang in my head. I'd helped the Americans fight the scourge of drug production in my country, not directly, but drug trafficking tainted everything in the Graveyard of Empires.

"Who?"

"His name doesn't matter."

"He traffics people too? He can get my family out?"

Farzana narrowed her eyes with concern.

"Maybe," Abdul said. "For a price."

"I can pay."

"We shouldn't do this," Farzana said.

I covered the phone with my hand. "We won't last in Kabul."

"But—"

"We have no choice."

"It's too dangerous."

"Be quiet," I said, a little too harshly. Everything depended on my decisions. Living under freedom or tyranny. Life or death.

I gazed out the window. Hiring a drug trafficker to sneak my family out of Afghanistan was fraught with peril. Would I be able to protect them from the clutches of a criminal group? Would that be more dangerous than living under Taliban rule again? I had few memories of their repressive regime, but every glimmer of childhood in my mind carried the weight of dread, as if monsters had lurked outside our home. The feeling wasn't just a manifestation of an active child's mind. Evil had surrounded us then, as it did now.

The monsters had returned.

I lifted the phone to my ear. "Call him."

9

Rahimya had left to brief the SAC, so Nathan and Bridget poked around inside the truck. They'd let the new agents officially discover anything they wanted to seize. Nathan moved deeper into the cargo area and lifted another box off a stack. A bolt of lightning fired through his clavicle where the bullet had torn through his muscle a year ago. He'd tweaked it during the incident, but his adrenaline had masked the pain. His inflamed nerves burned the muscles in his chest and shoulder, sending tingles down his arm into his fingers. The damn thing hadn't healed right.

"You're hurting?" Bridget asked.

"I'm fine."

Her eyebrows arched. "What's the deal?"

"Keep going. Let's find something. And fast."

Her forehead wrinkled. "I thought you said we'd skate on this. You said the shooting was solid."

"They'll clear us, but if we don't find contraband, it'll be a PR nightmare."

She surveyed the truck's interior.

Nathan ripped open the box and waited as pain sliced through his tendons, so intense it felt icy. He turned his head so she couldn't see the agony on his face.

Bridget didn't make a sound, which meant she probably watched him, so he didn't turn around. Tape ripped off a box as she continued the search.

He reached inside the box with his gloved hands and pretended to search, but instead, he waited until his pain subsided and colors stopped dancing behind his eyes. If management discovered how poorly his arm healed, they'd banish him to light duty, which meant sitting in an office answering phones or filing reports. That'd be worse than when his baseball coach benched him in college, but at least that time, he'd been able to watch the game. Being squirreled away in an office for an indeterminate amount of time—while China, Islamists, and other nefarious terrorist and criminal groups threatened the country—would crush his soul. He should see a doctor, but he'd keep it secret and pay on his own dime.

Nathan inhaled a deep breath and recovered, though his fingers still tingled with numbness and his shoulder throbbed. The bullet had done a real number on him.

Bridget slipped her Boston Red Sox hat out of her pocket. A scrunchie appeared in her hand, and she tied her hair into a ponytail then fed her hair through the opening in the back and fitted the cap.

"You love that cap," Nathan said.

"Go Sox."

"How long was your father a Boston cop?"

"Thirty-two years and counting. My brothers are lifers too. Tommy's a property detective, and Jimmy and Johnny both push squad cars. John's up for sergeant this year."

"You didn't want to get on the PD? I mean, you're . . ."

"Don't be shy," Bridget said. "You can say it. I'm a Southie girl. Born and bred. And yeah, I thought about it, real hard, but being a copper is harder for a woman."

"There are plenty of good female cops."

"Yeah, but you may have noticed, we're smaller and weaker. I can fight, a little, but no way I can hold my own without going to my ASP . . . or my gun.

"That's why the Bureau gave you weapons."

"It's more than that," she said. "I wanted to go my way, discover my identity. Dad's kind of a legend in the PD, and I would've stayed in his shadow, not to mention the shit I'd get every time one of my brothers acted up."

"They cause trouble?"

"Hooligans, all of them. If Dad had been in the mob, they would've fit right in, but he wasn't, so they became cops."

"The FBI's law enforcement."

"I may not be as strong is my dad or brothers, but I'm frickin' smarter, and doing big cases requires that."

"I know plenty of smart cops."

"Jesus, I'm not saying that. I know that. It would've been a good gig, an honorable one, but now I'm a Fed, and I've gotta make it on my own. I kinda like that. At least I did until this week."

"Yeah, well, things won't get better unless we get to work."

Bridget pulled a mat out as Nathan opened another box.

"Nothing else in here," Bridget said. "These mats are heavy. I guess they need to be thick and durable if people are kneeling on them every day."

Nathan stopped. Cognitive dissonance unbalanced him, as if he teetered on the edge of something. What was wrong?

Listen to your instinct.

He held the carpet in his hands. He squeezed it. Thick. Very thick. He parted individual threads with his fingers. The tight weave wasn't thick enough to conceal anything. He hefted the carpet. Bridget was right—it weighed too much. But nothing was inside it. He brushed his fingertips over the material. It wasn't soft, as it appeared, but stiff and thick.

He hefted the carpet out and dropped it on the floor, and a thump echoed off the walls. Bridget turned and watched him. Nathan knelt beside it and ran his palm across the surface. It looked like the carpet in his living room when Amelia had spilled grape juice on it and left it overnight. Sticky and hard.

Then it dawned on him.

He stood in dug into the box. The other prayer mat felt similar. He ripped open the box beside it, his excitement building. Those were heavy and rigid too. He nodded and smiled turned to Bridget.

"Be careful not to rip your gloves," he said.

She cocked her head. "Say again?"

"They soaked these prayer mats in something. My guess is some kind of opioid. Don't touch your hands to your face."

"You mean . . ."

"They didn't hide the drug inside the cargo . . . they saturated it."

10

Nathan rolled off Meili Chan and tried to catch his breath. Both their bodies glistened with perspiration. Her full lips, silky hair, and petite body attracted him like gravity. The clock on his nightstand showed almost midnight. They'd been dating since they'd broken open the Havana Syndrome case the previous year, but she'd been as busy with her China investigation as he'd been chasing Islamists, and that left infrequent, late-night trysts as their only time together. Long hours and unpredictable schedules—the burden of a career in law enforcement.

"I needed that," she said.

"Good for you?"

"Always." She flashed her coy smile that always drove him crazy.

"I wish you could stay all night."

Her smile faded. "I don't want Amelia to find me here in the morning."

"Amelia likes you."

"It's too soon, and I need a good night's sleep. I've got an early meeting with the CIA."

"They helping or just paying lip service?"

"Hard to tell, but they've given me access to intelligence I haven't seen before. Russia may be behind some high-energy attacks too."

"Will the administration impose sanctions?"

"The evidence is interesting but inconclusive. It's likely Russia targeted American personnel with directed-energy weapons, but the emails we intercepted require inference. It's not enough to prove anything."

"Russia's been running operations against us since the communists took over in 1917. Do you think they coordinated Havana Syndrome strategy with China?"

"Possible, but I doubt it. Havana Syndrome seems like a tiny piece of a much bigger Chinese strategy."

"Meaning what?"

"They're set on our destruction, and they're employing every means at that their disposal."

"Like the surveillance balloons they fly over the country?"

"That's part of it, but it looks more like a systematic attempt to degrade the United States."

"Our military readiness?"

"Everything. They want to damage our society." She looked at her watch. "I need to run soon. I have a meeting at headquarters."

"I wish I could investigate that with you."

"They won't put us in the same group since we're dating, especially with me as your supervisor."

"I'd still like to focus on China."

"After we stopped the attacks last year, you could have used your political goodwill with the director to get transferred."

"That was my intention, but then Frederick Richardson made all those accusations about me threatening him, and management kept their distance."

She wrapped her arms around his neck and pressed her body against his. "I'm FBI management."

He kissed her, and she parted her lips. He melted into her, and arousal stirred him.

"Maybe I should have tried this approach with the director."

She giggled and slapped his chest. "Seriously, will you try to transfer?"

"You know I want too, but I'm not done with terror prosecutions from the airport, and now this seizure and shooting will take over my days."

Her eyes softened. "How are you doing with that?"

"Shootings are traumatic, even when they're justified. We survived, but that always gets me thinking about what would have happened if it had ended differently."

"If they shot you?"

"If I died. What would happen to Amelia?"

"Your ex-wife would . . . hey, let's not talk about this."

He nodded. "Agreed, but you asked."

"Time's up." She slipped off the bed.

He climbed out of bed and moved to the door. "I'll walk you out."

"No need. Let's not wake Amelia." She kissed him, grabbed her gun off the nightstand, and slipped out.

11

The drug smuggler's truck, a tractor trailer with the flag of Afghanistan painted on its side, arrived four hours later and rumbled over the gravel to the dusty end of the parking lot. It parked and an obese man rolled out, his lard sliding off the seat in waves like a sand dune. His belly peeked out from beneath his tee shirt where the soiled cotton lifted over his hairy torso. He looked around and spotted us then headed over to our table.

I rose and met him. "You are Haji Jafar's man?"

"You have my money?"

I'd removed bills from the package taped to my stomach. I peeled them off a roll and counted for him. It wouldn't leave us much to continue our travel to the West, but even the Islamic Republic of Pakistan was safer than Afghanistan, and we had to flee the coming bloodbath.

He took the cash and counted it again, then grunted, seemingly satisfied, and stuffed the money in his pants pocket

"All three?"

"Yes."

"Follow me." He lumbered across the lot. Waves of heat shimmered over the hard-packed dirt.

Farzana and Tara looked at me with equal parts relief and fear.

"Is it safe?" Farzana asked with an edge. Her motherly protective claws had come out.

"Nothing in Afghanistan is safe. Not anymore."

"You trust these criminals?"

"No."

"Then why take the chance?"

"We have no choice."

"We could return home, and you could speak to your cousin Ahmed. He knows people. He could—"

"Enough. Nothing waits for us in the capital but torture and death."

Farzana pressed her lips. I'd seen that look before. She knew I was right, and none of our options came without risk.

I dropped rupees on the table for our tea. Farzana helped Tara out of her chair, and they followed me across the lot to the truck.

The driver pointed at me. "Get in front. Women in the back."

I froze. The trailer would get simmering hot. "Why can't they sit up front?"

"No visas. I have a compartment."

He clumped along the trailer to the rear door. He grabbed the handle then released it with a yelp. The metal had to be hot. He removed a filthy rag from his pocket and protected his palm as he wrestled with the metal hitch. The door opened with a creak, and heat wafted out. He put his hands on the floor and climbed up. He disappeared inside without offering to help.

"What should we do?" Farzana asked.

I mounted the metal step and extended my hand. She took it, and I lifted her and then Tara inside. We moved into the shadows.

"Papa?"

"Not now."

The driver shook a section of panel near the cab, and it popped out. He muscled it off the wall, revealing a concealed compartment—kilograms of either heroin or morphine stacked high against the wall. The plastic had black camel logos with the year and the name *Aziz* stamped on them.

The driver motioned at the one-by-two-meter open floor. "They hide in here."

I shook my head. "It's too hot and cramped."

"Just until we cross the border."

"I don't want them in back."

"They either hide or they stay here. It's it up to you, but decide now. I'm late."

I turned to Farzana. "It's this or we take our chances in Kabul."

She scowled and took Tara by the hand. She led our daughter into the cramped space. She looked up at me with glossy eyes. "See you in Pakistan."

The driver shut them inside, and I followed him to the cab.

12

Amelia perched in the Mustang's passenger seat as Nathan inched through traffic in Southeast DC—their daily commute to the Stephen Decatur Elementary School, located opposite the Congressional Cemetery. History surrounded every building in DC. With her auburn hair and confident manner, Amelia resembled her mother. She stared outside with those crystal-blue, intelligent eyes of hers. What was she thinking?

Amelia wore a gray dress with knee-high socks and black shoes, her private-school uniform, which made her look older—except for her pink Dora the Explorer backpack. At eight years old, she acted more like a teenager, part adult and part child. There were moments when glimpses of her future self flashed through, and other times when she exhibited the innocence of youth. Nathan's heart swelled every time he looked at her. People without children could never understand the connection he had with his daughter.

"Dad, do you like your job?"

He met her eyes. Despite her age, she didn't ask meaningless questions. This was going somewhere.

"My job challenges me, and the FBI's mission is meaningful."

"You slay, Dad, but you work such long hours."

Was that what worried her? Amelia spent half her time with her mother, Reagan Burke, and Reagan's fiancé, Vince Cabrera. Despite Nathan and Reagan's best efforts, maybe they weren't giving their daughter enough attention.

"I work hard, honey, because the cases I investigate involve high stakes, and they're always time sensitive. Besides, I love what I do, so it feels less like work and more like a privilege. That's the key to a good life. Find something you're good at doing, that you enjoy, and that pays. I'll never get rich as an FBI agent, but I make enough for us to be comfortable, and I'm proud of what I'm doing."

"Do you wish you worked less?"

He sighed. "I want more time with you but . . . well, you know. Your mom's and my situation is complicated, especially with her wedding coming up soon. I see you as much as possible. Am I not doing a good enough job finding one-on-one time for us?"

Amelia glanced out the window again. "Your job's dangerous too."

That was it. She worried about him. His job was dangerous, as the scars from the Chinese assassin's bullet proved. He told people he risked his life because being an agent was a noble calling to protect the weak, and that was true, but there was more to it.

The danger addicted him.

"It's not always perilous," he said. "But there's inherent risk. Bad people exist in this world, and it's my job to stop them."

Amelia's eyes softened. "It scares me when you leave for work. After that thing at the airport, I had nightmares every night."

"You didn't tell me that."

"Mom said you had enough to worry about."

He'd discuss that with Reagan. If anything he did caused his daughter grief, he had to know, and Reagan shouldn't keep secrets from him.

"Sometimes, I get so caught up in my job that I forget fear affects you and your mom too. I'm not the only one under stress. You can talk to me about this stuff anytime."

Nathan turned off Seventeenth Street SE and headed for the school. Amelia stayed quiet.

His phone chirped, and he glanced at the screen. Private number. That would be somebody from work, and the government could wait. Nathan had sacrificed enough, and they wouldn't spoil his twenty minutes alone with his daughter. He let it go to voicemail.

"Don't worry about me," Nathan said. "Nothing's going to happen."

"It's not always up to you."

Smart girl. "I can take care of myself. I don't take unnecessary risks, but sometimes taking chances is necessary to achieve what I want. There's another life lesson for you. You're getting your money's worth this morning."

"Oh, brother." She rolled her eyes, and the child came out again. Or maybe that was the teenager waiting in the offing like a monster in the woods.

"How's softball?" he asked. "You still their ace pitcher?"

"Coach said I throw harder than anyone on the team."

"That's my girl. Pitching is a thinking player's position, the perfect blend of strategy and physical execution."

"Whatever."

She'd sounded disinterested, but she loved softball. He glanced over and caught her smiling out the window.

Nathan pulled into the circular drive behind a line of parents' cars. School buses unloaded out front. Amelia could take the bus, but these moments alone with her were important to him. However fleeting.

All his sacrifice to get her into private school was worth it. The private institution offered a low teacher-to-student ratio and high level of individualized interaction, both of which fertilized learning. His real estate taxes paid for public schools, and he would've loved to send her there, but cramped classrooms with limited supplies and curriculums that catered to the lowest common denominator were not the environments in which children thrive. And then there was the social activism that had crept into the classroom. Private school took a bite out of his biweekly paycheck, but setting Amelia up for success was worth every penny. If she ended up attending college and majoring in gender studies, he'd kill her.

"Have a good day," he said. "Let them know Burke was there."

She rolled her eyes again. "I don't even know what that means."

"*Carpe diem.* Seize the day. Be good to people, engage with your classwork, and maybe most important of all, enjoy yourself."

"Not math."

"It's a new world, honey. Learn math. You're gonna need it."

Somebody moved to the passenger window, and Nathan instinctively reached for the .40 Glock on his hip. He touched his blazer but didn't expose the gun.

Lily Batchelder, Amelia's social studies teacher, wrapped her knuckles on the glass.

Nathan rolled down the window, and Lily leaned her elbows on the door. She was rail thin, but not frail, making her age hard to pin down. She wore inexpensive gold hoop earrings beneath short, curly black hair that showed flecks of gray. You had to respect the natural look.

"Good morning, Mr. Burke," she said.

Uh-oh. "Is there a problem?"

She frowned. "Why do you ask that?"

"You wouldn't be waiting for me outside otherwise."

She nodded. "No problem, just a concern. May we speak for a moment?" Her eyes darted to Amelia.

Nathan kissed Amelia on her head. "Head to your class and let me chat with your teacher."

"Don't embarrass me," Amelia whispered. She let herself out and skipped up the sidewalk toward the front door. A little girl again.

Nathan's phone chirped. He ignored it.

"Everything okay with Amelia's grades?" he asked.

"Her grades are fine," Lily said. "She's smart . . . brilliant."

Nathan raised an eyebrow. She was stalling, so whatever she had to say couldn't be positive.

Lily sighed. "That fight last week bothered me, and I thought—"

"What fight?"

Lily flinched. "With that boy. I know Principal Collins called."

"Nobody called me."

"I think he spoke with your wife."

Heat rose in Nathan's throat. A fight? Another thing he had to talk to Reagan about.

"What happened?"

"Amelia got into it with Teddy Hunt again."

Nathan clenched his fists. Teddy Hunt Jr. was the son of US Senator Theodore Hunt, a pompous dullard from New York who's ego barely fit into the school. "What happened this time?"

"Teddy made fun of Amelia's hair, then he started picking on Elmer."

That smug little prick acted exactly like his father. The boy's chubby face hovered in Nathan's mind. He shook off the urge to punch him, because he was just a kid. His father, on the other hand, had one coming.

"Teddy hit Amelia?"

"Actually, no. She socked him in the stomach with the entire class watching."

"Amelia punched him for making fun of her?" A wave of pride welled inside Nathan. Hitting another kid was wrong, and violence should never be the response to criticism, but . . . good for her.

"Amelia protected Elmer. That kid is half the size of the other boys, and Teddy always bullies him," Lily said. "Amelia jabbed Teddy in the stomach, and he doubled over. He went down hard. He must have been humiliated."

"I'm sorry she acted out. That's unacceptable behavior. I'll talk to her."

"I think it embarrassed Amelia too, but she hit him for making Elmer cry. From what I could reconstruct, Teddy was pretty abusive to Elmer, and everyone heard. He torments lots of kids."

"Protecting a student is one thing, but hitting someone is unacceptable. I didn't raise her like that. She needs to ignore Teddy's comments."

"Honestly, I think he was flirting with her."

That stopped Nathan cold. Flirting? They were only kids. Was he ready for that next phase of her life?

His phone buzzed. Rahimya.

"I've got to take this," Nathan said. "I'll talk to Amelia."

"She's a good kid," Lily said. She smiled and walked back to the school.

Nathan answered. "I'm dropping off my daughter. I'll be in soon."

"We've got a problem," Rahimya said.

Her tone took the humor out of Nathan's day. "What's up?"

"We intercepted a call on another case. It's about you."

"And?"

"They've targeted you for assassination."

13

2021: Surobi, Afghanistan

Wind whistled through the truck's cabin as the driver maneuvered along the two-lane mountain. He belched and farted without shame. Only a short, stone barrier rimming the cliff's edge separated us from a deep canyon. I pressed my face against my window and looked down. The steep mountain disappeared below into a slope of boulders, with only the occasional spot of color from cars that had gone over the side.

I leaned back into the safety of my seat and looked over my shoulder at the wall separating the cab from the concealed compartment. Farzana and Tara must be miserable in back. Were they angry, sad, or terrified? Maybe all three.

I rapped my knuckles on the wall. No response. The truck clambered over uneven road, and between the engine noise and rattling of bolts, metal plates, and cargo, my family probably couldn't hear me, but knowing they were okay would bring me some measure of peace.

My poor wife and daughter. What had my decisions done to them? My naïve belief that America could transform Afghanistan, bring my country into the twenty-first century . . . I'd been wrong. America had abandoned us, and now my family would pay the price.

I had to get them to Europe, but anywhere would be safer than Afghanistan.

The drive back from Surobi to Torkham was over 170 kilometers, and backtracking over treacherous roads would take us at least three hours. Nausea tugged at my stomach. Was it from roads serpentining along sheer cliffs beside us? Or from my guilt for subjecting Farzana and Tara to this ordeal?

The car pitched and swayed as our driver followed the ebbing contours of the pavement. He held the wheel with two fingers, seemingly unafraid of the precipitous drop feet away.

My spine tingled, and my stomach hollowed.

We rolled around a corner toward a yawning black mouth in the mountain's side—the entrance to one of the Mahipar tunnels. He didn't slow as we plunged into darkness.

Dark contours of rock flashed past, and I blinked to adjust my eyes. Then we burst out of the tunnel and back into the orange glow of the evening where shadows lurked in the mountain's umbra. The road curved sharply, and our driver swung around the bend at full speed.

A tractor trailer stacked high with lumber rolled toward us in the opposite lane, gaining speed in its decent.

"Do you think it's wise to—"

A bus with Afghans sitting atop it pulled around the trailer into our lane—blocking the road.

"Look out," I shouted.

Brakes squealed. Time slowed. Our driver yanked the wheel hard to the right.

Our front wheels hit the stone border with a thump that loosened my fillings. We launched into the air. The sky filled the windshield, then our hood pointed down the cliff face.

We plummeted into the abyss.

14

Nathan sat in his Bu-ride outside the mosque and turned up the volume on his laptop. The MPEG audio file's output bars twinkled as the recorded conversation between suspected jihadist Abdul Mohammad and an unknown male played through the speaker. The FBI's Joint Terrorism Task Force in New York had intercepted the call.

They spoke Arabic, a Gulf dialect either Saudi Arabia or Yemen. Years of working radical Islamic extremists had given Nathan a basic understanding of modern Arabic, but the audio instruction he'd studied only worked for Egypt, Lebanon, and the Levante. Arabic spoken by fundamentalists around the Gulf sounded markedly different, and he only caught words here and there. But still he listened, because he couldn't quell his curiosity at hearing men talk about his demise.

He enlarged the Word document with the draft translation of the call. And scrolled down to the pertinent part.

SUBJ 1 (Unidentified male): *Have you found the infidel?*

SUBJ 2 (Abdul Mohammed): A simple task. He does not hide from us.

SUBJ 1 (Unidentified male): The arrogance of the American gives him courage, but like all infidels, it will be his downfall.

SUBJ 2 (Abdul Mohammed): He works near the heart of the beast, and he comes every day. This will not be difficult.

SUBJ 1 (Unidentified male): Do not take this lightly. This man is dangerous. Ghulam learned that lesson through blood.

Nathan sat up in his seat. Were they talking about the same Ghulam he'd shot to death at the airport? He read along with the recording.

SUBJ 2 (Abdul Mohammed): I have passed the information.

SUBJ 1 (Unidentified male): Let the slayer plan this.

SUBJ 2 (Abdul Mohammed): Yes, of course. He knows the enemy better than they know themselves.

SUBJ 2 (Unidentified male): Then it will be done, if Allah wills it.

SUBJ 2 (Abdul Mohammed): Alhamdulillah.

The conversation switched to politics in the Middle East, and Abdul Mohammed sounded incensed about the tentativeness of the new Taliban leadership residing in Kabul. He sided with ISIS–K, who wanted to accelerate jihad and opposed the Taliban's long-game strategy. The international community would never afford them legitimacy, no matter how moderate they acted.

Two dark sedans entered the lot, and Nathan closed his laptop. The search warrant had arrived.

Normally, the seizure of drugs being delivered would create probable cause to search a building, but this was a mosque, a religious institution, which raised the bar for government agents to make forcible entry—if not in legislation, then in the minds of the FBI managers, DOJ attorneys, and the judge whose name would be on the warrant. But the driver had spoken to Imam Qadir, and then he and the passenger had unloaded boxes, which demonstrated their intent to bring the cargo inside. That coupled with the opioid-saturated prayer mats gave them probable cause.

The mosque's defense attorney would have a shot at overturning the search warrant, because the drugs had never entered the structure, but at least the judge had agreed to a limited search. The agents would have to take care not to damage anything and avoid throwing gas on the already flaming PR nightmare. Any government action against a religious institution raised Americans' hackles, but Muslims were a tiny minority, and many of them were brown, which ticked off the intersectionality box and gave them protection not afforded to other groups. If the mosque had been owned by neo-Nazis, no one would hesitate. Intersectionality explained why gay advocacy groups and godless communists supported radical Muslim countries and institutions, when they would be among the first people slaughtered under a Sharia government.

Nathan exited his car and intercepted Rahimya at hers.

Special Agent Tommy Henderson stepped out, waving the paper search warrant. "I got it."

Rahimya called over a dozen agents, and they formed a semicircle around her. They'd cleared the mosque hours before, as a safety precaution, and the Arlington police maintained the perimeter while crime scene techs investigated the shooting crime scene.

"We have the paper," Rahimya said. "We'll videotape the search. I don't want anyone coming back later and saying we violated the sanctity of this building. Keep in mind others may be videotaping also, so no laughing or snide remarks. Keep it professional. We'll go in, look for evidence, and get out. The only evidence we'll seize is what we can directly tie to criminal behavior. You find anything in a gray area, ask me, and I'll make a call. We're not looting a mosque. Everybody clear?"

Heads nodded around the circle.

"Nathan, you won't participate at all. You're the case agent, but until you're cleared, you can't take an active role. I'm only allowing you to be here because I want you to witness whatever we find. You need to know what happens, and we won't punish you for doing your duty."

"Got it, Boss."

"Harry, handle evidence inventory. Agents will photograph anything they find in place then bring it to you. Bag it, tag it, and maintain chain of custody. Remember, every second we're here, we risk protests and negative media publicity. Get in, get out, do your jobs."

The agents broke up and headed inside, with Nathan in tow. They entered through the back door, passed through a dimly lit anteroom and under an arch into a garden illuminated with skylights. Tranquility carried on the rays of light filtering through the thick glass above, reminiscent of so many churches Nathan had attended. Houses of worship had the same quality—a thickness to the air, almost a presence, like someone watching. The worn floors and ancient art invited flickers of the past. He couldn't hide his fear here, or falsely justify his actions.

They crossed the garden into the great prayer room, a marble-floored space where worshipers would spread out their mats and kneel in prayer. Well, not the mats saturated with millions of dollars of opioids. Passageways ran along both sides, separated by large columns, connecting the front lobby beyond the altar, or whatever the place where Imam Qadir gave his sermons was called. All houses of worship smelled the same, institutional and ancient.

Other than Rahimya, none of the agents present were Muslim, but they quieted as they moved about their business, showing the building the respect it deserved. The team spread out, and Nathan joined Bridget, who leaned against a wall.

"I can't believe getting paper took that long," Bridget said.

"I'm surprised we got it at all. Virginia is more religious than many states, and while it's historically Christian, its Muslim population is growing fast, especially in Northern Virginia."

"That doesn't click," she said. "Is it because immigrants follow other immigrants from similar cultures?"

"DC draws a diverse ethnic and religious population from around the world, but I think the increase in Islam has more to do with its proximity to Congress. Radical Islamists hammer the administration, congress, universities, and think tanks every day. They're looking to change legislation and influence public opinion."

Bridget scowled. "Fairfax county has over a million residents, but the Muslim population's tiny."

"Relatively, but they check the intersectional boxes, and they have a powerful voice through groups like the Muslim Brotherhood. They're protected by people they want to slaughter."

Bridget shook her head. "Radical Islam has kept the Middle East in the seventh century. Look how Hezbollah has destroyed Lebanon. It was once the Switzerland of the Mediterranean, and now their economy has shit the bed, inflation's out of control, and everyone is under the frickin' boot of Iran's proxy." She seemed pissed, and rightly so, but the lines in her face deepened more than unusual.

"How are you processing the shootings?"

She shrugged.

"Get any sleep?"

"Nightmares."

"Yeah, me too."

She met his eyes and smiled. "Let's shoot the shit about something else. How are you doing with Amelia? Being a solo dad must be tough."

"When I first became a father, everything I did for Amelia, I did for the first time. I was almost paralyzed with fear that I'd do something wrong, but over time, I got the hang of it. And I realized I could make mistakes and everything would work out."

"Kids are resilient," she said.

"And she's smart, but when Reagan left me, I became a single parent. Even saying that aloud—single parent—makes me cringe. I know how damaging it can be for child psyche to have a broken home."

"I've only met your daughter a couple of times, but it seems like you're doing a great job."

"I'm a mess of fears and concerns. And guilt. I grew up with loving parents in a stable home, and I still had my issues. What chance does Amelia have, shuttling back and forth between my and Reagan's houses? What kind of influence will that asshole have on her?" he said. "Amelia deserves the same stability, love, and predictability I had. I feel like I'm walking along a cliff with her in my arms—one wrong move, and she'll go over the edge . . . or we both will.

Three Balls burst into the great room, from a side office. "Holy cow," he said. "You gotta see this."

Nathan and Bridget followed him down a narrow staircase into the basement. He led them into a supply closet and stood beside a bookshelf on its rear wall. He grinned at Nathan. He grabbed the shelf and slid it back, exposing a cutout in the wall.

AR-15s filled the compartment.

"I didn't know they used assault rifles during their services," Three Balls said.

"Nice find," Nathan said. Relief and excitement battled for control.

"Give me a hand up," he said.

"I, uh . . ."

"C'mon." He put his hand on Nathan's shoulder and raised his leg.

Nathan couldn't say no without exposing his injury. Nathan cupped his hands, and Three-Balls stepped onto it and reached into the opening.

Nathan's shoulder burned, and crackles of electricity ran down his arm. He leaned against the wall and tried to absorb the man's weight with his legs.

Three Balls rooted around inside the compartment, and the pain gathered steam, like water breaking through a dam. A bead of sweat rose on Nathan's forehead.

"Okay, let me down."

Nathan bent his knees and lowered him. Searing heat spread through him. He let go, and Three Balls landed hard.

"Hey, you trying to kill me?" He eyeballed Nathan. "You sick? You don't look so good."

"I'm fine," Nathan sputtered. "It wouldn't hurt for you to pass on dessert now and then."

"Maybe you should get back in the gym, hero."

"I didn't know you knew what a gym was."

"Funny guy. We got at least three dozen rifles up there."

"Let's get everything photographed before you move it," Nathan said.

"Roger that."

Three Balls walked off to confer with Rahimya, and Nathan headed back upstairs, relieved to stop forcing a placid expression. He breathed rapidly through his nose to dissipate the pain. Would his chronic pain ever end? What if his shoulder never healed? Being an FBI agent was his life. His identity. Who would he be without a badge, without a mission?

He shook the thought away. He wouldn't lose his job if he kept his pain a secret. Nobody could know.

15

2021: Kabul, Afghanistan

The stale odor of death clung to the air as I sat on a folding chair in my kitchen. I listened to the wind howl through the alley between apartment buildings in the Macroyan Khan complex The cupboards were empty, and a film of dust covered everything. Kabul was perpetually filthy—a city covered in shit.

The image of Farzana's and Tara's broken bodies crumpled in the taxi's backseat had seared into my mind. Behind my eyes, blood poured from their bodies as their lives ebbed away. I saw it over and over on an infinite loop.

My daughter and wife had been dead for a month. The hospital released me two days ago, and I'd sat at home since then. Nobody could tell me what happened to my wife's and daughter's bodies after passersby pulled us from the wreckage, only to say they'd buried my family. Put my love underground. Life had lost meaning for the people of Afghanistan, and daily killings from criminals and the feud between the Taliban and ISIS-K had become commonplace. The sight of corpses on the streets grew far too common.

None of it mattered.

My life ended when my family disappeared, even if my heart and lungs refused to accept it. I would never feel happiness, never experience joy. Nor did I want to. The only people on earth I loved were gone, and the barren landscape of Afghanistan seemed colder than possible. My mind had become numb, an empty vessel that had once carried my spirit. The man I'd been no longer lived. I existed without love. Without purpose.

I waited for death to take me.

16

Bridget pulled her Bu-ride to the curb and shut it off. Nathan steeled himself for what they'd see.

"Locked and loaded?" she asked.

"I was about to ask you the same thing."

Nathan climbed out and leaned against the car. A few blocks away, restaurants, shops, and apartment buildings dotted the main drag in Clarendon, but here, residential homes lined the streets. The three-story, clapboard home had probably been built in the forties, and it had the dilapidated appearance that homes of that age always assumed, despite the care an owner gave them. Police cars double parked along the street and yellow crime scene tape roped off the front yard.

"I don't see how a bunch of ODs relate to our seizure," Bridget said.

"We're less than a mile from the mosque, and this is the most overdoses we've seen in Arlington, maybe ever."

Bridget grimaced. "How many juvies?"

"Maybe twenty."

The front door opened, and two guys in plainclothes with gold badges clipped to their belts walked out, chatting with a crime scene technician dressed in overalls. The shorter man spotted Nathan and waved.

"That's Detective Ramirez," Nathan said. "He gave me the heads-up."

Nathan strode into the front yard, and Bridget jogged to catch up. They met Ramirez outside the front door. Ramirez was a veteran, and Nathan had known him since he worked on a gang unit five years before, but the grizzled cop looked shaken.

"How bad is it in there?" Nathan asked.

Ramirez looked pale, and the skin around his face had stretched tight. "Eighteen vics. All freshmen at George Washington. Three of 'em lived here, and the rest came to party. It's ugly."

"Why aren't they in the ER?" Bridget asked.

Ramirez stared at her for a moment before answering. "You don't take bodies with lividity to the hospital."

Bridget blushed. "That's rough."

"From what we can ascertain, they partied last night, and most of the people left around eleven, probably because tomorrow's a school day. Timothy Langton—that's the name on the lease—and the other vics stayed here and broke into the Oxy."

"How do eighteen kids all take enough Oxy to kill them?" Bridget asked.

"The pills look like oxycodone and they're stamped, but they're counterfeit and probably laced with way too much fentanyl. It's like they're poison. It knocked them out, and the kids never woke up."

"How does that happen?" Nathan asked. "Did everyone take the pills at the same time?"

"Oxycodone's an analgesic," Rodriguez said. "People take it and lie back to enjoy the high. Maybe they dosed close together and didn't realize their friends were dead."

"They all took it?" Nathan asked. "I mean, didn't anyone abstain?"

"Not that we know of," Ramirez said. "It's possible somebody was here, saw what happened, and fled. Maybe they didn't want to get involved. We're checking phone records and videotapes. Maybe we'll get lucky. But even if someone had witnessed it, there's a brief window before brain death sets in. They probably couldn't have been saved."

"This shit is poison," Nathan said.

"It's an epidemic," Ramirez said. "It's like fifty 9/11s every year, only people don't perceive it that way because the victims voluntarily took drugs. What people don't realize is victims often think they're taking something else. Fentanyl and its analogues are used to lace everything. It packs a punch. We lost over a hundred thousand people last year."

A quiet settled over them, the destruction hard to contemplate. Over a hundred thousand victims. And the victims weren't as easy to dismiss as a death of a drug-addled homeless person or criminal. Fentanyl had tainted most drugs, including marijuana. The bigger infection was the social collapse that drove people to take prescription drugs recreationally.

"Want to see?" Ramirez asked.

"Not even a little bit," Nathan said, "but if this is related to the mosque, then I need to witness it with my own eyes."

Ramirez nodded and led them up the spongy steps. He opened the screen door with a creak and led them inside.

Teenage bodies slumped on couches and chairs, against the walls, and on the hardwood floor in the hallway. Beer bottles and red plastic cups littered the room, like any college party—except here, everyone was dead.

Nathan's breath caught in his throat. He'd seen plenty of bodies, but these were college freshman. Kids. Every year, college students looked younger and younger, and any premature death was a tragedy. Eighteen of them altogether was too much for his soul to carry . . . and they had done it to themselves. Sort of. Not intentionally, but with reckless disregard for their lives. People knew about fentanyl poisoning, yet they still rolled the dice. Unforced errors.

Bridget's eyes widened, and she covered her mouth with her hand. The sickly, sweet odor of rotting meat hung in the stagnant air. Even growing up hearing cop stories couldn't have prepared her for a house full of rotting children.

"Six in here, three in the kitchen, and nine more in the den."

Nathan and Bridget followed Ramirez down the corridor into the kitchen.

"This is what I wanted to show you," Ramirez said.

A duffel bag lay open on the counter, and brown medicine bottles spilled out of it. Half of them were uncapped and empty, and the rest remained sealed. Their opaque plastic revealed white oval shapes inside.

Ramirez pulled out a second pair of rubber gloves. He donned them with the deftness of an expert, then reached into the bag and removed a bottle.

"See the marking there?" he said, pointing to one of them.

"I'm not familiar with pharmaceutical markings," Nathan said.

"That's the number for commercially available oxycodone, which is what made these kids think they were taking the right thing. But look on the other side." He pointed to another tablet. "See that crescent?"

"What's that?" Nathan asked.

"It's what distinguishes the dealer's products."

"Why would they do that?" Bridget asked. "I'm deadass." Her voice sounded tight.

"It could be for theft control, to track their product, or branding."

"Branding?" Bridget asked.

"So customers know what they're getting."

"Seems counterproductive when your shit kills people," Bridget said. "Who would touch it after this?"

"Addicts want it strong," Ramirez said, "but you're right. These pills contain what I assume are lethal doses."

"Why would they make them lethal?" Nathan asked.

"Could be a chemist's accident, or maybe they're sending a message."

"What kind of message?" Bridget asked.

"That's why I called you here. This feels . . . intentional."

17

2021: Kabul, Afghanistan

They came at night. I watched from my third-floor apartment as two Hilux pickup trucks with shrieking brakes roared into the parking lot. A muffler coughed and backfired as a dozen Taliban dismounted and beelined for the entrance. They carried AK-47s, carelessly holding their weapons like umbrellas, and their barrels swept over each other as the gaggle stormed into the building. Arrogant, brutish, undisciplined.

And murderous.

Boots pounded in the enclosed stairwell like distant thunder and grew louder as they rose toward my floor. I waited. I had nowhere to run, and not enough willpower to take another beating like I'd done at the Khyber Pass.

I glanced at the bed, untouched since our trip to Torkham, and in my mind, Tara slept against my wife with her mouth open and her tattered teddy bear clutched in her hand, a gift from the US State Department two years ago. *Take one of the stuffed animals for your daughter,* the consular officer had said.

I pictured Farzana snoring like a goat. The corners of my mouth twitched from the memory—almost a smile—until their violent deaths washed over me like frigid water.

"Get up," I shouted into the empty room.

Farzana would always blink with confusion when I woke her. Her forehead would crinkle with annoyance and confusion until she saw me. Sometimes, she'd smile. My reward. All my hard work, everything I'd done had been to support her and give her the family she desired. All those times I'd snapped at her, complained about the food she'd cooked or her housekeeping . . . I hadn't been the man I could have been. And now it was too late. I was nothing without her. Without them.

Voices came from the hallway, loud and arrogant, without the need to keep quiet at night. The Taliban ruled with absolute authority. No one challenged them. Except the Islamic State.

They came to execute me, but I did not care. The hopelessness of Afghanistan manifested inside me, as if my soul and my country were one.

"They're here, my darling," I said. "I'll be joining you soon."

Farzana's face floated before me, her eyes wide with terror.

"Don't worry," I said. "I'm ready. I want this torment to end. I want to be with—"

Someone pounded on the door.

"Soon, *habibti*."

I stood and walked to the door to accept my fate.

18

Ahmed Darwish, a Syrian confidential informant Nathan code-named "Bluebird" because of his crystal-blue eyes, sat beside Nathan in the rear seat of Bridget's car in a parking lot off Eisenhower Boulevard in Alexandria, Virginia. The lot was unoccupied, except for three parked tractor trailers that lay dormant like sleeping beasts. Bridget parked in back, near the Holmes Run stream in the Cameron Run Watershed, which allowed a clear view of the Eisenhower Metro Station. Debriefing Bluebird—Nathan's only source inside the Al-Sahaba Mosque—required isolation. Most agents debriefed sources in designated rooms at FBI offices, but that had never made sense. All it took was for the wrong person to recognize a source to compromise a case. And get a source murdered.

"What do you have for us?" Nathan asked.

"I . . . nothing." A sheen of sweat glistened on Bluebird's forehead, but the temperature hovered in the mid-fifties, so something had shaken him.

"Don't give me that crap," Nathan said. "We seized weapons and a trove of tactical materials inside that mosque. They're planning something."

"Yes, yes," Bluebird said. "They have a program, but I'm not aware of its details."

"What kinda program?" Bridget asked.

"Something bad," Bluebird said.

"You better be more specific, and you better do it now," Nathan said. "If anyone dies because you're withholding information, I'll make you a co-conspirator, and you can do time with the rest of them."

Bluebird's eyes widened, and he blanched. "I've done nothing . . . it's the imam and the others."

"Which others?" Bridget asked.

Nathan grimaced. Whether questioning a suspect or a confidential informant, debriefings were more productive with one interrogator. Two agents pounding a suspect back and forth had a purpose, but a calmer approach with the subtle hint of a threat would bear more fruit. Threatening to indict him had been aggressive, but a storm approached, and the clock was ticking.

"They meet every few days in the basement," Bluebird said.

"Who meets?

"Islamists. I never saw them until a couple weeks ago."

"What do they do down there?" Nathan asked.

"Discuss things."

A vein in Nathan's temple throbbed. "What things? And I shouldn't have to drag this out of you. I offered to help your son stay out of jail on those drug charges, but only if you produce something of value."

"I'm trying—"

"Bullshit. You're not pushing hard enough. When will these men meet again?"

"Every few days, but after the raid, they only returned once."

"When?"

"Last night."

"Why were you at the mosque at night?" Bridget asked.

"I'm there as much as possible, helping the imam. Agent Burke instructed me to do that."

"Describe them," Nathan said.

"They look like everyone else—taller, shorter, fatter, thinner. How do I describe them?"

"Phone numbers? Vehicle licenses?"

"No."

Nathan sighed. "You need to do better. Call me when they return."

"It is difficult to—"

"Conceal your phone and slip into the restroom and text me."

Bluebird stared at his shoes and nodded. "Okay, okay."

"Can you get a picture of them?" Nathan asked.

Bluebird jerked his head up. "They'll kill me."

"Don't have them sit for a portrait," Nathan said. "Put your smartphone on camera and hold it to your ear like you're making a call. If nobody's suspicious, cant your body to point the camera at them and snap photos or video with your thumb. Practice in the mirror at home."

"I can't."

"If you want my help, you'll do this. These assholes are up to something, and you're in neck deep. You may not be on the planning committee, but you've assisted them—"

"You ordered me to do that."

"I recruited you because you've attended that mosque for years. You format their newsletter and plan events."

"That's not illegal."

"Don't give me shit. You're not innocent, but you're helping me now, and if your information prevents whatever it is they're planning, I'll go to bat for you. I'll do my best to keep you out of jail and help your son too. But if you're withholding anything, nothing will save you."

"What do you require?"

"Do your duty, your *Godly* duty, and help us catch them."

Bluebird hung his head. "I'll do as you ask."

19

Nathan met Meili outside his condo. The afternoon sun hung low, a harbinger of the coming winter. They hadn't seen each other in days, only communicating through texts and hurried phone calls, and seeing her even for a few minutes made a difference.

She flung her arms around him, and he kissed her.

"Your neighbors," she said. She nodded at Betty Baker's windows.

"Let's go upstairs for a quickie."

She slapped his chest playfully. "I told you I don't have time. I'm running a group meeting in half an hour."

"I'll take whatever time I can get." He embraced her again, and she melted into him. "This feels right."

"It does."

"You feel right. We've known each other for a long time."

Meili looked away. "We *knew* each other years ago. That's not the same thing."

"Were you interested in me back then, I mean, if we hadn't been in the academy?"

She blushed and smirked. "You know I was, but I focused on graduating."

"We could have tried. Imagine how things might have been different."

She hardened, the playfulness gone. "They sent us to different offices. It wasn't practical."

A blue Hyundai motored by with a middle-aged man driving, and Nathan's eyes fell to the license plate. He scanned the park across from his condo. A young woman studied something on her phone while her dog sniffed the base of a bush. Situational awareness kept Nathan alive.

He looked at Meili. "You've always been more practical than me."

"If we'd gotten together at Quantico, you wouldn't have Amelia."

That jolted him. "She's the best thing I've ever done."

"Practicality is a virtue."

"We're not in the academy now," he said. "You should keep some clothes here . . . and stay overnight."

Meili stiffened. "I'm not sure . . ."

"We have fun, and our sex is great. What's your concern?" He tensed, waiting for her answer.

Meili bit her lip, thinking. The seconds dragged by. His stomach churned.

"We're both consumed with our cases," she said, "and I'll be traveling a lot."

"We've navigated our schedules so far. We've made it work."

She frowned. "It's more than that."

Uh-oh. He swallowed hard. "You want to break up?"

She touched his arm. "It's not it. I have feeling for you too, but we're moving fast."

"We've been dating for months."

"And we haven't seen each other much during that time. We've both been working long hours and . . ."

"You don't feel the same way."

"It's . . . you have a daughter, and leaving clothes at your house is a big step."

"But—" Nathan started to argue, then pictured Amelia and stopped. Was Meili right? Amelia knew they were dating, but having Meili move things into their condo would reframe the relations. "I guess I hadn't thought this through."

"And you just got divorced."

"My marriage ended a long time ago."

"For her, but not you. You pined away for her until right before we started dating."

"I came to terms with her decision."

"It's still fresh. Let's take our time getting too serious."

Shit. He sighed. "Okay, but think about it."

She kissed his cheek. "I've got to run. You think about it too."

20

2022: Kabul, Afghanistan

I sat cross-legged on a tile floor in a windowless basement room in the General Directorate of Intelligence headquarters in downtown Kabul. I stared at a jagged crack running down the plaster wall and waited to learn my fate. This directorate purported to be the Taliban's version of the former National Directorate of Security under their newly formed Islamic Emirate of Afghanistan, but it felt more like fantasy camp for thugs.

Every day for a week, guards dragged me into this room, then my interrogator raged at me for an hour. If he wanted me to divulge American secrets, he didn't leave space for me to respond. I'd become his scream therapy. My will to live had long evaporated, and I couldn't summon the fear he hoped to evoke. I hadn't even bothered to lie about my position at the US Embassy.

The door opened, and a burly guard stormed in, followed by a short man with a trimmed beard—not my interrogator. He wore a tight black turban and a gold vest over black parahan tunban. His skin had a red hue, but not from the sun. This was a man who let others do his fighting.

He slipped into a wooden chair with the daintiness of royalty. "I am Mawlawi Jafar Mohammad, son of Haji Yousef Amadzai."

A Mawlawi was a religious teacher above imams and mullahs. His devotion to Islam involved many years of study. His name tickled a memory.

"You're from Achin?" I asked.

He stared a hole through me. "Yes."

"And your uncle is Ghulam Shinwari?"

"You know them?"

At least the fog of grief hadn't completely clouded my brain. I looked at the guard in the room then back at Haji Mohammad. He understood and motioned for the guard to leave. "Wait outside."

The guard closed the door behind him.

"Your uncle is a heroin trafficker," I said.

Mohammad tapped his fingers on the tabletop. "What is your point?"

"That cannot be acceptable to your new government. Or can it?"

"You should worry about keeping your own head."

I dismissed his comment with a flick of my hand. "My life is of no importance. I died when I lost my family."

He cocked his head. "We've all lost loved ones. You're here because you're a traitor."

"I'm a patriot. At least I was. Now all that is gone."

"You are an American spy."

"Who are you to judge me?"

"We are the law, your masters and protectors, and we will guide you back to the one true path. Everyone will submit to Sharia. It is Allah's will."

"I tried to save Afghanistan."

"By becoming a servant to Western infidels?"

How could I respond? I'd chosen sides and sought the dream of freedom and prosperity spewed by Americans, British, French, and the rest of our Western mentors. I'd believed it in my heart—all of it—but they'd abandoned us.

"I am Afghan, not American, not European, and everything I did was for my country. I'm willing to die for it."

"You are Muslim."

That was true, but my two identities were indistinguishable. The religion of Allah and the culture of Afghanistan had been linked. I'd always been religious, but not like this man—an extremist. He believed in a fundamental version of Islam, but I followed a moderate, watered-down interpretation of the Koran, compatible with modernity.

But how had that worked out for me? If believing in the secular ideas of individual liberty, economic freedom, and equality under the law had been a mistake, maybe my halfhearted embrace of Islam had been misguided too. Giving myself to Allah's will and expressing fidelity with my every action would honor him, honor my country, and my people's history.

Maybe all this time, I'd been wrong.

"You have nothing to say?" he asked. "Nothing in defense of your actions?"

"Everything I've done was to make Afghanistan stronger and our people healthier and happier. I wanted us to flourish."

"Happier? Our role is to serve, not feed blasphemous desires. You have fallen far from Allah."

I nodded. Every decision I'd made, all my choices, had led to my family's death, a decade of fighting, and my neck stretched beneath my executioner's blade. My vision dimmed, and I shook my head to clear it.

"The time has come for you to pay for your infidelity."

I met his eyes, my fear gone. The worst things I'd imagined had all happened. My life without my family had no meaning. I had not committed to Allah, and he would punish me when I passed. The government I fought for had disintegrated, leaving only this dichotomy between black and white—a choice.

"You are right."

He cocked his head. "Speak up."

"I've been a fool. I believed their lies. Their promises evaporated in the morning sun."

He narrowed his eyes. "It is you who speaks with a serpent's forked tongue."

"Then take my head. I've lost everything. It doesn't matter if you believe me. Use your blade and add my body to the pile of corpses behind the palace. Allah will see the purity in my heart."

"You seek death?"

"Life, death . . . the difference is inconsequential. I've destroyed my worldly existence."

"You lie to save your pathetic life."

"I speak the truth before Allah. If you don't believe my words, then stop me from talking. Relieve me of this burden and go on your way, or . . ."

He cracked his jaw and spit on the ground. "Or what?"

"Let me join you and do Allah's bidding."

His eye narrowed. "Doing what?"

"Killing infidels."

21

Nathan stood in his living room and watched Bridget parallel park and walk across the street toward his condo. He'd asked her to swing by for coffee before work to discuss their progress, or lack of it. Their politically charged shooting had laid a minefield, and they needed to navigate carefully.

He buzzed Bridget into the downstairs elevator and picked up the Washington Telegraph with another front-page story about the mosque shooting. His stomach cramped. What a disaster.

"Dad, oh my God, I can't believe it," Amelia said. She perched on the couch with her laptop.

"What?"

"Gloria Diaz is coming to DC."

"Who?

"Seriously, Dad, get with it. Gloria Diaz. She's the GOAT, the absolutely best. Emily just emailed me. Gloria's coming to the Capital One Arena. Everybody's going."

"Me too?"

"I can't even imagine. Let's buy tickets right now."

"Hold on. When is this? Who's going? What kind of music does she perform?"

Amelia clicked on her laptop, then spun it around and played a music video featuring a familiar-looking woman singing a song he'd never heard.

"This is her most popular song that has, like, a bazillion downloads."

"People used to buy CDs. When I was your age, I still played records."

"We don't have time to talk about the golden-oldie days or how ancient you are. I need tickets now. She's playing next month, and it's an unscheduled stop. This is my only chance."

"How much?"

She flipped her laptop around and tapped away like a court stenographer. "Emily said everyone will be in the mezzanine. She gave me the section . . . here it is. Tickets are only 300 bucks."

Nathan flinched. Money had been tight. He'd been a cop before being an agent, as his experience had allowed him to start as a GS-11 with the FBI. A year later, they'd promoted to GS-12, where he sat for three years, then he spent the last five years as a GS-13, the journeyman grade before management. As a Step 3, he made six figures. Barely.

And they spent it fast.

Education was important, and he'd do anything to set up Amelia for success, but private school cost a fortune, and now that Reagan had left them, he lost her income. Reagan wasn't working while she recovered from Havana Syndrome, but she'd promised to help with Amelia's expenses. Even if she contributed, Nathan still had to handle the mortgage alone, and DC was expensive.

"We'll see, honey."

"Da-ad, these tickets will be gone in an hour. We have to act now." The utter desperation in her voice, a window into her soul, proved too much for him.

"Fine, okay, but consider this an early birthday present."

She raced across the room and hugged him. Her love rejuvenated him. But how the hell would he make ends meet?

The elevator dinged, and Bridget stepped into his living room. Private elevators had advantages. She'd pulled her high hair back into a ponytail, but a few strands had broken free. Beneath her jacket, her taupe blouse had come untucked. Her disheveled appearance was unusual.

He smiled. "Morning."

She nodded and pursed her lips, her body wound like a steel cable.

"You've read the article?"

"My pop called me at six this morning and asked if I still had a job. Do I?"

"It's just bad PR. The *Washington Telegraph* has a far-left editorial page, and it's bled into their news coverage. This is nothing new for—"

"This hit the front page."

Nathan looked at the paper and skimmed down to the paragraph he'd read ten times. Byron Williams, a minister and black activist had eviscerated the FBI, and named Nathan and Bridget in his rant.

The FBI systematically targets Muslims, and not just foreign-born immigrants but American citizens. This horrific, racist shooting at the Al-Sahaba Mosque is a modern incarnation of Jim Crow targeting people of color. My ministry calls on the FBI to pay reparations to Imam Kareem Qadir *and fire Special Agents Burke and Quinn. Agent Nathan Burke has made killing minority Muslims a hobby.*

"They didn't mention the assault rifles we found until the twenty-ninth paragraph on the continuation page," Bridget said. "I counted."

Nathan nodded at Amelia. "Let's talk upstairs."

He led her up the curving steps past the floor with his bedrooms and into the turret.

"I feel like Rapunzel?" she said.

"This is my sanctuary."

"You're a wackadoodle," Bridget said, "and I'm not sure I wanna peek behind the curtain. Your inner psyche may be too much to handle if—" She stopped and looked out the former church's windows at Washington, DC, glimmering around them.

"Like it?"

"Wow. Just wow."

"I don't want Amelia hearing us. It's hard enough explaining the negative publicity."

"How you handling the single pop thing?"

"It's an adjustment."

She strutted around the room's perimeter, staring at the view. "What's going on with you and your boo?"

Nathan grimaced. Why did women always want to talk about feelings? "Meili and I are getting along, but . . ."

"Having troubles?"

"Things are fine."

"What's that supposed to mean? You getting serious?"

He sighed. Why did she analyze and categorize everything? "We're getting close, and we've been seeing each other whenever we can, which is hard with our schedules, but this may not be a long-term thing."

"Why wouldn't it be? You found somebody who shares your love of the job, and she puts up with your shit. What else you looking for?"

"Meili isn't ready for the next step. Maybe she's right."

"You scared of commitment?"

"My first marriage failed," Nathan said.

"Meili isn't Reagan."

"Yeah, well, Reagan and I were in love once, and she left. Maybe something's wrong with me." Where had that come from? He'd expressed feelings he hadn't known he had.

"Oh, there's plenty wrong with you." Bridget smiled.

She joked, but it still hurt. Reagan had cheated on him. The woman he most trusted, the mother of his daughter and his partner. If he wasn't enough for her, would be enough for anyone?

His thoughts must have shown on his face, because Bridget reached out and touched his shoulder. "Hey, I'm busting chops. You're a wicked catch. I'm not close to Meili, but she seems sharp, and she's hot. Don't get stuck inside your own head."

Nathan nodded. Easier said than done.

"How do we handle this frickin' political nightmare?" Bridget asked.

Time for business. "We push forward, but we must be delicate. The left smells blood in the water."

"I'm a Democrat," Bridget said, "and I don't understand how seizing opioids and weapons is racist."

"It's not a logical leap."

"Drugs do affect minority communities more than white communities."

"By percentage, but not in numbers. Police arrest more whites."

"Percentages matter," Bridget said. "Blacks are only 13 percent of the population."

"Of course, percentages are relevant. That's basic statistical analysis. The logical flaw is imbedded in looking at group outcomes when we target individual behavior. If a law is just, the color of the perpetrator's skin is irrelevant."

Bridget sighed. "My pop and brothers are wicked conservative. They've supported every Republican and voted red up and down the ticket in every election, but I've been voting Democrat since college. It's trippy being the target of these attacks."

"Revolutionaries eat their own. When we demonize others, it's hard to understand their true motivations. Both sides of the aisle do it."

"But I'm a card-carrying lib."

"I'm the true liberal," Nathan said, "in the classical definition."

"Meaning?"

"I'm libertarian."

"You've got a bunch of nuts in that party."

"I can't argue with that based on the candidates they've fielded, but I mean I'm philosophically libertarian, not a party member. Liberty, libertine. It's about freedom."

"Sounds simplistic."

"All core ideals are, but we have centuries of solid philosophy, economic, and natural experimental data to support it."

"Republicans want big government too."

"True again, but I think in terms of individualism versus statism. Is freedom a natural right or a privilege granted by government?"

"Either way, we're still being smeared as racist bigots."

"Let it go and focus on our case."

"You're shitting me, right?" Bridget said. "There's no way Rahimya gives us the green light to keep pressing."

"Something bad is going to happen."

"Nobody seems to care about terrorism anymore," Bridget said.

"People don't care about terrorism until it blows up in their faces. Especially when it involves a religious or ethnic minorities. White-racist terrorists are a minuscule number of people, but you'd think they were everywhere based on media coverage, yet radical Islam is excused or ignored. Everyone focused on Islamic terrorism after 9/11, maybe too much, but—"

"I joined the FBI because of that attack," Bridget said. "I was just a little kid, but I'll never forget those towers smoking over Manhattan, and when they came crashing down . . ." She gazed into the distance, and her eyes clouded.

"I know. It motivated many of us to join law enforcement. After the attacks, we took the fight to the enemy and most of the conflict stayed overseas. People felt safe. The fear of another incident diminished for most Americans. It became distant, unlikely."

"But the threat didn't disappear."

"When people watch soldiers being killed in distant land, it doesn't seem real. When civilians live in safe neighborhoods, they forget evil dominates the world. People demonize police and pretend their protectors are the problem, but when the wolf arrives at their door and they face nonexistence, they call the police for help. It's the same with the military and terrorism. It's only real when villainy challenges their existence."

Bridget adjusted her clothes. Agitated. "Everyone doesn't feel that way."

"Not according to the narrative coming from the media and politicians. The military are oppressors, and the police, racist."

"Bullshit."

"When people repeat a lie, it becomes perceptual fact."

Bridget sighed. "I agree something big is coming. How else do you explain those firearms in the mosque? They're planning something, and not in some foreign desert, but here, in the United States."

"It's our job to stop it."

"How?"

"We develop intelligence to convince people it's coming."

"Which people?"

"The FBI, for starters," he said. "We need resources and political will to investigate."

"A year ago, you stopped a terrorist from shooting down an airliner. Don't they see the threat?"

"Some do, but when we successfully interdict attacks, people feel safe.

Even the airport incident was out of the news after a few days. Targeting Islamists in a politically correct environment, where intersectional hierarchies paint every minority group as victims, is almost impossible. We get pushback when we interview Muslims, and chasing Islamists based in mosques will be a nightmare."

"It'll be a bigger shitstorm if they pull the trigger . . . whatever they're planning."

"Then we better solve this thing. And fast."

22

Nathan weaved through traffic down Route 1 and onto North Patrick Street in Alexandria, Virginia.

"You bang up this ride," Bridget said, "we won't make the meeting."

"Bluebird said it's urgent."

"You trust this guy?"

"Not at all, but whatever he gives us, we'll corroborate it."

"You know . . ." Bridget looked out the window. "Forget it."

"What?"

He felt her eyes return to him but kept his on the road to make it easier for her to unload whatever was on her mind—and to avoid wrecking the car.

"I know you put stock in snitches," Bridget said, "but people lie, and even when they're telling the truth, their memories suck."

"The best way to dismantle a criminal group is to have someone inside."

"That gives me agita," Bridget said. "We've been running criminal histories, credit checks, and backgrounds looking for weak links in the mosque, and we haven't found shit, except Bluebird."

"Your point?"

"He's our only snitch, and you rely on him too much. You need his info to be legit."

Nathan winced. She was right. Something was coming. He felt it is bones, but nobody seemed to care. The political tornado swirling around the shooting at the mosque had electrified their investigation like the Metro's third rail, and nobody at headquarters or Main Justice wanted to touch it. He'd used every tool in his kit to recruit sources, and he only had Bluebird—and Bluebird lied.

"I understand," Nathan said, "but we want probable cause to hang a wire on a phone to figure out what's happening."

"He hasn't done that for us yet."

"Nope. He's been giving me information I could've read in the newspaper."

"Then freakin' slow down before you whack us."

Nathan eased off the accelerator. "Sorry. He just . . . I heard a tinge of panic in his voice. He said he heard something serious, and he needs to talk now. He's waiting in a café."

"In public? This guy got a death wish?"

"No time for regular protocols. We'll scope it out before we approach."

Nathan turned onto Queen Street and parked outside Café Paris, three blocks from the water and King Street that drew tourists like a magnet. Being off the main drag reduced foot traffic, and the street was empty. They got out and walked up the red-brick sidewalk to an expansive picture window with *Café Paris* stenciled on it.

Nathan opened the door jingling the bell. A half dozen café tables dotted black-and-white marble floor across from an elegant wooden bar. Two middle-aged women sat by the window, oversized purses leaning against their chairs. A senior citizen read a newspaper and sipped coffee at the bar, and three men in business suits consumed croissants and espressos at a side table. No newspaperman, counterintelligence agency, or radical jihadists.

Bluebird sat alone in back.

Their source raised his hand in a halfhearted wave, and his eyes darted around the room. Was he concerned or afraid?

Nathan and Bridget crossed the room, and Nathan pulled out an iron chair with decorative coils and sat with his back to the wall. That forced Bridget into a seat where she couldn't see the door. She flashed him a nasty look, but her years of being an agent couldn't compare to his five years as a cop and a decade chasing terrorists. He couldn't face away from an entrance.

"You came," Bluebird said, his voice hoarse and dry.

"I don't like meeting this way," Nathan said, "not without pre-surveillance."

"I told you there's no time."

"Proper tradecraft will keep you alive. Us too."

"I just came from the mosque," Bluebird said. "Zabihullah was there."

"Who?" Nathan asked.

"Zabihullah Al-Afghani. The man leading the Phantoms."

"That's a terror cell?" Bridget asked.

"They terrify me," Bluebird said, "and they're planning something soon."

"What?" Bridget asked.

"A program. A deadly program. They . . . if they know I'm talking to you, I'm done."

"Your identity is safe with us," Nathan said.

"They'll slaughter my son . . . my wife."

"Tell us what they're planning," Nathan said.

"I volunteered, as you instructed. I've attended mosque every day. I—"

"Every day?" Nathan asked.

"Yes."

"That didn't make Imam Qadir suspicious?"

"I, uh . . . how would I know?"

Nathan glanced at Bridget and she returned his look with worry in her eyes.

"Until today," Bluebird said, his voice sounded far away, "they only spoke about the raid, but this morning, he arrived."

"Who?" Nathan asked.

"Zabihullah the Slayer. He came with three men, and they met with the imam in the basement."

Nathan's pulse increased. This was the break they needed. "Describe him."

"I couldn't see them. I crept downstairs and stood outside the door."

"They spot you?" Bridget asked.

"If they did, I wouldn't have made it out alive."

"Why do you think that?" Bridget asked.

"Because of what they discussed." A trickle of sweat ran down Bluebird's cheek.

Nathan glanced around the room. None of the other patrons paid attention to them. A security camera pointed down from above the bar. He may need to bribe an employee to get that tape.

"You got an overhear?" Nathan asked.

"The Slayer . . ." Bluebird removed a handkerchief from his pocket and wiped his brow. "He wants to murder many people."

A chill passed through Nathan. "How?"

"I didn't hear the details, but they spoke of revenge."

"Revenge for what?" Bridget asked.

Bluebird shrugged. "The imam told the Slayer his plan was brilliant."

"How do they intend to murder people?" Nathan asked.

"The Slayer said he possessed a magnificent weapon." More sweat trickled down his face.

"Which weapon?" Bridget asked.

"He didn't say."

"When will this happen?" Nathan asked.

Bluebird reached into his pocket and removed his *misbaha*. He fondled the Islamic prayer beads, and with the other hand, used a napkin to dab his brow. "The Slayer will strike soon. He spoke of the greatest jihad, the worst America would ever see."

"Did you record this?" Nathan asked.

"No . . . impossible. I . . ." Bluebird's eyes clouded over. He mumbled something.

"What?" Bridget asked, irritation seeping into her voice.

Bluebird opened his mouth then licked his lips. He started to speak, but only a strange slurring came out.

"You good there, chief?" Bridget asked.

Bluebird's eyes rolled back into his head. He collapsed out of his chair and crashed hard on the floor.

Bridget jumped to her feet. "Holy shit." She reached for him.

"Wait," Nathan said. "Don't touch him." He pointed at the barista. "Call 911. We need an ambulance."

Bluebird's arms extended rigidly, and a trickle of blood lined his forehead where he'd hit the tile. A bubble of foam popped between his lips.

"We gotta help him," Bridget said.

"Don't touch him. He's been dosed."

"What?"

"Poisoned." Nathan turned and ran behind the bar. "I need plastic gloves."

The barista pointed under the counter. Nathan ripped two pair of gloves out of box and tugged them on as he hurried back to Bluebird. The other patrons watched in silence.

Bluebird's body stilled, and his face turned blue. Nathan rolled him onto his back and tilted his head back open his airway. His chest didn't move.

"He's not breathing," Nathan said. "I'm starting compressions."

"Want me to do mouth-to-mouth?" Bridget asked.

"That'd be the last thing you'd do." Nathan knelt beside him, found his xiphoid process, then interlaced his fingers and began chest compressions.

"Don't die," Nathan said. "Not now."

23

2023: Nuevo Laredo, Mexico

I squatted in the sand on a desolate patch of desert somewhere south of Nuevo Laredo Mexico, near the border with the United States. At least that's what the cartel members who escorted our ragtag group of immigrants told us. I leaned into the thin shadow of a cactus for relief from the blazing sun. Kandahar had been far hotter, but our criminal escorts shared little water, and dehydration wrinkled my skin like a village elder's.

Rodrigo had mean eyes and long, oily hair, and he smelled of onions. A hard man, quick to anger, his subordinates feared him and grew silent when he approached. They followed his commands without hesitation. Rodrigo carried an FN semiautomatic handgun, which he kept pristine, unlike the dirt and filth that matted his soiled clothing.

During their first day the desert, Rodrigo had killed a young man, no more than nineteen, for complaining about maltreatment and demanding his money back. Rodrigo had shot him in the forehead without warning, then he turned to the group and glared at anyone who dared to make eye contact. After that, the twenty-three immigrants in our convoy had continued in silence. Rodrigo's demonstration of authority had worked, and no one needed to be taught that lesson again.

My fingers tingled with numbness. Weeks of travel from Kabul to Kandahar then over the border to a freighter in Karachi had worn me out. My Taliban escort had stuffed me into a cargo container with a dozen other emigrants—mostly military-aged men—and we'd stayed inside until the ship was safely at sea, but even then, they'd forced us to remain in a ten-by-ten section of aft deck. But at least we'd had fresh air and were alive. Not that my life meant anything anymore, but I needed to keep breathing long enough to exact my vengeance on those who'd abandoned us.

From Panama, a transportation group had separated me and three other men from the rest and taken us on a fishing trawler to Mexico, where a cartel representative collected us in Coatzacoalcos, a port city on the Gulf of Mexico.

They'd shuffled us into a panel truck with no ventilation, and we'd bounced over rough roads for eighteen hours before arriving in a barren strip of desert somewhere near the American border.

In this part of Mexico, the cartels controlled everything. They were the government, or at least the only authority. No one challenged them. They carried automatic weapons and drove around in armored vehicles. Their drones flew overhead. Rodrigo was one of these men, only harder the rest.

Rodrigo paused before a teenage girl, a vision with obvious beauty despite the days of dust that clung to her.

"Entrar en eso," he said.

"Entrar," he said again, pointing at a truck.

I didn't understand his Spanish, but the fear in her eyes told me she did, and we'd all seen the cartel members drag women into the truck, only to have them return different. Distant.

"No," a teenage boy said.

The boy had been with the girl the entire time. Were they friends, relatives, or lovers? It wouldn't matter. The cartel was the only law here.

Rodrigo turned and grinned at the boy. He pointed to him, and two of his thugs approached the boy, carrying planks. The teenager raised his hands, knowing what was coming. We all did. The fat trafficker swung his board, and it connected with the boy's forearm with a sickening crack. The wiry trafficker stepped up and delivered a second blow to the boy's head.

The kid collapsed, unconscious. The traffickers called this punishment *tableado.*

Rodrigo pointed at the girl. The men grabbed her and dragged her into the truck.

She'd suffer something far worse than *tableado.*

24

Jennifer Leigh leaned against the vertical grab rail on the Metro's Blue Line train, but didn't touch the metal with her bare skin, because *yuk*. How many dirty hands had held that pole already that morning? Children with food, adults who didn't wash after the restroom, homeless people with God knew what clinging to their soiled fingertips. She shuddered. Public transportation was no place for her or anyone with obsessive-compulsive disorder.

At least two dozen people filled the car, the regular crowd from the Virginia suburbs commuting into Washington, DC. Living in DC would have been easier than in Arlington, Virginia, but rent in the capital was higher, and college students needed to save wherever they could. At least she did.

The doors slammed shut, and the train lurched forward out of the Rosslyn Station and headed for Foggy Bottom in the District. Her physics class started in twenty minutes, and she'd cut it close.

The metal wheels clacked over the track as the car descended below the Potomac River, something Jennifer chose not to think about. The tunnel traveled eighty-five feet below the riverbed, a fact she'd researched before getting on the Metro the first time. OCD was enough to contend with, but claustrophobia tickled the edges of her mind every time she used a subway or stepped into an elevator.

She pressed harder against the pole, leaning back as the train dipped and they proceeded deeper into the earth. How had nature created phobias in the brain and why hadn't evolution eradicated them? Cool fear seeped into her belly.

Think about something else.

She had a test coming up that would determine half her grade, and she needed to ace it to make up for her lackluster performance on quizzes. The problem with physics was that it combined science with complicated theory and philosophy. She did fine with math in her other STEM courses, but anything that veered away from black-and-white answers caused her fits. Maybe she lacked imagination, or maybe she couldn't conceptualize anything she couldn't see, but whatever her deficiency, trying to understand quantum mechanics and differences with general relativity hurt her brain. If she—

What was that?

A high-pitched din broke through the background noise of electrical humming and clacking of the rails. Around her, passengers looked up with worried expressions. They heard it too. She canted her head and stared into the next car.

Red smoke filled the first car.

She gasped and jerked upright. The sound she'd heard had been shrieking, but it had stopped. The passengers had gone silent.

Her heart pounded.

The train's brakes squealed like a banshee. The car lurched and shuddered, sending Jennifer flying onto the floor. A fat man tumbled off his seat and belly flopped behind her, his girth just missing her.

The train jolted to a complete stop, and an electrical odor filled the car. Was the train on fire?

At the front of her car, two men in business suits peered through the windows into the first car and exchanged rapid, frantic words. They turned and hurried down the aisle toward her.

"Get off the train," one of them shouted. "Everyone off."

"What is it?" a guy wearing an army uniform and military crew cut asked.

"Fire. The first car's filled with smoke. Everyone's lying on the floor. They look dead."

Panic flashed through her.

"We should wait for the conductor to issue instructions," the soldier said.

"He's in the first car too... with the bodies. They're overcome by the smoke."

The soldier moved to a call box on the wall and pressed the red button. "Hello? What's happening." He released the button and waited.

No answer.

"Fuck this," the businessman said. "I know fire when I see it. I'm getting out of here."

Jennifer looked at the window, now completely opaque with crimson fog. "Smoke isn't red."

Everyone peered at the window. Wispy, blood-red clouds trickled in through cracks around the door. People stared as if watching television. Nobody moved.

A woman screamed.

That broke the spell. People leapt up.

The businessman shoved through the crowd to the center door. He flipped open the cover on the red emergency box and yanked down the handle. A bell chimed, then the doors hissed and cracked open.

"Wait," the soldier said. "Use the other door. We're supposed to exit on the lighted side."

Was any of this real? She'd stepped into a horror movie.

A woman near the front stumbled forward and collapsed. The elderly man beside her reached for her then coughed. He hacked again, and his forehead crinkled. He extended his hand, as if reaching for something. His eyes locked with Jennifer's. He fell back and bounced off his seat, and then crumpled to the floor beside the woman. Unconscious.

"It's poison," a woman screamed.

"Move out now," the soldier said. He activated the switch on the opposite side of the car. The doors whooshed and jerked, separating by a few inches, but they did not fully open. The soldier stuck his fingers into the space, grasped the rubber seal, and wrestled the doors apart.

Passengers moved toward the opening. Two middle-aged women near the front coughed and tumbled to the floor. More screams and frantic chatter.

A burly man pushed past Jennifer, almost knocking her down, and other passengers shoved past as they stampeded toward the open doors.

Jennifer turned to flee, then stopped and offered her hand to the fat guy lying on the floor. He grasped her hand and struggled to his knees but kept his other hand wrapped around his briefcase. Her elbow ached from his weight, and she let go.

"Thanks."

She opened her mouth to speak, but a young woman carrying a baby pushed past her, knocking Jennifer off balance. The soldier held the door open and helped passengers climb onto the elevated walkway. So brave. Soldiers took action.

Passengers seemed confused, panicked. Two men walked deeper into the tunnel, but most headed back the way they'd come, away from the affected car.

The guys on the walkway closest to the first car started coughing. One wobbled on his feet then stumbled and fell between the train and walkway. He disappeared into the dark. The other man turned to flee then toppled face first onto the concrete. People screamed and pushed. Everyone ran back toward Rosslyn.

Jennifer leapt onto the walkway and followed. She kept her feet moving and extended her hands for balance. How far away was Rosslyn Station? She followed the fleeing passengers along the length of the train. Passengers in the last cars had not evacuated, and many pressed their faces against the glass, staring at her and the others like animals in the zoo. Why weren't they getting out too? Hadn't they seen the smoke?

"Get out," Jennifer yelled. "Evacuate."

People gawked and didn't move. She shuffled forward as the line of fleeing passengers picked up speed.

Bang.

A bomb. Dark smoke, red like cherries, billowed through the car beside her. Passengers turned from the windows and covered their mouths. A lady screamed and collided with an elderly gentleman. Their legs tangled, and they fell.

Jennifer slowed, and someone crashed into her from behind, expelling air from her lungs. She stumbled forward, but instead of falling, she sprang into the air and leapt over the people laying on the platform.

She glanced over her shoulder. The fat man lumbered behind, but he hadn't bothered to drop his heavy attaché suitcase—and that coupled with his obesity took their toll. He fell on top of the woman and old man.

Jennifer stopped.

"Dammit."

She turned back. The older gentleman and the woman disentangled themselves, but the old guy clambered to his feet and lost his balance. He fell against the car.

Jennifer grabbed him and steadied him. The woman raced past, shouldering her as she fled. *What a bitch.*

Jennifer helped the fat man up for the second time. Did that make her a hero? Whatever, it had been the right thing to do. He nodded, and she turned and jogged along the walkway.

She was going to make it. What a story this would make when she returned to class to—

Boom.

Another bomb. This one in the last car. Crimson smoke flowed out of seams and cracks in the car and tinged the air with a hellish hue.

Jennifer sidestepped closer to the wall. Smoke poured out of the car as if from a smokestack.

She coughed.

Oh, God, no.

She held her breath, but numbness spread through her body like a warm wind. All her aches and pains vanished. A euphoric bliss welcomed her into an embrace. What had she worried about?

She withdrew inside herself, and the world disappeared.

25

Nathan stood in his group's common room with Bridget, Rahimya, and other agents and analysts as they gawked at images of the Metro terror attack. At least it appeared to be terrorism after first responders encased in HAZMAT suits had discovered two exploded suitcases. Early reports suggested toxic gas has been released inside the cars and contaminated the tunnel. Seventy-eight people were on the train, and almost all succumbed to the toxin.

Images of EMTs muscling gurneys out of the GWU Metro Station's elevator on the corner of Twenty-third and I streets NW filled the screen, captivating the room. Similar attacks hit transportation hubs in New York, Long Island, and Chicago. The coordinated attacks sent tremors through the population.

"We need all hands on this," Nathan said.

"Too early," Rahimya said. "They haven't established a link to Islamic extremism."

"The Mormons didn't do it."

She flashed him side-eye. "HQ has sent teams to assist since it looks like terrorism, but a variety of radicals could be responsible."

Grainy images taken inside the tunnel replaced the EMTs. Rescuers in Level A HAZMAT suits shuffled along the narrow walkway toward the trains. A hazy, red fog tinted the air, and maroon dust coated the concrete.

"If this is a terror attack, why give the gas color?" Bridget asked. "Wouldn't a colorless toxin be deadlier?"

"Maybe the poison gives it that hue," Rahimya said.

"I don't think so," Nathan said. "Even if it colored the vapor, I doubt it would be bright red. This seems intentional."

"That doesn't make sense," Bridget said.

"It makes sense if they want to intensify terror," Nathan said. "The video that will inevitably surface will appear scarier to spread fear."

"Okay, everyone," Rahimya said, raising her voice for the room. "Our group's terrorism targets aren't taking a break. Let's get back to work too."

"I'll task our CIs to see what we can find," Nathan said.

"That'll be my directive for our team, but I don't want anyone abandoning their cases to chase down something that could just as easily be a white supremacist group."

"Or a black nationalist group, or AntiFa, or . . ."

Rahimya rolled her eyes. "Put out feelers, but focus on your cases."

"Those may not be mutually exclusive."

Rahimya removed her glasses and rubbed the bridge of her nose. "I know I shouldn't ask, but . . . explain."

"Imam Qadir and his cohorts ordered a massive opioid shipment. They—"

"We don't know Qadir ordered it."

"It's a logical assumption," Nathan said, "but the question is why, and the obvious answer is they need money to fund something."

Rahimya's expression hardened. "We haven't determined they wanted to sell opioids versus storing it for a trafficker. Maybe they've warehoused this stuff for years. And we can't prove they used drugs to fund terrorism. Operations like what we just witnessed take years to plan, and it was funded before your seizure."

"That's what scares me."

"Meaning?"

"What else did Imam Qadir need to fund?"

"You're convinced the imam is involved?" Bridget asked.

"It's likely, considering the timing. I called Doug Cregar at DEA, and he set up a meeting for us this afternoon. I want their informants to beat the bushes. DEA knows every major trafficking group in the area, and maybe they can shed light on who ordered it and how it got here."

"And who plans to sell it," Bridget said.

"A shipment that size would require a significant retailer," Nathan said. "Using cutting agents to reduce toxicity and repackaging it for consumption takes knowledge, not to mention how many dealers they'd need on the street. I'm guessing they planned to send some to other cities."

"Then why bring it to the mosque?" Bridget asked. "Why not keep it concealed in prayer mats and drive it to its final destination?"

"Hold on," Nathan said. "Something just occurred to me. What if the mosque was its final destination, and what if they didn't plan to reduce its toxicity?"

"You mean they planned to sling it to a wholesaler?" Bridget asked.

"He's saying they wanted to use it as a weapon." Rahimya said.

"That's right," Nathan said. "The bombs on the Metro contained something poison, so why not opioids? Maybe that's what they intended to do with the drugs."

"But the operation's over."

"Then they're not done."

The room seemed to cool, and Rahimya and Bridget stared at each other.

"We should move fast," Nathan said.

"We're getting nothing from NSA," Rahimya said.

"How's that possible?" Nathan asked. "This is the biggest domestic terror attack since the Twin Towers came down. Whoever did this can't stay silent."

"Oh, radicals are celebrating all over the world," Rahimya said. "NSA's monitored databases are inundated with comments praising the attacks. The sheer volume overwhelms our ability to sift through it, even using algorithms."

"Then we've got leads?"

"That's the problem. Nobody has claimed responsibility."

"And who is that?"

"We've no idea. It must be Al-Qaeda, ISIS, Hezbollah, or one of the usual suspects, but none of our intercepts or data dumps has paid off. Whoever did this has gone silent."

Nathan scratched his chin. "That tells us something too."

"Yeah, that we're wire-tapping the wrong people, and NSA needs to adjust their collection parameters."

"More than that, our lack of intelligence indicates we're dealing with something new."

"I don't follow."

"They hit four targets across the country almost simultaneously. These operations required coordination, and a lack of communication suggests a new methodology. They may not be using computers or phones, or they're doing it through pictures, not words."

"That's guesswork," Rahimya said. "We dealt with plenty of cagey players smart enough to stay off phones."

"This is another level. What time did each of these attacks occur?"

Rahimya swiped her iPad and scrolled through a document. "They hit O'Hare at 0845 hours, Union Station at 0847, and the Rosslyn Metro at 0850—at least that's when they logged the first report—and the Jamaica Long Island Rail at 0849."

"That kind of precision is hard to pull off without expert planning, communications, logistics, and execution," Nathan said. "To do that without popping up on anyone's radar is incredible. This isn't just a smart organization being careful on the phones. It's a new beast entirely. Or an old one."

"Meaning?"

"They've gone old school using in-person communications only. No technology."

"Impossible. They couldn't pull this off like that."

"Sure they could, and they can do it again."

Alarm flashed in Rahimya's eyes. "There's more coming?"

"Guarantee it."

"For twenty years, law enforcement and intelligence have leaned harder and harder on technical solutions," Rahimya said. "If jihadists execute without technology, we'll sit our most effective weapons on the bench. They'll tie our hands."

"But a human chain of communication means they're vulnerable in a different way. The links in the chain are human, with all the frailties and mistakes that entails."

"How do we stop them?"

"Human intelligence."

26

Nathan waited for Bridget outside the DEA's Special Operations Division in Chantilly, Virginia. The Office of Professional Responsibility and the FBI had cleared them to officially return to work, and they needed to catch up. Bridget exited her car and breezed across the parking lot wearing a cinnamon-colored, V-neck dress that flittered above her ankles. He hadn't seen her in a dress. Her legs showed beneath the thin material below her slip. Why were woman sexier when they hinted at what lay beneath instead of showing skin?

She smiled and waved.

"You look nice today," Nathan said.

"Today?"

"No, not just today. I mean, you, uh, you always look good."

"Thanks." Her demeanor cooled.

"What I meant was, you look good in a dress. You're always wearing pantsuits, and I like your new look."

"Got it." She turned and opened the door.

Nathan's face burned with embarrassment. Had he insulted her? Did she think he was hitting on her? He'd been trying to be nice, but he wasn't hitting on her.

He cracked his neck. Then he cracked his jaw. Was this the new him, post marriage? Would women see him as a man on the prowl? Would he need to watch every comment he made? When he'd been married, nobody assumed he harbored lecherous thoughts. At least he didn't think so. He had them, of course, but he'd never cheated on Reagan, and despite Meili's hesitation to get more serious with him, he'd never cheat on her either. If the relationship didn't work out, he'd break up and then go find someone new. Did men cheat because they worried they wouldn't be able to find another woman if they broke up first?

Yep, this was his new identity—divorced guy. *Crap.*

They checked in with DEA's contract security office and waited until Intelligence Analyst Fernando Gomez collected them. Nathan had met him on a Taliban case the previous year.

Gomez, known as Mullet to his friends, appeared to be in his mid-sixties, based on the crevices in his face and weariness in his eyes. He'd been a cop at some Podunk department in the Arizona before becoming a DEA agent, and then he'd been forced to give up his gun for some reason, and he came back as an analyst pursuant to a legal settlement. Yeah, he looked his age, except for his hair which he dyed black, as if he didn't realize how it made him look. But despite his hairdo, poor attitude, and archaic belief system, at least he'd tell Nathan the truth. Mullet never held back.

"My GS told me you needed some intel," Mo said. "What ya want?"

"We're looking for an opioid briefing," Nathan said, "from soup to nuts."

"About time you Feebs came looking for the truth."

"Charming as ever," Nathan said. "Fernando, this is my partner, Bridget."

Fernando looked at her and shook his head with a smirk.

"What?" Bridget asked.

"Noth'n."

Bridget chewed on her lip. "You sure? 'Cause it looked like you got something to say."

"I'll let you know when I do. Follow me."

Mullet them upstairs in an elevator, but from the tire around his waist, he should have taken the stairs. He led them through an office and into his cubicle.

He plopped into his chair and swiveled around to face them. "What's this for?"

"We seized a huge load of opioids," Nathan said, "and—

"Get lab results back yet?" he asked.

"The Mid-Atlantic Lab is backed up. Since we haven't arrested anyone yet, they're not rushing our analysis."

"What are they, *retahded?*" Bridget said. "The subway attacks used carfentanil. How can they not expedite it?"

Nathan sighed. "Rahimya pushed a request up the chain, but we haven't heard back. Bureaucracy sucks."

Mullet smirked. "Ain't that right?"

"Anyway," Nathan said, "I need an education on what we're dealing with, because I've never worked drugs. Well, not directly. When I was in Afghanistan targeting high-value targets and Al Qaeda, it seemed like all of them were involved with the drug trade or protecting local labs and traffickers who supported them."

Nathan's cellphone vibrated in his pocket, but he ignored it. This meeting had been hard to set up, and it had to happen now. Without a better understanding of the drug world, they'd flail around in the dark.

"Opioids are a different animal," Mullet said. "Afghanistan may be the heroin capital of the world, but fentanyl is a hundred times stronger. They bleed poppy plants to create opium, which is smoked or injected. They synthesize opium into morphine and then refine it into heroin. Each iteration possesses higher potency."

"And opioids?" Nathan asked.

"They're synthetic opiates and exponentially more powerful."

"All I hear about is fentanyl," Nathan said. "Has it replaced heroin?"

"Market forces changed addicts' drug of choice," Mullet said. "Opioids don't require fields of poppies on mountainsides in hostile areas. Chemists engineer them to meet desired effects at reasonable price points, and with less wastage."

"Where are they produced?" Bridget asked.

Nathan's phone vibrated again. He slipped it out and checked the screen. Rahimya.

"Ninety percent of the opioids consumed in the US originate in China."

Mullet looked at Nathan when he responded, even though Bridget had asked the question.

"We should shut down trade with those fuckers," Bridget said, annoyance seeping into her tone. She didn't like being ignored.

"Opioids, as a class of drugs, are lifesaving," Mullet said. "Analgesics are used during surgery and to control significant pain. Opioids produced for legitimate reasons come from India, China, or wherever, and they're important and necessary, but we gotta stop illicit use."

"How do we tell the difference?" Bridget asked.

"Even legitimately imported opioids can be diverted by doctors or pharmacists out of pill mills. Diversion is an enormous problem. But the biggest challenge is the illicit manufacturing of opioids. Illegal mom-and-pop labs to massive factories in China produce and ship their chemicals overseas."

"And we snatch those shipments?" Bridget asked.

"That's the goal, but it's almost impossible." Mullet glared as if it was Bridget's fault the DEA hadn't won the War on Drugs. "China ships pills under different labels, so they aren't listed on cargo manifest and they pass through multiple transshipment countries to obscure the country of origin."

Nathan's phone buzzed a third time. Another call from Rahimya. She needed to speak with him—not a good sign.

"Excuse me," he said. He stepped into an empty cubicle. He dialed and Rahimya answered on the first ring.

"Answer your damn phone when I call you."

"We're in a briefing at SOD."

"Wrap it up and come back."

Nathan exhaled. "What's happened? Did we get the arrest warrant for Qadir?"

"Far from it. DOJ won't green-light the application. They claim you can't link the drugs to him because—"

"That's bullshit. The driver carried a box of opioid-soaked carpets toward the back door, and the imam was inside."

"Listen," Rahimya's tone warmed. "I know that would be enough under normal circumstances, but that was a house of worship, and he's a prominent Muslim leader."

"We wouldn't get this resistance if it was another religion," Nathan said. "DOJ's worried about the backlash."

"Being tarnished as Islamophobic isn't in DOJ's best interests, or those of the FBI."

"Maybe we should be more worried about enforcing the law than political correctness. Isn't that what American citizens pay us to do?"

"Islamophobia is a real thing."

"That's crap, and you know it. Sure, there are bigots on all sides, and don't get me started on the supremacy built into radical Islam, but that's not why we're being stonewalled by DOJ. Their decision is driven by intersectional hierarchy. There are fewer Muslims, so they're protected. Not holding them to the same standard as everyone else is its own form of bigotry. Isn't equality under the law our directive?"

Rahimya sighed. "Just get back here. The ASAC just called me into his office to defend our actions."

"You've gotta be kidding me."

"Activist groups are gathering their resources. The ASAC told me to expect a demonstration and a lawsuit."

"What we did is defensible in court."

"This is reality, Nathan. We need to fight in the court of public opinion too. Come back to the office."

"Roger that." He hung up and waited for his rage to dissipate before he walked around the corner.

Mullet continued to lecture Bridget. "China also sends precursor chemicals to Mexico and other countries where criminal groups manufacture the pills. They don't have quality control, so a single pill may have ten times the amount of active ingredient the user expects. Traffickers use fentanyl to intensify the potency of other drugs too."

"Where's the bulk of it coming in?" Bridget asked.

"From Mexico. It comes across the border hidden in tractor trailers with legitimate goods, by sea in the holes of ships, or even in jury-rigged submarines. Human smugglers swallow balloons containing the product, and since the border's wide open, drug mules cross with impunity."

"You think our dope came over the southern *bordah?*" Bridget asked.

"A chemical signature may point to a known producer or region, but barring that, yeah, it probably came through Mexico."

"What happens after drugs cross the border?" Nathan asked.

"Cartels control everything. They influence the Mexican government and control regions like fiefdoms. The drugs enter in wholesale amounts, either as powder or pills, and they're picked up by cartel members in the border area and transported to distributors around the country. Distributors traffic in large amounts and sell to lower-level traffickers. The drugs pass from group to group until they reach users.

"Where does DC fall into that hierarchy?" Nathan asked.

"DC's not an importation city—it's a secondary distribution center. Most of the drugs sold on the street around here come from New York, Philadelphia, or LA. In DC, gangs sell to users. The city must have sixty open-air drug markets."

"That explains drug-related violence," Bridget said.

"Gangs are responsible for much of the violence, which is why DEA labeled them domestic cartels," Mullet said. "Violence is rampant throughout the drug trade. Groups that engage in illicit drug trafficking can't go to the police when thieves steal from them, so they're forced into vigilantism."

"Who are the players in Arlington?" Bridget asked.

"Could be any of a dozen known groups, from MS-13 to local crews."

"They'd diluted the drugs we seized in a water solution," Nathan said, "then they soaked carpets with it and let 'em dry. It'll take a while for the lab to recover all the drugs and give us a final weight and profile of substance, but it's an opioid, probably fentanyl."

"They make plenty of analogues."

"Analogues?" Bridget asked.

"Chemists try to stay one step ahead of the laws. For a synthetic drug to be illegal, it must have a certain chemical composition, so producers tweak a few molecules so it's different and then sell it and wait for legislation to catch up. The analog law criminalizes structurally similar chemicals that produce similar outcomes."

"The libertarian in me feels uncomfortable with that," Nathan said.

"Boo-hoo. Lots of Libs get their panties in a twist over that one." Mullet said.

Bridget scowled. "It's a slippery slope to arrest somebody for a substance that's not illegal until we determine it to be similar to another drug. How far removed can they go?"

"Up to the judge."

"That's why I'm uncomfortable with it, but these tested positive for opioids, and the perps who shot at us knew their conduct was illegal."

"We'll see what the judge says," Mullet said, "but sometimes these guys get off. Too much, ya ask me."

"The guys we caught are dead," Nathan said. "I took out one, and Bridget offed the other one." Nathan used blunt language to push back against Mullet.

Mullet looked at Bridget, as if reassessing her. His eyes carried more respect than before.

"Guess justice was done," Mullet said. "Why the need for a class on drugs?

"We're having trouble pinning the load on the imam."

"Can't help you with that," Mullet said.

"Seems no one can," Nathan said. "Hey, that was our boss. We have to skate."

"I hope you whack more of those assholes." Mullet lumbered off across the office.

"Great attitude," Nathan said. "What's his problem with you?"

"He's a chauvinist pig. He doesn't like a chick with a badge. I seen it before, but when you told him I capped that asshole, he changed his mind."

"You don't need his respect."

"What did Rahimya want?"

"There's political trouble."

"No warrant?"

"Nope, but what worries me most," Nathan said, "is what they planned to do with the money they made from the sale."

27

Nathan turned into the Al-Sahaba Mosque. Their meeting with Rahimya had been unpleasant, and he needed to get away from the flagpole. He raised his cellphone, pressed it against the driver's window, and hit record on the video. He rolled down the line of cars taping the license plates.

Bridget groaned beside him. "For the third frickin' time, this is a shit idea. Didn't we take enough of a beating from HQ and the press the last time we came here?"

"I have all my sources beating the bushes, but they've found nothing. Our adversary's using low-tech methodology, and we'll counter it by returning to basics. Their plans require human beings, so we find the weak leak and exploit it."

"You said jihadists don't cooperate with boys in blue."

"True believers don't, but it's one thing to preach radicalism and another to strap a bomb to your back and return to Allah."

"What's the plan?"

"The registrations will tell us who own the cars, and they're all connected to the mosque. We'll background them and see what turns up."

"Is it legal to run names for attending services?

"They used the mosque as a cover to store drugs and weapons, and that links anyone here to a crime. Sort of."

"The dope we seized may have nothing to do with terrorism."

"The imam's connected to the Slayer, and the opioids are too much of a coincidence."

"I doubt the special agent in charge will see it that way. Or the director."

"Then we better uncover evidence."

"How?"

"We find someone who knows what's going on, preferably someone on the fringe, like a transporter who has inside access but isn't as radical as the others."

"And then what?"

"We find their vulnerability and apply pressure. We balance the carrot and the stick. People have needs, and we have resources."

"You're freakin' whacko if you think the front office wants us poking around a mosque again."

"After yesterday's attack, they have a choice. If we locate a way into this group, we'll have the resources of the entire US government behind us. Our next challenge will be to protect our source."

"Who we don't have yet."

"Nobody said counterterrorism is easy."

He drove around back where another three dozen cars parked in the rear lot.

"I thought we were between prayer services," she said.

"Next one's not for a couple hours."

"Then why all the cars?"

"We're at war. We uncloaked them, and they're planning how to handle it."

"You can't know that."

"Nothing's for sure." He filmed the first row of cars.

"That's new," Bridget said.

"What?"

She jerked her chin up at the mosque. Two giant security cameras aimed at the parking lot.

"Shit. Smile for the cameras."

"Will that be a problem?" she asked.

"If we let them know who we are."

The back door opened, and a dozen men sauntered out, shielding their eyes from the morning light. They'd been inside a while.

"We better get outta town," Bridget said.

"Almost done."

"Not worth the risk."

Nathan sped up, but not too fast to avoid blurring the video. Three men stared across the lot at his car.

"Done," he said.

"Thank, God. Let's skedaddle. Why isn't there a rear exit? We're forced to drive right past them."

"Keep you sun visor down and turn your head as we pass."

He started to pocket his phone when it rang. Rahimya. He put it on speaker.

"Hey, Boss."

"The lab just emailed me with the chemical analysis," she said.

"Fentanyl?"

"Carfentanil. It's much stronger."

Nathan's pulse raced. "The same as the drug in the Metro attack."

"They used it in all the attacks. It's fentanyl on steroids. We were lucky none of us were exposed."

"Another link to terrorism."

"Not necessarily," she said. "We may be seeing an increase in carfentanil usage, and if we are, be prepared for a massive spike in ODs."

"Or a spike in terrorism," Nathan said.

"Let's talk about it. Where are you?"

Nathan looked at Bridget. "On our way back to the office. See you in thirty." He hung up.

"What does this mean?" she asked.

"Our evidence is growing against Qadir. Let's get back and check out the report."

The men watched them. Nathan sat erect, so his visor obscured his face. He wanted to look away, but anyone of them could be a terrorist, and the cop in him refused to be blindsided by an attack. He squinted and watched their hands, hoping the glare would obscure his face. If anyone recognized him, there'd be trouble. He scanned the last three men.

Recognition jolted him.

Nathan lifted his foot off the gas. His eyes lingered on the last man, a guy with black hair and a wiry frame. Something about that guy. A memory tickled his mind. He'd seen that man before, but out of context, he couldn't place him.

"Why are you slowing down?" Bridget asked.

"I know that guy."

"Who?"

It came to him—Hamid.

Nathan accelerated out of the lot then turned to her and smiled.

"What the hell are you doing?" she asked.

"We just caught a huge break."

28

2023: Laredo, Texas

We trudged over scalding sand through clapweed, juniper, and saddlebush. Fifty meters away, the murky-green Rio Grande River crept by, a moat protecting our destination—the United States.

Rodrigo led our caravan of immigrants up a dusty dirt road littered with empty water bottles and torn clothing, and his men bracketed us, more captors than protectors. Six of the nine women in our group, all teenagers stared at the ground with dead eyes. Their *sessions* alone with Rodrigo had left scars.

My rage simmered.

I'd stood by and done nothing while that animal had defiled these women. Every day of our week-long journey from the Gulf, this man had taken a woman. The Koranic law made them man's property, but Rodrigo hadn't even bothered with temporary marriages to legitimize his conquests. He'd raped them, which was also allowed—if they were infidels.

Tara's image appeared in the shimmering reflection of the sun off the water. She gazed at me with desperate eyes, pleading for something. Farzana had not come to me in days, and only my daughter stalked my movements, appearing in moments of doubt or conflict. What message did she have for me? What did she want?

Rodrigo pointed at the river. *"Nosotros cruzamos esta noche."*

I'd picked up enough Spanish to understand we'd sneak into the United States tonight. I had the address and telephone number of my contact in my pocket, but Islamic State jihadists would collect me in Texas. They'd take me to Michigan, where I'd be given a group of martyrs to exact my revenge. It hadn't taken me long to deduce that my interrogator in Kabul, Mawlawi Jafar Mohammad, held loyalty to ISIS over the Taliban. He preferred their aggressive strategy, and that suited me.

The time for vengeance was now.

The cartel men congregated around a knapsack and dug out food, none of which would trickle down to us. The girls huddled together, knowing what would happen. Rodrigo took his reward after each day's march.

A scrawny thug handed Rodrigo a stick of salami, and Rodrigo bit off a piece and chewed it as he walked toward the girls. They shriveled as he neared.

Rodrigo snared a young girl's wrist in his hairy mitt and dragged her into the brush. She looked over her shoulder at the others, her eyes desperate, like Tara's.

My stomach hardened, and Tara's face filled my vision. That girl was only a few years older than my daughter. She could be her—not Muslim, but defenseless and innocent. At least she had been before she met Rodrigo. And this monster wasn't Muslim either. He had no right.

They disappeared around a stand of cacti, green melons with spikes. I glanced back at his men, who lounged in the sand, eating and passing a bottle of tequila, oblivious to us or the plight of the girl.

I stomped after Rodrigo and the girl. My fight lay across the border with the people who had forsaken me and my country, and venting my anger endangered my mission, but Allah's wrath flowed through me.

I could be impotent no more.

The girl squirmed beneath Rodrigo beside a yellow, flowering rabbit-brush. His pants collected around his ankles and his .357 revolver lay beside them in the sand.

Disgust foamed up from my stomach into my throat. My muscles tensed on their own, and I reached for the gun.

A twig snapped beneath my sandal.

Rodrigo cocked his head. He looked up and scowled. Then he must have recognized the look in my eyes because fear flashed over him.

I snatched the silver revolver off the ground. I shoved the barrel in his face.

His eyes widened. *"Te mataré—"*

Allah's will flowed through me.

I pulled the trigger, and flame exploded out of the barrel. His head jerked back, and a piece of his skull flapped off his head.

The gunshot echoed over the Rio Grande Valley. The girl gaped at me, Rodrigo's blood splattered over her face. Tiny pink flecks of his brain stuck to her hair.

I looked back through the cacti at the hollow where the caravan rested. The immigrants cowered. The cartel members all stood and faced me.

I could fight it out with them, but my destiny lay in America.

I pushed through the underbrush toward the river.

My head swam. Murder. Killing. Death had surrounded me in Afghanistan, and I'd supported American missions which resulted in the loss of life, but I'd never caused it. Not directly. Rodrigo lay at my feet, blood running out of his head and pooling on the ground. A river of vanishing life seeping into the sand.

I should feel something, but I didn't. Where was the fear, the regret, or even triumph? I felt nothing—only numbness. Was I a servant of Allah, or had I lost all my humanity? The Koran approved killing infidels, and not only was Rodrigo not Muslim, he was a rapist and murderer, so his death counted as jihad.

Whatever I'd become, I bore no resemblance to the man I'd been. Not to the husband of Farzana nor the father of Tara. I was a warrior in Allah's army, and I could never return to the world as I'd know it. If only . . . Why didn't I feel satisfaction?

Farina's image hovered before me. She moved her head from side to side, either disapproving or dissatisfied with my efforts. I hadn't joined ISIS and traveled this far to kill cartel members. I had one mission. Only one thing would avenge the deaths of my family.

I waded into the river.

I looked back. The immigrants watched me, their expressions a combination of awe and fear. Even Rodrigo's men kept their distance and made no move to confront me. Did they fear me, or were they glad to be rid of their unstable and violent leader? They'd face difficult questions about his death when they returned to the cartel, but I wouldn't be there to refute their story.

I held the pistol above the water and stroked toward the shore. I'd find my contacts and make my way to Michigan. My jihad had begun, and I had one goal before me.

I would destroy America.

29

Nathan and Bridget established surveillance on Washington Boulevard and watched cars exit the Al-Sahaba Mosque.

"Who is this guy?"

"Hamid Mangal."

"A suspect?"

"Ally. He was our best foreign service national at the Kabul Embassy. Hold on, here he comes."

Nathan scrunched down as Hamid's decrepit Honda Accord pulled out of the mosque's parking lot. Nathan fell in behind it, and they followed him westbound onto Wilson Boulevard.

"You know him from the Stan?" Bridget asked.

"State assigned Hamid as our foreign service national, and I used him as my interpreter whenever we went into the field. He acted as a fixer more than anything. We would have been useless without him and our other FSNs."

"What's he doing at the mosque?"

"He's Muslim, and there aren't many mosques around here."

"Where's his pad?"

"I didn't know he'd moved to the US. I tried to help a bunch of our guys after the withdrawal, but I lost touch with him. This could be our chance. I debriefed dozens of informants with him. He could be our key to getting inside Qadir's inner circle."

"But he's an interpreter, not a source."

"Hamid was more than a linguist. He knew our investigations better than some agents, and his intricate understanding of Afghan culture and tribal nuances helped us recruit sources and interrogate prisoners."

"He's attending a pretty radical mosque. You trust him?"

"Most of the mosques in Northern Virginia have radical elements. I put my life in Hamid's hands all over Afghanistan, from Helmand to Mazar-i-Sharif. I trust him, and he trusts me . . . at least he did."

"How will he help us—"

"Hold on. He's stopping."

The Honda turned into a strip mall and parked. Nathan entered behind him and parked two spaces away.

"What's our play?" Bridget asked.

"We ask for his to help and hope he still believes in me."

The Honda's door opened, and the driver got out.

"That's Hamid," Nathan said.

Nathan slipped out and scanned the lot before he approached. A handful of shoppers shuffled in and out of a supermarket, bracketed by a Vietnamese restaurant and a nail salon. Hamid headed for the entrance.

"Hamid," Nathan called out.

Hamid flinched and whirled around. His eyes narrowed.

"It me, Nathan Burke."

Hamid's shoulders relaxed, and he grinned.

Nathan extended his hand, and Hamid took it and pulled him into a hug. They slapped each other on their backs, the way warriors did.

"My friend," Hamid said. "It has been too long. How is your health?"

"I'm good." Nathan looked him over. "You look thinner."

"I don't get free chow here like we did at the airfield."

Images of the Jalalabad Airfield flooded Nathan's memory, and he smelled the dust and jet fuel. He'd spent many months in Nangarhar debriefing sources with Hamid, such a long time ago—a memory from another life.

"How'd you get that scar above your eye?" Nathan asked.

Hamid's face hardened. "After you left, things became . . . difficult. They slaughtered those who worked for you."

A wave of guilt sickened him. "But you survived."

Hamid nodded. "I was lucky."

"How is your family?" Nathan gritted his teeth as he waited for the answer. Too many Afghans had suffered after the botched withdrawal.

A cloud passed over Hamid's face. "They are well . . . I think. I try to speak to them every day, but they lose power in Kabul, and their phones are often off."

"Will you bring them here?"

"I've applied for visas, but State hasn't approved them."

"How is that possible? You worked for the embassy for what, four years?"

"Six. They tell me my family is on the list, but there's a backlog . . . and difficulty getting anyone out."

"The immigration system is a mess. I'll call HQ and see if I can get them moved up in the queue. The logjam may be at State, but a call from the Bureau may help."

Hamid shook his head. "Thank you for offering, but there's no need. Other agents have called for me. I just need to wait."

Nathan's guilt deepened. He should have stayed in touch, helped more. He nodded. "Listen, I'm glad I spotted you. I didn't know you attended mosque."

Hamid turned serious. "My father took us every day when I was young, but after I had my family, we only went weekly. I came here because I felt homesick, but it was a mistake."

"Why?"

"Imam Kareem Qadir and the religious leaders try to control us. They demand we attend every day, sometimes multiple times. They push us to embrace fundamental Islam. It's too much."

"Tell them to fuck off."

Hamid flashed a sad smile. "It's not that easy. Beyond the social pressure, they make veiled threats. Sometimes, they get physical.

"What? This is America. If someone threatens you, call the cops."

"They have much influence, and not just here. Many of us are immigrants, and the leaders know Taliban in Afghanistan. They have radical connections in many countries, and they threaten that if we're not good enough Muslims, something bad will happen to our families."

"That's bullshit. Go to a different mosque."

"Most are like this. Mosques in areas with large Muslim communities draw radical imams like magnets."

Bridget cleared her throat behind them.

"Uh, sorry," Nathan said. "Hamid, meet my partner, Bridget."

Hamid placed his palm over his heart. "Very nice to meet you."

"Hamid saved my life in Afghanistan," Nathan said. "He's a patriot and a true hero."

"Good to meet ya, buddy," Bridget said. She knew enough not to offer her hand to him in public.

"You know what happened at Al-Sahaba?" Nathan asked.

"Of course. Everyone talks about it."

"Yet you still attend," Bridget said.

Hamid frowned. "I have no choice. I explained that—"

"I'm glad you're still there," Nathan said.

Hamid cocked his head.

"I need someone on the inside. We have one source, but it's important to recruit more."

"Too dangerous," Hamid said.

"We've been through much worse together."

"If they know I'm helping . . ."

"Our meeting today is destiny," Nathan said. "I need a source who can help me uncover whatever is going on inside there, and you need money. We can pay you well."

Hamid looked down at his shoes. He scratched his chin then met Nathan's eyes.

"Then once again, we will fight the enemy together."

30

Ali Hafeez rested his elbows on the steel table in the Alexandria Police Department's interrogation room on Wheeler Avenue. He adjusted the handcuffs on his wrists and stared at Nathan with bloodshot eyes. Detective Ramirez, who'd called Nathan as soon as he realized Ali attended Al-Sahaba, leaned against the back wall. Bridget waited outside, at Nathan's request, because Bluebird had said Ali was a radical Islamist who met often with Imam Qadir, and the presence of a female agent would incense him. That could come in handy later, if done intentionally, but it wouldn't help with recruitment.

Brain chemicals fired synaptic connections and drove anger, a powerful emotion that clouded reason and allowed the lizard brain and its primal urges to take over, turning the tongue and body into weapons to inflict violence. For Ali Hafeez, that had meant unleashing his inner demons on his wife, Samara, a heavyset, plain-looking woman with a unibrow that peeked out from beneath her hijab. Now she had two broken ribs, a missing tooth, and an eye swollen shut. Love took many forms.

Ali was an asshole.

"Your wife's injuries make this a felony," Nathan said.

"What a man does with his wife is none of your concern."

"You're not in the Middle East anymore." Nathan glanced at the file in his hand. "You're a long way from Jeddah."

"This is my home."

"Then you know our judicial system takes spousal abuse seriously."

"Why does the FBI care about a wife's discipline?"

Revulsion bubbled inside Nathan. Protecting those who couldn't help themselves was why he'd gone into law enforcement, and he'd seen the worst in humanity.

Ali scowled but seemed smart enough to understand his predicament. He pretended civility, but his actions at home betrayed the savage inside him, and he couldn't hide the simmering hatred in his eyes. Anger wasn't Ali's worst character trait, but when he'd acted on it, he ventured into the criminal world—Nathan's territory—and that created leverage to turn him into an informant.

"You're worried about the FBI's venue?" Nathan asked.

"A dispute between a man and woman should not worry the FBI."

"Let me decide which crimes are of interest."

"As you wish," Ali said with a disdainful wave.

"But you're right. I won't charge you with aggravated battery for beating your wife."

Ali looked up with a shimmer of hope.

"I won't," Nathan said, "but my friend here, Detective Ramirez, is happy to do it."

Ali's face hardened. "A common dispute. I metered out the punishment my wife deserved. She's used to it. All women are . . . at least *our* women."

"Maybe under Sharia law," Nathan said. "However, in the US, everyone has equal rights, no matter their genitalia. You're not allowed to strike a woman, and not with your shoe. That counts as a weapon, and her fractured ribs and concussion bump this up to a felony. You know what that means?"

"I have a master's degree from Al-Azhar University."

"In Cairo?"

"We both know my attorney will negotiate this down to a misdemeanor."

"Did you get your law degree in Cairo too?" Nathan asked.

Ali smirked. "This is shit."

Nathan wanted to smack that smarmy grin off his face, but the wife-beater was right. Calling a shoe a weapon was a stretch, and while a couple of cracked ribs certainly qualified as felony battery, without prior convictions in the US, a prosecutor would allow a plea deal. Ali would get off with probation. But that outcome wasn't guaranteed, and Ali couldn't be certain either.

"Plea deals are common," Nathan said, "but one word from me, and the prosecutor will ask the judge for the maximum penalty." He paused to let that sink in. "But that's not what should worry you most."

Ali raised an eyebrow. "What other fake crimes will conjure?"

"I'm referring to your immigration status. You're here on the work visa, and a felony conviction will violate the terms. ICE will deport you."

"I haven't been convicted yet."

"A plea deal will require an admission of guilt."

Ali shifted in his seat, less confident.

"And not just that," Nathan said, "but I researched your background since Detective Ramirez contacted me, and your name popped up in some databases."

"Which databases?"

"That, I can't tell you. It's classified. But it appears you weren't forthcoming on your initial visa paperwork, and lying on official documents is another crime. If I pursue this, your gone."

"I didn't lie."

"You lied by omission when you claimed you didn't know anyone affiliated with terrorism."

"Telephone records?"

"I can't confirm or deny that, but intelligence has documented your association with people seeking our destruction. One call from me, and DHS will deport you, assuming you don't have to finish your year in jail first. Unless . . ."

Ali ground his teeth. "I'm listening."

"If I don't recommend a stiff sentence or open an investigation into immigration fraud, you could receive a slap on the wrist."

"Let's not haggle like we're in a bazaar," Ali said. "What will make these stupid charges go away?"

Nathan's cheeks warmed. "First, fuck you. You beat a poor woman so severely, she'll have scars. The charges aren't going anywhere, and a jury will convict you because you're a guilty piece of shit. What I'm offering is to not push the court to sentence you more severely or dig further into your background. Give me what I want, and I won't make this worse."

"Should I guess, or will you eventually tell me?"

"I'm not anxious to spend that much time in your presence. Give me information about Imam Qadir and his connection to the opioid attacks."

"What are you asking?"

"I need inside information to stop the next incident."

"I know nothing, and why do you think there will be more?"

"Knock off the bullshit."

Ali rolled his tongue inside his cheek. Nathan wanted to punch him.

"If what you say is true," Ali said, "I'd be dead the moment I opened my mouth."

"You'd be killed if they knew you talked. I'm promising you confidentiality. I give you a codename, and sign you up as an FBI informant, with a number. We'll only refer to you by that number in reports, never by your name. I'll sanitize my paperwork so anyone who receives judicial discovery can't identify you."

"You must think these people you chase are idiots. If I give you information, and you take action, they'll know they have a traitor in their midst, and I'm the only one with a recent public arrest."

"Unless we keep it quiet."

"I'm not stupid either."

"They won't know for certain," Nathan said.

"These men, whoever they are, don't need absolute certainty to protect their jihad."

"You pass information, and I'll wall it off."

"Meaning?"

"If, for example, you give me information that a load of carfentanil is arriving, I'll hide your involvement with a random traffic stop. An illusion."

"It won't work."

"I'll sweeten the pot," Nathan said. "If what you give me stops further attacks, I'll submit you for a massive award. The government has funds for people who provide significant information."

"Too risky."

Nathan stared at him. Ali's reaction proved he knew something, as they'd guessed, and he considered cooperation. This was the moment between either a recruitment or more deaths.

"You can take your chances in court. By the way, I'm happy to go into court with Detective Ramirez and publicly recommend lenience. Everybody can note the FBI has an interest in your case."

Fear flashed across Allie's eyes. "They'll kill me."

Nathan looked at him. "I don't care. It's your life or the lives of innocents around the country. You choose."

31

2023: Hamtramck, Michigan

I followed two black men wearing white *taqiyahs,* which they referred to as *kufis,* through a dark hallway in the Al-Saleh Mosque in the City of Hamtramck, Michigan. Interaction between Arab and black Muslims had fascinated me in the few days I'd been in Michigan waiting for instructions.

The men, both over six feet tall, stopped outside an ornate oak door. One knocked and opened it then motioned for me to enter. I did, and he shut the door, leaving me alone with a thin man with flowing gray hair and a wispy beard that hung to his waist.

Sheikh Omar Yemeni.

"As-Salamu Alaikum," Omar said.

"Wa Alaikum As-Salam."

"Welcome to the United States."

"I've been here for ten days."

Omar stared holes through me. As one of the highest-ranking Islamic State leaders in America, he was not used to people standing up to him, but I'd traveled long and hard to exact my revenge, and every day I waited, the chance of my capture increased.

"You are unhappy?" he asked.

"I am ready to fight."

Omar was the Islamic leader who would issue my assignment. Or execute me, if he didn't trust my motivation. At least coming from Afghanistan and with the blessing of Yusuf Rehman, one of the top lieutenants of Khorasan ISIS leader Sanaullah Ghafari, had given me credibility. But reputation depended on perception, like the value of a rupee, and when it plummeted, my life would be nothing but currency for them to spend.

He poured tea from a worn silver pot and offered it to me. I took it, as custom required, and sipped the warm liquid.

"How do you like our city?"

Hamtramck had roughly thirty thousand residents and the only all-Muslim government in the US. Omar Yemeni operated with impunity here, as he executed the Muslim Brotherhood's strategy of co-opting academia, government, and media to further Islamic infiltration.

"I am not a tourist. I wish to prosecute jihad against the infidels."

He nodded. "You rush, but it is not wise to take off your shoes before investigating the water." All religious men spoke in proverb.

"Allah blesses action," I responded in kind.

He smiled. "I'm told you conceived of this plan."

"Yes."

"And it will work?"

"If Allah wills it."

The idea had first come to me in a dream, then I'd added flesh to the bones using my knowledge of Americans—and Allah revealed it to me. The operation would be simple, elegant, and deadly. And my weapon of choice had a cosmic justice to it. I would strike at their Achilles' heel, using their own strength against them.

"You must begin at once," Omar said.

My pulse increased. This was happening. I'd get my revenge.

"May I ask a question?"

"Of course," he said.

"Mawlawi Jafar Mohammad recruited me for the Taliban in Kabul, but the men who arranged for my travel were loyal to the Islamic State. The

Taliban still skirmishes with the Islamic State in Afghanistan. Do you approve of the Islamic Emirate of Afghanistan?"

Omar held his cup with both hands as he sipped. He set the cup on its saucer. "Their leadership has no vision. They take half steps when Allah demands total devotion."

"Why do you refer to the Taliban as 'they' when you work for them?"

"I seek a global caliphate."

"As does the Taliban."

"Yet they do not bring the attack to the enemy," he said.

"You criticize the Taliban, but they sent me here for a mission."

"Mawlawi Jafar sent you."

"He is a ranking member of the Taliban leadership."

"He is Allah's servant." A gleam shone in his eyes. Did he and Haji Mohammad not feel loyalty to Hibatullah Akhundzada and the rest of the Afghan government? Was a rift developing between the former Haqqani member and the Taliban? They were old wounds that—

The thought hit me like a thunderbolt. Omar Yemeni was not Taliban at all. He spoke and acted like a Salafist. So did Haji Mohammad.

"You're Islamic State Khorasan," I said.

"Now, you understand."

"You want to replace the Islamic Emirate of Afghanistan?"

"I want to destroy our enemies," he said. "Loyalties shift like sand. Only Allah's will unites us. He will slay those who proceed with weak hearts."

An image of Tara floated in the air before me. She smiled, then the corners of her mouth drooped into a frown. Her chin melted away, leaving only the white bone and teeth. She appeared, simultaneously before me and behind his eyes, existing inside and outside my mind. Was she a *jinn* or a delusion?

I blinked to clear the fuzziness. Omar watched me. How long had I been inside my head? Every day, I experienced moments of lost time, when my mind wandered on its own. Grief had ushered in emotional apathy, a psychological purgatory devoid of human feeling.

"What worries you?" Omar asked.

"Inaction."

Omar nodded. He seemed in no hurry. "You worked for the infidels for so long, why do you choose jihad now?"

My life had been wasted. I needed to embrace Omar and do Allah's bidding. If fighting jihadists who sought an Islamic caliphate had been the wrong decision, then embracing fundamental Islam was the answer. The most fundamental were the Salafists, and they controlled ISIS-K. The Taliban thought they were too extreme, but ISIS-K was more dedicated. More intent on forming a caliphate, as Mohammad had ordered. They were ideologically pure, without reservations, and their doctrine hadn't been tainted by the half-hearted. Their commitment was complete. The purity of their cause could only come from Allah.

"I made many mistakes. My choices led to loss . . . and grief. I need to return to the righteous path."

"I know your story. A skeptic would say this was a ruse to save your neck."

"My life is meaningless, other than as a tool for the one true way."

"Should I trust a man who fought with the enemy? Someone who passed our secrets to those who would destroy us? To infidels who occupied Muslim lands?"

"Trust me or do not. It doesn't matter. Allah has shown me the way, and I'll follow it."

"Would you martyr yourself for our cause?"

"I am here. I have already committed my life to jihad. I seek death."

"You will fight?"

"I will make them pay."

"Who?"

"The Americans."

32

Nathan reclined in the passenger seat of a Border Patrol Jeep Wrangler and stared through the inky blackness at Mexico. They'd parked under thick netting, close to the border. Bridget reclined in the backseat with her eyes closed, and her breathing had slowed. Was she asleep? Nathan kept his window up, because the temperature hovered around thirty degrees, colder than usual for November in southern Texas. He hadn't brought a warm enough jacket, a stupid mistake, but instead of acknowledging his ignorance, he pretended the cold didn't bother him. It did. Denton Springer, the assistant chief Border Patrol agent in the Eagle Pass office sat beside him.

"What time do mules usually cross the border?" Nathan asked.

"They used to be more tactical, but now they come across in waves, sometimes dozens at a time, and often in broad daylight."

"Doesn't that make them easier to catch?"

"Would if we had the personnel to patrol properly, but they reassigned most of our resources to handle processing. Besides, the illegals know we'll release them into the country with court dates."

"Then what?"

"We'll never see them again."

"Shit."

"Yep. Catch and release. Millions have crossed since the Remain in Mexico policy changed. We catch hundreds of thousands every month.

"How many do you miss?"

Denton shrugged. "Unknown. We estimate we interdict 68 percent, so more than 100,000 illegals slip past us each month. Sometimes, we see them on CCTV, but most of these fellas get through undetected."

"And how many carry drugs?"

"Only the good Lord knows that, but fentanyl seizures are at record levels, so do the math."

Nathan nodded. "Tonight's shipment is supposed to be significant."

"Good intel?" Denton asked. His eyes narrowed a bit, betraying his skepticism.

"I wouldn't be here if it wasn't."

"Don't get your britches in a wad. I'm just asking 'cause a lot of our tips turn into noth'n."

"I'd be skeptical too" Nathan said. "Our new source said to expect hundreds of kilograms to replace what we seized in Arlington. Another proven source confirmed a load was destined for Virginia. It left China weeks ago and diverted from its original destination."

"Which was where?"

"Chicago. The source with the Chinese info has provided reliable information in the past. No guarantees, but I'm pretty confident."

"Pretty?"

"Fifty-fifty. A lot of things can go wrong. The intel may be accurate, but something else could have happened before we set up here."

"Ain't that the truth." Denton chuckled. "How long you been in the game?"

"I'm new to drug interdiction, but I've been investigating terrorists for over a decade, and I was a cop before that."

"Yep, me too. El Paso PD. Gotta couple of decades doing the Lord's work. My old lady is used to me being out all hours."

Law enforcement took a toll on cops, from the sleep deprivation, confused circadian rhythms, and uneven schedules to the families left alone at home, wondering if their loved ones would return to them. Being a cop could be exciting, and the work was meaningful, but it chewed up the men and women who wore badges. Those who didn't consider law enforcement a calling rarely lasted.

"I appreciate you and your guys being out here," Nathan said.

"No problem, amigo. Maybe we'll get lucky."

"Be careful what you wish for." An image of the driver's twisted body, crumpled on the asphalt behind the mosque, flashed in his mind. He turned away and looked out at the thin line of horizon. Bad guys were out there, men who'd kill him, given the chance. Electricity crackled through his body and tingled his fingertips.

Denton went quiet too, not that he'd been a man of many words. They'd set up within sight of the border, about thirty miles south of Eagle Pass. Denton had a dozen agents spread out over half a mile, circling the ten-digit grid Kei's source had provided as an entry point for the massive opioid shipment.

A low buzzing echoed across the sand, and Nathan squinted into the dark. It came from the border.

"You hear that?" Nathan asked.

"It's a drone," Denton said.

"Can you have your guys fly higher? That'll scare the bad guys away."

"Nope."

Nathan looked at him. "If I can hear it, so can the traffickers."

"Ain't our drone."

Nathan cocked his head. "Who else is watching this?"

"The cartels fly drones along the border looking for us. It's why we're parked under netting."

"I thought that was for shade."

"Ain't no sun at night. It's camouflage."

"You're telling me cartels operate drones in US airspace."

"They locate our patrol units then send the traffickers where we ain't. That's why I've got two CBP Broncos cruising fifteen miles north of us.

"Decoys."

"Yessir."

"How do we allow a foreign criminal group to fly over US soil?"

"We'd shoot 'em down, but by the time we get permission, they're long gone. Only a matter of time until the cartel arms them."

"That's bullshit. I can't believe—"

The car radio crackled. "Got a sensor warning," an agent said. "Movement near 3258, west side."

"Someone's a coming," Denton said. He unhitched the mike off the center console and transmitted. "BP-One, copies. Everybody wake up and git ready."

Nathan leaned into the backseat and tapped Bridget's knee.

She bolted upright and looked around. "I wasn't sleeping."

Nathan smirked. "I believe you, but you may want to wipe that drool off your cheek."

Bridget turned her head and dried her face with her sleeve. "Funny."

The radio chirped again. "Camera's got nine pax moving single file toward the fence."

Excitement coursed through Nathan's veins. Kei's Chinese source had been spot-on. He, or she, had identified the crossing point within half a mile of where someone had cut the fence.

"Any cargo?" Denton asked.

"Affirmative. Our eye has all of them wearing knapsacks."

"Hmmm." Denton scratched the back of his head.

"What?" Bridget asked.

"We see people carrying bags, everything from Hello Kitty children's bags to full-fledged military rucksacks, but it's unusual to have everyone with a knapsack."

"Not if they're mercenaries," Nathan said.

"Or organize drug traffickers," Denton said, "though it feels too uniform, even for the cartel boys."

"They're at the fence," the agent's voice came over the radio.

"He's flying a drone?" Bridget asked.

"Negative," Denton said, "but he's relaying camera and sensor data from the comms center. Don't worry—I got a dozen agents on the ground and K-9 and air support on call."

"I mentioned this in the briefing," Nathan said, "but it bears repeating. These guys are dangerous."

Denton rubbed his chin. "You're looking for fentanyl, right?"

"Or carfentanil."

"This related to the attacks? I mean the stuff those A-rabs done around the country?"

"Officially, no. But the source led us to another shipment tied to a radical mosque in Virginia. I couldn't prove it in court, but I'm certain the opioids we interdicted were destined for jihadists."

"Then we better make sure we stop this one," Denton said. He picked up the radio again. "BP-One to all units, tighten your circle around the entry point."

"Two perps pulling the fence back . . ." the agent transmitted. "Hold on . . . okay, I've got the pax moving through the opening.

"Here they come," Denton said. He transmitted, "Y'all be patient. Don't move in until they get at least a hundred yards from the fence. I don't want them burrowing back under and making us wait all night. Hey, Tommy, any sign of a vehicle this side of the border?"

"Negatory, Boss. I've got all pax through the fence and moving north through US territory."

"All right, gents," Denton said. "Start creeping up, but don't light 'em up till I give the word."

Bridget shuffled around in the backseat. She seemed antsy. Pre-operation adrenaline had awoken him too.

"Fifty yards," the agent broadcast.

"Keep containment," Denton responded. "These fellas are the real deal, so be ready."

Denton looked at Nathan and nodded. "You set?"

"Yes, sir," Nathan said.

The backseat illuminated with a flash of light, then the cabin returned to darkness. Nathan blinked to recover his night vision.

"Sorry," Bridget said. "Just checking my flashlight."

"Well, that done lit us up like a lighthouse," Denton said. "No sense waiting." He raised the microphone to his mouth and paused for a moment, the way people often did before giving orders that sent their men into harm's way.

He depressed the plunger. "All units, move in. Go git these sumbitches."

33

Denton manhandled the Jeep Wrangler's wheel as they bounced over uneven terrain on a course to intercept the smugglers who raced away from the secondary fence and into American sovereign territory. The headlights illuminated ten men, all dressed in black and wearing heavy backpacks. They split up, scattering to evade the Border Patrol—but too late.

Spotlights from eight government vehicles approached from three sides and lit the area like daylight. Two Jeeps sped behind the traffickers, cutting them off from the hole in the fence. The men had nowhere to flee.

Nathan clung to the dashboard and braced his palm against the ceiling to keep from banging his head as the vehicle lurched over bumps. Despite Denton's age, he drove like a drunken teenager.

The traffickers scattered like cockroaches in the light, but the Border Patrol agents had spaced themselves perfectly, allowing no room for escape. The net closed.

Vehicles slid in the sand, and agents poured out with firearms drawn. The men turned erratically then slowed. Several raised their hands, realizing there was no avenue of escape.

Denton stopped and jumped out. He drew and moved toward the group, with Bridget behind him. Nathan leapt out on the passenger side.

A trafficker with tangled brown hair hanging over his shoulders walked between their Jeep and four-wheel-drive Border Patrol vehicle twenty yards away. A heavyset, middle-aged Border Patrol agent climbed out and headed to intercept. Nathan closed on the suspect too.

The smuggler kept his hands up, but he angled between the vehicles. Nathan had read that same body language many times as a cop. The perp was about to—

The long-haired trafficker took off and darted across the desert. The chubby agent reached for him, but Longhair dodged him like an NFL running back and disappeared out of the headlights and into the dark.

Nathan didn't hesitate.

He bolted after him, digging his toes into the soft sand and lifting his knees high to avoid tripping on the scrub brush. The terrain melted into the flickering shadows cast by the scrum of humanity wrestling by the vehicles.

A young border patrol agent wearing desert boots and armor flew past like Nathan was standing still. Another stud that could have been a professional athlete if he hadn't gone into law enforcement.

Nathan churned his legs over faster, and the cool air tousled his hair as he picked up speed. Longhair sprinted ahead, twenty yards in front, but he struggled under the weight of his heavy load.

The junior agent closed the distance, and Longhair must've heard his approaching footsteps, because he glanced back and stumbled. He regained his footing, feinted left then broke to the right.

The young buck closed on him.

Longhair probably sensed his imminent apprehension because he shrugged off one shoulder strap and then the other. He glanced at the fast-approaching agent. He cocked his arm to throw the knapsack, as that would immunize him from criminal charges.

The agent lowered his shoulder and plowed into him, catching Longhair under his arm. They collided with an audible thud as air forced out of Longhair's lungs. Longhair went horizontal, and the knapsack flew into the air. The agent drove him into the earth, crashing his full weight onto him.

The knapsack landed a few feet away with a pop.

A cloud of red powder wafted out of the knapsack's partially open zipper. Longhair's face crinkled with pain as he struggled with the agent.

He froze when he saw the cloud.

Longhair's fear spread to Nathan like an airborne virus. He slowed and stopped.

"Look out," Nathan shouted.

The agent had his handcuffs out and Longhair's arm twisted behind his back. He looked up, and his eyes followed Nathan's outstretched finger to the cloud of dust settling around the knapsack. Tiny twirls of powder curled in the faint night wind like dust devils. The agent's eyes widened.

"Mask up," Nathan said. He reached into an outer vest pouch and dug out an N-95 mask.

The agent looked from the cloud to Nathan, then back again. His head shook like he was trying not to fall asleep.

Shit.

The agent collapsed onto Longhair as if someone had yanked his power cord out of the socket. Longhair's eyes closed too. They were unconscious.

Nathan strapped on his mask. He had to take care of himself first. He kept his distance and keyed his radio to the multiagency tactical channel the Feds used on the border.

"Agent down," he transmitted. "We're north of . . ." He glanced around him at the outline of the mountains against the night sky. "Make that northeast, about eighty yards from the scene."

"Status?" Denton responded. All the humor had gone from his voice, and the strain of responsibility raised his tone an octave.

"Looks like an exposure overdose. Got a cloud of drugs in the air."

"It's the damn knapsacks," Denton responded. "They're filled to the brim. Keep your distance."

"I got a naloxone autoinjector in my kit," Nathan said.

"Negative," Denton said. "Your mask won't protect you. That chemical touches your skin, and you'll go down."

"Copy."

Denton was right. If Nathan rushed in to help, he'd become a victim too and worsen the crisis. But not trying to save the men ran contrary to his every instinct. It was what had drawn him into law enforcement. Not to be a hero—though that was ingrained in male DNA—but to protect those in need. Defend the tribe. And a fallen officer only intensified his urge.

"Dammit."

Nathan ripped off the autoinjector that he'd attached to his vest with a rubber band. They'd designed it to be carried in a box for safety, but tactical medical interventions required speed. Every officer on site had one for personal use, and protocol dictated he use the injector on the agent's body and save his own for himself, but it was critical to minimize time in the danger zone. If even a particle of that cloud touched him, he'd lose all functioning and collapse.

Nathan hesitated and considered the bodies. The powder drifted away on the wind, no longer visible, but if the deadly toxin had landed around them, and Nathan came into contact with it, he'd be finished.

Time slowed. He'd need to direct agents to the victims. Even now, they'd be donning HAZMAT suits, but every second counted. Opioids depressed breathing and heart rate. The victim's hearts wouldn't pump fast enough to oxygenate their blood, and every second organs and tissue were undernourished could create permanent damage. After a few minutes without proper oxygen, brain damage set in. But how much toxin had affected them? People didn't stop breathing immediately. Not usually.

He looked back at the arrest scene, where an orange glow from the headlights created a fuzzy sun, and the silhouettes of agents and suspects passed before it like demons. It would take them at least three minutes, maybe more, to suit up, then another three or four to hustle across the desert in their restrictive gear. Medical intervention would be delayed for ten minutes.

Too long.

Nathan turned back toward the men. Neither moved. They'd suffered significant exposure.

Nathan bent and tucked his cargo pantlegs into his boot socks. It looked ridiculous, but it protected his skin. He tightened the Velcro straps around his wrists on his military tunic, the uniform he'd worn on operations in Afghanistan, then he donned two sets of rubber gloves from his medical kit. Nathan yanked off the injector's orange safety cap and approached the bodies from the side opposite the knapsack.

He aimed his flashlight at the ground and looked for any sign of the toxin, but in the inky desert blackness, the chance of seeing almost microscopic particles was low.

He held his breath, despite his N-95 respirator. He stopped beside them and bent at the waist to avoid kneeling in the contaminated sand. He jabbed the autoinjector against the agent's leg over his clothing. He pushed the injector until it clicked and vibrated in his hand. Inside, 0.4 milligrams of naloxone hydrochloride flowed through the needle into the fleshy part of the agent's thigh. Nathan held the injector flush against him, making sure every ounce of drug entered his body.

The agent flinched and jerked. He moaned.

That confirmed it. Opioid overdose. The naloxone wouldn't have worked if another toxin affected him.

"Stay still," Nathan said. "Don't move. Help is coming. Nathan glanced behind him. Shadowy silhouettes approached like specters. They had fifty yards to go. Nathan flashed his light three times to direct them.

The suspect lay still.

The agent had a naloxone dose on his belt. Touching him would be dangerous, but trafficker or not, the suspect's life had value. Nathan ripped the injector off the agent's belt.

Nathan raked his light over the area then tugged off the safety and moved around the agent. Nathan pressed the autoinjector against the suspect's thigh and administered the naloxone hydrochloride.

Longhair's hand moved, and his eyes opened. He blinked.

"Don't move."

The man squirmed beneath the agent, both of them conscious but confused.

Nathan stepped back and drew his Glock. The agent had been in the process of handcuffing the suspect and hadn't searched him. The last thing he needed was for Longhair to draw a weapon. Nathan sidestepped and aimed at Longhair's head so he could shoot without hitting the agent.

Nathan had just saved Longhair's life, and now he contemplated killing him—the nature of law enforcement. A lifetime of hard choices. Life or death. Ultimate consequences.

Overhead, the cartel's drone flew over the scene. There'd be no hiding the seizure. Nathan held his position and waited for help to arrive.

34

One hundred kilograms of suspected carfentanil—a synthetic opioid one hundred times more potent than fentanyl and five thousand times stronger than heroin. A particle the size of a grain of sand could kill.

Nathan stood beside a table covered with the seized drugs. Agents had double-bagged each kilogram in plastic to prevent the opioids from going airborne. The young agent and the suspect had both survived, but no one wanted to risk injury.

"How much is this worth?" Nathan asked Denton.

"Wholesale, around fifty grand per kilo, more in cities up north and on the East Coast. Gotta factor transportation into it."

"And how many doses does that mean?"

"Again, depends on the quantity. Pills contain 0.2 to 5.1 milligrams, so it's a range. Each kilo should contain one million user doses. The scary part is, 2 milligrams will kill you. One kilo of fentanyl could wipe out five hundred thousand people.

Nathan did the math in his head. "The powder on this table could murder fifty million people?"

"If they overdosed the pills, it would do serious damage."

"How much do we seize each year?"

"Over 115 million pills last year."

"This is an epidemic," Bridget said.

"It's a crisis," Denton said, "but it doesn't get the proper attention."

"Something bad is coming," Nathan said.

"Something bad's already here, partner."

Nathan nodded. "Thanks for your help."

"Anytime." Denton joined a group of his officers.

Nathan turned to Bridget. "Better call this in."

Bridget nodded.

He reached for his phone then stopped. "You do it."

She smiled then narrowed her eyes. "Why?"

"You deserve the chance to give Rahimya good news. You work with me long enough, you'll have plenty of uncomfortable conversations. Take the win."

Her smile returned. "Thanks." She put the call on speaker.

Rahimya answered. "What happened?" Her voice sounded tight.

"All good, Boss," Bridget said. "The intel was accurate. CBP seized 100 kilos."

"Fentanyl?"

"Something that tests positive for opioids, possible carfentanil or an analogue."

"Good news," Rahimya said. "You keep making seizures like this, and I'll transfer you to DEA. Is Nathan on?"

"Right here. Bridget did a nice job."

"Don't make me wait too long for your report," Rahimya said. "Document everything and have them preserve the evidence for us, in case you can link it to your case."

"Roger. This intel came from our source, so it's related. We may to link it to the mosque. Imam Qadir is up to no good."

"We don't know that," Rahimya said. "The *Shaykh* could be behind the load we seized."

"Shaykh?" Bridget asked.

"Elders," Nathan said. "They help run the mosque."

"What about the assault rifles," Bridget asked. "Religious institutions don't require weapons."

"Don't be so sure," Nathan said. "Fundamental Islam is a supremacist ideology that allows violence against infidels. It demands it."

"Not all Muslims support violence," Rahimya said, an edge in her voice.

"Of course not," Nathan said. "But many do around the world, according to polls."

"We can't trust polls anywhere in the Middle East," Rahimya said. "People say what they think the government wants to hear."

"Almost 20 percent of American Muslims believe Islamic terrorism is justified," Nathan said, "and with close to five million Muslims here, and that's a lot of radicals."

"There's a difference between responding to a poll and strapping on a suicide belt."

"Most Muslims aren't radical," Nathan said, "but it doesn't take many to create chaos."

"Keep your eye on the ball," Rahimya said. "We're investigating specific crimes by individuals, not group demographics."

"The Al-Sahaba Mosques trafficked in carfentanil worth millions of dollars," Nathan said. "Will the AUSA support a weapons charge?"

"It's not illegal to possess carbines," Rahimya said. "The ATF check came back while you guys have been on the road, and the firearms were legitimately purchased from a gun dealer in North Carolina."

"Who's name is on the paperwork?" Nathan asked.

"Hold on," Rahimya said. Papers rustled over the phone. "Ali Hafeez."

"Shit," Nathan said.

"What?" Rahimya asked.

"That's our source," Bridget said.

"Then Mr. Hafeez isn't being honest," Rahimya said. "Bring him in."

35

Nathan exited the George Washington Parkway onto Daingerfield Island and drove through the parking lot of the Washington Sailing Marina. He parked at the end, near a dozen trailered boats, and faced out so he and Bridget could watch the street. Across from them, sailboats bobbed in slips along the inlet. The Potomac glistened through the trees, but no boaters braved the cool morning air.

"We gonna ask Ali about the guns?" Bridget asked.

"No sense waiting, but whatever he says, we need him."

"But he lied about the carbines."

"He omitted the information, and we can use that as leverage. We don't work with angels, and we don't have anyone else inside. I still want to sign him up."

"We should have done that when we first debriefed him," she said.

"I've been doing this long enough that I know most of these guys never follow through, and every CI comes with quarterly reporting requirements and reams of paperwork. If we signed everyone who provided intel, we'd be chained to our desks."

"Rahimya on board with this?"

"What she doesn't know won't hurt her."

"I don't want to get suspended."

"Trust me. We're documenting what's important. The bureaucratic beast only gets hungrier. If we follow every rule, we'll turn into bureaucrats with perfect paperwork and no arrests. The American people pay us to catch bad guys."

Bridget looked across the park. She didn't appear convinced.

"We'll sign him up, and everything will be kosher."

"Is Hamid joining us?"

"Don't need him," Nathan said. "Ali's English is passable."

Ali drove his white Toyota Camry into the lot and headed for them. Nathan scanned the parkway. He'd changed the meeting location from the cargo terminal at the airport to the marina at the last minute—tradecraft that made countersurveillance difficult. Cars whizzed by. If anyone showed signs of interest, Nathan would have aborted the meeting.

Ali pulled into the spot beside him and turned off his car. Nathan glanced around then waved him over.

"I'll jump in back with him," Nathan said.

Nathan got out and climbed into the back seat. He opened the passenger-side door. Ali moved around the front of their car, and Nathan watched Ali's hands and looked for the telltale bulge of a weapon.

Ali sat beside him and shut the door. "Why did you move the meeting?"

"Too many people at the cargo terminal," Nathan lied. Telling a source he'd moved the meeting to avoid an ambush would damage the trust he had to cultivate. Ali was providing information that could get him killed, and Nathan needed Ali to believe he'd protect his identity. Relationships between sources and handlers drove intelligence gathering. Nathan would never trust a source, but sources needed a safety net or they'd be too afraid to help.

"This is very dangerous for me," Ali said.

"We won't meet in person often, but we're required to fill out your paperwork and take photos and fingerprints."

"You said you'd keep my name secret."

"This is how we do that. Once you're signed up, you'll become a number in our reports, and we'll lock your true identity in the most secure safes in the FBI. We'll give you a codename."

"Code?"

"We'll refer to you as Falcon and communicate with you by phone."

Ali scowled. "If they spot your number in my phone, I'm dead."

Nathan dug a prepaid phone out of his pocket—an over-the-counter purchase Rahimya had approved—and handed it to Ali.

"I have a phone," Ali said.

"This won't come back to you. I bought it with cash. Only use it to call me or Bridget. If you call anyone else, you'll compromise your identity."

Ali pocketed it.

"Bridget will print and photograph you in a minute, and I also need you to sign our confidential informant paperwork."

"A contract?"

"It lays out our relationship. You tell us the truth, and we keep your involvement secret. It says we can't promise anything."

"You said you'd help with my case. My wife won't press charges, but the prosecutor says the state doesn't need her consent."

"Keep helping, and we'll ask the judge for leniency. If your information stops an attack, we'll submit you for a significant reward. You be straight with us, and we'll fight for you."

"Straight."

"Don't make things up."

"I didn't."

"Where did Qadir acquire the carbines in the mosque?"

Ali looked at the ground. "I don't—"

"You lie to us and we're done," Nathan said.

Ali nodded. "He gave me cash, and I bought them for him."

Nathan relaxed. "Where?"

"North Carolina."

"Why didn't you tell us?"

"I didn't want to get into trouble."

"You withhold information again, and I'll charge you. Be on our team."

"Yes . . . I understand."

Nathan scanned the lot, letting the tension subside. "Your tip about the drugs was accurate. We seized a big load."

Ali's shoulders relaxed. "Yes, yes, as I said."

"One hundred kilos."

His eyes widened. "Where?"

"At the border."

"I didn't tell you exactly where it would come into the country," Ali said.

"You're not our only source. We collect human and signals intelligence all over the world. The FBI has thousands of investigations and surveillances ongoing. Your information is a small piece in a gigantic puzzle."

"Then you will tell the police to stay out of my business?"

"I'll call the prosecutor today and tell him you're working with us, but if you touch your wife again, I'll tear up the contract and tell them to throw the book at you."

Ali scowled. "Very well."

"Now, I need to know who at Al-Sahaba was receiving the opioids."

"I overheard the imam and two elders talking about the shipment you stole. An elder said more was coming."

"Who said that?"

Ali shrugged.

Nathan stared at him. "Don't bullshit me."

"I'm not . . . I—"

"Who ordered the drugs?"

Ali hung his head.

"You can either work with us, and your legal troubles will disappear, or you can face jail time. The choice is yours."

"He'll kill me." Ali's voice had softened to a whisper.

"Who?"

"One of the Phantoms."

"Phantoms?"

"They'll murder me . . . and my family."

Ali had already come close to murdering his own wife, so his concern had to be more about himself, but this was the moment where he'd either fully commit or Nathan would lose him.

"I'm trying to save lives," Nathan said. "Stopping poison from coming into our country will do that, but I think this is bigger."

Ali nodded then seemed to catch himself. "I'm not part of it."

"I don't think you're involved, and I don't want to prosecute you. Help us stop them, and I'll protect you,"

"They're planning something."

"What?"

"Something big."

"Who is behind it?"

"Zabihullah is in charge," Ali said, his voice low.

"Who?"

"Zabihullah Al-Afghani."

"Who calls him that?"

"Everyone."

"Everyone who?"

Ali dabbed a bead of sweat off his forehead. "The imam."

"Kareem Qadir?"

"Yes, and the elders . . . everyone who regularly attends mosque. Men with power."

Bridget scribbled on her pad, taking notes while Nathan focused on Ali's body language.

"Have you met him?"

"I saw him from a distance."

"Description?"

"He stood in shadow. He's a powerful man with a scar on his face and anger in his heart . . . a dangerous man."

"Who are the Phantoms?"

"The Phantoms of the Khorasan. Zabihullah's men. Islamists."

"Can you describe them?"

"They come at night, but I haven't seen them. Only rumors in the mosque."

"But you know this Zabihullah."

"He is a very hard man," Ali said. "They call him the Slayer."

36

2024: Washington, DC

I sat in the vestibule of the Al-Sahaba Mosque and listened to men entering the prayer room. My men. Warriors in our jihad.

I reached for the kettle of hot tea and wrapped my fingers around the handle. The ceramic warmed my skin and transported me to the Surobi café were I'd dined with Farzana and Tara when my girl was only three years old. Tara had touched the hot cup on the table and squealed as her eyes widened.

Yes, it's hot, I'd said. I mouthed the words now. I felt the distant moment. I was no longer present in the mosque but in downtown Kabul during one of those perfect days when the searing sun remained weeks away. A rare breeze blew between the mountains carrying the last vestiges of winter, and the odors of the city dissipated, removing the usual foul stench that scented the air. The spring breeze coated everything, like a backdrop of pastel on a canvas. It tasted like honey.

Tara's image smiled at me and shook her head, slowly at first, the faster. Emphatic. Her eyes darkened, and her brow furrowed. Her eyes threatened to pull me into them like a black hole. They'd capture me, if I let them. I blinked, then closed my eyes. Guilt washed over me for breaking my trance.

I opened my eyes, and she was gone.

I sighed and strolled into the prayer room. I stopped before a table made from a giant slab of marble and stared at each of the men as they entered, keeping my face impassive, void of emotion—but strong and confident. Omar Yemeni had appointed me himself, but it was my responsibility to earn the respect of these Islamists. Like all leaders of violent groups, from pirates in the Gulf of Aden to guerrillas in the Colombian mountains, I had to be tougher and more committed than the jihadists I led into battle. How else could I ask men to martyr themselves if I appeared weaker or wavered when death hovered over us? They must accept my word as if it came from Mohammad himself.

These men needed to fear me.

Three dozen operatives filled the space before me, with another four guarding the locked doors and patrolling the mosque's exterior. An unnatural quiet filled the room, and I let it hang there, growing in weight, as every man watched me. I made the silence my ally, and I'd only break it when I was ready.

My lieutenant, Khaled Mousa, lingered nearby, as if afraid to wake a sleeping lion, then he approached and leaned close to my ear.

"The doors are secure. All the men are present, except Abdul Abdullah from New York. He's not answering his phone."

I dismissed him with a wave of my hand, not taking my eyes off the group before me. One of our men was late, and there could be a simple explanation, but I hadn't survived in this world of jackals by expecting the best-case scenario. I'd deal with Abdullah later.

Khaled stepped back and stood behind me and to the side. Rage radiated off him. Omar Yemeni had assigned Khaled as my second-in-command. A Palestinian, Khaled had grown up in Gaza and come to the United States on a university scholarship. He had a sharp mind and had studied engineering at Princeton. He'd have led the newly formed cell, but his high IQ and troubled background didn't afford him the life experience he needed. But I'd been on the inside of investigations and knew Americans as well as they knew themselves. I'd wanted to be one.

But no longer.

I took a breath and addressed the men. "We've chosen you as messengers—to deliver the will of Allah." I paused and watched them fill with purpose. "I come from Afghanistan, with the support from our leaders who have a direct line to Allah. Our Islamic allies provided financial backing for me to lead you on our greatest victory. This is the moment when everything changes.

"Give us our orders," Khaled said.

I glared at him.

I returned my attention to the men. "Starting tonight, you are no longer individuals. From this moment, you are one, a collective weapon for Allah that must remain whole."

I stepped to the edge of the platform and looked down at them. "For the rest of your lives, you are Phantoms."

37

Nathan checked his watch then glanced out the window of the Courtyard hotel in Old Town Alexandria. Bridget waited out front for Hamid. He approached her, and they spoke before she headed into the lobby. Nathan closed the blinds then dragged a chair against the wall. He'd make Hamid sit in the hot seat.

Bridget entered alone. "I gave him the extra key. He'll be right up. I didn't want the clerk seeing us together."

"Good idea." He checked his phone.

"Expecting a call?"

"Meili. We keep missing each other's calls. Our schedules haven't aligned."

"That's a copper's life. My father missed every soccer game I played for twelve years of school. I can't get my brothers in the same room, not even at Christmas."

He stuffed his phone into his khakis. "I asked her to store some clothes at my condo and stay over more."

Bridget smiled. "That's great. It's time you—"

"She said no."

"Meili waiting for you to put a ring on it? She wants to get serious, but you don't?"

"Other way around."

Bridget raised an eyebrow. "She's blowing you off?"

"It's not like that. I've been attracted to her since the academy, and I don't plan to waste time now that we're together. But she doesn't want to move that fast."

"She wants to see other people?"

"Nothing like that. She's worried about Amelia and that I haven't had time to process the divorce."

"Have ya?"

He blew out a long stream of air. "I thought so, I mean, yes, but now I'm not so sure."

"You still have feeling for Reagan?"

"I still love her, sure, but it's not romantic love. Not anymore. We have a history, and she's the mother of our daughter, but I accept the divorce, and I'm into Meili."

"Then why push her? Keep it causal."

"Yeah, maybe. It's just my natural inclination. I've been in relationships since high school."

"You afraid to be alone?"

He shrugged. "I like the idea of seeing lots of women, but when I date someone, I want to get to know them better, and intimacy is better than a series of shallow relationships. I mean, when I'm with Meili, I feel like I have a partner, someone who gets me. Someone who—"

The door lock clicked, and Hamid came in. He hesitated when he saw the look on Nathan's face.

"Hey, Boss."

"Sit."

"Where's the source?" Hamid asked.

"We're talking to you today," Nathan said.

Hamid stiffened. "Something wrong?"

Nathan pointed at the chair, and Hamid shuffled across the carpet and slouched in the wooden seat. He dropped his chin, sullen.

"You told us about *Ashbah Khorasan,* the Phantoms of Khorasan, but you never mentioned Zabihullah Al-Afghani."

"Where did you hear that name?"

"Our source."

"Who?"

"Ali. You haven't met him yet, but you will. I need more detailed information, and I can't lose anything in translation. He told us the mosque's leadership all know Zabihullah."

Hamid nodded.

"You're familiar with that name?" Nathan asked.

"Yes."

"Who is he?"

"Zabihullah is the Phantoms' leader."

Rage bubbled inside Nathan's gut, like a boiling pot. "Why the fuck didn't you give us his name?"

"I'm sorry. He's . . . everyone is afraid."

"We have hundreds of dead Americans, and you withheld the name of the man responsible?"

"Zabihullah means 'the slayer,' but it's not just his jihadi name. They call him that because he's ruthless. Anyone who threatens him disappears."

Nathan tapped a pen against the desk. "Do you realize you suppressed the most important piece of information from us?"

"Yes."

"Do you understand how significant this is?"

Hamid looked at his shoes.

"Hamid?"

He nodded.

"How can I trust you after this? Did any of our sources mention his name during our debriefings?"

"They never said his name."

"Do they know him?"

"Probably. Nobody outside the Phantoms has seen his face, but everyone in the mosque has heard his name. They just won't say it."

"Why didn't they tell me?"

Hamid looked up and met Nathan's eyes. "They are afraid."

"Why didn't you tell me?"

"I'm frightened."

What about this man terrified Hamid? "I don't get it. We hunted Al-Qaeda in Afghanistan. We fought in combat together. Why fear the Slayer?"

Hamid mumbled something.

"Speak up," Nathan said, unable keep irritation out of his voice. If Hamid wasn't on board, how would they recruit more sources?

"This man is different. He's smart. Elusive. He'll fight until his anger is gone."

"Anger at whom?"

"America. He seeks vengeance. He won't stop until he brings America to its knees."

Nathan paced. He caught Bridget's eye and jerked his head at the door. She followed him into the hallway.

"He's scared," she said.

"I don't care."

"You can't change how he feels."

"There is no place for feelings in this war. This is the real world where bad guys want to murder us."

"We need him."

Nathan looked at the ceiling. She was right, of course. "Okay."

They went back in, and Nathan stood near Hamid, a little too close for comfort.

"I should charge you with obstruction of justice."

Fear danced in Hamid's eyes. "I'm sorry."

"I don't want an apology, and I don't care about your fucking feelings. We're in an existential fight with radicals who want to destroy the West and subjugate everyone under Sharia law. They want to enslave half the world and murder anyone who resists. Of the world's forty-nine Muslim-majority countries, fifteen implement Sharia law. Extremists are on the move, and all it'll take is a shake-up of the world order, like after a war, natural disaster, or global depression, and these monsters will fill the vacuum. We must stop them, and I need your help to do it."

"Yes, Boss."

"Stop cowering like a victim and help me catch the Slayer."

Hamid nodded.

"I'm not fucking around."

Hamid stood and offered his hand. "I'll go with you into this fight."

Nathan grasped it. "Let's find Zabihullah and put him in a cage."

"I'll be with you till the end."

38

2024: Manhattan, New York.

I hunkered down between the seats of an old Ford van that had been hit more times than a Christian orphan in Kandahar and stared down the block at the New York City Police Department's First Precinct. Nerves tickled my abdomen, a reminder of my pre-operation nerves in Afghanistan when the Americans had used me, but this time, my anxiety didn't come from worry about death.

I feared failure.

The van's metal floor had ridges, making it impossible to sit comfortably, but shifting around kept the blood flowing in my legs, so I'd be ready. I wasn't supposed to directly engage the enemy—like Malik and Omar who both fidgeted in the front seats—but I would. My planning and leadership had a broader impact than fighting, but I couldn't miss the chance to pull the trigger and fire my anger and resentment out of an AR-15 and into the flesh of the men who defended America.

Malik reached down and patted the stock of his Mossberg shotgun on the floor beside him. It wasn't as lethal as a high-capacity carbine at this distance, but Malik would initiate the attack, and nothing was better at close range than a 12-gauge shotgun loaded with double-aught buckshot.

He wouldn't live long enough to reload, but this operation didn't require his survival.

We sought to sow confusion, create chaos, and deter first responders from the primary attack scene. Later, when the after action was complete, and the public realized the police had responded to defend their own instead of helping civilians whose lives ticked away with every passing second, citizens' confidence in the police would erode, and we'd have planted seeds of discontent. And Allah willing, revolution.

Khaled Mousa led a team that waited outside the hospital with orders to fire on any ambulance leaving, and Abdul Al-Wazir, a Palestinian holding a grudge as big as his head, would shoot patients in the Emergency Department, shutting it down. More critical patients would strain the city's medical resources. I could have been there, but firing on police officers was far more challenging, so I depended on Khaled. If he screwed the camel, our entire operation would suffer.

I grabbed the handheld radio and twirled the volume knob between my thumb and forefinger. We couldn't strike until the first wave began. I depressed and released the transmitter, and static hissed back at me. It worked.

The First Precinct was a three-story, gray-stone fortress on the corner of Ericsson Place and Varick Street in Southern Manhattan, about a mile and a half from Wall Street. My deep understanding of the American psyche had informed my decision to target it. The primary assault would hit Wall Street, drawing police from numerous precincts. Cops would rush to help, making this an all-hands event.

That's what made attacking the First Precinct vital.

Any ambush on police would slow the response, but attacking their precinct—a building filled with managers who hadn't worked the streets for years—would divert resources from Wall Street. Officers would race to the precinct to save their own, like workers bees protecting their queen.

Light reflected off the precinct's front door as it opened, and three patrol officers walked out with a guy in a suit, probably a detective. They smiled and laughed with a jocularity that would be impossible for them to find in the coming days. If they lived that long. Death swept away optimism like a sandstorm. It had happened to me, and soon, they would suffer too.

Salman, a vicious Chechen with an unquenchable thirst for blood, waited in a rental car half a block away with his motor running. I'd tasked him to blitz NYPD headquarters, a monstrosity near the Brooklyn Bridge. He'd fire from behind the brick pillars facing One Police Plaza and take out as many cops and civilians as possible before his inevitable death—an outcome he eagerly sought.

I lifted my radio and transmitted, "Salman, can you hear me?"

"Naeam." Yes.

"Make your sacrifice."

He didn't respond, but his car pulled away from the curb, and he drove down the street toward his destiny. Most of my men sought martyrdom. Whether seventy-two virgins awaited us in heaven, at least Allah knew our devotion was real. What was the alternative? The materialism and emptiness of the West?

Tara's face flickered in my vision, but I shook her away. *Stay present.*

The streets grew more crowded as people commuted to their jobs, and a din of horns drifted over the city.

My radio squawked.

"Mudiri," Khaled transmitted in Arabic. I'd told him to use his native tongue in case police intercepted our transmission. It would take them time to translate and the not-knowing would inflict more terror.

"Tell me," I said.

"The birds attack their prey."

Adrenaline coursed through my veins. It was time.

39

Nathan crossed his legs in a leather chair in the lobby of the Fairwinds Hotel in Northwest DC and pretended to read the newspaper as he scanned the faces of guests entering through a revolving brass door. Because of the hotel's proximity to the White House, it catered to guests with money. Nathan could have rented a cheaper room to debrief Ali, but criminals frequented those kinds of hotels, increasing the chance some nefarious gangster or terrorist would spot his CI. Rahimya had balked at the cost, but their massive drug seizure had been the largest in DC and showered the FBI with positive publicity, at least until the press labeled the incident a minority shooting.

Nathan had yet to link the Al-Sahaba Mosque to the horrific Metro attack that killed eighty-nine people, but a chemist confirmed the drug in the toxic gas was carfentanil—the same opioid Nathan and Bridget had seized.

Nathan's phone vibrated with a text from Ali: *I'm here. Which room?*

Nathan texted back: *321 My partner is upstairs. Keep your sunglasses on and take the elevator. Don't speak to anyone.*

A thumbs-up glowed above Nathan's text.

Nathan straightened and peeked over his newspaper as Ali pushed through the revolving door. Ali's face was drained of color, and his shoulders slumped as he dragged across the tiled floor to the elevator. Either he had bad news, or the stress of being an informant had worn him down. Ali passed by without noticing him and disappeared into the elevator.

Nathan casually folded his paper then hurried up the stairs to the third floor. Bridget opened the door for Ali, and Nathan followed them inside. Hamid rose to greet them.

"Plop down in the chair," Bridget told Ali. "We're grinding today."

"Hamid, this is Falcon," Nathan said. "Falcon, meet our linguist, Hamid."

"I know you," Ali said. "You've been to the mosque."

"As-salaam-alaykum," Hamid said. "Sometimes I attend prayer there."

"He's okay," Nathan said. "I've worked with Hamid for many years."

"What happened to only talking by telephone?" Ali asked.

"I need to be with you to collect evidence, especially the first time," Nathan said.

"Which evidence?"

"I want you to call Imam Qadir and discuss the attacks."

Ali shook his head. "I do not speak to him about such things."

"We think another attack's coming. Our carfentanil seizure and the terror attack are too coincidental, and the snippet of conversation you heard between the imam and Zabihullah cements it."

"What did you overhear?" Hamid asked.

"They spoke of a great weapon," Ali said, "and glory coming to Allah."

"That's why I need to record the imam," Nathan said. "We have nothing else to corroborate your testimony."

"I never agreed to testify."

"We can cross that bridge later," Nathan said, "but we need corroboration, and that means getting the imam on tape."

Ali crossed his arms over his chest. "This will end with my death."

"I'll protect you."

Ali looked at Hamid. "If word of this reaches the Slayer, we're both dead men."

"I won't speak of this to anyone," Hamid said. "Our secrets remain with us."

"Imam Qadir won't talk to me about his program," Ali said. "I'm not involved."

"Say you overheard them talking, and you want to help."

"He'll know I'm an informant."

That was a distinct possibility, and under normal circumstances, Nathan would never ask a CI to push this hard, but a train full of dead passengers required aggressive tactics. They needed results.

"Explain you're angry about police invading your mosque, and—"

"That is true."

Nathan's chest tightened. "If they don't want us to raid them, maybe they shouldn't traffic drugs or stockpile weapons."

"Muslims must protect themselves."

"Yeah, yeah, that's their defense," Bridget said, "but I call BS. I ain't buying it."

"Listen," Nathan said, lowering his voice to defuse the confrontation, "You don't need to be explicit. Tell him you can't sleep at night, and you need to do something—"

"That is not a lie."

"—and leave it open to see what he says."

"And if he says nothing?"

Nathan rubbed his chin. This was the tricky part, and cognitive dissonance tickled the base of his skull, the way it always did when something felt off. This was too risky, but what choice did they have?

"Dangle your offer, and if he doesn't bite, tell him you overheard them, and you want to be part of it."

"He will never accept this."

"Make him believe."

Ali looked down, audibly grinding his teeth. "If I do this, my charges go away?"

"I'll do my best."

Ali stared at Hamid. "Should I call?"

"The choice is yours," Hamid said.

"You're already on Team America," Nathan said. "You chose your side when you signed your confidential informant agreement. Now I'm asking you to do what you promised."

"I never said I'd record the imam."

"We need this. Help us gather the evidence to stop an attack or we're done here."

Ali sighed. He lifted his phone. "I am ready."

"Not the phone I gave you," Nathan said. "That's just for us. Use your personal phone. You want him to know it's you."

Ali switched phones, and Bridget took out a digital recorder with a suction cup dangling from a cord. She attached the suction cup to Ali's cell phone and connected the suction cup.

"You straight on what you'll say?" Nathan asked.

"I'm angry and want to help."

"And if he doesn't agree?"

Ali sighed. "Then I tell him I know about the program."

"Don't say you know about it. Say you overheard people mention a plan, and you want to assist."

"Very well," Ali said. "I don't have the imam's number."

Nathan had every number Qadir had used for the past ten years, but he wasn't about to share that information. He checked his watch. "We're between prayers now. Call the mosque."

"I've got those digits," Bridget said. She plugged them in and hit record. "You ready?"

Ali scrunched his face but nodded.

"This is Special Agent Bridget Quinn, and I'm here with . . ." She listed their names with Ali's confidential informant number and the time and date. She looked at Nathan, and he gave her the thumbs-up. She dialed and flicked on the speaker.

"Al-Sahaba," a man said.

"This is Ali Hafeez. Put Imam Qadir on the phone please."

Rustling came over the line, and a minute later, Qadir came on. "Yes, Brother Ali, what can I do for you?"

"Imam, thank you for taking my call."

"Of course, Brother."

"I am sorry to bother you, but . . ." Ali looked up.

Nathan nodded and pointed to the phone.

". . . I must speak to you."

"You sound troubled."

"I can't sleep. This ugly business with the police . . ."

"What about it?" A tinge of wariness entered Qadir's voice, or had Nathan imagined that?

"These people persecute us. I will stand by you."

"And do what?"

Ali sucked in a long breath. "Join the jihad."

The line stayed silent, and Ali looked at Nathan. Nathan raised his palms, indicating Ali should wait.

Imam Qadir cleared his throat. "I understand you are stressed. There are many ways to fight jihad."

"I wish to hurt infidels."

"You can serve Allah by being more pious. Be more devout. Live a righteous life."

Qadir wasn't taking the bait. Ali might be more persuasive in person, but that would mean wiring him with a recording device and sending him inside the mosque—a risky proposition. Nathan circled the air with his finger, telling Ali to continue.

"I, uh, I heard things in the mosque."

"What things?" The imam's tone cooled.

"I heard men speak of a program. A way to praise Allah."

"What are you talking about?"

"The program."

"Whatever you've heard, I don't know about any program."

Nathan drew a finger across his throat. The imam was too cagey to speak over the phone.

"They said they had a great weapon," Ali continued. "They—"

Nathan shook his head and touched Ali's shoulder.

"Uh, perhaps I misheard," Ali said. "I am here if you need me, ready to fight."

"Submit yourself to Allah," Qadir said. "Pray, fast, and give charity. Live your life to praise him."

"Yes, Imam. I will do that. Perhaps I can do more."

"Perhaps."

"Thank you, Imam."

Nathan pressed end, and the call disconnected.

"He said nothing," Ali said.

"He won't talk over the phone," Nathan said.

"That fucker is wicked smart," Bridget said. "He knows what he's doing."

"The imam didn't mention the weapon," Ali said.

"He didn't say you were crazy either, and he didn't dissuade you from jihad," Nathan said.

"This is evidence?"

"Not yet, but the next time you go to the mosque, thank him for taking your call. Tell him you're available if he needs you for anything, but don't mention the program. You push too hard, he'll know it's a trap."

"This will work?"

"He knows you want to join. The next move is up to him."

40

Rahimya hurried into the conference room where Nathan and the rest of his group waited around a mahogany table that had been polished to a shiny gloss. Nathan sat between Bridget and Otis Gray, a 130-pound analyst whose brain probably accounted for half his weight. A fire burned in Rahimya's normally placid face, and her body vibrated with energy.

"We have our first break in the Metro attack," Rahimya said, "and it looks like Islamists."

Nathan's pulse increased as everyone exchanged glances.

Rahimya slapped a thick manilla folder on the desk and removed a stack of photographs. "We've identified four perps who delivered the bombs, but as you and everyone with a television knows, they concealed their faces with sunglasses and what we thought were N-95 masks but now know were respirators."

"Did NSA find something in their metadata?" Otis asked. Their team analyst loved numbers more than anything.

"They're still identifying numbers that hit the cell repeaters in the Metro. They've got thousands of hits, and even if they ID the right phones, they'll probably be burners."

She handed out the photos. "Take one and pass them down. The terrorists were careful to stay covered, but we traced them back to the King

Street Metro in Alexandria. Agents conducted a neighborhood survey of nearby businesses and recovered video from a credit union three blocks south."

Nathan looked at the flyer which contained six photographs. The first three depicted men exiting a white van and walking up the street. The other three photos were enlargements of a suspect adjusting his mask and revealing half his face.

"Our Next-Generation Identification System used advanced facial recognition and produced an ID with 85 percent certainty. Meet Rafiq Al-Din. He—"

Bridget sat up straight. "I've seen that name."

Everyone looked at her. Rahimya raised an eyebrow. "Care to share?"

"I don't remember where, but I came across it recently. I've been running dozens of vehicle registrations and parishioner lists from the mosque. It could have been on one of those or . . . hold on."

Bridget pushed back her chair and raced out of the room.

Otis banged away on his secure laptop beside Nathan. The screen's privacy tint hid whatever he worked on, and Nathan resisted the urge to look over the guy's shoulder.

"I'll brief you while we're waiting," Rahimya said, "Rafiq Al-Din, DOB February 1994. He's a Syrian national and suspected ISIS member. He popped up on an Egyptian National Police database when he requested a US visa four years ago. His name is flagged as having extremist connections."

"ISIS?" Nathan asked.

"ISIS-K. The Coalition intercepted his name in Kabul, and foreign intel from the UAE and Egypt linked him to the Muslim Brotherhood."

Otis stopped typing and peeked over his laptop screen. "The Secure Flight Program has a hit on the same name and DOB traveling on United Airlines from El Paso to DCA on the first of November."

"He's not a citizen, and he doesn't have a valid visa," Rahimya said. "How did he get into the country?"

"That's no mystery," Nathan said. "The border's wide open. Al-Din may have been down there organizing delivery of the drugs coming across the border."

"Maybe," Rahimya said, "but let's not get ahead of ourselves. Allow the evidence to drive theory."

Bridget burst back into the room waving a paper over her head. "Found it. Rafiq Al-Din received an $800 check from the Al-Sahaba Mosque two weeks ago. He's listed as a vendor in the mosque's checkbook."

"There's our smoking gun," Nathan said. "We've got a participant in the Metro bombing receiving funds from the mosque."

"What did Al-Din give them?" Rahimya asked.

Bridget scanned the papers in her hand. "The checkbook entries don't list what they purchased. There's jack shit for detail. I'll double check their inventory log, but it's sloppy."

"Is this the same Rafiq Al-Din?" Rahimya asked.

Bridget shrugged. "How many can there be?"

"More importantly," Nathan said, "this implicates Imam Qadir. They paid a terrorist before they received a load of opioids."

"We don't have evidence connecting Qadir to the attack," Rahimya said, "and we don't know if the Rafiq Al-Din on their books is the same man. Even if it's him, association doesn't prove guilt."

Nathan threw up his hands in frustration. "How many more coincidences do we need linking the mosque to terrorism? Qadir funded this."

"Find me evidence, not coincidences."

"We can convict on circumstantial evidence," Nathan said.

"We don't have enough."

Nathan's phone vibrated on the table, drawing a glare from Rahimya. Falcon's number displayed on the screen.

"Sorry, gotta take this." Nathan snatched the phone off the desk, caught Bridget's eye, and nodded at the door.

She joined him in the hallway. "What's up?"

"It's Falcon." He answered. "Hello?"

"I can't talk long," Ali whispered.

"What's happening?"

"Something big."

Bridget leaned her head close to the phone. "Put it on speaker."

Nathan glanced around at people marching through the hall and shook his head no.

"What's going on?" Nathan asked Ali.

"The imam said they're planning a big program. He asked if I was serious about jihad. I said yes, and he told me they're planning a historic attack to bring down the Great Satan."

"What kind of attack?"

"He called it *amaliyya istishhadiyya.*"

A chill ran up Nathan's back.

Bridget looked at Nathan. "What's that in English?"

He covered the mouthpiece. "It's a martyrdom operation. There's no other way to take that than terrorism."

"Should we pick up Qadir?"

Nathan raised his finger to tell her to wait. He spoke into the phone. "What did you tell him?"

"Why, yes, of course."

"We should meet. Where are you?"

"I just left the mosque. I'm headed to Alexandria to meet a guy."

"Who?"

"He didn't say. He told me to go to Jones Point under the bridge and wait. Someone is coming to give me instructions."

"Hold on." Nathan hit mute and looked at Bridget. "Get surveillance out to Jones Point."

"I think Tommy's at the mosque."

"Keep him there and have him take photos of everyone coming and going. Roll our team to the park to cover the meeting and see who shows up to task Falcon."

"And arrest them?"

That was always the question. Should they show their cards and hope to delay the martyrdom operation, or stay in the shadows and attempt to develop enough evidence to make a prosecutable case? With an imminent attack, they'd have to act. The stakes were too high, especially in the wake of the Metro bombing.

"We stick like glue to whoever shows up and hope he leads us to their operators. If he spots us, we arrest him."

"And charge him with what?"

"Whatever we can find. We'll debrief Falcon after the meet. His testimony could be sufficient to charge a crime or to detain the players long enough for us to unravel the conspiracy."

Bridget jogged back into the conference room, and Nathan took the phone off mute.

"Don't miss the meeting. Get there and wait for him. Listen to whatever he has to say, ask questions, and agree to everything. Any chance you can record it with your phone?"

"Not unless you want me dead. If they—"

"What?"

"I'm at the park. I need to go."

Falcon disconnected, and Nathan stared at his phone. They needed to hurry.

41

The interior of Nathan's car smelled like burning rubber, and his engine ticked like a time bomb as he sped down Army-Navy Drive to pick up Hamid at the Pentagon City Mall. He'd driven as fast as the heavy traffic allowed while half his group raced to the mosque to back up Tommy and Carlos, both newer agents without prior law enforcement experience. The other half, including Bridget and Three Balls, hurried toward the Woodrow Wilson Bridge.

Setting up a tight surveillance on whomever Falcon met would be critical to identifying members of the terror cell. Without Falcon on the inside, they wouldn't have had any indication a second attack was coming. But would ISIS-K target the Metro again or something bigger? He had a sick feeling the Metro was only a test. The body count would have been higher in more crowded venues.

Nathan screeched to a halt on South Hayes Street, near DEA headquarters. Hamid hustled over and climbed in.

"What's the emergency, Boss?"

"Falcon's meeting a terrorist. They're planning an operation for tomorrow."

Hamid's eyes widened. "Where?"

"Falcon's heading to receive instructions. Qadir asked Falcon to join a martyrdom operation."

"Who's Falcon meeting?"

"That's what we must determine. We'll surveil the meeting, and with luck, he'll led us to the other jihadists."

"How can I help?"

"I'll use Falcon's intel to show probable cause. As soon as he finishes the meeting, we'll debrief him, and I want you with me. His English is good, but our warrants will be based on his words."

"Whatever you need, Boss."

Nathan weaved through traffic like a running back dodging linemen. He didn't use his dashboard and wigwag lights to avoid heating up the area. No telling how many terrorists covered the meeting, and the bad guys he couldn't see were the most dangerous.

He passed through Old Town's Historic District to the Woodrow Wilson Bridge, which crossed the Potomac River and linked Virginia with Maryland. The massive bridge spanned almost a mile and a half and supported twelve lanes of northbound and southbound traffic on I-95 and I-495. It rose high above Jones Point Park, where Falcon would meet his contact.

Nathan continued down South Washington Street and turned into an apartment building's parking lot that overlooked the confluence of Hunting Creek and the Potomac.

"Twelve, Oh-Two," he transmitted. "I'm in the vicinity."

"Oh-Two, Twelve," Bridget responded. "Falcon's in the park beneath the bridge on a path that runs along the water. I'm close by in a parking lot."

"You have eyes on?"

"Affirmative."

That meant Nathan and Hamid were a couple hundred yards away. Nathan pulled in beside an SUV and shut off the engine. They couldn't see Falcon, which meant they were out of sight too.

"Oh-Two to all units, sit tight and let Bridget call the ball."

Hamid turned in his seat and faced Nathan. "You trust Falcon?"

"No, but he's taking a huge risk for us."

"Do you have proof he's telling the truth?"

"That's why we're here."

"Huh."

"What?" Nathan asked.

"It seems convenient. You offered to keep him out of jail if he finds evidence of terrorism, and he comes up with this."

"Qadir is funding the attacks," Nathan said. "The drugs we seized are connected."

Hamid nodded. "Makes sense, but he may be telling us what we want to hear."

Nathan's stomach knotted. Hamid made a good point. Was Nathan's desire to bring justice to the monsters who'd killed those Metro passengers clouding his judgment? He wanted the imam to be involved so he could stop another attack. One was coming. He felt it deep in his gut.

"We'll corroborate what we can before we—"

"Oh-Two, Twelve. Someone's walking up the path from the south. They came out of the woods."

Nathan's heart raced. "Description?"

"Hold on . . . disregard. It's a woman, middle-aged."

"What's she doing?" Nathan asked.

"Wait, she's stopping by Falcon. It looks like they're talking . . . yeah, they're shooting the shit, er, engaged in conversation."

"This is it," Nathan broadcast.

"Break, break," Bridget transmitted. "They're walking south together."

"Give us a better description."

"Female has dark, shoulder-length hair, heavyset, dark overcoat."

"See anyone else?"

"Negative . . . they're out of my sight now."

"Shit," Nathan said to Hamid, then into his mic, "Get eyes on the subject. They're heading toward the point. Perimeter units, she has to come out near the entrance to the bridge."

"Oh-Two, Oh-Seven," Wilson broadcast, "I'm on Washington covering the pedestrian walk. I'll see them when they come out."

"Oh-Nine," Brown chimed in, "she can double back and come through the parking lot to the north."

"He's right," Nathan told Hamid. "I don't like this. She could leave the path and cut through the old cemetery."

"Maybe she's parked near us," Hamid said.

"We'll see her if she approaches the apartment building," Nathan said.

"Break, break," Bridget transmitted. She sounded breathless. "I'm out of the car. They're moving south toward the point. No sign of anyone else."

"Keep a distant eye," Nathan broadcast, now mad at himself for not taking over the primary position. Bridget had little field experience.

"We'll spot her," Hamid said.

"I'm worried she'll double back, and Bridget will miss her. Those woods are thick." Nathan pressed transmit, "Let's get two more units out on foot. I want one by the water and one in the center. Make sure you can see each other. We can't let her slip away."

A chorus of transmissions followed as two more units disembarked on foot.

"Subject and CI are near the point. They're making the turn back west . . . now. Out of sight again."

Nathan pulled up Google maps on his phone. The path continued west, past the Jones Point Lighthouse, then bisected with paths heading west and north. They'd see them when they emerged from the path, unless they dipped into the woods. That would be unlikely, but he had to be prepared for the worst case. If she entered the woods, they should hear her moving through the thick brush.

"Twelve, Oh-Two, give me your status."

"I don't see them. I'm approaching an old building now."

"Anyone have eyes?" Nathan asked.

No answer.

"Shit, shit, shit," he grumbled. He keyed the mic. "Twelve, Oh Two, close the gap. I don't care if you burn it. We can't lose her."

"Copy," her breathless words came over the air.

"Everyone stay alert," he broadcast. "Be ready to move in."

The woman was in a tiny park, and they had six agents spread out, covering each path. They should see her exit—not to mention Falcon was with her, and he would call when they finished. Even if they lost her, Falcon should possess information to help them deter the next operation. But that was hopeful thinking, and not the worst-case scenario. Not by a long shot.

Nathan turned to Hamid. "I don't like this. Stay here and keep your head down. I don't want her spotting you . . . and if you see her, call my cell.

"I'm not going anywhere."

Nathan climbed out and hurried through the lot to the path that led into the park. He took long strides but didn't run. If Falcon and the suspect rounded the corner, he had to appear casual, out for a stroll. He should have brought Bruno for cover.

A figure moved out of the shadows. Nathan slowed.

Bridget.

He stopped, and she did too. He raised his palms in a question. She did too.

He hurried to her. "No sign of them?"

"They came down this path."

Nathan looked to the north across and open field. They hadn't had time to cross it. He would have heard them stomping through the woods, not that Falcon would follow the woman in there. He canted his ear and listened. Nothing.

"Let's backtrack and—"

The distant sound of an engine vibrated through the woods behind Bridget. She heard it and looked at him.

"What's that?" she asked.

"A motorboat."

Nathan jogged down the path toward the old lighthouse building. The sound of the engine increased as its driver applied throttle. It echoed over the water.

Nathan sprinted past the building to the shore with Bridget right behind him. He stopped and squinted at the river. The sound evaporated into the distance. It was too dark to see anything away from the shore.

"Oh, my frickin' God," Bridget said.

"They're gone," Nathan said. "She's in the wind. Where they hell is Falcon?"

"No, I mean look."

Nathan followed her outstretched hand to a body floating face down in the river.

Ali.

42

Nathan jumped into the water and stumbled over the rocks and rotting logs strewn across the river bottom. Ali floated with his face submerged, not moving. Nathan wedged his foot against a rock for balance, grabbed Ali's shoulders, and rolled him over onto his back.

A plume of crimson spread through the green water as blood gushed from Ali's neck. A deep laceration ran from his clavicle to his chin, and ivory cartilage of Ali's Adam's apple poked through where his skin peeled back.

Nathan dragged Ali toward shore, stumbling on the incline. Bridget jumped in and helped pull Ali onto the bank. Out of the water, Ali's body became dead weight. Nathan's back strained as they pulled him onto the gravel lined the shore. Ali's eye remained open and unseeing.

He was dead.

Nathan dialed 911 and requested an ambulance and police to respond. The FBI's air wing wouldn't be available on short notice, but that's what Nathan needed to catch that murderous bitch. The borders of Virginia, Maryland, and the District of Columbia intersected at a stone marker on Jones Point. The Potomac off Alexandria was mostly owned by DC, and Maryland's boundary ended at its shore, except where it crossed the river at the Woodrow Wilson Bridge. Any of these jurisdictions had venue when chasing a fleeing suspect, as long as Virginia requested assistance.

Nathan took out his handheld radio and switched to the interagency emergency channel shared by DC-area law enforcement agencies and broadcast an alert. He requested an MPD airship and was told to standby.

The sound of the motorboat had disappeared. Nathan strained to listen, but only heard chirping crickets and a croaking bullfrog in the distance.

"We gotta catch that frickin' woman," Bridget said.

"She's in the wind."

"I was right there. I could have arrested her."

"That was my call, not yours. We needed to let the meeting play out to gather evidence and intelligence about the next attack."

"Did Ali record the conversation?"

"He said he it was too risky." Nathan knelt and searched Ali's pockets. He took out Ali's cell phone. It was off. "Damn."

"What now?"

"Organize the team and hold the crime scene until Alexandria PD arrives. I'll call Rahimya."

Bridget took a last look at Ali and scampered up the bank. A siren wailed somewhere to the west.

Nathan dialed Rahimya. "They killed our CI."

"He's dead?"

"On the way to the hospital, but yeah, he's gone."

Rahimya groaned. "What happened?"

"He was compromised, obviously. He met a woman to receive his tasking. She killed him and fled off Jones Point by motorboat. MPD's got a helicopter en route."

"How did this happen?"

"Falcon . . ." Nathan hesitated. Using the man's codename seemed childish now that the tradecraft intended to protect Ali had proved worthless. They'd continue to maintain his confidentiality for the sake of his family, but the terrorists knew his name.

"Give me the short version so I can brief the ASAC before I get down there."

"Falcon told us Imam Qadir agreed to use him for jihad. Qadir sent him here to receive instructions."

"That's corroborated?"

"Tommy confirmed the imam and Falcon were at the mosque, but we can't corroborate their conversation."

"That's thin."

"It's enough to bring in Qadir for questioning."

"That'll compromise the case."

"They know were investigating them."

"Okay, do it, but stay at the scene until I arrive. This is a clusterfuck."

"It's worse for Ali's family . . . well, maybe not for his wife. At least she won't suffer any more of his beatings."

"Coordinate with Alexandria PD. It's a homicide, so it's their scene."

"Copy."

Nathan hung up and stared out across the river. Rotors from an approaching airship thumped over the water. The helicopter's lights blinked red as it approached from DC—MPD's air wing.

The motorboat had disappeared into the darkness. Once the woman disembarked, they'd never find her. Not through a manhunt.

He joined Bridget beside the blood-coated rocks. "Think you can give enough of a description to help a sketch artist?"

"I can do better than that. I took a few shots with a digital camera. The telephoto lens isn't great, and the lighting sucked, but it captured them together."

"You checked out a camera?"

"It's my own. I've been champing at the bit to get into a serious investigation. I came prepared."

Nathan smiled. "Let's get those images to the PD." Blood dripped off the rocks, and guilt washed over him.

"What's wrong?"

"I don't get it," Nathan said. "First, someone poisoned Bluebird, and now, Falcon's dead."

"What frickin' happened?" Bridget asked.

"Don't know. Either we burned him, or he burned himself."

"Maybe he pushed too hard, and Qadi got suspicious," Bridget said.

"That's possible, but there's a big difference between suspicion and murder. Falcon's offer to join the jihad may have raised suspicion, but Qadir didn't know he was insincere. Why not test Falcon or shut him out? All Qadir had to do was plead ignorance. Killing is extreme."

"These a-holes don't give two shits about murdering innocent people," Bridget said. "Murder seems to be their point."

"This will bring plenty of heat on them. We're gonna pick up Qadir and sweat him. Maybe he'll say something incriminating."

"Doubt it."

"Detaining him may preempt whatever's coming."

"If they're planning anything. It could all be bullshit."

"People don't kill to cover up nothing. Another terror incident is imminent. I feel it in my bones, but that's not the worst thing troubling me."

Bridget raised her eyebrows. "What the fuck could be worse?"

"We've got one CI dead and another in the hospital fighting for his life. That's not coincidence."

"Meaning?"

"We've got a mole in our house."

43

Dan Lamonte had a black cloud following him. His day had sucked since his boss's call had awoken him. Receiving a call outside of business hours was never a good sign, and this had been no exception. He'd botched his last financial report, and their client was raising hell.

Dan brooded near the front door of the M15 Metropolitan Transit Authority bus as it stopped at another red light. Traffic had been heavier than usual all the way down Second Avenue from his apartment on East Ninetieth Street. Dan checked his watch—almost nine o'clock—and his boss wanted him at his desk before the bell rang for the core trading session. Worse, today was the final day before the markets closed for Thanksgiving. He made six figures as a junior trader at Latham & Winchester, barely enough to afford a studio apartment, and if he lost his first job in finance, he'd screw his career.

Dan shifted on the blue plastic seat. Blue-collar employees packed the bus, and if any of his colleagues saw him disembark, he'd never live it down. The subway was acceptable transportation, but a bus? No way. He should get his shit together, or he'd never move up and earn more moola, the key to the lifestyle he deserved.

He sighed. Starting his day with his boss yelling at him had been awful enough, but then Dan had stepped onto the bus and spilled his coffee on his lap—of all days to wear a light-colored suit. It looked like he'd pissed his pants, not to mention scalding his private region. He couldn't afford to burn his Willie Wonka, not that he had any realistic shots at getting laid. He hadn't had a date in a month or done the horizontal dance in . . . what? Six months. Could it have been that long? Man, he should get his life in order. No money, no pussy, and already, the day wasn't trending in the right direction.

The bus jerked to a stop at the corner of Water Street and Maiden Lane, and Dan pushed through the crowd and stepped out into the cool morning. Escaping the confines of a packed bus always felt like a jailbreak. He inhaled the fresh air. The scent of candied nuts wafted off a street cart, the first sign that Christmas approached.

Buildings towered around him, a canyon of metal and glass shielding the dim light that filtered through clouds on another gray November morning. He walked under a metal walkway protecting the sidewalk from construction above and headed south toward his office. The day before Thanksgiving, tourists swelled the regular crowd. Dan weaved through the throng, then bladed his body and slipped between two plodding fatsos. He crossed Pine and turned onto Wall Street as the sun poked out from behind a cloud and illuminated Wall Street—as if God recognized the epicenter of the universe.

Cars honked as traffic inched forward in gridlock. Dan skirted a woman who pushed a high-end baby carriage with enormous wheels that had probably cost more than his mountain bike. A narrow stream of yellow liquid slithered over the sidewalk toward the gutter, and he leapt over it without losing steam. The odor of urine burned his nostrils. The homeless were animals. He continued along the curb toward the row of flags where his office occupied three floors of a skyscraper.

Half a block ahead, a battered pickup cut off a taxi and jerked to the curb. Its tailgate slammed open, and four maintenance workers in back climbed out carrying leaf blowers. Thousand-dollar suits packed the sidewalk and traffic jammed both lanes. *Just great.* Maintenance work would cost him another five minutes.

And maybe his job.

Three Mexican-looking cleaners wearing matching overalls spread out along both sides of the street. They had tanks strapped to their backs like scuba divers. *Weird.* Maybe they planned to suck up leaves and garbage, another green initiative the city wasted millions of tax dollars.

A scrawny worker yanked the cord on his leaf blower, and its engine sputtered to life like a motorcycle without a muffler. The others started theirs too, and the machines growled, filling the morning with a mechanical din. Screeching lawn equipment was one reason Dan had moved out of the suburbs after graduating college.

The odor of gas and oil polluted the air. Those damn things were so dirty, and they caused global warming too. Why the hell did they muck up rush hour, and which bureaucratic numskull decided sidewalks needed to be free of leaves at nine o'clock in the morning?

Dan slowed behind two woman who wore designer tracksuits and sipped from venti Starbucks cups—probably stockbrokers' wives planning to gossip all day while their nannies raised their children.

His watch beeped. Nine o'clock. Dan groaned. What would make a good excuse? Maybe he could say the police had set up a bag check and detained him. They did that sometimes, but everyone else in the office would have been caught in it too. Maybe he could sneak in and pretend he'd been in the bathroom with stomach issues. His boss would understand a night of debauchery, and—

The wiry guy reached into a pouch on his belt and donned a face mask. What the hell? Now he really looked like a scuba diver. Farther down the sidewalk and across the street, the other workers tightened their masks in a coordinated movement.

Something's wrong. Dan's stomach twisted, and he slowed.

A man bumped into him from behind. "Watch it, asshole," the guy said.

Dan turned and looked at him. The guy had slicked-back hair and a Cartier briefcase.

"Sorry, I—"

"First time in the big city?" the guy said as he brushed past.

Another group of men clad in the same uniforms rounded the corner onto Wall Street. They spread out too. What the hell was happening? Two started their leaf blowers then pushed through the glass revolving door into Dan's building.

Alarm bells went off in his head.

Ten yards away, the closest maintenance worked touched something on his tank, then aimed his leaf blower at head level, not down at the sidewalk.

Dan stopped. A flutter of panic tickled his insides.

A crimson cloud of smoke mushroomed out of the leaf blower—directly into the faces of the nearby pedestrians.

A frost chilled Dan's body and froze his feet to the sidewalk.

A businesswoman dropped her attaché case and collapsed, as if someone had flicked off a switch. The two women in pantsuits crumpled to the sidewalk beside him. Then a man in a jogging suit.

A gust of wind carried the red fog gusted across the sidewalk, and the bloom drifted over the street. A woman screamed. Another shrieked something unintelligible. Bodies tumbled into each other and fell to the ground.

Primal fear shocked Dan's body back under his control. He couldn't think, couldn't make sense of the scene before him, but he needed to escape.

Run.

He spun around and ran back toward Water Street. The crowd gawked, like spectators at a football game. Their curious expressions morphed into horror and shock.

A pickup double-parked at the end of the street, and two more men dressed in coveralls and carrying leaf blowers jumped onto the sidewalk. Their machines simultaneously roared to life. They discharged dark gas into the faces of people around them. A car passed through the toxic smog. It drifted toward the curb and smashed into a postal truck.

The scarlet cloud blew over Dan, a penumbra of death that blotted the sun and turned the city street blood red.

His fear vanished. A total calm embraced him. Pain and worry flittered away, and he floated on a blissful cloud. Terror gave way to euphoria, and then numbness.

Then death.

44

The moment of vengeance had arrived.

I placed my walkie-talkie on the floor of the van and looked up at the two men in the front seats.

"It's time."

Malik nodded and grabbed his Mossberg shotgun off the floor, a pump-action weapon with an extended tube that carried eight shells. Every shell contained nine pellets of double-aught buckshot, each the size of a 9mm bullet. At close quarters, it would inflict maximum damage, and its booming noise enhanced the terror.

Part of me wanted to assault NYPD headquarters with Salman, because it would garner the most media attention, but that attack would have little effect. Barricades blocked the streets around One Police Plaza, limiting entry to pedestrians and authorized vehicles, and security cameras stationed around the building would spot Salman long before he penetrated the perimeter. He'd die, but his efforts would create chaos, and divert officers headed to Wall Street.

But this attack against the First Precinct, whose officers covered Southern Manhattan, would affect cops on a visceral level. Putting the lives of officers' comrades in jeopardy, would penetrate professional defenses and shake officers' hearts.

I slipped on a surgical mask and pulled a Yankees cap low over my eyes. If cameras recorded me, facial recognition software shouldn't capture enough to identify me. Anonymity allowed me to lead the campaign. I shouldn't risk myself, but I hungered to draw their blood with my own hands.

My family demanded justice. All Afghans did. Farzana held Tara and floated before me. Their eyes hardened, criticizing my chosen path. But what did women know? War and killing was the province of men. I'd avenge their deaths, and then they'd understand.

Malik and Omar exited the van, and neither covered their faces. They knew this was their final act, and they ballooned with pride in anticipation of their glorious jihad.

Malik held his shotgun by its pistol grip and kept it against his leg. A dozen civilians strolled along the sidewalk, most with their faces buried in smartphones, and nobody noticed. Malik strode toward the precinct.

Omar stayed near the passenger door and waited. I'd tasked him to engage any threats coming from police vehicles parked nearby, and once he'd done that, he'd fire on the precinct.

I sought anarchy.

The precinct's blue door opened and two uniformed officers exited. Malik was halfway across the street when the officers hit the steps. He saw them and stopped. A green Prius braked then honked. Both officers looked up. They stared at Malik. He stared back. Time froze.

"Gun," an officer yelled.

He reached for his holstered weapon, but in his hurry, he grabbed the front of his holster instead.

Malik raised his Mossberg with one hand and fired. The pattern spread, and balls of hot lead struck both officers. The blast echoed down the street.

The shotgun recoiled, and Malik grabbed it with both hands.

The first officer clutched his thigh and grimaced. His handgun clattered to the steps. The other cop twitched and looked down at his stomach, below his vest, where blood stained his shirt. He clasped his stomach, then turned his palms upward and stared at the red glistening liquid.

A man shouted for help. The Prius driver gawked.

Malik ejected a shell and racked another round into the chamber. The loud clack seemed to refocus the officers' attention. The first officer scooped his gun off the ground.

Malik fired again. Half of the first officer's head splattered against the door. The second officer stumbled back and drew his gun. Malik jettisoned another shell and fired a third time. This one caught the officer low, and his leg twisted at an odd angle before he spun and collapsed on the steps.

I watched, as if it played out on television, but this was different. I was present, with both my life and freedom in jeopardy.

"Police, drop the gun," another officer yelled from across the street.

Omar stepped around the van and loosed six rounds from his AR-15.

I exited the van as Malik jacked another round and sprinted toward the precinct's door. The on-duty sergeant probably sat behind bulletproof glass at the front desk, but it didn't matter. The point was for disruption, not for Malik to survive. Two dead police officers on the front steps meant we'd already achieved our limited goal for this part of the operation.

Omar's carbine cracked. A three-round burst. Then another. The detective in plainclothes sprawled in the street holding his chest. He reached beneath his wool jacket for his handgun, his face twisted in agony.

Omar had turned and fired down the street at an approaching police car. His bullets peppered the windshield and slammed into the cops inside. He didn't see the detective.

I raised my weapon. Despite planning and directing the first terror attack in Washington, I hadn't acted as an operator. I lay my front sight over the man's prone body and centered it in the rear sight, just like the Americans had trained me. How ironic. I fired, and the carbine jerked in my hands. The detective's torso spun, and he flailed onto his back. His handgun clattered onto the street.

Malik burst into the precinct. His shotgun boomed. A cascade of small-arms fire popped inside the building. Malik's shotgun stayed silent.

He was dead.

Sirens came from multiple directions. I'd come for the visceral experience of combat, but if I stayed, I'd end up either in handcuffs or bleeding out on the street. I swiveled and raised my AR-15 above the van and aimed it a tiny window on the precinct's second floor. A handful of faces peered out, trying to figure out what was happening.

I fired.

Windows shattered, and bodies dove for cover. A mist of blood indicated I'd hit someone, but I didn't wait to confirm it. I moved to the next window. Another burst. More broken glass.

I aimed at the third window and fired. Nobody was visible behind it. They'd seen the threat. A bullet smashed into the roof of the van and winged off with a high-pitched whine, like tapping a wineglass with a fork.

Time to go.

I ducked behind the van, as incoming rounds slammed into the opposite side. I raised the carbine above my head and fired wildly at the building. Bullets clanged off brick.

My bolt slapped back empty, and I tossed the spent weapon onto the sidewalk.

Emergency lights twinkled everywhere. The intensity of fire coming from the precinct picked up, and bullets peppered the van. Omar fired burst after burst, alternating between the building's front and side doors and targets in the distance, probably police cruisers.

I stayed low, making myself a smaller target, then I sprinted down the sidewalk. If anyone saw me from the windows, they'd only have a brief second to identify me, decide to shoot, and pull the trigger. I ran, but none of the incoming fire followed me.

I made it to the next street and looked behind me. Civilians scurried for cover, and I blended into the panicked mob. Nobody gave me a second look. I stopped at a trash receptacle, stripped off my rubber gloves, and threw them inside. Then I jogged north at the next avenue. I needed to get to the train station and out of New York before authorities shut down the island.

If all went well, the next thirty minutes would be the worst New York City had experienced since 9/11.

45

Terror struck Manhattan.

Nathan stood with members of his group before the television and watched death consume Wall Street. He was as helpless as every other American, and guilt crushed his chest. This was the attack Ali had warned about, and Nathan had been unable to stop it.

The screen filled with fuzzy images of rescue personnel moving through Lower Manhattan wearing Level A protective gear. News crews shot the scene from blocks away using telephoto lenses. Experts estimated the death count at over one hundred.

Nathan gazed out the window, impotent and nauseous. Every life lost would weigh on him forever. He'd been called to protect the weak, and whether his urges came from culture, evolution, or God, they controlled him.

"Shit," Bridget said.

Nathan looked up, and she pointed to the television monitor. Panicked people ran across a parking lot near a glass facade and the colorful star-shaped sign. The scroll running across the bottom of the screen said, "Suspected Terror Attack Strikes Mall of America."

"They hit Minneapolis too?" Nathan asked.

"Bloomington," Bridget said.

"It's coordinated," Rahimya said. "They also struck the Galleria in Houston. They're spreading terror across the country."

"Wall Street I get," Bridget said. "It's our financial hub, but why a mall?"

"It scares the average American," Nathan said. "Most people have never set foot on Wall Street, but they've been to the mall. And . . ."

"What?" she asked.

"What's the date?"

"Wednesday. Tomorrow's Thanksgiving."

"That's it."

"What's it?"

"Wall Street won't open again until Monday, which creates days of economic uncertainty, and these incidents will decimate sales on Black Friday."

"And the Mall of America is one of the world's largest malls," Rahimya said, "but one mall won't hurt our economy."

"It's not just one mall," Nathan said. "Who will take their family shopping after watching images of an attack?"

"But the chance of—"

"Statistics don't matter once fear seeps into the public consciousness. People react with their hearts. Their desire to live supersedes statistical likelihood. These attacks will spread terror, chaos, and economic ruin."

"Frickin' pricks," Bridget said.

On the television, police officers in a mishmash of protective chemical suits carried liters with unconscious patients through the mall's parking lot. Medical personnel set up a decontamination center made from tents and plastic dividers. Bodies piled up, and yellow police tape fluttered in the wind.

"They finally figured it out," Nathan said.

"Figured what out?" Bridget asked.

"How to attack a free society. Our culture's built on individual liberty, at least it used to be, and that leaves an uncontrolled populace. By definition, an open society is more dangerous than one with a central authority controlling behavior. And by dangerous, I mean open to attack from outside and with higher levels of crime."

"How is ISIS exploiting that?"

"With an elegant solution. Whoever planned this has realized that low-tech attacks are almost impossible to stop. We have sniffers for radioactive material, and we guard our aircraft and political buildings, but citizens retain freedom of movement, which makes it almost impossible to spot and interdict teams carrying small arms."

"They're not flying planes into building, so how much damage can they do?"

"Lots, if they're coordinated and if the operation is well-planned and executed—and more with biological or chemical agents."

"Carfentanil."

"If we could stop someone carrying a baggie of powder, the war on drugs would've ended decades ago."

"Ffrickin' evil."

The news switched to a split screen with the chaos of Wall Street juxtaposed with the growing body count at the Mall of America. Medical teams stood outside the mall waiting for HAZMAT teams to bring them patients. Frustration showed on their faces. Every minute they waited, more people died.

"The genius of the plan is its simplicity," Nathan said. "My grandfather was alive when the Wright Brothers took flight, and half a century later, man walked on the moon. It's hard to contemplate the rapid advancement, but technology and innovation have become the norm. There isn't a person alive who experienced the technological stagnation of the past."

"But it's not enough to stop a low-tech attack."

"Our reliance on technology . . . no, it's more than reliance, it's an expectation. We believe technology makes things easier, so we hang wires, install tracking devices, and sift through metadata. The more sophisticated we get, the more we turn to computers to solve our problems."

Bridget nodded. "They knew that."

"They've gone primitive. They learned it from the jihadists hiding in the caves of the Hindi Kush. Being a seventh-century warrior provides some natural immunity from modern law enforcement, because they don't exist in the digital world."

"Because we can't intercept emails or tap their phones?"

"It's way deeper than that. We can't charge conspiracy without a record of their plotting to do evil. How do we prove collaboration when they only communicate face-to-face?"

"Surveillance, bugging."

"That won't work unless you already know who they are and what they're doing."

"Flip one of them."

"Yeah, except were dealing with radical Islamists who seek martyrdom. We can develop CIs around the edges, but when terrorists meet at a coffee shop to plan detonating a dirty bomb, our options for recording that conversation are minimal."

"We're fucked. These guys' lack of sophistication is screwing us."

"I don't think it's luck they've taken this tack. They're operating here, which means they have access to technology. They've gone primitive by choice."

"You may be overthinking this."

"They're foregoing technology to seal themselves in a bubble."

"If your theory is right."

"We know it is, because we haven't intercepted them. They're employing simple tactics, like a lone gunman would, and they're using drugs to rub it in. We been trying to win the war on drugs for decades, and they're proving our impotence."

"Frickin' evil," Bridget said.

"And brilliant."

The scene on television switched back to Wall Street, and the juxtaposition of EMTs carrying bodies beside expensive buildings created cognitive dissonance. Watching terrorism ignited Nathan's need to protect, as if the murders had happened in his office. Television did that. His muscles hardened as his body prepared to fight, yet the tragedy occurred hundreds of miles away, and there was nothing he could do. Absolutely nothing. He could only watch images on the flickering monitor.

Those bastards.

Bridget shook her head. "This is a historic intelligence failure. We're hearing about attacks from the media."

"Phones are everywhere. Everything's recorded."

"Why aren't local authorities reporting to us?"

"They will," Nathan said. "They've got their hands full, and calling the Feds is the last thing on the minds."

Rahimya hung up her phone. She looked glum. "They used a carjacked pesticide truck in Tampa and dumped its chemicals behind a kindergarten. They refilled it with a water-soluble, opioid solution. They believe it's carfentanil, but we will know more by tomorrow."

"How bad?"

"At least 300 overdoses. Most of those didn't make it. The cops are still finding victims."

Bridget shook her head. "This is our fault."

"Maybe," Nathan said, "but our enemy's killing soft targets. We can't protect hundreds of millions of people in an open society. We need to bring the fight to ISIS."

"Military action?"

"Sure, but that's out of our control. We can develop intelligence to give the administration the ammunition they need to take action overseas, but we can also develop sources and run stings here. If we go offensive, we can keep them looking over their shoulders and maybe discover what they're doing next."

"Isn't NSA combing through chatter?"

"They use algorithms, but they're limited to communications involving foreign nationals . . . at least in theory. They're monitoring almost everything, but when it involves American citizens, it gets dicey."

"We're at war," she said. "We should ignore those rules."

"It's a terrorist organization, not a hot war, but once Congress gives us more authority, we'll keep it. Trading privacy for security is a delicate balance, and we can't trust the government. I learned that the hard way during my Havana Syndrome investigation."

"We should pick up Qadir again," Bridget said.

"Agreed," Nathan said. "If we can find him again."

Alexandria PD had detained the imam as a person of interest in Ali's murder. Unfortunately, the only recorded conversation contained nothing incriminating, and the police had to release him. Qadir had disappeared immediately.

Nathan turned to Rahimya. "We cleared to talk to him?"

"Talk, but no arrest. The AUSA won't approve a warrant. We have nothing linking him to these attacks . . . at least not yet. Maybe we'll get lucky with a telephone intercept."

Her phone rang, and she answered. "Uh-huh . . . uh-huh . . . we're on the way." She hung up.

"Qadir?"

"Negative. They took one of the terrorists alive in New York. JTTF's talking to him now. I want both of you there."

"On it."

Nathan snatched his tactical bag off his desk, confirming his heavy vest, tactical belt, and raid jacket were inside. Where was his FBI cap?

Bridget walked up carrying her bag. "We going?"

"Let's see what that asshole has to say."

46

Yusuf Mubarak lay in bed in the intensive care unit of New York Metropolitan Hospital and glared at Nathan and Bridget. The day-shift doctor and head nurse hovered beside them didn't appear much happier. They'd insisted on monitoring the conversation, because medical regulations prohibited interrogations inside the ICU, but the horror of the transportation attacks had loosened the rules. Collective memories of the World Trade Center collapsing on 9/11 may have added to the medical staff's acquiescence, and they'd agreed to a brief interview. However, if Yusuf asked them to leave or if his vitals deteriorated, they'd stop the meeting.

Yusuf, an Egyptian national, had arrived on a student visa, despite his name popping up in NSA metadata. Islamic State affiliates had been in contact with him, yet authorities had never officially labeled him a terrorist. What the hell were State Department officials doing letting someone with his associations into the homeland?

Nathan glanced at the door, anxious for Hamid to arrive and interpret. Yusuf didn't speak a word of English, an inconvenient fact the FBI's JTTF had discovered when they first spoke with him earlier in the morning. Luckily, an NYPD task officer assigned to the JTTF was fluent in Arabic and had facilitated the interview.

Yellow liquid sloshed through a drainage tube sticking out of Yusuf's chest. He'd taken two .40 slugs to the abdomen, courtesy of an NYPD patrol officer, and he'd almost died from blood loss because it'd taken EMTs over an hour to enter the scene. Six EMTs who'd first arrived had succumbed to clouds of opioid gas dancing on the wind.

"Let bet kalem Arabi," Nathan said, diving deep into his limited vocabulary to say he didn't speak Arabic. "*Ayyaz* an, uh, interpreter."

Yusuf sneered. Would he even agree to speak to them? He'd spoken to JTTF but had not given them anything they could use.

They'd handcuffed Yusuf's arms to the gurney, which made it a custodial arrest. Nathan would need to read him the Miranda warning again, despite the earlier interview. Yusuf wasn't an American citizen, but why give ammunition to whichever slimy defense attorney represented him? No, that wasn't fair. Many defense attorneys Nathan had jousted with were honorable people, smart and caring, and everybody needed a proper defense. With all the violent confrontations Nathan had endured, sooner or later, someone would levy serious criminal charges against him, and then the attorneys he callously called *slimy* would become his protectors. Still, how could anyone defend a piece of shit who murdered innocents?

The door opened, and Hamid entered. Yusuf's eyes widened. Despite Nathan's attempted Arabic, Yusuf was probably just realizing he was about to be interrogated again. Using foreign languages without proficiency was always a minefield. Once in Haiti, Nathan had told a suspect "*kushay*" to order him to lie down, not knowing it was slang for "I want to fuck you." Boy, had that guy fought hard.

Hamid stood beside Nathan. He crossed his arms and stared daggers at Yusuf. Hamid had fought beside Nathan as Taliban bullets had whizzed over their heads. Now, the Taliban had destroyed his country and trapped its population beneath the boot of oppression. Time would tell whether Yusuf worked for ISIS or the Taliban, but the ugly truth was, little difference separated all radical Islamists. In the end, they proselytized a supremacist religion that repressed people under Sharia law and murdered anyone who resisted.

Yusuf didn't take his eyes off Hamid.

Jihadists held a deep and fiery hatred of Westerners, especially military members they perceived as crusaders, but that anger paled compared to their visceral disgust at Muslims who enabled the West—people like Hamid who facilitated military and law enforcement operations. Islamists manipulated diplomats, and many Americans expressed sympathy to anti-Western ideas, but cops and soldiers needed to fight, and Hamid and his fellow interpreters increased the Coalition's effectiveness. Islamists hated them most. And now Hamid presented himself before the injured and handcuffed Islamist. If the man had the ability, he'd climb across the bed and attack.

"Before we begin," Nathan said, "I have to read you your rights." He slipped his laminated Miranda card out of his credential case. "You have the right to remain silent. You—"

Hamid simultaneously interpreted, and they quickly fell into a rhythm they'd enjoyed running sources in Jalalabad.

"Do you wish to be interviewed without an attorney present?"

Yusuf spat something out in Arabic, but Hamid didn't translate.

Nathan looked at Hamid. "What did he say?"

Hamid's face had a reddish hue. He looked from Bridget to the nurse.

"Hamid?"

"He said something very vulgar . . . about your sister."

"Nathan doesn't have a sister," Bridget said.

"Not the point," Nathan said. "Will he answer our questions?"

Hamid and the man exchanged words. Yusuf seemed to defer. "Yes, he will talk to you."

"Voluntarily?"

"Yes."

Nathan had reviewed hours of recording from dozens of security cameras that had captured the death and destruction on Wall Street and the First Precinct. None of the men were identifiable, but Yusuf had been arrested at the scene, so his guilt was self-evident. What they needed was information to find the terrorists who had escaped.

Nathan moved closer to the bed. "Where will your group attack next?"

"America."

Nathan didn't need Hamid to understand that.

"Where?"

"Everywhere."

"That's impossible. Are you afraid to tell us?"

"We will strike where you are weakest."

"And where is that?"

"Your people."

"What will you do?"

"We will use your vices against you."

"How?"

"Everything is jihad."

"Who is your leader?"

"Allah."

"Who is the Slayer?"

Yusuf looked from Nathan to Bridget to Hamid. "You will never catch him."

"Why?"

"Because he's more clever than you. And more driven."

Nathan cocked his head. "We catch monsters every day."

"The hatred in his heart runs deep. You will suffer his wrath. He implements the wrath of Allah."

"Why does he hate us?"

"You will learn that . . . in time."

"We'll catch him, with or without your help, and when we do, you'll have lost your chance to earn leniency from the court."

"I only seek Allah's grace."

"Why did you do this?"

Yusuf leaned back and grimaced. "I do not feel well."

"Who is supporting you?"

"I must sleep."

"Have you been to the Al-Sahaba Mosque in Virginia?"

"I am done talking."

"You'll never get out of prison."

"Allah will release my shackles."

47

I stood beneath a coffee-shop awning and stared across the park at Amelia and Nathan exiting the elevator in their home. *Elevator.* How privileged, these Americans. Elevators in Afghanistan were a rarity, an exclusive benefit to those in the capital city, and even then, you took your life in your hands by entering one. Even the lifts that worked took an eternity to ascend. I'd been stuck in my cousin's building enough times to know not to use it. Americans took their wealth for granted. Nobody in human history ever lived under such safety and in such luxury.

That would change—I'd see to it.

When I finished this operation, Americans would never again vote without thought to foreign affairs, without concern for those poor souls around the world who suffered the consequences of US policy. May Allah help the foreigners gullible enough to ally with the United States. I was a living example of what would happen.

Nathan looked both ways then strode across the street with his hand on Amelia's head. He moved as if he owned the street. American bastard. He stopped at a sporty Mustang. Of course Nathan would own an expensive car with an enormous engine and bold style. Who did he think he was? Nathan must be in his thirties. Maybe forty. So hard to tell. Afghanistan aged men, unlike the soft existence Nathan and his countrymen experienced, being serviced by immigrants. Their government took care of everyone's basic needs until people talked of universal incomes and complained that the government wasn't providing Wi-Fi. If they only knew. Americans on welfare earn 100 times the median Afghan income, and all they had to do was dial 911, and men with guns would arrive to protect them. Yet they complained. These rich, entitled donkeys criticized the very people who protected them. The reality of the dangers in the world became foreign to them—so much that when bad things happened, Americans went into shock. What other cultures watched horror for pleasure? In Kabul, poverty was the norm, and horror his daily existence.

Nathan's daughter lived under the protection of his privilege. She walked around the car, and Nathan opened the door for her. She looked across the park, and her face transformed into Tara's. She stared at me, her face full of sadness.

I stayed still. What was this magic?

Amelia's face returned. She scanned the street, looking through me without recognition. She climbed inside and closed the door.

What did her transformation into Tara mean? Had that really been my daughter? Was Tara trying to tell me something? I shook the thought away. She was but a girl. What did she know of adult things? Manly things?

Nathan jogged around to the driver's side and got in. He didn't have a care in the world.

That wouldn't last for long.

48

Nathan and Bridget approached the front door of the Al-Sahaba Mosque as Three Balls and Tommy ran around back. The combination of carfentanil, radical Islamic beliefs, and intelligence from Bluebird and Falcon, put Qadir atop their suspect list. They didn't have probable cause to arrest Qadir for the coordinated attacks that stunned the country, but they could apply pressure—and the rising death count gave them leeway that didn't normally exist.

Nathan shoved open the door and entered the mosque. He didn't need a warrant to enter a building that allowed public access, but forcing Qadir to come in for another interrogation required his consent. They hoped for an incriminating statement that would give them enough to arrest Qadir, but as an American citizen, the constitution afforded him full rights. Qadir had immigrated legally ten years before and had recently been granted citizenship, and now he used his rights to shield his nefarious activities as he acted on his hatred of America and the West.

The clip-clopping of Nathan's and Bridget's shoes echoed off the marble in the empty vestibule. They continued into the Great Hall, also vacant. Nathan stopped and allowed his vision to adjust to the dim lighting.

"Where is everyone?" Bridget asked.

"Something's off. I expected them to be in here, armed and barricaded behind sandbags . . . figuratively."

Nathan crossed the hall and knocked on the door leading to the administrative offices. Those were private spaces, and their legal footing became tenuous. Violating Qadir's rights could get make his statements inadmissible—if he was there.

And if he agreed to talk.

Nathan glanced around. During previous visits, the imam and his staff had been present. But now—nothing.

"Screw this," Nathan said.

He turned the knob, and the door opened. He kept his body out of the threshold, a tactic ingrained from years in law enforcement, and he quick-peeked. Darkness shrouded the interior hall, and the office doors were closed. A staircase led down to the basement where they'd found the cache of rifles.

Bridget bit her lip, wary. "This is creepy."

"C'mon."

Nathan flung open the door to Qadir's office. The dark room was tidy, unlike last time when papers had littered the desk. Nathan stepped inside.

"We can't search," Bridget said.

"I'm not searching, I'm looking for the imam. No one's answering, and he could be hurt. Exigent circumstances."

"But—"

"We see anything with potential evidentiary value, we'll apply for a warrant."

Nathan rounded the desk. A drawer was cracked open an inch. He illuminated the interior with his SureFire light. Empty.

He opened the other drawers. Nothing but a paperclip and a handful of rubber bands.

"Shit," Nathan said.

"What?"

"He's gone."

"On the lam?"

"Check the other offices."

Bridget's eyes darted around, clearly uneasy with their search, but she nodded and walked into the hallway.

The computer monitor remained black. Nathan scanned the ceiling and furniture for cameras. Nothing obvious, but any recording of them conducting an illegal search would hurt their case. He continued anyway. He strolled around the room using a single finger to open drawers and cabinets, as if a casual technique made the search acceptable. No financial records, no membership lists, no legal documents.

Nothing.

He entered the adjacent room used by Qadir's second-in-command. The man had vacated too.

Nathan exited into the hall as Bridget came out of the last room.

She shrugged. "Zilch. They're ghosts."

"Let's check the basement." He pulled out his portable radio. "Oh-Three, Oh-Two."

"Go ahead," Three Balls responded. He sounded irritated, perpetually grumpy.

"Nobody's here, and it looks like they cleaned out. We'll keep looking."

"Want us out here?"

"Keep watch. Any cars out back?"

"Nope."

"We'll be out in five."

Nathan led Bridget down the hall, and he shined his flashlight into the stairwell. They climbed into the dark chamber. The floor had been littered with papers and ripped cardboard boxes. The imam had taken everything.

"Why'd he flee?" Bridget asked. "He must know we don't have jack shit on him after we couldn't hold him for Ali's murder."

"Why wait around for our investigation to catch up?"

Nathan moved to the wall behind the bookcase where they found the carbines. He peered into the chamber behind the plaster. Barren.

"Let's get out of here," he said.

"And do what?"

"Check Qadir's residence. I'll put a lookout on him."

"Moving is legal."

"EPIC can issue a silent lookout, and they'll notify us if his name pops on a manifest."

"We can't do shit if he leaves," Bridget said. "He's an American citizen and free to travel."

"Then let's find evidence to detain him. Anything. If he returns to the Middle East, he'll be gone."

"But if our charges won't hold up—"

"I'd rather lose a case later than let this monster disappear into the desert."

"If he's guilty."

"We'll figure this out eventually, and if our suspects are in the wind, there won't be anyone here to charge. And we won't prevent more attacks."

"You think more are coming?"

"America is still standing, and Islamists won't stop until they've brought us to our knees."

49

I double-parked my car and stared down Pennsylvania Boulevard at the FBI's Hoover Building. The concrete fortress that symbolized American hegemony. The monstrosity dominated the surrounding buildings like the United States bullied countries around the world. Anger built inside me like hot steam. But I wasn't sightseeing—I came to plan.

Taking life wasn't hard when the moral justification became clear to me. Killing Rodrigo had taught me that. And taking life became easier the more I did it, like that detective in New York, but killing a special agent would be difficult. Despite the complexity and risk, one thing had grown crystal clear to me.

Nathan Burke must die.

Everyone on earth was vulnerable. If assassins could murder presidents, then people without bodyguards stood little chance. But Nathan was an FBI agent, acutely aware of his surroundings. The Taliban tried to kill him in Afghanistan, and he'd foiled a terrorism attempt at the airport, so he understood deadly force. He'd be harder to take out than an ordinary citizen, and he couldn't see me, in case he survived.

Cars inched by on the street. I couldn't sit there for long.

My first decision was where to assassinate him. Nathan wasn't a head of state with a published schedule, but he commuted into his office every day.

His erratic schedule would require surveillance, but that invited attention, and doing it near an office brimming with security guards, surveillance cameras, and armed FBI agents seemed foolhardy.

I could ambush him before he reached his office, but that would depend on his taking the same route to work, and he probably varied his routine. Following him without exposing myself would prove challenging.

That left his home. Finding it would be hard because the FBI wouldn't provide it, and even if I used a ruse, I'd still need to surveil his home. That entailed serious risk, because he'd be more security conscious around his home, and he might have employed countersurveillance.

Alternatively, I could lure him to a neutral location.

A calm spread through me the way it did whenever I solved a problem. Getting Nathan away from his most protected spaces would make everything easier and would allow me to prepare. Yes, that was the answer.

A parking enforcement officer walked up Pennsylvania and stopped at another double-parked car. She pulled out her citation book and took down the vehicle's license plate. The driver bolted out of a coffee shop and raced up the sidewalk, waving his arms. I needed to leave before she reached me.

Which weapon to use? I had many options at my disposal, but infinite choices only made it more difficult to choose. I could poison him, or blow him up, or tamper with his brakes, but the more complicated I made it, the more likely I'd forecast my intent to murder him.

A gun seemed the simplest choice. I could use a rifle and shoot him from a distance, but those logistics were more complicated than they initially appeared. The Phantoms had carbines, rifles, and handguns stashed in other mosques, so acquiring a weapon would prove easy, but I wasn't an expert shot, and distance shooting required skill. How would I adjust for wind, temperature, ammunition, and other variables?

But distance would provide anonymity. And safety.

The parking enforcement officer handed the man a ticket and turned toward me. I should leave. Or I could kill her.

That thought jolted me. Was I fantasizing about murder, or was my rage guiding my thinking? Maybe I'd become reckless.

I started the car as she approached. I pulled into traffic, but I had my plan.

I'd lure Nathan to an unfamiliar spot, one that afforded me concealment and an avenue of escape—and then I'd shoot him. The FBI would assume his death was related to the recent terrorism incidents, but the exact connection would elude them. They may consider retribution for stopping the airport attack last year. But they'd be wrong.

This was much more personal.

50

Nathan exited the Capital One Center and strolled down Seventh Street NW toward the District Chophouse and Brewery to meet Meili for a quick lunch. They'd both been working grueling hours and hadn't been together in ages.

His phone rang, and he answered.

"We hit the Mega Millions and got a lead," Bridget said.

Optimism filled him. "What's up?"

"Some chucklehead called in. Said he attends the Al-Sahaba Mosque and overheard the elders talking. He knows where they're planning the next attack."

"Set a meet."

"Already did. He's driving down from Philadelphia. I told him to call when he arrives and we'll give him the meet location."

"Get a name?"

"Wouldn't give it."

"Telephone number?"

"Came back as private."

"Run an emergency subscriber with the carrier."

"Already sent the subpoena."

Nathan looked at his watch. Meili would arrive any minute, and he had to eat. "Give me forty-five minutes and meet me at the office. Round up a couple of guys to cover our debriefing."

"Mint."

Nathan hung up as Meili approached. She grinned and waved when she spotted him.

His heart filled.

They met in front of the restaurant, and he kissed her.

"Hello, stranger," she said.

"We should've skipped lunch and met at my condo."

She flashed a sly smile. "Wish I could, but I've got a briefing in thirty, so let's make this quick."

"I was hoping for a quickie."

She grinned. "Seriously, gotta make this fast. I'll get a salad."

"You eat like a bird."

"You hiding a fat fetish?"

"Definitely not."

He tugged open the restaurant's thick, wooden door for her and followed her inside. His phone rang again as the teenage host greeted them. Rahimya calling.

"Give me a sec to take this."

She rolled her eyes then spoke to the hostess.

He stepped away and answered. "What's up, Boss?"

"Where are you?"

"Grabbing a bite. Back in thirty."

"I scheduled an appointment for you with medical services."

His core chilled. "Why?"

"To get your shoulder checked."

"My doctor cleared me six months ago."

"I want you to see a Bureau physician, in-house."

Had Three Balls noticed Nathan favoring his arm, or had Bridget said something?

"Where's this coming from?" he asked.

"I went to HQ this morning and bumped into Agent Chan. Naturally, our conversation migrated to you. She mentioned you were still in pain."

Nathan's gut hardened. "I'm fine."

"Good, then you'll have no reason to avoid the doctor."

"But I—"

"Your appointment's at two o'clock today."

"I'm meeting a source this afternoon. We're trying to stop terrorists from blowing up the country."

"Don't tell me what we're doing . . . or what we're failing to do. See the doctor and don't be late."

Rahimya hung up.

"Table's ready," Meili said. She looked at him, and the smile slid off her face. "What happened?"

"You told Rahimya about my shoulder?"

"You need medical attention."

"I told you that in private. You betrayed my confidence. You betrayed me."

She flinched. "I didn't—"

"If I wanted Rahimya to know, I would've told her myself."

Meili's eyes flashed with angry fire. "I did it for you. You think I'd hurt you?

"She's sending me to med services and—"

"You need to see a doctor."

"Once they evaluate my shoulder, they'll put me on light duty."

"Then go on admin leave and heal."

Nathan burned with anger. He closed his eyes. "And what if I don't heal?"

Meili pursed her lips. "I . . ."

"You what?"

"I'm worried about you. I hate seeing you in pain."

"What you did may get me fired."

"I don't want you to lose your job, but you can't bury your head in the sand. You sustained physical trauma. Whatever damage the bullet did is fixable."

"You don't understand."

"Then explain it to me. Why won't you go back to the doctor?"

Nathan sighed. "Because it's causing other problems . . . pain."

"A doctor can fix it."

"It's not just the torn muscle and ligaments or the shattered clavicle. I hurt everywhere. It's systemic."

Her eyebrows knitted. "What's that mean?"

"The trauma triggered reactive arthritis. My joints ache—"

"Trauma can't do that."

"Not the bullet, but maybe the bacterial infection. I've researched it to death . . . poor choice of words."

"They gave you antibiotics after surgery."

"That wasn't just prophylactic. I had a serious infection either from the bullet or bacteria growing at the zoo. Whatever caused it, I haven't recovered. The pain's bad."

Meili squeezed his hand. "I understand you're scared about your health and losing your job, and I know your injury brings back traumatic memories, but the solution is medical attention. You need to confront your phobia."

"Reasonable fear isn't a phobia. Losing my job is likely."

"It's . . ." Meili teared up and looked away.

"What?"

"I'm not talking about losing your job. I mean, that's part of it . . ."

"What are you telling me?" Uncertainty bubbled inside him.

"The few times we've spent the night together, you mumble in your sleep and jolt awake. You're having nightmares."

Heat rose in his face, and he looked away.

"Don't be embarrassed."

"People have bad dreams."

"Not like that."

"People are dying, and I can't stop it. Chasing terrorists stresses me."

"You had trouble sleeping after that animal shot you. I think it's PTSD."

"We didn't spend the night together before that. Maybe I have a sleep disorder."

"I noticed a difference in you after the shooting. Little things, like jumping when you hear a loud sound. You're crankier than usual."

"This conversation isn't helping that."

She smiled. "It got worse after you killed those guys at the mosque."

"Bridget took out one of them. You can't give me all the credit. If she hadn't, I wouldn't be here talking to you."

Meili bit her lip. "You almost died, and that's enough to give anyone PTSD, but if you didn't fully process being shot, your latest incident may have amplified your trauma."

"My shootings were justified. I don't worry about them—legally or morally."

"But you think about them."

He sighed. "Yeah, sometimes."

"You killed a terrorist who was trying to down a passenger plane, and now you're hunting Islamists who are targeting civilians. You don't see the connection?"

"I'm assigned to an extremist group. Of course there's a connection."

She crossed her arms. "You know that's not what I mean."

"What do you expect from me?"

"You need to talk to someone."

"That's what we're doing now, and so far, I'm not loving it."

"A psychiatrist."

Hearing the word felt like a gut punch in his ego. Was she right? Were his nightmares a manifestation of his inability to resolve the trauma he'd experienced? He'd killed his first person in Afghanistan during hand-to-hand combat with a Taliban commander, then he'd shot three terrorists who were trying to bring down a plane at DCA, and then a Chinese assassin. He'd also done nothing to stop a tiger from mauling the national security advisor to death, but the big cat got the credit for that one. Did he have unresolved issues?

"What are you thinking?" Meili asked.

"None of my critical incidents bother me, and if they did, I can handle it."

"Getting help isn't a sign of weakness."

"It ain't a sign of strength."

She smirked. "Yes, it is. Asking for help requires courage."

He saw red and wanted to lash out. His temper took control. "Thanks for looking out for me."

He stormed out of the restaurant and headed for his office, feeling more like an asshole with every step.

51

Nathan sat in the passenger seat beside Bridget as she headed for Rock Creek Park, where they planned to debrief their new source. Nathan fumed over his conversation with Meili. She'd been wrong to tell Rahimya about his shoulder, and despite her good intentions, her betrayal of their private conversation stung him. Worse, his reaction to her suggesting he had PTSD had been immature. Why had he reacted like that?

Maybe she was right.

Bridget's phone rang, and she glanced at it.

"Private number," she said. She pulled over and answered on speaker. "Hello?"

"I am here," a man said with a thick Arabic accent.

"It's him," Bridget whispered to Nathan. She hunched over the speaker. "We spoke on my office line. Who gave you my digits?"

"What do you say?"

"My number. How'd you get my number?"

"From a friend who wants to stop this massacre."

"What massacre?" Nathan asked.

"A big program is coming. Many will die."

Another tragedy. More death. A chill passed through Nathan. Islamists had infiltrated the country. They could be anywhere. He glanced at passing cars. "Who are you?"

"I cannot give my name," he said. "They will break me if they know I speak to you."

"Meet us in Georgetown at the entrance to Rock Creek Park," Bridget said. "We'll put you in my car. My windows are tinted."

"I am waiting for you. I have a paper with the information you need."

Nathan glanced at Bridget. She shrugged.

"Where are you?" Nathan asked.

"West Potomac Park, by the river. Nobody is around."

The park paralleled the Potomac between the Lincoln and Jefferson Memorials and was accessible off Ohio Drive. The area drew crowds during tourist season, but this close to Thanksgiving, it shouldn't be busy.

"Meet us on the steps of the Lincoln Memorial," Nathan said.

"I will only meet here, and I can only stay for a few minutes. Come now, or I must leave."

Nathan's gut twisted. Moving meet locations was protocol, because letting bad guys or informants call the shots created hazards. Under normal circumstances, Nathan wouldn't agree, but nothing was normal anymore. The country burned, and fear gripped its citizens—the goal of terrorism.

"How do we know your information is real?" Nathan asked.

"You arrested twelve AR-15s inside the basement."

Arrested? English wasn't his first language.

Nathan sighed. "What are you wearing?"

"A blue windbreaker."

Nathan looked at Bridget and shrugged. "Give us half an hour."

She hung up, cut the wheel, and gunned the engine.

"Who is this frickin' guy?"

"We'll find out soon," Nathan said. "Let's get there fast and do a pass-by."

Their emergency subscriber request had turned up nothing. Their tipster used a prepaid cell phone purchased from Walmart, with no record of its user. They might get more information from the store, but that'd take time.

Nathan picked up the microphone, then thought better of it and replaced it on its hook. He snatched his cell and dialed Rahimya.

"Tell me you're at the doctor," she said without preamble.

"We diverted. We're meeting a source who claims there's an imminent threat."

"Related to Qadir?" Rahimya asked.

Nathan's face warmed. He had assumed that but hadn't asked. What if the Muslim Brotherhood had issued a general order, and terror groups launched independent attacks? That thought didn't make him feel better.

"We don't know," he said. "He wouldn't give his name, but he knew about the carbines we seized. We're meeting him at West Potomac Park."

"If he has anything substantial, bring him in."

"Roger. I'm calling to see if anyone's free to cover us."

Rahimya was quiet for a beat. "You want backup for a meeting?"

"We know squat about this guy, and it doesn't feel quite right."

"I'll roll whoever's around. Keep me posted."

"Roger."

"Oh, and Nathan?"

"Yeah?"

"Be careful."

He hung up as they turned onto Ohio Drive SW. A woman wearing black running tights and a pink jacket jogged along the shore, and students played softball across the street. Otherwise, the area appeared quiet. Nathan had told the source they needed thirty minutes to arrive to create an artificial advantage. Debriefing sources took skill and attention, from the initial recruitment, to the mechanics of clandestine meetings, to the delicate dance of persuasion. Federal investigations took expertise, and like all complicated professions, they were fraught with failure. But in law enforcement, failure brought death.

"Slow down," Nathan said, "but keep a steady speed."

"I've surveilled sketchy perps before," Bridget said.

"Don't get your panties in a bunch," Nathan said. He chuckled to show he wasn't serious. "Following money launderers is different than terrorists. These people are in the business of death."

"That doesn't make them good at it."

"Many develop a sixth sense, a feeling when something's wrong. I have it too, and this guy worries me."

They approached the Tidal Basin. A man in a blue windbreaker sat at a bench where the bank sloped down to the river. He stared at the water, facing away from them. A ferry chugged westbound on the river headed toward Georgetown, and a tiny motorboat anchored the Virginia shore.

"There," Nathan said. He pointed at the man.

"Should I pull over?"

"Keep going. Find a place to park, and we'll come back on foot."

"Think he brought someone?"

"I don't know anything about this guy or what motivates him. That's a problem."

No vehicles had parked along the road, and no unsavory characters loitered around. Another group of young people played kickball beside the Tidal Basin, and a woman led two children across the Ohio Drive Bridge. Both kids leaned over the edge and stared at the murky water.

Bridget motored past, and they continued under the Fourteenth Street Bridge and parked. They hustled out of the car past the George Mason Memorial. Beyond it, tourists disembarked from a bus parked outside the Jefferson Memorial. They fast-walked past the family on the bridge as the kids pointed at something in the water and giggled. If only people knew the evil that surrounded them. The recent terror attacks had been a wakeup call for ordinary citizens who lived in a wealthy country immunized from the barbarity that pervaded the world—savagery deeply rooted in human nature.

Bridget and Nathan skirted the grassy edge of Ohio Drive and then shuffled down a riverbank's brown grass to the path.

Bridget motioned to the man on a bench at the water's edge. "What's he doing?"

"No idea."

Their source hadn't moved. He faced the water, possibly watching the boats. If he worried about being seen with them, why wasn't he looking around? A man somehow affiliated with the worst domestic terror attacks since 9/11 prepared to meet two FBI agents. Any normal person would have difficulty sitting still.

The hair rose on Nathan's neck. Something didn't feel right.

"This a-hole's a *pissah,"* Bridget said.

"I don't like it," Nathan said, "but we can't pass up the chance to stop another incident."

Few people braved the cool weather, and the scant, midday crowds concentrated around the monuments. Only a single jogger was in sight, a man trotting toward them at a leisurely pace. His hands appeared empty.

"Cover me, while I approach," Nathan said.

"Let's wait for backup."

"It'll take them fifteen minutes. If this guy's for real, we can't blow our chance to recruit him. Keep your eyes on the road."

Bridget nodded.

Nathan sidestepped down the embankment until he was even with the bench. The jogger closed on them, still moving slow.

Nathan crept toward the bench. The man didn't move.

"You called us?" Nathan asked.

No answer.

Nathan stepped into the man's vision—but it wasn't a man at all. A mannequin clothed in blue jeans and windbreaker rested on the bench.

Nathan's heart raced, on alert. The jogger kept coming.

"It's a trap," Nathan yelled.

He drew his Glock.

52

I crouched in the bobbing fiberglass fishing boat and watched Nathan approach the mannequin. I peeked over the center console, careful to stay low. Beside me, Haji Makhmud inserted his fishing pole into the rod holder and unzipped his waterproof duffle bag.

Nathan moved around the bench and shouted something back at the female agent, though the words carried off on the wind.

Makhmud dug into the bag and removed his rifle. A combat-hardened Chechen, he'd assassinated three Russian politicians and one particularly sadistic district mayor in Chechnya. All Makhmud's kills had come out of the business end of a SVD Dragunov sniper rifle, but I couldn't acquire that Russian weapon in the United States, which was why he held a Remington Model 700. Hunters and cops used the center-fire rifles all over America. An ally with fake identification had purchased this one from a private seller on Craigslist, so police couldn't trace it back to me.

Nathan drew his handgun.

Makhmud braced his elbow against the gunwale and elevated the rifle. He stared through the Leupold 4-20x52 scope, not the best for a sniper but good enough for this distance. Nathan was 482 meters away, according to Makhmud's rangefinder. We stayed close to the Virginia shore, still a reasonable shot, but too far for me to execute.

Nathan scanned the passing traffic then pivoted and surveyed the entire bank. The woman drew her firearm too. Women with firearms . . . I snorted with contempt.

Makhmud had sighted the scope for this distance, so he only needed to acquire the target. He hunched his shoulder and melted around the stock. His body stilled.

A ferry motored down the center channel and approached the Fourteenth Street Bridge Complex. I lingered on it to gauge its progress. We should have time before it passed between us.

"Hurry," I said.

Makhmud didn't respond. He didn't move. Pure concentration. The boat rocked gently, pivoting on its anchor line.

Fire exploded out of the Remington's barrel, and the shot shattered the crisp air.

I flinched. The boom echoed with overlapping acoustic waves and moved down the river, reflecting off the banks. A blue heroin took flight along the shore, its flapping wings chugging hard as it skimmed over the water.

Makhmud ejected the cartridge and slammed the bolt forward, inserting another cartridge into the chamber. I squinted to see the results of his work.

Nathan lay on the ground.

Had Makhmud killed him? A wave of elation bubbled through me, followed by a pang of regret. What was that about?

"Did you hit him?"

Makhmud remained silent. The boat rocked. Ripples ruffled the surface.

Nathan crawled behind the bench.

Makhmud fired again. He mumbled something unintelligible.

"Is he wounded?" I asked. My words sounded muted. I should have brought hearing protection. What other details had I missed?

"The boat moved," Makhmud said. "I miss."

"Keep shooting. He can't escape."

"That is in Allah's hands."

Makhmud inhaled and held his breath. He fired a third time. The bullet hit the bench and with a satisfying *thunk*. At least he was on target now.

"Finish this," I said. "Kill him."

53

Nathan peeped over the bench. The shot had come from the Virginia shore, not from the District. Was the sniper hiding in the bushes along the opposite bank?

A muzzle flashed on the deck of the fishing boat anchored offshore, and a round smacked into the bench. The bastard had been waiting for him. A pre-planned ambush using a life-sized doll as bait.

Nathan curled into himself, getting small. He looked back at Bridget, who'd retreated up the slope and hidden behind a thin tree.

"Stay down," Nathan yelled.

"You hit?" she asked.

"Negative. Shooter's on the boat. Crawl away and dial 911. Get an airship and river patrol to respond."

"I can't leave you."

"You can't help either. Stay out of the line of fire."

The rifle's discharge filled the air again, and a bullet cracked over Nathan's head.

That shooter was good—not good enough, since Nathan continued to breathe—but a round would eventually hit its mark. Unless Nathan disrupted the sniper's rhythm. The longer he drew this out, the better his chance of rescue. Time was the shooter's enemy.

Nathan leaned around the bench and fired twice at the boat. His shots probably fell short—a feeble attempt, but maybe enough to keep the sniper's head down.

The Potomac was over 1,000 feet across, and the boat anchored about 500 yards away. A Glock's maximum range could reach it, but the effective range was closer to 100 yards, and Nathan wasn't a marksman.

But he must try.

The sniper fired again A muzzle flashed just above the boat's gunwale, and the bullet cracked beside Nathan. The soft breeze of overpressure touched his cheek.

Nathan lined up his sights on the boat and canted the barrel into the air. A forty-five-degree angle should give the bullet its maximum arc, but the rifle's barrel had been sloped for efficiency, so Nathan depressed it another inch. He didn't know enough about long-range shooting, but at least he wouldn't die like a lamb.

Nathan fired then adjusted the angle and fired again. He raised the barrel a quarter inch and fired a third time, walking his rounds toward the boat. Even if his calculations were off, he had to be close.

The sniper's rifle flashed.

Wood shattered on the bench beside him, sending splinters into the air. The round hadn't punched through, but it had splintered the end piece. Whatever rifle the assassin was using delivered a serious punch.

Nathan's counterfire seemed to have no effect, and the bench provided scant cover. Should he bolt for safety?

Sirens wailed behind him. *Good job, Bridget.* Nathan peeked at the boat. It hadn't moved. If they heard the sirens, they'd know their time was limited and flee—unless they were jihadists who wanted to martyr themselves. What if they waited for the police to arrive and killed the first responding officers?

Bile rose in his throat.

"Screw it."

He lifted his gun and fired.

54

The distant pop of Nathan's handgun echoed over the water, faint, like a child's toy. The round blooped into the water a few yards away. How had he come so close?

Makhmud fired again, and his body jerked back before rolling back into his previous position. He seemed like a professional, but he hadn't finished Nathan yet.

Another round from Nathan's pistol buzzed past as it lost velocity. His chance of hitting the boat seemed impossible, and Makhmud had promised they'd be out of range, but stranger things had happened. My life was a carpet woven from tragic threads. A gun battle on the Potomac confirmed that.

Red and blue lights flashed on the road behind the park where Nathan hid. Hundreds of people must have heard the gunfire. The police were coming. That much was certain.

I turned and scanned the Virginia shore. Cars flowed down the George Washington Memorial Parkway like an army of ants. Traffic was as constant and prevalent as corruption in DC. Life continued as normal, but Arlington police would soon respond.

We needed to flee before then.

Our getaway depended on a fast strike and hasty exit. A car waited at the Columbia Island Marina behind us, but we'd have to reach it before police prevented us from disappearing into the George Washington Memorial Parkway traffic.

"Enough," I said.

Makhmud looked at me.

"Put that away. We're leaving."

I tightened the drawstring on my hood and scrambled on my hands and knees to the bow. My plan was to use the tiny engine mounted on the deck to retract the anchor, but I'd assumed Nathan would be bleeding out on the bank of the Potomac, not taking shots at us and drawing the attention of every law enforcement agent in the capital. I unsnapped a knife from my belt and used its serrated edge to saw away at the nylon anchor line. The tension did half the work, and the line snapped and slithered over the side. The boat's bow turned as the current took hold of us.

I climbed behind the center console and turned the ignition key to fire the single 250-HP engine. It growled to life, a sign Allah wanted us to escape.

I squeezed the gear release and edged the throttle forward. The prop churned the water, and I spun the boat around.

The ferry's engines rumbled, and white water bubbled around its props as its captain tried to avoid the crossfire. The boat stayed in the channel. Three crew members stood on the lower portside tier and pointed at us.

I gunned the engine, and the bow raised as we accelerated. I followed the shoreline as it curved to the south, careful not to get too close to the rocks, logs, and garbage in the shallows.

Makhmud dumped his rifle over the side as we buzzed past the Navy Merchant Marine Memorial. A shame to lose a sniper rifle, but we couldn't have it and still blend in with civilians.

I cut the wheel hard at Kendall Point, and the boat canted hard to starboard. We slipped into the channel that led into the Pentagon Lagoon Yacht Basin. Car tires drummed against the bridge overhead like thunder. I slowed as we passed the Columbia Island Marina Gas Dock, but our wake rocked the dock and drew a glare from the attendant. I took a wide turn to avoid rows of berthed boats and entered the Boundary Channel. A dozen boats bobbed in our wake. I yanked the throttle back and turned into the last row of empty slips. The dock was vacant at this time of day.

The metal pier ground against our fiberglass hull. I jerked the throttle into reverse, and the engine whined and lifted.

Makhmud climbed onto the dock as I wiped down the steering wheel, throttle, and other surfaces. The police would identify the boat soon, but my men had stolen it, and that search would reveal nothing. Hopefully.

Distant sirens wailed over the river from the police response in DC. The Arlington police would arrive soon, and if we weren't clear of the marina, our lives would end there. I followed Makhmud through the parking lot, and we climbed into an old, powder-blue Nissan, also stolen.

More sirens. On our side of the river.

I started the car, and we flashed between parked cars. Its bald tires squealed and centrifugal force pushed me against the door as we whirled around the looping driveway.

Louder sirens. Close.

I paused at the parkway. Blue lights twinkled in the distance, approaching fast.

I stomped on the pedal and accelerated. We merged into moderate traffic. I sped, but not much. Pentagon Police were close too.

I kept my eyes on the rearview mirror as we crossed the bridge and approached the I-395 overpass. Behind us, police cars turned into the marina.

We made it.

55

Nathan and Bridget exited FBI headquarters after meeting with OPR. The last five hours had been a whirlwind of investigators from multiple jurisdictions as the manhunt for the sniper locked down Northern Virginia and the District. They walked up Ninth Street toward their office.

"I can't believe you didn't tell OPR that you returned fire," Bridget said.

"Another shooting would have taken me off the investigation for days while they investigated."

"But you lied."

"I omitted a minor fact."

She raised an eyebrow. "Shooting at a sniper on the Potomac is a minor fact?"

"I didn't hit anything, and you can't be sure I shot. You were hunkered down behind a tree. Maybe you heard an echo."

Bridget stopped and looked at him. "When I came to the unit, they told me to fasten my seatbelt. I mean, I heard about what you did at the airport last year—everyone heard—but I wasn't ready for this."

"You left white-collar crime to see more action," Nathan said.

"Yah-huh, but I didn't expect counterterrorism to be the Wild West, and I didn't ask for Wyatt Earp as a partner."

"It's not normally like this . . . but we're under attack and business as usual won't cut it."

"How do we stop Phantoms?" Bridget said.

"We overturn every rock until we win."

The FBI had tasked all hands to the terror attacks, as police around the country pivoted to defend the homeland, but Ali's murder had to be related, and Imam Qadir and the Al-Sahaba Mosque were the key to unravel the conspiracy. Unfortunately, the imam remained in the wind, and the search for Ali's killer hadn't been any more fruitful than their terrorism case.

"We're spinning our frickin' wheels," Bridget said.

"That's how we'll catch them."

"How?"

"Old-fashioned police work. We run down every lead, flip anyone related to the mosque, and use every technique at our disposal."

"We've found squat so far."

"Not true, and we'll get Qadir . . . eventually."

"Unless he slips over the border."

Nathan nodded. That would be easy for him to do. Border Patrol couldn't stop the massive influx of illegal aliens, and nobody looked for Americans sneaking into Mexico.

A truck stopped on the corner and backed up. Its high-pitched beeping cut through the air. Nathan jumped, his every sense on alert.

"You okay?" Bridget asked.

"Yeah, fine." His heart pounded like he'd just sprinted the obstacle course at Quantico. What the hell was wrong with him?

"You don't look fine. You've been jumpy."

"I'm not sure what's happening to me," he said. "I feel like I'm in Afghanistan again. It was tense over there. We were on edge all the time, always searching for threats, and that constant vigilance took a toll. By the end of my tours, I'd be a shell, completely worn out."

"Some a-hole just tried to murder you."

"What's your point?"

"Maybe being back home in your safe place isn't as secure as before.

You'd come home from deployments and be able to unwind . . . recalibrate. But DC's been as dangerous as Afghanistan."

"I don't need to scan the road for IEDs here."

She touched his arm. "But you do, don't you? I've seen it."

Nathan nodded. "It's habit."

"PTSD is a real thing."

"I just need a vacation."

"Want to take a few days?"

"You're kidding, right? We're trying to stop terror attacks."

Bridget sighed. "You can't do that if your head's not in the game."

Nathan tensed. "You can let me know if I fuck up, but being jumpy doesn't make me incompetent."

"I'm not saying that. I just think—"

"I'll take a break after we find the monster behind this. I won't stop until we identify the Slayer. Let's get Hamid and approach the *Jama'ah*."

"What's a frickin'—"

"The mosque's congregation. Let's squeeze their elders."

"Squeeze how?"

"Whatever it takes. We'll do interviews, looking for the imam, but if we sense an opening, we'll stick a knife in."

Bridget shrugged. "Better than sitting around with our thumbs in."

Nathan called Hamid.

"What's up, Boss?" Hamid asked.

"Where are you?"

"I had some personal business to attend to . . . with my lawyer."

"What kind of business?"

"Immigration. Filing more paperwork for my family's visas."

"This is too important—" The cognitive dissonance that had been needling him lifted as pieces of the puzzle came together, hazy but connecting. A tingle climbed Nathan's spine as the realization formed in his mind. How had he been so blind?

"Hold on a minute."

He muted his phone and pointed at Bridget. "Call headquarters and find out where Hamid's family is on the visa list."

"Why?" Bridget asked.

"Just do it. I've got a twist in my gut, and I've learned not to ignore my instincts."

"But what—"

"Get his info from our CI coordinator and determine his family's status."

Bridget's forehead wrinkled, but she opened her phone as she walked up the sidewalk.

Nathan unmuted. "Hamid, I want you to help us find the imam. We've been completely reactive, but that's about to change. I plan to grill the mosque's membership."

Bridget spoke on the phone but kept her voice down, and Nathan couldn't hear what she said.

"I'm busy this afternoon," Hamid said.

"We're at war," Nathan said, his stomach hardening into cement.

"My family is my priority." Hamid's voice had taken on a sharp edge, like a blade.

Nathan wanted to reach through the phone and strangle him, but he kept his voice even. "When can you be here?"

"Two hours."

Bridget walked toward him as she pocketed her phone in her purse.

"Hold on again," Nathan said.

He put the phone on mute and looked at her. "What did you find out?"

"Hamid applied for visas for himself and his family about a month before we pulled out of Afghanistan. They were put on a list with close to sixty thousand other Afghans."

"How close to the top are they now?"

"That's the thing," Bridget said. "He never submitted the required paperwork after US forces left. HQ sent him emails and even called, but he didn't respond."

The knot in Nathan's stomach clenched like a fist. "What's their status?"

"Pending. They're waiting for Hamid to send the requested information."

Nathan closed his eyes and breathed out. "Thanks for checking."

"Didn't he say he'd had other agents call for him? Why didn't they tell him he was holding up the process?"

"Because he's not waiting for visas?"

"What are you—"

Nathan held up his finger and spoke in the phone again. "Meet us at the mosque as soon as you can."

He ended the call and dialed Rahimya.

She answered immediately. "I'm in a meeting."

"I need an emergency check on a phone number and see if it comes up in the toll record data dump the phone companies gave us from the Wall Street bombing."

"We've had analysts combing through that for days."

"Can you check a specific number to see if it pinged off a cell tower? I doubt it was used to make a call, but maybe a tower recognized it nearby."

"I can send a request to—"

"It's urgent. It requires an emergency tasking."

"That's for imminent danger to life or limb."

"It's related to the attack."

Rahimya sighed. "Send me the number."

Nathan texted it to her, and she put him on hold while she ran it down.

His pulse thumped in his temples. Was he being crazy? Energy coursed through him, a mixture of excitement and dread. And guilt. If he was right, what did that mean? It was too crazy to conceive.

What information had he shared?

He removed his notebook from his pocket and flipped to his last debriefing. He pictured the meeting, trying to see it through the lens of his new theory. Nothing jumped out at him. The stakes were so high, the case made him paranoid. That's all it was—paranoia.

"Got it," Rahimya's voice came over his cell phone's speaker.

Nathan picked up. "Got what?"

"The number you gave me connected with a cluster of towers in Manhattan on the day of the attack."

"Anything near Wall Street?"

She clucked her tongue, like she always did when she was thinking.

"Yep, here it is. It pinged off the southern side of Verizon Cell Tower KNKA 209 on Monday.

"What time?"

"Several times. Starting at 8: 45 a.m.," she said. "Hey, that's fifteen minutes before the attack. Whose number is that?"

Nathan swallowed. "Hamid's."

56

Nathan clutched his phone so hard it creaked. Lightheadedness trickled his consciousness, and his stomach flipped. He wanted to vomit.

Bridget raised her eyebrows then leaned closer to the phone to hear.

"What did you say?" Rahimya asked over the line.

"That number is Hamid's," he said. "Our linguist."

"In Manhattan?" she asked. "I don't understand. What was your terp doing in NYC?"

Nathan sighed. He gazed up at dark clouds moving over Northern Virginia. "Hamid has been lying to us. He's one of them."

"That's preposterous," Rahimya said. "He's worked for us for years. What would motivate one of our FSNs to turn on us?"

"You're kidding, right?" Nathan asked. "We cut and ran. We stabbed them in the back."

"Walk me through this," Rahimya said. Her tone wasn't friendly.

"Hamid applied for visas for his wife and daughter before the US withdrawal, but he never followed up."

"You're certain?"

"Bridget just confirmed it. I'm putting you on speaker."

"It's true," Bridget said. "Hamid requested visas for himself, his wife

Farzana, and his daughter Tara, but he never responded to document requests."

Nathan scratched his chin. "Maybe he became disillusioned and didn't trust us to evacuate them."

"He's wicked right," Bridget said. "We left tens of thousands of them behind."

"Or something happened to his wife or daughter," Rahimya said.

The Taliban raped women and took child brides. Nathan's stomach churned, and his body unsettled. "The Taliban would've targeted him. Maybe they hurt his family."

"Animals," Bridget said.

"How did I not see Hamid had turned?" he said.

"It's a radical shift," Rahimya said, "from risking his life for Americans to embracing ISIS."

"I understand his sense of betrayal," Nathan said, "and he's not wrong to be outraged. We asked Afghans to embrace Western ideals of freedom and individual liberty, and hundreds of thousands of them bought into it. They risked their lives for a better future, and the administration abandoned them for a political win."

"But ISIS is killing innocents," Rahimya's voice took on a sharp edge. "How could Hamid join the enemy?"

"He snapped."

"If the Taliban victimized his family," Bridget said, "why fight for them?"

"ISIS and the Taliban are at odds," Rahimya said.

"They're all Islamists," Bridget said. "Different teams in the same league."

"Unless the Taliban didn't target his family," Nathan said. "Maybe something else happened."

"Whatever it was," Bridget said, "how does he frickin switch sides like that? You said he fought side by side with you, and he joins the people who tried to murder him? He turned his back on everything he believes?"

Nathan's mind reeled. "Anger . . . betrayal . . . grief? His world crashed around him, and everything he fought for had disappeared."

"If he's involved," Rahimya said. "This is only theory."

"His phone data is real."

Nathan leaned against a cement vehicle barrier. "It all makes sense now, like examining a chess matches. Now that I know the endgame, I can spot the attack unfolding. He quietly advanced his pawn, and now we've got a queen in our back rank."

"We've been stumbling around chasing shadows," Bridget said, "and our target's been right there beside us."

"Understanding Hamid's involvement made the cognitive dissonance that's been nagging me disappear. The assassination attempt against me wasn't retribution for the airport. That motivation didn't feel right. I mean, why target an FBI agent and bring down more heat? It's been Hamid all along. He doesn't just want vengeance against America—he wants to kill me."

"He takes the withdrawal personally?" Bridget asked.

"It *is* personal. We sold him a political, economic, and moral ideology, and then we turned our backs on him. We endangered his family and obliterated his vision of the future."

"And his hope," Rahimya said. "And optimism is a scarcity in places like Afghanistan. I know. But this is all conjecture. You've heard me say this a million times, but show me the evidence."

Nathan paced to help him think, and Bridget followed with her eyes glued to his phone.

He stopped. "Did NYPD ever fingerprint those rubber gloves they recovered from the trash can downtown?"

"They recovered thousands of pieces of evidence," Rahimya said. "We can check with their liaison."

"I thought those grainy video images of the man fleeing the First Precinct looked familiar, and now that you confirmed the cell tower hits . . . it's Hamid. He tossed the rubber gloves. They need to compare prints from the rubber gloves to those on his 249 in our CI file."

"If they lifted any," Rahimya said.

"It's proof that would convict him."

"We'll never take that a-hole alive," Bridget said. "Every cop worth a salt wants a shot at the Phantoms."

"I still can't believe it," Rahimya said.

“I’m more in shock than you,” Nathan said. “I promise.”

“How did this happen?” Rahimya asked.” How did we let a terrorist inside our investigation?”

“*We* didn’t,” Nathan said. “I did. I brought him in, and I gave him access.”

“If you’re right about Hamid,” Rahimya said, “this is a political disaster. Congress will shred us. This could tear the FBI apart.”

“Then we better lock him up before he helps the Slayer strike again.”

57

I slumped in my seat as the Arlington Transit Metro bus lumbered down Washington Boulevard past the Al-Sahaba Mosque. Something in Nathan's voice had been off. More than suspicion, rage had tinged his tone. He knew. Somehow, he knew.

I lowered the brim of my Washington Nationals baseball cap. Two cars parked in the mosque's rear lot, Nathan's and another vehicle I hadn't seen before, then the bus barreled past, and they were gone from sight.

I leaned into the aisle and peeked through the opposite windows. I surveyed the cars and buildings. No sign of more agents, but they were there. I sensed it. Knew it. My body tingled from danger, and my senses heightened. Colors looked richer, and I heard everything inside the bus, from hushed conversations to music leaking out of headphones. My mind prepared my body for a life-or-death conflict. That was all the confirmation I needed to believe they'd compromised my identity.

The bus edged through traffic. I leaned back in my seat. The danger was behind me, but nothing would be the same again. I'd always known this moment would come. The Americans identifying me, hunting me, forcing me to evade. I'd accepted that. Martyrdom was the ultimate jihad, and I'd known joining ISIS would lead to my demise. But now that I engaged in my jihad against them, I didn't want to die. Not that I craved life. Existence brought no joy. Nothing did, not since I lost my loved ones. I hadn't smiled since the Americans packed up their materials and fled, leaving behind only empty promises and dashed hopes.

I delayed death . . . not to live, but to continue jihad. I knew Americans better than anyone. We'd lived together, fought together, drank together. I knew how they thought, what they wanted, and more importantly, their weaknesses. Americans could not tolerate conflict. They sought a rapid end to war but were unwilling to do what was necessary to achieve total victory. They grew queasy at the sight of dead civilians, and they transposed their own morality and epistemology onto their enemies. I understood them, but they didn't understand me, and because of that, I knew how to hurt them. We had to push where they were soft.

But I couldn't do that if they killed me.

The Metro bus slowed, then pulled to the curb and hissed to a stop. I got up and followed a young mother with her child down the steps and onto the sidewalk. She bent to tie the girl's shoe, and I continued past her and headed into Clarendon on foot.

How had Nathan discovered my complicity? What had he uncovered? What loose ends, what mistakes had I made?

I stopped outside a restaurant and took out my cell phone. I sighed. This began a new chapter. My life as a fugitive, a terrorist fighting from the shadows, like those men I'd helped Nathan pursue in Afghanistan. I shook away the thought and dialed.

"We're here," Nathan answered.

"I can't make it."

"Why not?" Icicles clung to his voice.

"I have other priorities." I couldn't lie anymore.

He was quiet for a moment. "I need you here. If you can't stay, that's fine, but I want to talk."

"Then talk."

Quiet again.

"Where are you?"

The pretense was gone. He knew I had betrayed him, and now he knew that I knew. But neither of us said it. I wouldn't confess to a federal agent, and he didn't want to ruin his chance of luring me into a trap.

But my hesitancy came from something more. I'd fought with Nathan, risked my life for him, and he'd done the same for me. He remained a paladin in the war, but I had changed sides. The weight of that tickled something deep inside me, something I'd buried with my family. A flicker of my former self.

I crammed the feeling back into the dark recesses of my mind.

"I must go," I said.

"Hamid, we have to meet."

"I'm sorry. I can't."

"Whether you want to meet me or not, I'll see you soon."

I sighed again. Long and sorrowful. My energy waned. "*Ilhumdilala.* If Allah wills it."

I hung up.

I looked around. Nobody paid attention to me, but this anonymity wouldn't last long. Nathan would launch a massive dragnet for me. They'd geo-locate this call, but I'd be long gone by then. I needed to disappear and prepare to finish what I'd started.

I headed for the parking lot where one of the mullah's elders had left his car for me. It was a risk, but everything carried risk now.

I replayed my conversation with Nathan in my mind. I'd said nothing that could incriminate me, not that I would live to see a courthouse. But why had I apologized? I hadn't abandoned the United States, but it had forsaken me. Anger rose inside me.

They'd pay for their betrayal. They'd all pay.

58

Nathan's carotid artery thumped in his neck. His worst fears were becoming reality. He hung up the phone and stared at Bridget in the passenger seat.

"And?" She cocked her head.

"Hamid knows," Nathan said.

"How?"

"He knows me. Must have heard the truth in my voice."

"You sounded fine to me."

"When I called from outside headquarters, I was suspicious, and he may have noted my stress. Or my anger. We lived in the same Special Forces base for months at a time. He knows my mannerisms as well as my wife . . . I mean my ex-wife."

"What'd he say?"

"He can't come. He has other priorities."

"Maybe he's busy scheming."

Nathan chilled. "Being on the inside of our investigation gave him a tremendous advantage, and he wouldn't break contact unless he knew we were onto him."

Nathan picked up his mic and transmitted on the tactical channel he'd reserved. "Oh-Two to all units, target canceled. Break it down and head home."

A chorus of agents responded with their unit numbers.

Nathan transmitted again. "Be stealthy on the way out. It's possible they have countersurveillance in the vicinity of the meet location."

Bridget's eyes darted around. "You think he's nearby?"

"It's possible, or he could have sent someone."

"That fucker."

Nathan rubbed him face. Not getting a clear shot at his enemy built frustration that required release, but he battled ghosts, and they were winning. He could punch something.

"Let's watch his pad and wait for him," Bridget said.

Nathan rubbed the bridge of his nose. "Yeah, we'll check all the boxes, but he won't be there. He's in the wind."

"How can you be sure?"

"He wouldn't blow us off without being prepared to vanish. Calling me was his way of telling me he figured out we're onto him. He's not dumb enough to admit anything, but he wanted me to know."

"Why risk a call?"

"Because this is personal, and he holds me responsible."

"For the US pulling out of Afghanistan?"

"Yep."

"You complained about the withdrawal to anyone who'd listen."

Nathan nodded. "I wrote memos predicting that our sources and allies would be slaughtered if we abandoned them. Without maintaining our source networks, we'd be blind—and that's what happened."

"That's my point. You were against the surrender, and you helped dozens of the Afghans get out."

"Only a handful escaped."

"But you tried. It's not your fault."

"I'm the United States to him. He sacrificed and risked his life for me as much as for Afghanistan and the ideals we fought to protect."

"You really think he tried to kill you?"

"I do."

"For what purpose?"

"I think he lost his mind. Whatever happened to him after we relinquished the battlefield pushed him over the edge."

"I didn't peg him as a *nuttah*. Not even a little whacko."

"He's smart as hell. Whatever broke inside him spawned something dangerous. Something evil."

"We gotta collar that fucker," Bridget said.

"It'll be harder than you think, but we've no choice. I heard it in voice . . . whatever he's planning, we need to stop him before he destroys the country."

59

Ammar slouched behind the wheel and gazed out the van's passenger window, lost in thought. I glanced over my shoulder into the cargo space. Turki glowered at me, and Rashid crouched on his haunches beside him, both crowded by a dozen metal tanks with CO_2 stickers. Gas was weightless, but the thick tanks were heavy to keep the poison inside. We'd parked beside our second utility van in the facility's employee lot outside a wide maintenance gate.

Turki kept staring at me, silent and intense. The hair stood up on the back of my neck, but I kept my expression placid. They were already afraid of me, and keeping silent let the worst of their imaginations roam free, conjuring dark punishments.

Turki's dense beard, leathery skin, and bulging muscles projected strength. And evil. His sunken black eyes stared back at me like pools of tar. A flicker of doubt tickled my skull. The choices I'd made ensconced me in a gang of dimwits and monsters. Too many took pleasure in killing. If not for our jihad, how many would have become serial killers? But who was I to question how Allah chose his warriors?

We needed hard men for what would happen.

I reached into a cardboard box between the seats, grabbed a padded envelope, and ripped it open. I removed official identification passes and handed them out, offering three extras to Ammar. He was a Saudi, like Turki, two men sent by a member of the royal family who funded Sheikh Omar Yemeni's operations. The Saudi's were well-equipped, but neither Turki nor Ammar had come from money. They acted like peasants and could easily have been raised in the slums of Kabul. Both possessed the deep-seated rage common among jihadists. I couldn't tell whether they fought to achieve a caliphate and celebrate Allah's domain or if the violence they inflicted came from somewhere darker.

I nodded at the other van.

Ammar snatched the IDs out of my hand with fear in his eyes. He nodded—an apology or deference, I didn't know—then he slipped out and headed to the second van.

This operation would be the most dangerous. And the deadliest. We would strike fear into the heart of America.

I turned to Turki. "You're certain those tanks won't leak?"

"The seals are good," Turki said. "I tested them."

He wasn't bright, or eloquent, but he'd proven to be an efficient technician. Many of the men Omar sent me craved violence but lacked technical expertise and common sense. I could only count on a few—but I trusted Turki's expertise.

Ammar climbed back inside and looked at me with pride, like a child who'd finished his chores.

My daughter's eyes appeared, large and close, filled with despair. Was she in a terrible place now? She had nothing but goodness inside her, and she'd been too young to do anything to attract Allah's ire. Nothing serious, just kid stuff that everyone did. We were all bad. Maybe that's why we needed to martyr ourselves for Allah to make up for our human condition.

Tara continued to stare at me. Her image had been staying longer and longer. I hadn't seen Farzana in days, but my daughter came frequently now, and she stayed longer than before. Was my mind slipping into dementia? Or was she trying to convey something?

I blinked the image away.

I scanned the parking lot. No police. No FBI hostage rescue team fast-roping out of helicopters. No signal from my lookouts that we'd been compromised.

Turki watched me, waiting.

"Open the gate and load the canisters onto the dolly," I said. "No talking once we're inside."

"It will be done," Turki said.

I addressed the others. "Install the devices, set the timers, and get out."

"Yes, Zabihullah," Turki said.

"Act like you belong. You're busy workers doing a hard job. Nothing more."

The men nodded. I looked at each one, holding eye contact for a beat longer than comfortable. They had to trust me. And fear me.

"The time has come."

"Allahu Akbar," Rafi said.

"Allah Akbar," Turki and Ammar repeated in unison.

"Strike with vengeance against the Great Satan," I said. "Do it now."

60

Nathan juggled two venti black coffees as he shoved open the Starbucks door with his hip. He waited for a bright-red bus to rumble past, and a picture from a children's book came back to him, something he'd read at five or six years of age. Flashes of his childhood often materialized under stress. Love and warmth imbued his memories of youth, and they came back frequently since he'd been shot. He longed for the past. Did he miss the security his parents had provided, or did he hunger for life unburdened by complexity?

Maybe memories were lies he told himself.

He jogged across Seventh Street into the Navy Memorial. Meili came from the other direction. She spotted him and waved. He waved back, confused.

He intercepted her beside the fountain and kissed her. "I thought we were meeting at your office."

"Change of plans," she said. "I have to travel, and it's time sensitive. I'm running around, putting out fires."

"LA again?"

"Taipei."

That surprised him. "Why the urgency?"

"I'm meeting a new source."

He handed her a coffee. "I'm crazy busy too. These attacks have everyone working around the clock. Can you swing by late tonight?"

She pouted her lips. "My flight leaves early."

"I miss you." His heart ached.

"I know. Me too."

They stared at each other for a beat. "I don't like the idea of this trip," Nathan said.

Meili's eyes darkened. "I didn't ask for your approval."

He'd seen that look before. Had she dealt with overprotective boyfriends before, or did she not appreciate having to justify her actions to a man, especially in a profession dominated by testosterone?

"Don't get mad. I'm worried you can't protect yourself in China."

"Taiwan."

"Anywhere inside China's sphere of influence is hazardous."

"I'm a big girl."

"They attacked you before." The memory of Meili collapsing on the walkway outside the White House chilled him.

"That's more reason to go. Our Havana Syndrome investigation will save lives, and it's vital to national security that we uncover what China's planning."

"How long will you be gone?"

"Eight or nine days, maybe longer if her information is good."

"Her?"

"Better if you don't know any more."

"I'll come with you," Nathan said.

"It's not your case," she said, "and you almost got fired the last time you wormed your way onto our charter. Besides, I'm flying commercial."

"I'll take annual leave and fly on my dime." The thought of shelling out a few thousand dollars clenched his stomach, and he couldn't abandon his case, but he wanted to go. And he needed her to know that.

She took his hands in hers. "Our country's under attack. Rahimya won't give you time off . . . and she shouldn't."

"China's sourcing the opioids, which makes my investigation related."

"That's part of my motivation, but my goals are more strategic than tactical. I'm playing the long game."

"You think China knew what the Phantoms wanted to do with the carfentanil?"

She bit her lip. "Maybe. The opioid connection confuses me. Why not use bombs or shoot up public areas instead?"

"Carfentanil's a weapon of mass destruction."

"Using opioids seems a needless complication."

Nathan nodded. "If they figure out a better delivery system, they could devastate our economy."

"Seems weird, that's all."

"Agreed. There's something more behind it."

She sighed. "Thanks for the coffee."

"Last chance. Want me to come?"

"What I want and what's pragmatic are rarely the same. Stay here and stop these attacks."

She was right. As usual. "Be safe. I'll be thinking about you."

Her face softened. "Now, that's how adults say goodbye."

"I'll show you how adults do it." Nathan kissed her hard on the mouth. He filled with warmth. He broke the kiss.

"Please be careful," he said.

"I should be telling you the same thing. Try not to shoot anybody while I'm gone."

"Yeah, okay." She'd made a joke, but the thought of killing someone again made him want to hide under the covers.

"You okay?"

"Peachy."

61

I parted the curtains in the back office of the Community Center for Islamic Studies and peeked into the lobby. Fifteen men mingled after prayer for a community meeting. Sameer Attallah stood in the rear corner, and his eyes flitted around the room like a cornered rat. Greasy hair hung over his eyes, his shirt had come untucked, and his wiry frame twitched. He seemed unable to stand still.

I stepped out where he could see me and motioned for him to come. He scurried toward me, and I slipped back out of sight. Sheikh Omar Yemeni had arranged for me to stay at the community center since I'd become a fugitive, and I'd slept in the basement and stayed concealed, only meeting Khaled Musa when I needed him to relay orders to our team, and no one else. But Sameer wasn't a member of the Al-Sahaba Mosque or known by the Muslim community—the perfect messenger to relay communications from Hamtramck.

Sameer slinked into the back room. He didn't make eye contact. Was he trembling from fear or did he shake from his normal kinetic energy? If he hadn't been so devout, I'd suspect methamphetamine. He may suffer from some disease, probably a psychological disorder.

"You have it?" I asked.

His eyes darted in my direction, never landing on me, then he returned his attention to his shoes. “The sheikh told me to fly like the wind.”

I stared at him, waiting. He shifted on his feet. His abnormal behavior unsettled me.

“Give it to me.”

Sameer dug into his jeans and extracted a bulky cell phone, more outdated than anything I’d used in Afghanistan. He handed it over with a toothy grin, like a dog bringing a ball to its master.

“Shokran.”

He looked up and cocked his head.

“Thank you,” I said again.

Sameer stared at the floor and rocked back and forth.

“Do you have something else for me?” I asked.

His body stiffened, and a hint of fear tingled through me—an ancient genetic warning. His eyes reached my chin, then he shook his head and shuffled back out through the curtain.

Psycho.

I stopped, shame weighing me down. Sameer probably had an IQ below eighty and an obvious mental illness. Jihadists often used people with cognitive impairment as suicide bombers because they would do anything without worry about deadly consequences. That tactic had always repulsed me, yet now I engaged in it.

Tara’s presence touched me but without warmth.

I shook my head and stretched. The strain of being outed muddled my thinking. I wasn’t strapping C4 to Sameer’s chest. He’d merely carried a phone from Omar, and being a messenger for the sheikh gave Samir’s life meaning. He’d become a tool to enact Allah’s will, instead of wasting his time on earth without purpose.

I powered on the cell phone and scrolled to the address book, which only contained one number. The sheikh’s private cell.

I dialed, and he answered without preamble. “Are you safe?”

“Thank you for the refuge.”

“Everywhere you go is dangerous now.”

“We only have two planned operations left,” I said.

"That is incorrect. We have three."

The hair rose on my neck. "I've set the trap, and my plan to escalate the body count is on schedule. I didn't expect any deviation."

"Plans change," Omar said. "We anticipated Americans coming together to mourn the tragedy and express anger, but we didn't expect Democrats and Republicans to come together so fast. I thought the members who infiltrated Congress would control the narrative . . . but I was wrong."

My body tensed. I'd missed something. "What happened?"

"The foreign affairs committee met last night and discussed a legislative response. They—"

"How did you learn this?"

"Our people are everywhere. Some lead committees."

"How can legislation alter our operation?"

"The senators' colleagues in the House are crafting a bill that will authorize the president to take terminal action against ISIS leaders around the world. In fact, it would require such action."

"Terminal?"

Worshipers murmured in the other room. Their meeting breaking up. I watched the curtain.

"The bill authorizes and funds assassination," Omar said, "though it's couched in doublespeak and buried deep within an omnibus proposal."

"I don't see how—"

"I let our success cloud my judgment," Omar said, "and I became too comfortable. Our enemy has scrambled a rapid legislative response to our glorious jihad because they feel invincible. They sit in their expensive limousines and luxury apartments, spending American tax dollars with impunity, but their actions have consequences. It's our job to show them that."

I squeezed the phone tighter. "You want to target elected officials?"

"Assassinating a congressperson or two, would only paint them as noble victims and confer more authority upon them. It would invite the infidels to strike back even harder. Besides, they're on alert and protected, and we need our devout warriors to execute our plan."

"What do you suggest?"

"We must terrify them, trigger primal fear, until they cower in their homes. I want them to hesitate before they raise a pen to sign legislation."

"How?"

"You're going to murder their children."

62

Nathan parked half a block from Hamid's residence, a tiny studio in a three-story brick apartment building in Woodbridge, Virginia. Nathan had requested a surveillance team cover the location, but he wanted to check it himself. He scrunched down and watched the building in his side-view mirror. Central American immigrants and poor blacks populated the transient neighborhood. Thick stalks of dead grass lined the base of the building, and the property suffered from neglect. Hamid rented a basement apartment with bars affixed to a tiny window. A soiled curtain covered the glass, but the lights remained off inside.

Hamid was gone.

Squealing tires drew his attention as a car careened around the corner. Nathan sat up, and his hand moved to his Glock as the car approached.

Bridget sat behind the wheel. He relaxed as she pulled alongside him and rolled down her window.

"That's a good way to burn a surveillance," he said.

"Get in the frickin' car," Bridget yelled.

Nathan's core turned to ice. "What happened?"

"We nabbed Imam Qadir. They're bringing him in now."

"Who?"

"Smitty's with SWAT. They got Qadir and his deputy in custody, and they're headed to our office to process him."

"I thought he'd slipped into Mexico by now. Where'd they get him?"

"He's been hiding in the basement of one of his supporters. Our drone spotted him sitting in the backyard, and the surveillance team hooked him up."

Nathan's cheeks burned. "Why didn't you call me?"

"I did. Nine times. Check your phone."

Shit. He had sixteen missed calls. He'd put his cell on silent before meeting Meili and forgotten to flip it back.

"I'll follow you."

He fell in behind her car as they raced to the office. They couldn't charge Qadir with terrorism, but based on their source's information, the carfentanil seizure, and timing of the attacks, the AUSA had convinced a judge to sign an arrest warrant for conspiracy to possess carfentanil. One hundred kilos put Qadir atop the sentencing guidelines, but securing a conviction would be tough since nothing directly linked Qadir to the shipment. The two assholes who delivered the drugs were both dead, and Qadir denied knowing anything about the drugs. Without a confession, a defense attorney may convince a jury that someone else at the mosque had ordered the drugs. Reasonable doubt wouldn't be hard to sow, especially with a DC jury.

But Nathan needed to talk to him, look into his eyes. The chance of the imam cooperating was basically zero, but people uttered things they shouldn't under interrogation, and it wouldn't take much of a slip to convince a jury. The attacks dominated the news and enraged Americans across the political spectrum. Nathan couldn't claim the seized drugs were destined for terrorism, but jurors would make the connection themselves.

A trial verdict would be a coin flip.

They arrived at the office, where agents had fingerprinted, photographed, and processed Qadir. The imam waited for them in an interrogation room.

Nathan paused before entering. "I'll take the lead."

"Want me in there?"

"We need an incriminating comment, and talking with a female agent will infuriate him."

"He won't be the first crook I've driven into a rage. I have that effect on men."

"Work your magic."

Nathan opened the door, and they entered. Qadir sat handcuffed in a plastic chair opposite Agent Timmy Wilson, another new agent in their group. Qadir glowered at them, hatred simmering in his eyes.

Nathan slid a chair in front of Qadir and sat too close for comfort.

"You cannot hold me," Qadir said.

"I'm happy to explain everything to you, but before I do, I need to read you the Miranda warning." Nathan took the laminated card out of his credentials case and read it aloud. "Do you wish to speak to us without an attorney present?"

"Ask your questions. It's only an inconvenience. You've tried this before."

"This time, we have a warrant. You're under arrest for conspiracy to possess with intent to distribute carfentanil in violation of 21 USC 846 and 21 USC 841."

"I didn't buy those drugs. I never touched them. We've been through this already."

"Only now, a federal judge agrees we have enough to go to trial."

Qadir shifted in his seat, almost imperceptibly. The thought of being tried in a DC court had hit home.

"We're charging you with the firearms too, since you constructively possessed them when the drugs arrived. That's a big sentencing enhancement."

"You can't prove the rifles were there with the drugs."

Qadir was right, because the search warrant came later, but the carbines had been dusty, and circumstantial evidence might sway a jury. The AUSA hadn't verbalized his concern—he didn't want to taint Nathan's testimony—but they both knew the AUSA had only considered the gun charge because the country was under attack. Americans wanted to fight back, and Qadir was involved, whether they could prove it or not.

"You could spend the rest of your life in prison," Nathan said.

"Your courts do not scare me."

"What we do next is up to you."

Qadir stared daggers. "Then I choose to be released."

"Not on the menu. You can plead guilty, go to trial, or cooperate and cut a deal."

Qadir shook his head. "I know nothing about the drugs you found."

"Help us," Nathan said, "and we'll ask for a reduced sentence."

"The weak man reaches for ripe fruit as a camel leans toward the riverbank."

"What are you frickin' talking about?" Bridget asked.

"I see crocodiles waiting in the water," Qadir said.

Nathan leaned forward. His face close to Qadir—provoking him. "Cut the shit. You ordered those drugs, and we'll prove it in court."

"Then do so."

"But it's worse that. You're involved with terrorism, and I'm going to nail you to a wall."

Qadir cocked his head. "A threat?"

"A promise. You're going to pay for all those deaths."

"We shall see."

Qadir was a cool cucumber. Nathan had to give him props for that. The imam wouldn't barter for his freedom, which meant their interview would go nowhere.

"If we go to trial, we'll ask for the maximum penalty, but if you cooperate, you'll do less time."

"Drugs are prohibited in Islam."

"That's not exactly true, is it?" Nathan asked.

Qadir's eyes glimmered.

Bridget approached him. "Even if you beat these charges, you'll need to worry about your friends who are behind these attacks."

"And why is that, Special Agent?" He spat the words, his misogyny on full display.

"They'll think you're working for us."

"It doesn't matter."

"Why?"

"Because you'll never defeat them," Qadir said.

"We caught you, you frickin' motherfucker," Bridget said.

"You're weak. Americans don't have the stomach for what needs to be done. You'll pay, and so will the next generation."

"Piss off," Bridget said.

Nathan's gut hollowed. "What do you mean, *next generation?*"

Qadir smiled. "We've brainwashed your children for decades, but the Slayer will take a more direct route."

"What makes you say that?"

"An educated guess."

"What's that direct route?" Bridget asked.

Qadir sneered. "I'll speak with my lawyer now."

"Good luck," Nathan said.

He slid his chair back and walked out with Bridget. She shut the door behind them.

She leaned close. "Do you—"

Nathan held his finger to his lips and pulled out a digital recorder. He held it to his mouth. "That was an interview of Imam Qadir at the FBI Washington Division by Special Agent Bridget Quinn and Special Agent Nathan Burke. Also present was Special Agent Timothy Wilson." He gave the time-stamping information and turned it off.

"What good will that do?" Bridget asked. "He didn't say much."

"We'll let a jury decide if those are the words of an innocent man."

63

Jack Snyder loved the Philadelphia Flyers more than anything on earth. Well, not more than his mother, but she was gone now. Maybe his wife was on par, but she couldn't hide the contempt in her eyes when she talked to him. At least she pretended. His teenage daughter outright hated him. Both suffered his drinking and foul moods, but that wasn't his fault. How could anyone be pleasant after twelve-hour shifts in a smelting operation? Extracting and refining copper was men's work, dirty and painful, and his back perpetually hurt. Life sucked.

But not the Flyers. They were awesome and always would be.

Jack exited bus 17 onto Broad Street and headed for the Wells Fargo Center. The Eagles and the Phillies stadiums occupied the same complex in the shadow of the city's skyline. He joined the throng of fans, all wearing orange and white jerseys. They laughed and spoke in loud tones as anticipation electrified them.

The Flyers were matched in a Metropolitan Division game against their rivals, the New Jersey Devils. The teams' proximity heated their rivalry, as did their high-octane head-to-head battles since 1978, when the Devils franchise played in Colorado. To catch their next game, Ralph would need to drive ninety miles up the Jersey Turnpike to the Prudential Center in Newark—the belly of the beast. Jersey fans were the worst.

The battle of the Jersey Turnpike was not a game to miss.

Jack's heart accelerated as he approached the Wells Fargo Center, like a Roman citizen entering the Coliseum. At least that's how it looked in the movies.

"Let's go, Fly-ers," a man chanted, enunciating each syllable.

Others joined in, and soon, hundreds of voices boomed across the parking lot. This was his tribe. He moved into the entrance, and their chorus echoed off cement walls. Jack handed his ticket to an attendant, who ripped it and returned the stub, another trophy to tape to his bedroom wall. God, his wife hated them.

He pushed through the rotating gate and entered gallery. The game hadn't started, but beer already stained the floor, and the rich odor of barley and hops wafted through the air. Jack scanned the numbers painted on the wall and turned left toward the ramp that would lead to his seat. Fans pulsated with energy around him. A man pushing ninety held a chili dog with both hands and stared at it like it would disappear if he blinked.

A moment of sadness fluttered through Jack. He'd attended as many games as he could afford, and while sometimes the guys from work would go as a group, he usually came with his cousin Davey. But Davey had overdosed and died three weeks before. Jack didn't have many friends, and no one he'd known since kindergarten, so coming alone would be his new normal. At least at the stadium, Jack was surrounded by his extended family—a community of people who loved the Flyers.

Jack shuffled up a ramp, and the hockey rink revealed itself before him. Cool air rose over the ice and washed over him, as the blinking neon lights and the sea of orange jerseys filled him with excitement. And hope. He climbed a steep flight of concrete stairs. Up and up. Nosebleed seats. That's all he could swing, but being there and seeing his boys in person was worth a day's pay.

Even if it wasn't, what else did he have?

He slowed behind a fat guy who would barely fit between the rows of plastic seats. The man checked his ticket and turned into a row. Jack continued past him, higher and higher. Two rows from the top, he stopped and looked back down. The ice was a long, long way away, but Philadelphia's warriors would soon take to it and defend his city's honor. His heroes. And he would cheer loudly so they could hear him. Being there was like touching greatness.

Jack sidled down the row, making a couple curl their legs under them. Another guy about his age, with a similar-sized gut, looked annoyed as he stood to let Jack pass. Jack pushed the folding seat down and plopped in beside him.

"Big game," the guy said.

"Biggest."

Jack's pulse pounded in his temples, and his breath came hard. He engaged in strenuous physical labor at work, which gave him forearms like Popeye's, but he should start running—or some other kind of cardio. If he didn't, he'd drop dead of a heart attack like his father had at about the same age. Grim thought. Yeah, he'd join a gym . . . one of these days. Then maybe fix his relationship with his wife. Or leave her. Maybe spend more time with his daughter.

Jack's chest tightened. Why was he worrying about all this now? He'd paid for this ticket. Paid dearly. This was his time.

The lights dimmed, and a deep bass pounded out of the speakers. "Ladies and gentlemen," the announcer's voice bellowed, "welcome to the Wells Fargo Center."

Fans applauded, and a few yelled, but the reaction was tepid.

Then the lights went out, and people screamed with anticipation. Music reverberated through the rink.

"Ten, nine, eight . . ." The announcer counted down as corresponding numbers flashed on the jumbotron above the ice. Fans counted with him.

". . . three, two, one."

The image on the giant screen changed to Gritty, the seven-foot orange mascot, as he skated onto the ice waving a Flyers flag. He circled the rink and disappeared into a side tunnel as digital images projected onto the rink's surface.

Waves of music pulsed through Jack's body. The ice glittered with flashing lights, and strobes projected across the stadium, turning it into a disco.

The guy beside Jack turned to him and said something, but his words disappeared into the clatter.

"What?" Jack asked, leaning close.

"I said, it's like Vegas. I thought this was a hockey game."

Jack scowled. This wasn't just a game. It was the biggest contest in years, and the players deserved the celebration.

The referees skated out onto the ice, circling like vultures to a chorus of boos. Then the music changed.

"The New Jersey Devils," the announcer said.

The hated enemy took the ice, skating in circles.

The jumbotron lightened. "Give a big hometown welcome to your Philadelphia Flyers."

The center exploded with cheering and applause.

"Tonight's first line is . . ." The announcer read the names of the starting players as their images flashed on the screens.

Fans leapt to their feet as the gate on the ice opened, and the Flyers streamed in, glittering across the surface like birds. People whistled and cheered. Someone blew an air horn.

Jack's chest swelled with pride. These were warriors, men who fought the toughest game on ice, crashing into each other at twenty miles an hour and pummeling the enemy into the boards. These men wouldn't put up with the lack of disrespect from their wives.

"Kick some ass," Jack screamed.

The music stopped. "And now, please stand and direct your attention to Master Sergeant Michael Davis, as he sings 'The Star-Spangled Banner.'"

Jack took off his cap and held it over his heart. A carpet rolled out of the gate, and a man in green Army uniform stepped onto it.

"Oh, say can you see . . ." his baritone voice echoed through the rink as his image showed on the screen. An American flag projected onto the ice.

The crowd sang along, loud and robust. Patriotism lived in hockey fans. These were Jack's people. Real Americans.

Red smoke poured out of the ceiling, the same color as the flag. The Flyers had gone all out with this introduction. They—

Smoke wafted out of a vent one section away. It blew through the people standing at their seats. Why would the Flyers organization do that?

Something was wrong.

Jack scanned the rink. Smoke continued to seep out of vents along the top row and ceiling. The master sergeant stopped singing halfway through the anthem. He stared up at the red cloud, and his quizzical expression filled the jumbotron. The music kept playing.

Jack looked back at the ceiling. Smoke flowed in billowing scarlet clouds. Something about the color tickled his memory. Hadn't there been some kind of cloud on television? He glanced down the row. People ducked and crouched. The fans in the first two rows didn't react. Jack stared. They weren't moving.

The odor of burnt popcorn tingled Jack's nostrils. Who was eating during this?

A woman screamed. People stood and rushed for the aisles. A heavyset man in a Metallica shirt shoved a young boy to the ground. The boy's father punched the man, and they grappled.

Red clouds merged into a mist that obscured the other side of the stadium. People trampled each other. A fat woman fell and rolled down the concrete steps, taking out half a dozen people like bowling pins.

Jack remained sitting and watched. It seemed funny. Everything had become hilarious. He turned to laugh with his neighbor, but the man beside him had slipped down in his seat. His tongue drooped out of his mouth, and white foam bubbled from his lips.

They were going to die.

The thought consumed Jack, but he wasn't afraid. His wife wouldn't have him to take care of her anymore. He wouldn't be her slave. A part of him welcomed death.

He shut his eyes and drifted off.

64

Rahimya rushed into the open area between cubicles known as the bullpen. "I need everyone. Something's happening. Another attack."

Nathan looked over his cubicle and locked eyes with Bridget. "Let's go."

Rahimya stood beside the Moser safes that held their active case files, and she powered on the television that suspended from the ceiling by a crooked metal frame. The half dozen members of their group who were in the office crowded around her. Nathan checked his phone, which had two notifications from news apps breaking the news about multiple terror attacks.

The television came to life, and the dour face of an anchor at a twenty-four-hour news network filled the screen. The banner above him read, "Gas Attack at Wells Fargo Center."

"This will be bad," Nathan said.

"How many people does the stadium hold?" Rahimya asked no one in particular.

"Over nineteen thousand," Otis said. He scrolled furiously on his laptop.

"Frickin' disaster," Bridget said.

A news helicopter provided aerial shots of ambulances, fire engines, and police cars surrounding the hockey rink. Their emergency lights bathing the exterior in red and blue.

"A hazardous materials incident has taken life at a Philadelphia Flyers game against the New Jersey Devils. Authorities have yet to classify the incident, but all signs point to another terror gas attack. Images from the pregame telecast are horrifying, so viewer discretion is advised."

The screen showed a soldier singing the national anthem before an arena packed with fans. Red clouds gushed out of the ceiling vents.

"That looks like the same shit on Wall Street," Bridget said.

"Zabihullah," Nathan said.

"That fucker."

A talking head suggested the possibility of a chemical leak, but anyone watching understood it was another opioid gas attack. Images of the rink before they suspended the broadcast flashed on the screen. Through the red haze, ticket holders rushed for the exits, trampling each other. Hundreds of people in the upper rows collapsed in their seats.

"The death toll will be horrific," Nathan said.

Rahimya turned to him. "The Philadelphia Division has the lead, but I want you there before rescue workers contaminate the scene."

"How can it get more contaminated?" Bridget asked. "The whole place is a HAZMAT cluster."

"I'm talking about the evidence. Get up there and find a link to our case."

Nathan sighed. "I still don't understand why they chose opioids."

"Isn't it obvious?" Bridget asked. "They're highly toxic."

"So is cyanide and a hundred other poisons."

"Illicit drugs don't leave a trail," Bridget said.

"Their choice feels more deliberate," Nathan said. "The elegance and simplicity of their plan was well thought out, and they didn't choose opioids on a whim. Islamists use symbolism in their operations, like constructing a mosque on a former church site."

"Or an Islamic Center at Ground Zero," Rahimya said.

"Using opioids was intentional," Nathan said. "Afghanistan is the opium capital of the world, and China produces most synthetic opioids—two countries seeking to destroy the United States. It can't be coincidence."

"You make it sound personal."

A lightbulb clicked on in Nathan's head. "Nothing's more personal than killing. I think they used opioids to send a message."

"For who?"

Nathan frowned. "That's the question."

"What would motivate Zabihullah to use opioids?" Rahimya asked. "He could find easier ways to kill. If you hadn't intercepted those drugs, we'd have no clue who was behind this."

Nathan scratched his rubbed his neck. "Hamid I'd understand. He helped us find links between drug traffickers and Al-Qaeda in Afghanistan. There'd be a simple elegance to using it."

"You said that before." Bridget said.

"What?"

"Elegance. You said the low-tech plan had elegance, and now you're saying it about their ironic choice of weapon."

"It's only ironic if Hamid chose it."

"You think he has that much influence with Zabihullah?"

Nathan's body chilled. "Unless . . ."

Rahimya's eyes widened.

"Unless what?" Bridget asked.

"He has that scar over his eye," Rahimya said.

"Ali told us Zabihullah Al-Afghani's face is scarred," Nathan said.

Bridget gawked. "You mean—"

"I think . . ." Nathan could hardly form the words. "It's possible Hamid is Zabihullah Al-Afghani, the mastermind behind these attacks."

Bridget gasped.

"He matches the description," Rahimya said.

"Shit," Nathan said. "I never put that together."

Bridget snorted. "Scars in Afghanistan gotta be as common as bruises on a Southie street punk."

"Still, I missed it. All the clues were there."

Rahimya shook her head. "This is crazy, Nathan. Even for you. You're saying your FSN didn't just pass information to the enemy or even join them. You think he's the brains behind all these attacks?"

Nathan knew it in his core. "He knows us. He knows me. Hamid's using carfentanil against us because he sacrificed everything to help us combat drugs in Afghanistan. It's ironic . . . his private joke."

"With who?"

"Me."

65

A knock on the office door jerked me out of my daydream. Or nightmare. Or whatever hell on earth existed inside of me. I looked up and rubbed my face.

"Enter."

The door swung open, and Sheikh Omar Yemeni stood in the threshold.

A flash of adrenaline shocked me, and I jumped to my feet, knocking my chair over.

"As-Salamu Alaikum," Omar said.

"Wa Alaikum As-Salam," I said, returning the greeting. I blinked to orient myself. Seeing people out of context did that to me. "I wasn't expecting you. What has brought you to Washington?"

Omar surveyed the room, his eyes darting from the phone to the lamp to the window's drawn shades. "Perhaps we should speak elsewhere, where no one can overhear."

"I can assure you this room is safe to—"

"Walk with me."

Omar turned and slipped into the hallway. I hurried after him. What urgency had brought him to the capital? My abdomen hardened.

I walked beside Omar as he crossed the prayer room's marble floor. A handful of men spoke in hush tones, so we skirted them and moved to the back. I led Omar through a double door into the *sahn,* a manicured courtyard punctuated by a center fountain and plum trees ringing the walkway.

I stopped in the garden, and he glanced around. Seemingly satisfied we were alone, he turned to me.

"Why have you come?" I asked.

His eyes sparkled. "To oversee the final operations."

"Everything is prepared in Philadelphia. I supervised preparations myself."

He nodded. "That will be a glorious victory for Allah."

"It will shock them and—"

"A magnificent tribute, yes," He placed his hand on my shoulder, "but I've come to see you deliver a cataclysmal blow."

"The aerial attack will terrorize them, make them cower in their homes. It will decimate the economy when we—"

"Yes, yes," Omar said, waving his hand as if shooing away a fly. "But they've recovered from our other attacks. They're resilient."

Farzana's perfume floated on the air, the scent she'd worn on the day she died. I dared not look around, for fear of seeing her.

"Our operations injure them. These next strikes will be an escalation. They rely on their police and military to protect them, but no one can shield them from Allah's wrath." A note of desperation had crept into my voice as my chest and larynx tightened. I knew what he wanted.

"America remains strong. More united than before."

"I understand these people. When the body count continues to rise, they'll see no end in sight. They'll turn on their police and their leaders and demand change. Many politicians will blame America, and they'll withdraw from the Middle East."

"I know you've lived with them, broken bread together . . . fought with them against your Muslim brothers." Disgust tinged his voice.

"I know what I've done. I . . ." I looked at my sandals, unable to meet his eyes.

"Your experience inside the infidel's camp is why I chose you for these operations. You can anticipate their reaction, avoid detection and escape their dragnet."

"Perhaps . . ."

"Your standing here is proof I was correct."

"Then why do you seek to alter my tactics now?"

Omar's face hardened. "You forget your place. I've lived in America for a decade and listened to their whining, their self-hatred. I've witnessed their weakness with my own eyes.

"But—"

"Your operations scared them. That is true. Now they fear death from you when they are in more danger of dying in their cars than from your gas. But we must amplify their terror, make it visceral, and force them to demand change."

"We have already walked down that path. We—"

Omar held up his hand to silence me. "I know how to strike dread into every man, woman, and child in the country."

"You're talking about their children." My body cooled.

Omar nodded. "Their fear of death is irrational, but threatening their children supersedes everything."

Tara's breath tickled my neck, and I flinched. I quickly recovered. If Omar learned insanity clawed at me and threatened to smother me in its grip, he'd murder me. Or have me killed. Leaders rarely bloodied their own hands.

I cleared my throat to cover my distraction. "What about the backlash? The world will unite against us—"

"Presidents worry about their own country's children . . . and about their jobs. This pivotal moment will force fat, lazy Americans to stop thinking of war as something in a far-off land. They will reap the consequences of their heresy."

I had trouble breathing. Why did this bother me? Children had died on the Metro. I hadn't specifically targeted them, but the carfentanil bombs had killed teenagers. Why did the idea of killing children affect me now?

Farzana and Tara stood close, and their warmth radiated into me.

"What do you wish me to do?" I asked.

Omar glanced around then reached into his jacket and removed an envelope. He handed it to me.

"What's this?"

"The program for Operation Reckoning. You will begin with the most visible children."

"Whose children?"

"The offspring of their vile leadership. Then we will target elementary schools. Then preschools. It's time to decapitate the next generation of infidels and make the world fear Allah."

66

The Wells Fargo Center's parking lot danced with red and blue emergency lights from police cars, ambulances, fire trucks, and a host of city, county, state, and federal agencies. Every HAZMAT team within a hundred miles had responded. An estimated 20,000 people had attended the Flyers-Devils game, and the loss of life made it one of the worst terrorist attacks in history. Not since the collapse of the World Trade Center had so many Americans died in a single incident, and as emergency personnel recovered more victims, the body count grew.

The death toll staggered the country.

Nathan stood still with his arms extended while Special Agent Chuck Hillary checked the seals on Nathan's Level A Totally Encapsulating Chemical Protective Suit. Chuck was a senior member of the FBI's Hazardous Materials Response Unit and an expert in moving through toxic environments. Nathan wore inner and outer gloves and thick, chemical-resistant boots that made movement awkward. His full-face SCBA mask connected to an oxygen tank on his back, and his breath fogged his face shield, shrouding his vision with clouds. He could have been walking on the surface of the moon, but instead, he was about to enter the Wells Fargo Center. Nathan focused over Chuck's shoulder at the entrance to ignore his creeping claustrophobia.

Bridget approached. "This is awful." Her voice crackled through the speaker in her suit. They carried handheld radios, but they hadn't brought the TCI TTMK III throat microphones they needed. The hazards of packing in a hurry.

"Ready?" Agent Hillary asked.

Nathan nodded, a gesture impossible to see while buried in his protective suit.

"Burke?"

"Lead the way."

Nathan had locked his and Bridget's firearms in their trunk, and being unarmed left him naked with the nagging thought he'd forgotten something. Even if he had carried his weapon, he wouldn't be able to draw from inside the suit.

But there shouldn't be any threats in the arena.

Everyone inside was dead.

Nathan steeled himself for what he was about to witness. Despite all the emergency-response training he'd done over the years, he'd never thought he would need it. Agents, troopers, and cops wandered around the staging area like astronauts.

Surreal.

Nathan followed Hillary through the ground-level door at the Broad Street entrance. His feet swam in the rubber boots, which were at least two sizes too large. He'd barely trained in HAZMAT and wasn't prepared to enter a contaminated environment, but seeing the crime scene firsthand would be essential to their investigation. And as difficult as it would be to observe the overwhelming loss of life, he deserved to suffer. He'd failed to stop the onslaught, and he'd never forgive himself. He should have been better.

They passed between crowd-control dividers and metal detectors and entered a wide concourse with beer and snack stands on either side. The tile was littered with naloxone caps and medical gauze, detritus from the initial medical response before EMTs and police officers had been overcome by the tainted air or surface residue. They had pulled out, dragging their overdosed colleagues with them, and waited for HAZMAT to respond. By the time they'd safely reentered the building, it had been too late.

Everyone affected died.

A dozen people in the attached office buildings had succumbed too. The incident kept revealing more death, like peeling back layers of a poisoned onion.

"I'll check with our tech at rink side," Hillary said. "Wait here."

Nathan flashed him a thumbs-up, too emotional to talk. Bridget plopped into a chair beside him. Her face had pulled back tight.

"Doing okay?" he asked.

"It's . . . unbelievable. All those people . . . families."

He patted her shoulder then turned and scanned the arena. Bodies remained in the upper rows, sitting there like mannequins. Rescue teams had moved through the entire complex, checking vitals and for any sign of life, but they only found three concession workers alive. They'd survived by hiding in a storage room with no ventilation.

The arena's capacity for hockey games was 19,541, and the place had been sold out for the big game, but authorities hadn't ascertained the exact number of victims yet. People who bought tickets may not have shown up, and vendors and other people may have been present but unaccounted for. Determining who had been there would take days.

Over 600 spectators had escaped the clouds of death, mostly those sitting in the middle rows. Fans near the top had been doused with direct gas streams, and people closest to ice were overcome by the ceiling vents above the jumbotron. Over 200 casualties had been admitted to local hospitals, overwhelming their emergency departments and exposing their inadequate preparation for a mass casualty event.

Nathan bumped into a seat. The damn suit made it almost impossible to function. How did HAZMAT guys perform in them? The confinement inside layers of sealed material caused mild claustrophobia, which was bad enough, but the thought of poison particles drifting through the area threatened to trigger a full-blown panic attack.

He climbed onto a concrete step and scanned the seats across the ice. A similar horrific tableau. Bodies everywhere. It would take firefighters days to recover them all. Public safety departments didn't possess sufficient HAZMAT suits, and organizations from around the country had shipped equipment, creating a logistical nightmare.

Nathan glanced back at Bridget. She sat still in her chair, and if she was freaked out, she didn't show it. How did she keep her composure? Another area where she excelled.

"You doing okay, Bridget?"

No answer.

Damned radios hardly worked inside on a good day, but add feet of concrete and then smother the signal in rubber, and they became worthless.

"Ready to head to the engineering facilities?" Nathan asked.

Nothing.

He shuffled over to her and tapped her shoulder. Bridget leaned away from him, farther and farther. She toppled onto the floor and rolled onto her back.

Panic bubbled inside him like a wave. *What's happening?* He knelt beside her and shook her shoulder. "Bridget, what's wrong?"

No response.

He leaned his face close to hers. Bridget's eyelids hung half closed, and her pupils had constricted into tiny points.

Opioid intoxication.

"Officer down," he yelled. "I need help."

67

Nathan crouched over Bridget with a knot in his throat. He ran his gloved hands over her suit, searching for compromise. Her left sleeve had torn beneath the wrist, exposing a few millimeters of skin. She must not have noticed, but that's all it had taken to let the poison inside.

Nathan scanned the stadium looking for help. Hillary chatted with an FBI Crime Scene tech, who examined residue on a board along the ice. Their backs were to him.

"Hillary, help."

Around the stadium, dozens of emergency person lifted bodies onto gurneys, but none were in his section. Nobody noticed his distress.

Time equaled life. Opioids would slow her breathing, then her heart. Once she wasn't pumping blood fast enough to oxygenate her organs, her brain would starve. He had to get her out of the hot zone, remove her HAZMAT suit, and render aid.

Every second counted.

Nathan moved to Bridget's head. He grabbed her under her arms and lifted her upper body, so her head rested against his stomach. He glanced up at the ramp leading to the concourse six rows above.

He shuffled backward, dragging Bridget by her heels. She didn't respond at all. She probably only weighed 120 pounds, but the suit, oxygen tank, and other gear, added thirty more. Dead weight. He stepped up and lifted her behind him. One step. Then another.

The timer on her life ticked down.

His quads and calves strained, and his back ached. He grunted with exertion. A bead of sweat ran down his forehead.

Hillary raced up the stairs beside him, followed by a firefighter.

"What happened?" Hillary asked.

"Suit ripped," Nathan said. "Help me carry her."

Hillary grabbed her legs, and the firefighter grabbed Bridget's arm and supported her oxygen tank.

They stomped up the steps, Bridget's weight easily handled between the three of them, and he struggled to keep up. They all understood the urgency.

They reached the ramp, and a group of EMTs and firefighters met them with a gurney. The response to a fallen emergency responder felt different, more emotional. It broke through barrier of personal detachment that professionals needed when dealing with life-and-death careers. This could be any of them, at any time.

"What we got?" an EMT asked.

"Exposure," Hillary said.

"Stay with me, Bridget," Nathan said.

He held Bridget's hand and pressed his fingers against the tear in her suit. He should have carried electrical tape to seal rips, another failure of preparedness. Never again.

Nathan jogged beside the gurney as they raced across the concourse, then through a gate and into the fresh air.

"Head to the decontamination tent," Hillary said.

Nathan's muscles screamed under her weight. He gripped the stretcher until his fingers ached. They angled through the warm zone toward the decontamination area, a series of stations where workers stripped off a victim's gear and hosed down the skin before a more detailed cleaning. The process prevented cross-contamination into the safe zone. In theory.

An EMT ripped off Bridget's hood while another tugged down her suit to expose her chest. He tilted her head to open her airway and placed two fingers on her carotid artery. A petite doctor wearing a white lab coat, rubber gloves, and respirator met them as they rolled across the pavement.

"Status?" she asked.

"Ripped suit, likely overdose," the EMT said. "She's got bradycardia with shallow respirations. Can't get a good pulse."

"Inhaler won't work," the doctor said.

She had a naloxone nasal spray injector in her hand, but she dropped it into her lab coat pocket and withdrew a syringe and vial. She ripped off the orange cap, inserted the needle, and pulled back the plunger as she eyeballed the dose.

"Administering naloxone," she said.

The doctor stretched the skin back on Bridget's shoulder and stuck the needle into the muscle. She pushed the plunger until the contents of the syringe emptied. The toxin may or may not be an opioid, but giving naloxone couldn't hurt. Either it would help, or it wouldn't.

The doctor felt for a pulse in Bridget's neck as another EMT produced an AMBU bag. He slipped a face mask over Bridget's face, sealed it around her mouth with one hand, and squeezed the bag with the other. Bridget's chest rose as he forced air into her lungs.

"Start compressions?" the first EMT asked.

"Pulse is around fifty-five," the doctor said. "Keep rescue breathing and finish decontamination. Let's see if the naloxone works."

They reached the tent and stopped behind a privacy screen. Nurses and firefighters manhandled Bridget as they stripped off her protective clothing. She wore a gray tee shirt and boy shorts.

She'd soiled herself.

Nathan gasped. Involuntary urination meant her muscles had lost rigidity, and if the opioid, or whatever had infected her, had loosened her bladder and sphincter, then it affected her breathing muscles too.

"C'mon, Bridget. Hang in there."

Rescuers removed her clothing and scrubbed her skin while another responder directed multiple shower heads to rinse her. Nathan stepped back and averted his eyes as they began decontamination. Concern about modesty seemed ridiculous, but he knew her, and he wanted to respect her privacy.

Even if she never woke up.

An ambulance's air horn bellowed as it backed up to the yellow tape bordering the support zone. An EMT opened the door from inside and prepared to take her. They would have called Jefferson Hospital's Emergency Room, and ER staff would be standing by to receive one of their own, a fellow emergency responder.

Medical personnel raced around Bridget as they lifted her onto a clean gurney, then moved her to the next station. They worked like a NASCAR pit crew.

Nathan stripped off his suit and followed Bridget as she progressed from cleaning to disinfection to sterilization. He walked around the tent and met them in the final stage close to the ambulance. Someone had covered her groin with a sheet, a nod to her humanity and the fact that she was one of the rescue workers.

Bridget kicked her leg, and Nathan's heart leapt. She'd moved on her own.

An EMT pumped the AMBU bag.

Nathan stepped closer. "Bridget, you're okay."

She didn't respond.

They rolled her out from under the tent, with the doctor and six medical personnel continuing to work on her. They loaded her into the ambulance.

Hillary came up beside Nathan. "How did that happen?"

"No idea. She was beside me one minute then sitting down the next. She must have felt it coming on."

"The naloxone helped, so it's an opioid."

'This is way nastier than fentanyl. It's probably carfentanil, and whoever made this intended for it to kill."

"She gonna be okay?" Hillary asked.

"She's breathing on her own, but—" His throat spasmed with emotion.

"But what?"

"She hasn't breathed adequately for a while. The question is, will she have brain damage?"

68

Authorities suspected my complicity in the attacks, but if I made smart decisions, they'd have trouble catching me. Even if they did, the FBI couldn't possess much evidence linking me to the attack. Maybe circumstantial evidence at best, if anything. They may never get a conviction.

But Nathan knew I'd become a jihadist. I was certain of it. He knew me better than anyone in America. At least he knew Hamid, the person I'd been before America's betrayal had snatched my country and my family away from me.

But did he know I'd become Zabihullah the Slayer?

The FBI would need Nathan to build a case against me. The years Nathan and I had lived together on Special Forces bases in Afghanistan meant he knew how I thought—or used to think—and he'd anticipate my moves, despite his failure to see the fire burning inside of me. Nobody else understood me like him, and no one would be as motivated to catch me.

That's why I needed to kill him.

This was more than revenge, more than making the man I'd trusted pay for his country's betrayal. With Nathan gone, I'd be safer and free to continue my jihad. We had much left to do, and I wouldn't rest until Americans suffered the way I had. Sheikh Omar Yemeni's plan to kill their children would do that.

A shudder passed through me. *Killing children.* American deserved it because their government represented them, but children didn't vote. They didn't understand the world. They owned no guilt.

Tara's image came to me, more real than ever. She flashed those eyes, her beautiful brown eyes. Sad eyes.

"I need to do this," I said.

She pouted.

I reached my hand out to touch her, and my fingers wiggled in air. She evaporated. Had she really been there? Was I crazy?

"I'm sorry."

I unfolded the cloth in my lap and lifted the Smith & Wesson .357 revolver. Six shots with serious knockdown power. Revolvers were old school, but they didn't jam. If six bullets weren't enough to take Nathan down, then I would die.

I'd failed to kill him before because I worried about concealing my identify. Now that he knew, I was free to get closer and do it the right way. As long as I escaped with no one witnessing the deed, I'd be better off than before, freer to pursue jihad. I should have killed him when Omar's assassin, Mona al-Busiri, slit Ali Hafeez's throat. That traitor. But agents had known Nathan and I rode together, and they would have arrested me. Besides, I needed Nathan as my alibi to prove I had no role in the killing. They couldn't know I'd planned the entire thing.

But I didn't need Nathan anymore.

I wouldn't make the same mistake I did on the river. I'd tried to be too clever. A mannequin doll as bait. How ridiculous. And planning to shoot from the deck of a boat had lessened the chance of success. I couldn't blame Makhmud. We'd been too far away and shooting from an unstable platform. It was a low-probability attempt. Makhmud had come close. I felt badly for him.

It wasn't his fault that I'd had to put two bullets behind his ear and dump him in a landfill. I couldn't have anyone tie me to that attempt, and he'd seen too much.

Killing Nathan would be hard. He'd be more guarded now. Every time I glimpsed him, his eyes darted around. He knew another attempt was coming. I'd followed him twice, but only in spurts. I knew where he lived and worked. He also occasionally drove his daughter to his ex-wife's house, but I never knew when, and following him that long would never work. My choices were home or work.

I leaned back in the seat and fondled my prayer beads.

Eventually, he'd show himself, and next time, I'd do it up close and personal.

69

Nathan sat in his car outside his ex-wife's residence, preparing to pick up Amelia. He reached for the door as Rahimya called. The demands of being an agent never ceased. He leaned back into his seat and answered.

"I have an update on Bridget," Rahimya said, her tone cold and impersonal, like a teacher delivering a failing grade.

Nathan froze. "How bad?"

"She responded to the naloxone, as you know, but . . ."

"But? Just tell me."

"She's functioning fine . . . physically, but she hasn't woken up yet."

Nathan sank into his seat, falling farther and farther, disappearing into the earth. "What does that mean?"

"She's still in a coma."

"Is there brain activity?"

"The doctors haven't finished her neurological testing. The verdict's not in yet on brain damage."

Nathan's stomach turned. "Is this normal? I mean, does this happen with overdoses?"

"It's not a good sign. They're transporting her to a facility in DC tomorrow."

"What are her chances of recovery?"

"I asked that too." Rahimya's voice softened. "The doctor wouldn't put a number on it, but I pressed him. He said the longer she doesn't respond, the worse the outcome. He estimated she had a 25 percent chance of waking up."

"Shit, shit, shit."

"Don't give up hope. He'll know more later today."

"You'll call me when you get an update?"

"Of course."

Bridget's family. Pain pierced Nathan's chest. "What about her father and brothers?"

"They're with her at the hospital."

"All of them."

"Yes."

Not a good sign either. At least Bridget finally found a way to drag her family away from work and into one room together. He wanted to cry.

"Nathan?"

"Yeah?" His voice had softened. He wanted all this to end.

"I don't know if you're religious, but pray for her. The doctor said we should."

"I will."

Nathan hung up and closed his eyes. *Please, God, help her. She's fighting evil for you. She's one of the good ones.*

Nathan gripped the steering wheel hard, the weight of the world on his shoulders. The possibility of losing Bridget loomed, but even if she woke up, the life she'd known could be over, depending on how much brain damage her oxygen-deprived body had incurred. Everything seemed to be falling apart. Hamid's betrayal would never leave him. The lives of those victims in New York, Philadelphia, and around the country were on his head. Maybe they'd have been killed anyhow, even if he'd never spotted Hamid at the mosque, but Nathan had brought Hamid inside the investigation, which at a minimum, resulted in one of his CIs being murdered and the other critically injured.

I fucked up.

Nathan steeled himself, then he exited his Mustang and turned for the house. The front door swung open as he reached the sidewalk, and Reagan stepped onto the stoop. She frowned when she saw him, and the crow's feet around her eyes deepened. Nathan's heart fluttered.

"Is Amelia okay?"

"She's fine," Reagan said, holding her hands up to calm him. "But we need to talk."

She intercepted him halfway up the walk.

"What's wrong?" he asked.

"You've been gone for three days, your allotted time to have Amelia."

Anger welled inside him. "I was in Philadelphia. I watched hundreds of corpses carried out of the Wells Fargo Center. Our country's under attack and—"

"I know, I know," she said, her tone softening. "Listen, I don't want to fight, and I know how important your work is, but . . ."

His anger wasn't as quick to dissipate. "But what?"

"This constant whisking of Amelia between us, sometimes in the middle of the night . . . it's not good for her. It's scary."

"For you or her?"

Her face hardened. "Amelia needs stability. With everything's that happening in the world, she's terrified. All her friends are freaking out too. It's all anyone can talk about. Waking her up and shuffling her from my house to yours creates anxiety. Her teacher said—"

"Yeah, I heard about the fight. Thanks for mentioning that."

"You were busy, and it's not the fight. Her grades are slipping, and her teacher said she can't focus. None of the kids can."

"I'm trying to prevent these attacks from happening again."

Reagan crossed her arms and pulled them into her chest. She bit her lip and looked at her sandals, then met his stare. "I think it's best . . . best for Amelia, if she stays with me and Diego.

"You mean—"

"Just temporarily, until your schedule becomes more regular and our country returns to normal."

Nathan put his hands on his hips. "We may never get back to normal, and if you take full custody of her, the judge may accept those arrangements as a permanent fix."

"It's what's best for Amelia. For now."

"I'm not losing my daughter."

"I'm not asking you to give her up, and I'll make it clear to the court. We can type up an informal agreement."

His traps hardened into monkey's fists. "We can manage—" Nathan's phone vibrated in his pocket. He pulled it out to shut it off.

A text from Kei displayed on the screen. *Call me. 911.* Kei hadn't used that code before.

"I've got to return this."

Reagan scowled. "See what I mean?"

"The bodies are piling up."

"Take it." She tapped her foot and looked away.

Nathan dialed. "What's happening?"

"Hey, Boss," Kei said. "We got a problem."

Frustration tightened Nathan's chest. "Tell me."

"It's my friend in Shanghai. They sent a big shipment to the States."

"Carfentanil?

"Yeah, but it's been altered."

"Altered how?"

"Enhanced. It's the deadliest opioid ever made."

Nathan grimaced. Things couldn't get any worse. "When will it arrive?"

"It already crossed the border into California. Something bad is about to happen."

70

Nathan parked outside a two-story townhouse with dusty brick and faded blue shutters and waited for Jim and Tom to jog around back. The residence belonged to a charity affiliated with the Muslim Brotherhood, and phone tolls linked the organization to several of Imam Qadir's benefactors. Public records indicated no tenant had lived there for over a year, but fugitives didn't sign leases, and the dwelling was in Falls Church, close to the mosque. It was worth a shot, because even the slightest of chances had to be checked out. The cost in lives for failure grew too high.

Nathan nodded at Three Balls. "Let's see if this asshole is here."

Nathan adjusted his ballistic vest as they exited the car. Body armor had a way of riding up on him in vehicle seats. He tugged up his belt and tapped his Glock with his elbow to confirm its position. Nathan scanned the windows as they approached the front door. Dark and dusty. The place didn't appear inhabited, but Qadir wouldn't advertise his presence.

They mounted the front steps and stood on either side of the door. Three Balls knocked. No answer. He tried the knob. Locked.

Nathan leaned over a shrub and peeked through a window into the living room. No furniture, no sign of life. He dismounted the steps and skirted the scraggly bushes sticking out of mulch. His image reflected in the dusty windows. The overgrown grass had turned brown. He examined the steps where a thin film of dust coated the concrete. If Qadir had used that door, his shoes would have left imprints.

Nathan keyed his radio. "No answer. Door's secured."

"Copy," Jimmy responded. "The back door is locked too. Looks empty."

"Guess that's it," Three Balls said.

Nathan observed the house. There wasn't a single thing that proved Qadir or any radical Islamist had ever visited it. The charity probably owned a rental property, and they'd let their investment fallow. Nathan couldn't get a search warrant, because the linkage to Qadir was too weak, but they weren't looking for evidence anyway—just a fugitive. And a terrorist one at that.

Jim and Tom rounded the corner with their shoulders sagging. None of the group's tips had led to anything.

"This was a long shot," Jim said.

Nathan sighed. "Still, I was hoping . . ."

A hopeless, impotent sensation infected him and bled his energy. He carried a gun and badge and had sworn to defend the constitution, yet he'd done nothing to protect his fellow citizens against the rash of terrorism. He'd been relegated to watching it unfold on television like everyone else. The images spread terror through the population, but a different emotion consumed Nathan.

Rage.

"We're searching this fucking house," Nathan said.

"Where's our warrant?" Jim asked.

Three Balls smirked at Nathan. He knew what Nathan was thinking, understood the stakes.

"They're murdering innocent people all over the country, and they own this place. I don't give a shit about a piece of paper. I'm checking inside. If we don't stop them, more people will die. Those victims could be us or our loved ones."

Jim crossed his arms. "That doesn't give us the right—"

"I didn't ask you to go inside," Nathan said. "Wait here."

Nathan jogged around back, pressing on the side windows as he went. The owners had buttoned up the place.

He climbed onto the weathered deck and knelt beside the sliding door.

He whipped out his knife and jammed the blade underneath the door. He pushed hard and lifted the door off its metal track. Dr. Jacob Mandel's killer had used the same technique.

Tom and Jim came around the corner. Nathan glanced back at them then pried the door away from the frame. He stood and wrestled it out of the way. The room was dark and quiet.

"Not a good idea," Jim said.

"Stay here," Nathan said.

Nathan drew his gun and stepped across the threshold into the kitchen. The space smelled of abandonment—dusty and still, like a tomb.

Tom and Jim entered behind him with their weapons out. Three Balls probably waited out front, in case they flushed a suspect.

This was an illegal search. They all knew it, but no one said anything more on the subject. They weren't searching for evidence, just trying to find a killer. If Qadir hid inside, it wouldn't matter how they'd found him. His arrest warrant would stand, and they'd only lose whatever evidence they found inside as fruit from the poisonous tree.

Tom and Jim split left and right, moving through the living room and hallway. Nathan slipped into the kitchen. He cracked open the refrigerator, and a sour odor punched him in the face. Mold covered the inside of the empty refrigerator. His heart sank. If Qadir had been there, he would've used a working fridge.

"All clear," Jimmy called out.

"I'm going upstairs," Tom said.

Nathan hurried down the hall and followed him up the steps. The bathroom door was open, and the shower curtain, missing. Empty. They popped open the master bedroom door and flooded into the room. Nathan raked his barrel across the empty space.

He nodded at Tom, and they moved across the hall to the last bedroom. Nathan flung the door open.

The room was devoid of furniture or any sign it had ever been occupied. Nathan walked across the floor to the open closet door. Empty too.

Nobody home.

"Shit," Nathan said.

Another dead end. How high would the body count reach?

"Uh, guys," Three Balls radioed. "Meet me out front when you finish."

"The place is abandoned," Nathan responded.

"Open the front door," Three Balls said.

Nathan and Tom exchanged looks then pounded downstairs. Jim unlatched the door and opened it. Three Balls stood on the stoop, watching something on his phone.

"Holy shit, guys," Three Balls said.

"What you got?" Nathan asked.

"Another attack."

Nathan moved beside him. A live camera feed from a news traffic helicopter showed the Vegas Strip, and the angle wobbled. The scroll read, *Terror in Las Vegas.*

Bodies littered the sidewalks along the street, and traffic had stopped. At least a dozen cars had crashed into each other. Police lights flashed around the city, and faces filled hotel room windows as people watched the scene.

"What happened?" Nathan asked.

"Hell if I know," Three Balls said. "There's gotta be 200 bodies—"

A black drone flashed across the screen beneath the helicopter, and the camera bobbed as the pilot took defensive action. The frame righted, and the drone came back into view. The drone descended close to the street, and a thick stream of dark-red vapor poured out of its tail.

"That fucking thing is gassing them," Three Balls said.

Nathan wanted to vomit. People were dying—civilians, innocents—and he watched from over 2,000 miles away, powerless to stop it.

Maroon clouds billowed over the street. None of them spoke. There was nothing to say. A second helicopter came into view, this one belonging to the Las Vegas Police Department, and the news crew filmed it chasing the drone. But what could it do? They could shoot it down, but any bullets that missed might kill someone below.

"Damned nightmare," Three Balls said.

"Only it's real," Nathan said, "and it won't end until we kill Zabihullah."

"You mean catch him," Jim said.

"Nope. There's only one way to stop these monsters."

71

Nathan stepped off the elevator into his dark condo. City lights glowed outside, casting shadows on his wood floor, and he stood there listening to the silence. The place didn't feel like home without Amelia. The same thing had happened after Reagan left him, but Amelia's presence had kept him human. Now she was gone too.

He sloughed across the floor and plunked onto the couch without turning on the lights. He wanted a scotch. Badly. But he couldn't drink and be effective. He'd only come home to catch a few hours' sleep before returning to the office. Booze might buoy his spirits, but it would be a fake mood, and it would disrupt his sleep, which he needed more than anything.

Jihadists were out there, scheming and preparing. He was obligated to work harder than them, especially since he played defense. They knew their plan, and he didn't. He may not prevent the next attack, but if he failed, it wouldn't be from lack of effort. Every moment he did anything but investigate was lost time. And time meant saving lives. How hard would he work if the next victim was a friend or family member? He owed the citizens who entrusted him with a badge. He would work himself to death to save them.

But so far, he'd failed.

Over 270 people dead in Vegas, according to early estimates, and that number would soar once area hospitals reported admissions and rescuers discovered more bodies.

He needed to talk to someone. But Meili was in Taiwan, Bridget still hadn't awoken from her coma, and Reagan had made a play for full custody.

He dialed Meili's cell.

It took a few seconds to connect, then the strange double ring of a foreign cell-service carrier rattled in his ear. Someone answered, and the din of traffic came over the line.

"I only have a moment," Meili said.

"Where are you?"

"Can't say."

"You coming home next week?"

She was silent. Cars honked and tooted in the background. A tuk-tuk?

"Meili?"

"I'll be back sooner. I . . . something happened, and I needed to leave."

He tensed. Was she in danger? "What happened?"

"Not over the phone."

"Are you still in Taiwan?"

"We left. Fast."

His protective urges took hold. He flexed his muscles, ready for combat. "I'll meet you wherever you are and escort you back."

"The agency, er, we've got it covered. I'll be back in a day or two."

"Who's with you?

"Please don't worry."

"Are you hurt?"

"I'm fine. We had a close call, but we got out. I'll tell you everything when—"

"Meili?"

"I've got to run."

The line disconnected. Nathan checked the screen. She was gone.

He cracked his neck. What kind of incident? Had the Chinese government come after her? Or the Triads?

Nathan paced.

Things looked dark, grim. Threats came from every angle, and he remained powerless to stop them. Someone imperiled the woman he cared about, and he couldn't do anything to help her. A massive load of supercharged carfentanil had crossed the border, but Kei didn't know exactly where. Bridget may never recover. Hamid had double-crossed him and betrayed everything they'd fought to create. The Phantoms had murdered hundreds of Americans, and a bigger attack appeared imminent.

Nathan couldn't fix any of it.

The room tightened around him, as if the air pressure had increased. It squeezed him, making it hard to breathe.

Reagan had ripped Amelia out of his life, insisting she keep Amelia until his schedule normalized—but would that ever happen? Would she retain sole custody? He could fight her in court, but Reagan was right. He'd been working eighteen-hour days, barely eating or sleeping, and that wasn't a suitable environment for his daughter, which is why he'd agreed to give her up for now. That was best for her, but would he lose her forever?

Nathan's life was falling apart.

He stopped pacing and breathed in deeply. He had agency. He couldn't protect Meili wherever she was now, but she'd be home in a couple of days, and then he'd watch over her like a sheepdog. His team had missed the carfentanil shipment, but if he could arrest the Slayer and the Phantoms, he could defend the country he loved. If he stopped the attacks, he may get Amelia back. Nathan nodded to himself. He knew what had to be done.

He must stop Hamid.

72

Nathan rested his elbows on his cubicle desk and blinked to focus his weary eyes. He'd been there since five o'clock, after he'd given up his feeble attempt to sleep—a nightmare-filled three-hour wrestling match with his sheets.

Rahimya walked into his peripheral vision.

A dart of fear flashed through him. "News about Bridget?"

Rahimya smiled. "She's awake."

A weight lifted off him. He inhaled deeply and filled his lungs for the first time in days, as if breaking the surface after a deep dive where he'd almost drowned.

"Her mind . . . is she cognitively sound?"

"She's groggy, and they're still testing, but the doctor said she answered their questions appropriately. He seemed very positive."

Nathan covered his face and focused on his breath. *Bridget's okay.*

"I wanted you to know right away," Rahimya said.

He grinned. "Thank you."

"By the way, you look like death. Did you go home last night?"

"I came in early to formulate a plan. It's incredibly difficult to catch a terrorist in a free society, and Hamid knows our playbook."

"He needs to conspire with others to plan, obtain materials, conduct surveillance . . . everything that makes him vulnerable."

"It hasn't so far," Nathan said. "He has ISIS supporting him, which means funding from Qatar or Iran, or both. And his team executes like professionals. The Phantoms have experience killing. We're not chasing a lone wolf with psychological problems. These guys are the real deal."

"We've caught monsters before, and you've taken out formidable adversaries yourself. If the SEALS can kill Osama bin Laden, we can reach out and touch anybody."

"In some ways, catching Hamid will be harder. He helped us take down high-value targets in Afghanistan. He's familiar with all our tools."

"He has to come out from under a rock to fight," Rahimya said.

"Yeah, but we will pay for every operation with American lives. He knows us. He knows me. He understands how we investigate, but more importantly, he's familiar with our limitations. He . . ."

A germ of an idea sprouted in Nathan's mind.

"What?" Rahimya asked. "I don't like that look on your face."

He looked at her. "Hamid knows our limitations."

"I heard you the first time."

"We can use that against him."

"Meaning?"

"He won't expect me to do things we're not allowed to do."

"Right, because we're prohibited from doing them."

"Catching him is what matters. I can't get ahead of him by following procedure."

Rahimya tensed. "Catching him will stop the attacks, but if you break the rules, he could walk free."

"I'm not talking about violating the law . . . not exactly, but I don't plan to follow the FBI handbook to the letter. We should act differently, do the unexpected."

Rahimya shook her head. "That sounds good in theory, but how—"

Nathan leapt to his feet. "I'm an idiot."

She smiled. "No argument here. What is it?"

"We have something Hamid wants as much as he wants to destroy America."

"And what's that?"

"Me."

"Nathan—"

"He tried to kill me. I know that was him behind the shooting in West Potomac Park. He wants me dead."

"Why would he single you out?"

"Because we abandoned him and his family."

"You're not responsible for failed US foreign policy. I know you think you can control everything, but our withdrawal from Afghanistan was miles above your pay grade. Even our generals couldn't organize an ordered retreat. Politics drove that train off the cliff."

"It's irrational, but emotion drives Hamid's actions. What he experienced after we left unbalanced him. He wants to hurt America, and I'm the face of the country that left him to die."

"You did your job."

"Combat is more than a job. You know what it took to convince foreigners to risk everything to fight with us. I convinced him he was saving his country. I sold him on freedom, and he bought in. Then we fed him and his countrymen to the wolves."

"Not your fault."

"I bought the lie too. I trusted our government to follow through with its promises."

Rahimya tapped her tongue against her teeth. "You want to use his hatred against him?"

"I want to give him what he wants."

"Meaning?"

"If he wants to murder me, let's give him a shot."

"The FBI would never approve that."

Nathan smiled. "Exactly."

73

I sat alone in a panel van on Seventh Street across from the Capital One Arena and stared through Tara's face floating before me. Farzana and Tara stayed with me most of the time now. They hovered in my vision, forcing me to look through them to conduct business. They glared, their disapproval palpable.

But I fought for them.

I waged jihad for all Afghans, and for Muslims around the world. I'd tasted the bitter fruit of freedom with the constant requirement to produce to survive, and I'd seen the fragility of governments based on the will of the people. They required free-thinking citizens with the courage to sacrifice for their values, but political corruption and weakness crumbled that dream.

I killed the infidels to strengthen the Ummah. One day, Islam would rule the world under the total authority of an Islamic caliphate, and all men would live under Sharia. Allah's will shall reign on earth.

"We will be victorious."

That was why I risked coming out of hiding when the FBI hunted me. At least I assumed they did. I concealed myself in a van with food-delivery placards affixed to the door so I could watch the exit until I saw him.

Eventually, Nathan would emerge.

His office was upstairs in a commercial building inside the arena complex. Nathan parked in the underground garage, and I'd considered shooting him there, but I'd spotted security cameras inside, and the garage offered few avenues of escape.

But Nathan went out for lunch sometimes. Approaching him on the street was a possibility, though it entailed too many variables and carried uncertain risk. Best to follow him into a restaurant and kill him inside. Just walk up to his table and shoot him in the head, then flee through the pandemonium. I could—

Nathan exited his office onto Seventh Street, between Clyde's and the Capital One Arena. My heart raced with excitement.

He stood on the sidewalk and glanced around. I stayed still. He turned and strode down Seventh Street at a good pace.

This was it. I'd do it here. Now. The moment of my revenge had come.

74

Nathan wandered down the west side of Seventh Street, heading toward Pennsylvania Avenue at a leisurely pace. He'd taken the same route around the same time, three days in a row, even taking pictures and posting them on Facebook. If Hamid had Nathan's office under surveillance, he'd have discovered Nathan's "vulnerability."

For the first two days, Nathan had rented adjoining rooms at the Hotel Monaco, but Hamid hadn't bitten, and he'd had to pull the plug on his private-lure operation that cost him over $350 per day, plus the time away from their investigation. Rahimya had refused to sanction an operation to lure Hamid into a trap because it knowingly put Nathan in jeopardy, though down deep she had to know it was worth the risk. So, Nathan did this on his own.

A reckless act.

But this wasn't the first time he'd put himself in peril to catch bad guys, and if he survived, it wouldn't be the last.

He waited for the light at Pennsylvania Avenue and glanced around. No indicators of surveillance, and no sign of Hamid. Was Hamid crazy enough to still be in DC? Would he waste time coming for Nathan?

Nathan's gut told him that's exactly what Hamid would do.

Nathan fast-walked past the National Archives to Constitution Avenue.

Ironically, using himself as bait was self-preservation, because if he failed to address Hamid's attempt to assassinate him—something he knew in his heart was true—he'd end up dead. And he couldn't investigate anything from the morgue.

Nathan crossed Constitution Avenue where the National Gallery of Art's Sculpture Garden spanned the entire block, and on the far end, across Madison Drive, the National Mall stretched out from the Capitol to the Washington Monument. Finding a place to lure a terrorist without endangering civilians was next to impossible in Washington, DC—yet another reason Rahimya had nixed Nathan's plan—but victory went to the bold.

So did death.

Nathan continued west along Constitution Avenue, increasing his visibility and giving any potential watchers a better chance to find him. He'd been trained not to follow a routine and expose himself like this. He intentionally made himself vulnerable. *Idiot.*

He paused on the sidewalk and took out his phone, pretending to make a call to give him cover to spot surveillance. Still no sign of the enemy. They could be present and concealed, but what were the chances these jihadists had proper surveillance training?

But Hamid did.

The thought chilled him. Hamid had been with Nathan on dozens of surveillances in Afghanistan and knew the basics. If Hamid joined the assassination team, he could avoid detection—at least for short distances. That realization settled into Nathan's bones, and a flicker of fear tickled his belly.

Nathan pretended to talk on the phone as he ran his fingers through his hair and paced back and forth. If the roles were reversed, Nathan would wear a disguise and use a vehicle, in case his target left the office in a car. Unless Hamid had observed Nathan's route and waited for him to arrive. That's how Nathan would have done it.

Nathan continued west, following the wrought-iron fencing that surrounded the Sculpture Garden. If Hamid's men took the bait, Nathan would lead them inside the maze of art and greenery. He would—

There. Across the street, a man wearing sunglasses and a baseball cap stood outside the archives and glanced his way. The movement had been intentional. The man watched him. Nathan felt it. Knew it.

Hamid.

Nathan looked away to avoid signaling he'd spotted his tail. His heart raced. His trap had worked. But was it really Hamid? The man concealed his face beneath the brim of his cap and mirrored glasses, but he couldn't change his body size and shape, not without significant effort, and Nathan hadn't shown Hamid how to do that. The shape of the man's face and skin tone were right too.

The man watched him, following from the opposite side of the street, a decent technique, but he seemed unable to restrain himself from looking directly at Nathan. That was human nature, but a rookie mistake. It took willpower and skill to appear like a disinterested pedestrian, far more than people realized.

Trust your instinct.

Would this be the Slayer's assassination attempt? Nathan's body tingled.

He dialed Rahimya.

"What is it, Nathan? I'm in a meeting and—"

"It's Hamid. I found him."

"Where are you?"

"Constitution between Seventh and Ninth, beside the Sculpture Garden. He's paralleling me outside the Archives."

"You lured him? I told you not to—"

"You can yell at me later. He's here now. Send everybody."

"Give us ten minutes. Keep him on the hook and stay on the phone to vector us in."

A van pulled to the curb near the Seventh Street garden entrance. Hamid looked at the van.

"Nathan, are you listening?"

"It's too late. The hit team is here."

"Get inside. Can you make it into the Archives?"

"Negative. I'll lead them into the Sculpture Garden. Surround it, then come in and get him."

The van rolled toward him.

"Gotta go."

"Nathan—"

He slipped the phone into his pocket and walked toward the garden's western entrance.

The van closed.

Nathan reached the gate, and his heart jolted. The gate was padlocked. The van was only twenty yards away. Hamid watched from across the street. This was it.

Nathan broke into a trot.

75

Ahead, the traffic signal at Ninth Street changed, and southbound traffic flowed across Constitution. He sprinted across Ninth, just ahead of the traffic, drawing a honk from a taxicab. He looked over his shoulder. The van screeched to a stop at the light.

Nathan had become both predator and prey. He had the opportunity to escape, but these were the men who had killed hundreds of Americans. The urge to turn and confront his assassins welled inside him.

But that would be suicide.

Hamid paralleled along the north side of Constitution, but he hadn't made the light, and he stared through traffic at Nathan. Did he know he'd been burned? Nathan had run, but they might assume he'd hurried to beat oncoming cars. Nathan needed to keep them on the hook.

He slowed to a walk. He approached the National Museum of Natural History, which extended all the way to Twelfth Street. Nathan turned south on Ninth Street and took out his phone. It had disconnected, so he called Rahimya back.

"What happened?" she asked, breathless.

"Change of plans. The Sculpture Garden was locked. I'm outside the Natural History Museum."

"They still following?"

Nathan surveyed Constitution out of the corner of his eye. The light changed and westbound traffic resumed. The van was the first vehicle, and it turned onto Ninth.

"The hit crew's coming. They're in a white panel van. The DC plate starts with *FN*."

"Is Hamid still on foot?"

Nathan chanced a look. "Yeah, he crossed Constitution, but he slowed. He's suspicious."

"Get indoors."

"I can stay out here as a decoy until you arrive . . . maybe."

"Take cover in the museum, and that's an order."

The van neared.

"Yeah, okay. That's my only play unless I shoot it out right here."

"Nathan, I'm warning you—"

"I'm headed inside. They won't try anything in a government building with armed security guards. I'll try to monitor them, and if we're lucky, they'll wait for me to come out.

Nathan turned onto Madison Drive toward the museum's main entrance. The van approached, and the sound of its engine reached him.

He increased his pace, trying to appear unworried, and climbed the stone stairs opposite a vehicle barrier. He approached towering pillars, and his neck tingled with vulnerability, but he couldn't turn or they'd know he'd spotted them and flee.

Nathan reached the front door with its long, tinted windows in brass settings. He squinted at the fuzzy image of the white van in the reflection. It had parked opposite the entrance.

Nathan pushed through the heavy door before the jihadists had time to shoot. He entered a vestibule where bored security guards monitored two metal detectors. A woman and two small children shuffled through the detector on his right. The machine chirped, and the red lights blinked, but the heavyset female officer didn't react, and they continued into the atrium.

Nathan looked back out through the glass. The van hadn't moved.

He put his phone to his ear. "I'm inside, and our suspects are out front."

"Where's Hamid?"

Nathan scanned the street. "I can't see him."

"We're five out. Every agent in the office is headed your way."

"Have them hunt for Hamid. The hit crew's secondary. Hamid's wearing blue jeans, a black jacket, Nationals baseball cap, and sunglasses. He's the prize."

"Stand by," Rahimya said. Her muffled voice came through the speaker as she broadcast Hamid's description.

The van remained stationary. They wouldn't dare come inside, but would they wait to ambush him when he left?

"We're spreading out to contain him," Rahimya said. "It'll delay our arrival, but I don't want him slipping past us."

"Don't let him get away. We may not get another chance."

"Copy. Sit tight and stay indoors."

Nathan's stomach knotted. What did Hamid think Nathan was doing in a museum in the middle of a workday? The only logical explanation would be to meet a source. What if Hamid wanted to identify—

Hamid stepped into view.

Nathan's senses heightened. He heard everything, saw everything, sensed everything. He called Rahimya.

"Hold on," she said. "We're casting a net over."

"Hamid's standing outside the main entrance."

Hamid headed for the doors.

"Where exactly?" she asked.

"He's coming inside. He's hunting me."

"Hide."

"I can take him."

"Don't provoke a confrontation until we arrive. He wants to kill you, but let's avoid violence inside. We'll surround the place and take down all of them simultaneously."

Nathan hurried to the metal detector. He could flash his credentials and explain the Glock beneath his jacket, but that took time, and he needed to get out of sight.

He trusted his initial assessment of the seemingly disinterested guard and stepped through the detector. It beeped and flashed. He dug his keys out of his pocket and jingled them for the guard.

"Go ahead," she said.

Nathan rushed into the atrium with its fifty-foot ceilings, white marble, and open balconies on the second and third floors. A life-sized elephant statue stood on a pedestal, with its tusks pointed at him and its trunk raised high. Twenty tourists milled around.

Where to hole up?

Behind the elephant, two wide stairwells rose to the second floor. Nathan raced past the statue and mounted the stairs on the left. He paused halfway up and glanced over his shoulder.

Hamid scanned the crowd in the lobby.

He stared directly at Nathan.

76

Nathan turned away without looking—which was hard to do—and climbed the steps. He pretended to be consumed with his call. He needed Hamid inside where they could trap him.

Nathan turned and used his peripheral vision to check the lobby. Hamid eyed the front door then passed through the metal detector. It flickered but didn't beep. Was he unarmed?

Hamid moved into the atrium with purpose, his body a coiled spring.

Nathan called Rahimya.

"What's happening?" she asked.

"He's through security," Nathan said. "He spotted me."

"Why the hell would he follow you inside?

"Because he knows me. I taught him how to enter a building then flee out another exit before surveillance can react. He came in to ensure I don't escape. He doesn't realize he's the one being hunted."

"Stay out of sight until we arrive. We're one minute out."

"Negative. I'm leading him upstairs."

"Listen to me—"

"He came in so he wouldn't lose me," Nathan said. "He knows it's easy to slip away in the crowd, and he can do the same to us. I can take him."

"Too many civilians. Don't confront him."

"How many people will die if he eludes us?"

"I'm telling you—"

"Call me when you're here. Send a team inside but take out the van first."

"They still out front?"

"I can't tell."

"I'm calling MPD for backup."

Nathan reached the top and looked back at the lobby. Hamid headed for the stairs.

Instinct urged Nathan to draw his weapon and make the arrest, but if he confronted Hamid alone, the Phantoms might escape, or worse, come in with guns blazing. He should wait for Rahimya to set a cordon and send a team inside.

Only a few more minutes.

Nathan slipped into Bone Hall. Life-sized skeletons behind the thick glass of shadow boxes stared back at him. He hurried into the next room, past the fossils of apes, humans, and dinosaurs.

Footsteps tapped up the stairs. Hamid followed, but would he watch Nathan or assassinate him?

Nathan kept moving through the exhibits. Distance meant safety. If he avoided Hamid long enough, agents would trap him and possibly take the Slayer alive. Hamid would know what operations the Phantoms had planned, but whether he'd give them up was another matter.

Nathan entered a room with Egyptian mummies lying prone on tables. A group of girls, no older than his daughter, milled around pointing and whispering.

Shit. A school field trip. Bad luck. Nathan edged through the students headed for the exit on the far side.

Hamid rounded the corner before him.

Hamid jerked to a stop, as surprised as Nathan. Neither moved.

Nathan stared at Hamid, or Zabihullah, or whoever the hell he was now. The man he'd once known, his partner in combat, had vanished and been replaced by the Slayer—a killer of innocents and the mastermind behind the worst terrorist attacks in American history.

Nathan had to arrest him. Or kill him.

Hamid glared back at Nathan with those brown eyes Nathan had seen every day in Afghanistan, but now, fire raged behind them.

Murdering another human went against Nathan's genetic code, but killing in self-defense did not. If Nathan didn't shoot first, he'd be dead.

He brushed his jacket back and reached for his Glock.

Hamid ducked behind two girls, both of whom wore plaid skirts and white shirts with school crests over their breasts. A chrome revolver appeared in Hamid's hand.

Nathan drew.

Hamid grabbed a girl by her neck and yanked her off balance. She cried out and stumbled. He drew her against his body. A human shield.

The girl screamed. Her friend screamed. Children shouted and ran, but a few rooted to the ground, immobilized by fear.

Nathan fingered his trigger. "Drop it."

Hamid's stare cut into him as if the photons of reflected light were lasers, his darkness and hatred tangible.

Time slowed. Nathan's vision narrowed. Everything in the room faded into a hazy blur, except Hamid's revolver. Nathan's mind processed every detail. Saw it all.

Hamid jammed his barrel into the girl's neck. "Lower your gun."

"You can't escape," Nathan said. "It's over."

"It's only the beginning."

Nathan shivered. "Let her go."

"Throw your gun on the floor, or I'll splatter her brains all over the wall."

The girl gasped, and tears streamed down her face.

Nathan aimed at Hamid's forehead. He applied pressure to the trigger. If she didn't move, he could make the shot. Maybe.

Hamid wrestled her between them, as if he'd read Nathan's thoughts. He stayed in motion, making a precise shot almost impossible.

The cavalry would arrive soon. Nathan needed to stall.

"You're Zabihullah the Slayer."

Hamid smirked. "Your arrogance made you blind. The man you hunted stood beside you the entire time."

Nathan rotated to his right, looking for a shot. Hamid mirrored him, always in motion.

"Using low-tech weapons to avoid detection was brilliant. You knew we're tech focused."

"You Americans think you're so smart, but you know nothing."

People screamed downstairs. Had FBI agents entered the lobby? *Keep him talking.*

"Why opioids?"

"You came to my country spewing ideals of freedom, as if we could embrace individualism after thousands of years of tribalism. Only your pompousness allowed you declare opium a great evil."

"Drug trafficking *is* evil. It ruins lives. Over a hundred thousand Americans overdose every year."

Hamid spat on the floor. "Listen to your indignation. Your pharmaceutical companies make billions."

"Opioids are a medicinal miracle. It's their misuse that's wrong. Afghan traffickers create poison for people to abuse."

"We use it to escape our lives."

"There's no escaping reality. Traffickers don't alleviate pain, they cause it."

Hamid's barrel came off the girl and swung in Nathan's direction.

Move.

Nathan dove for the corner as a deafening explosion pierced his ears. He landed hard as glass shattered and bones clattered against the shadow box.

Nathan rolled around the exhibit and scrambled to his feet. He leveled his gun sights at the corner and waited for Hamid to appear. Where was Rahimya?

The girl whimpered.

"Such noble ideals," Hamid shouted, "yet your country is the biggest consumer in the world."

Nathan quick-peeked around the corner. Hamid dragged the girl toward the shattered glass, closer to Nathan—stalking him. Hamid wedged his barrel under the girl's chin. Everyone else had fled the room.

"Give it up, Hamid."

"Hamid is dead. You killed him. I'm Zabihullah now."

Hamid kept his head behind the girl's as he backed up toward the hallway on the opposite side. Nathan tracked him with his sights.

"You've lost your mind," Nathan said. "You've betrayed everything we've fought to achieve."

"You are the hypocrites. You trumpet morality, but your people consume the drugs."

"There's a difference between having ideals and not achieving them."

They circled each other. Sweat streaked down Hamid's face. The room reeked of perspiration and fear.

"Carfentanil exposed your weakness for the world to see."

"You dosed women and children."

"I gave you a taste of the death I've suffered."

"I thought you did this for your people."

"You can't understand what we've endured."

Footsteps pounded up the steps. Help was seconds away. Hamid had reached the far wall.

"How could you join those animals and hurt us?"

"Hurt you? You abandoned us and destroyed our country. You destroyed me."

"We fought side by side. You saved my life, and I saved yours."

Hamid's face hardened to stone. "That's when I thought you were my friend."

"I was your colleague *and* your friend."

"America brought this on herself."

"What happened to Afghanistan was unconscionable. What you suffered was . . . beyond horror. But killing innocent people won't bring your family back."

"Innocent people die in war."

"The Taliban and ISIS killed your family. They were the ones who—"

"Drugs killed them. America killed them. You scurried away in the night and sacrificed us."

Nathan nodded. "The administration poorly planned the withdrawal and badly executed it, but they didn't seek to kill civilians."

"Your politicians and the Americans who voted for them are responsible for betraying us. People died. My family died."

"Civilian deaths weren't our intent, unlike Islamists who seek their murder."

Hamid's eyes flared. "Either way, my wife and child are gone."

"Civilians shouldn't suffer, especially women and children."

"We're coming for your children next."

Hamid's words hatched dread inside Nathan. A cold fear seeped into his heart. "What does that mean?"

Hamid looked at his sandals. He said nothing.

"You daughter's innocence makes her loss worse, right?"

"Yes."

"Then why commit these crimes against God? The children in American are innocent too. Why destroy other families and make them suffer like you did?"

Hamid looked up. His eyes glistened.

"Hamid?"

Tears flowed down his cheeks. "I . . ."

Footfalls clomped down the hall behind Nathan. Had the SWAT team arrived? Nathan glanced behind him.

Five keffiyeh-wearing jihadists raced into the hallway carrying long guns.

Nathan looked back at Hamid.

He shrugged. "My people arrived first. As Allah wills it."

77

Nathan swung his Glock toward the approaching Islamists. He dropped his sights onto the first man's chest and double-tapped.

The man screamed and dropped his shotgun. The terrorist beside him slowed and pointed an AK-47 at Nathan. Flame flashed out of its barrel as the bullet cracked overhead and the shot echoed down the hall.

No time.

The overpressure of the 7.62 mm round whooshed past Nathan. He spun into the exhibit and charged Hamid.

Hamid's eye's widened in surprise.

Nathan extended his Glock without slowing. He aimed a foot over Hamid's head to avoid hitting the girl.

He fired.

Nathan's rounds punched into the exhibit's plexiglass and shattered a light inside.

Hamid ducked and dragged the girl backward. He raised his revolver, and flame shot out of the barrel. Dust puffed into the air where the bullet hit the drywall.

Nathan sprinted around the corner into a cell phone exhibit with Vegas-style billboards everywhere. He knelt behind cover and aimed at the corner, waiting. He couldn't confront Hamid until he dealt with the approaching jihadists. Even though he'd taken out the lead man, that still left four terrorists with carbines. They outgunned him.

Footsteps pounded on the other room as the men closed on him. Nathan peeked around the corner, staying low.

Hamid had regained his feet, and he held the girl with her neck in the crook of his arm. Two jihadists stood behind him with their carbines mounted and searching for their target.

Hunting him.

Nathan leaned out just enough to keep his barrel away from the wall. He punched his Glock toward a heavyset jihadist carrying a black-barreled rifle, not taking the time to aim. He fired twice.

Nathan dove back around the wall as a fusillade of gunfire erupted. High-velocity rounds punched through the wall, and a cloud of detritus sprayed the room. Digital screens exploded in flashes of glass and sparks.

He crawled away, keeping his head down. The visitors had fled the immediate area, but the museum had been full of people, and Nathan had to be careful not to hit civilians. Every shot he took came with a life-or-death responsibility.

But terrorists didn't care. They sought death for Americans and themselves.

He couldn't shoot it out with a group who had superior firepower and numbers, especially when he needed to watch every shot. He needed help.

Nathan scrambled to his feet. Time to escape and evade until reinforcements arrived. But where were they?

He slipped around a digital screen the size of a billboard and concealed himself. Despite the terrorist's advantage in numbers and weaponry, they'd need to move slow and ease around each exhibit to avoid getting ambushed.

Why weren't they using suppressing fire? Were they worried about conserving ammunition?

Nathan sprinted across the open center of the room into the Cellphone: Unseen Connections exhibit. Carbines erupted behind him and bullets smashed through digital screens, paper signs, and walls. A bullet ricocheted off a metal frame and a graph illustrating cell phone usage crashed beside him. Nathan juked, making himself a hard target. They couldn't see him and probably fired at the sound of his footsteps, but he couldn't slow down. He rounded a corner into the Objects of Wonder exhibit.

A boy, only a toddler, stood alone sucking his thumb. A wet spot soiled his pants.

Nathan bounded past glass cases that protected indigenous masks. He angled for him, and the child's eyes widened as he approached. Nathan bent and scooped the child into his arms. The kid struggled and kicked, but Nathan squeezed him against his hip, afraid to let go. He raced for the exit.

The gunfire silenced. Men shouted in Arabic behind him. They took their time stalking him. Being careful.

Nathan hefted the squirming boy and weaved past rows of ancient pottery. The child whimpered, and Nathan held tight. The boy would die if Nathan left him behind.

They approached the Garden Lounge, and Nathan stepped into a room filled with benches and plants. Greenery everywhere. He headed toward an elevator and stairwell in the far wall.

The elevator dinged. He stopped.

The doors opened, and two jihadists stepped out.

Nathan stood in the open. Exposed. They leveled their guns at him. Nathan swiveled and dove behind a bench as the gunfire shattered the silence. Bullets smashed into the bench, splintering wood. Leaves popped off the potted plants beside him.

Nathan landed hard on his elbow and side, protecting the boy. Pain flashed up his arm. He hunched over the child, shielding him with his body.

Nathan raised his Glock, ready to fight. More shots came from the area of the stairs. Duller pops—handguns.

The shooting stopped.

"Watch their hands," a man said.

Nathan peeked around the bench. Two agents in FBI parkas moved from the stairs with their guns pointed at the elevator. They crossed the room, aiming low.

"They're dead," the agent said.

"Blue, blue." Nathan said, letting them know he was a good guy.

The agents whirled around and headed to him. “We have Burke,” one said into his radio.

Nathan climbed to his feet. The boy stayed on the ground with his palms pressed against his ears. How much therapy would he need to recover from this?

“Four more are right behind me,” Nathan said. He pointed his Glock at the Objects of Wonder exhibit. “Zabihullah has a hostage.”

“What are they—”

Shouts came from the cell phone exhibit, followed by shooting. Then more gunfire. Carbines and handguns.

Nathan moved forward with his gun up.

“Watch the crossfire,” the agent said. “We’ve got teams moving through the stairwells.”

Nathan stopped at the entrance and covered the room. More shouts came from out of his sight. A man peered around the far corner.

Three Balls.

Nathan lowered his gun. “We’re good here.”

Three Balls came around the corner. He gave a thumbs-up then wiped the sweat off his forehead.

Nathan turned to get the child, but an agent had taken the boy by the hand and veered for the stairs.

Rahimya joined Three Balls, and Nathan hurried to them.

“Hamid?” Nathan asked.

“He’s not here,” she said. “Teams searching the bottom floor now.”

“He had a girl.”

“Brown hair and school uniform?”

He nodded.

“We found her curled into a ball in the bones exhibit. She’s fine.”

“Seal the exits,” Nathan said. “He can’t escape.”

“We have the perimeter covered,” Rahimya said. “He must be hiding in here.”

Nathan followed her back the way she’d come.

Her radio crackled. “Oh-One, Oh-Seven.”

“Go for One,” she said. “You have Jackpot?”

"Negative. First and second floors are clear. We moved everyone into the auditorium."

They passed through the cell phone exhibit where three jihadists lay handcuffed in pools of blood. All dead.

"Keep them there," Rahimya said. "Zabihullah's in the building. Make sure he's not hiding among the civilians."

They crossed through Bone Hall into the O. Orkin Insect Zoo. Rahimya held her radio to her mouth. "All units, we have our primary suspect in the building. I need a thorough search. He's in here somewhere. Check cabinets and closets. He must—"

Nathan touched her arm, and she looked at him. He pointed to the emergency stairwell exit. Hamid's black windbreaker, baseball cap, and sunglasses lay in a pile beside the door.

"He fled," Nathan said. "Alert the perimeter team."

"All units, Oh-One," Rahimya broadcast. "Target subject used an emergency exit on the west side."

"Who's out there?" Nathan asked.

"Murphy's on Twelfth," Rahimya said. She keyed her handheld radio. "Oh-Four, Oh-One."

No answer.

"Oh-Four, you on?"

Nothing.

"Can any unit get eyes on Oh-Four?"

"Break, break," an agent cut in, his voice high with adrenaline. "Agent down. Agent down. Murphy's hit."

Nathan looked at Rahimya, his stomach in a knot. "Hamid escaped."

"Not yet," she said. "Every cop in the city is bearing down on us."

"It's too late. He's out, he's smart, and he knows us too well. Besides, he has a mission to . . ."

"What?"

"He's going after our children." An icy chill tickled his spine. The Phantoms planned to kill politicians' offspring, and the best place to do that would be at the Stephen Decatur Elementary School—home to a dozen children of cabinet members, US representatives and senators.

And Amelia.

78

Lily Batchelder stood before her fifth-grade class and enjoyed the rare moment of silence as her students mulled over today's surprise exam with their heads down and pencils scribbling in blue exam notebooks. Tests that impacted students' grades were her only tool for tempering their usual unbridled energy.

Movement in the back row drew her attention. Amelia sat beside Teddy Hunt and Maria Hernandez, both children of US senators, which meant they should take a test on the constitution seriously. Teddy leaned over and read Amelia's paper.

"Eyes on your own paper, Mr. Hunt," Lily said.

Teddy looked up like a burglar caught in a spotlight.

"Do your own work please."

A few children snickered. She cast a stern look around the room, and the children's attention returned to their tests.

She glared at Teddy, and he stared at his desk. His shoulders slumped.

Teddy wasn't the sharpest tool, but she'd never say that aloud or hold him to a lower standard. Work ethic mattered as much as intelligence, maybe more. If he tried harder, he'd succeed—a good life lesson. Besides, the poor kid had inherited bad genes. His father, the senator from New York, acted like a functional moron. What was the average IQ in the

Senate? It couldn't be much above the norm. The Founding Fathers would vomit if they witnessed what had happened to the government. And to the constitution.

Her cell phone vibrated in her drawer. *Damn.* She'd forgotten to silence it. She forbade her students from bringing electronics into the classroom, and she always hid hers to demonstrate the rules applied to everyone. Half these kids were addicted to their phones. Social media used neuroscience to trick users' brains into releasing endorphins to keep their eyeballs on the screen, and it worked exceptionally well with children. No one knew what the long-term effects would be on their cognitive development after kids spent their formative years seeking immediate gratification. Shorter attention spans seemed to be the first unintended outcome. Or maybe that had been intended. People who couldn't concentrate could be easily manipulated.

She cracked open her drawer and checked her phone.

Nathan Burke was calling.

She slipped her phone into her pocket. "Children, I need to step outside for a moment. I expect you to stay quiet and keep working. If anyone causes a problem while I'm gone, they'll receive a zero on their exam."

A few of faces whitened.

Lily scanned the room again to let them know she was serious, then she stepped into the hallway. The call had gone to voicemail, but she didn't bother waiting for it to finish. Nathan Burke was a serious man, and he and his family had been targeted by criminals or spies or other nefarious forces before. If he called when his daughter was in class, it must be serious.

She hit redial.

"Ms. Batchelder?" he answered.

"Sorry, I missed your call. We are taking a test on—"

"You've got to get the kids out of there," Nathan said.

Icy water trickled down her spinal canal. "What—"

"Terrorist are targeting the school. I called 911, and they're activating an emergency response, but these assholes want to kill my daughter. You need to escort every student out of that building."

"They're supposed to lock us down if there's a threat."

"That's why I'm calling you. This isn't coming from a disgruntled kid. The Phantoms are coming for you."

"Who?"

"ISIS. They may use drones."

"This school is solidly built. If we stay away from the windows . . ." Her voice trailed off as images of the aerosolized opioid attacks of the past days flashed in her mind. She couldn't breathe. "It's like the other incidents?"

"Probably another chemical attack. Evacuate everyone."

Fire alarms clamored through the halls.

The principal's voice came over intercom speakers mounted high on the wall. "Attention, all faculty. This is an emergency. Shut your doors and windows and barricade in place. This is not a drill."

"Mr. Burke?" Lily pressed the phone against her ear but couldn't hear anything over the clanging bells. What more did she need to know? Terrorists were coming to kill the kids. Her kids.

She flung open the classroom door. The children looked up in horror. Several had moved away from their desks. Amelia stared out the window.

"Amelia, get away from there," Lily said.

Lily's job was to follow her principal's direction and barricade themselves inside, but her duty was to her children. And Nathan was a special agent with inside information. Amelia was the target. If the principal wouldn't listen to reason, her only option was to act out of policy—a decision that could cost her the career she loved.

But her students came first.

"Ms. Batchelder," Amelia said, continuing to peer through the glass.

"Amelia, come here now. Students. Listen to me. I need everyone to line up in a row. We're going to file out of the school and—"

"Ms. Batchelder?" Amelia pointed outside. "Look."

Lily raced across the room. She dragged Amelia away from the glass and shielded the girl with her body. She looked out the window.

Two black drones raced toward them.

Too late.

79

The expression on that FBI agent's face when I'd burst through the museum exit doorway had imprinted itself on my mind. His surprise. His horror. What had he felt in that split-second before I pointed my revolver at his chest and shot him?

My .357 had bucked hard in my hand as the agent stumbled backward. Had he fallen because of my gun's knockdown power, or had he panicked? I'd pulled the trigger a second time as he went down. My ears plugged, so I hadn't heard his skull connect with the vehicle barrier. Had my shots snuffed out his life—or was it the blow to his head? Either way, I'd taken another life.

My wife and daughter judged me. Their presence smothered me and made it difficult to breathe.

I'd slipped into the agent's vehicle, a brown Ford that screamed *cop car* even without the blue bubble light on the dashboard. His keys remained in the ignition, and he'd left the engine running. The FBI had responded fast. Nathan must have spotted me long before I entered the museum. I should've known. During my years supporting the FBI in Afghanistan, I'd joined operations and debriefed informants, but I wasn't an agent. I'd learned by observing, but nothing replaced training and practice.

My success as a cell leader had only resulted from my intense hatred and thirst for vengeance.

I drove slowly up Twelfth Street. They'd be looking for the agent's car once they discovered his body, but until then, I didn't want to draw attention. Police lights flickered across the mall, down by the Capitol, and behind the Washington Monument. Emergency response vehicles had turned the city into a light show, like I'd seen in Dubai. Firetrucks, ambulances, and police cars merged with unmarked units from unrecognizable agencies as they descended on the museum.

I dug into my back pocket and pulled out an FBI baseball cap, the one I'd liberated from Nathan's car the night we killed his source in Jones Point Park. That, combined with my white Oxford shirt and official vehicle, should be enough cover—at least until they broadcast the car's description. Knowing the FBI and their procedures gave me an edge, but only a slight one.

I drove north on Twelfth Street and stopped at the light. Dismounted Metropolitan police held up traffic. An obese black woman in an MPD uniform saw my flashing blue light and waved me onto the street. I crossed Constitution and headed north, picking up speed. I turned onto Pennsylvania using my light to skirt traffic and headed east toward the Capitol.

Decision point.

I could return to the mosque and hole up, but they'd track the car, so I'd have to spend significant time on foot then sneak into the building. I could also take down the dashboard light and leave the city. That made sense, if saving my skin was my only goal. But my team remained in DC. Those who hadn't been killed amidst the volley of gunshots that had echoed in the museum. It was better that way. They were martyrs. All of them.

The sheikh's attack would launch at any minute. They'd need my support, though my heart wasn't in it.

A shadow flickered in my vision, and I turned to the passenger seat. Farzana sat in the seat with Tara in her lap, their bodies dark, cloudy images. Both stared daggers at me.

What?

A tear rolled down Tara's cheek.

"My darling, don't cry."

Her face continued to melt.

Panic rose in me. "I'm doing this for you. Both of you. And if the Americans had just stayed, or given us visas, or delayed their withdrawal until fighting season ended, you'd be here now. Alive—

A lump closed my throat, and tears filled my eyes. What was this? What brought on their anger? Didn't they understand I did this for them? I fought for Afghans betrayed by our masters.

Police cars flew past me in the other lane. The next attack may have started. I should head for New York to prepare for the second round, but something pulled me to it. What could I possibly do on the ground? Death would come from the air.

Still . . .

I glanced back at the passenger seat. Farzana's image had disappeared, but Tara remained. She scowled at me. Her eyes flared, black as night.

A chill passed through me. What did she want?

A thought huddled at the back of my skull, hiding from my conscience. It peeked into my heart and mind, and my stomach knotted.

What have I done?

80

Nathan sped across DC, headed for Stephen Decatur Elementary School. He had nothing pointing to the school as a terrorist target, other than his gut. Was his instinct accurate, or had parental love clouded his judgment. Either way, he'd protect his daughter—whatever the cost.

Rahimya had all the help she needed. Washington, DC, had become a chaotic mess as a multitude of law enforcement agencies sprang into action. Hundreds of MPD cops and FBI agents converged on the city to establish a perimeter and launch a manhunt.

He careened down Pennsylvania Avenue into Southwest DC listening to emergency traffic clog his radio. The capital would lockdown harder than it had since Union soldiers searched for John Wilkes Booth. He exited before he hit the Anacostia River and wormed through side streets toward Amelia's school.

Guilt threatened to draw him back to the manhunt, but protecting Amelia meant everything, and if he ignored his instinct and anything happened . . .

He shook away the thought. If anyone hurt his little girl, he'd never recover.

He drove up Seventeenth Street, and the school appeared in flashes between buildings. Nothing looked amiss. He was being paranoid. He'd get there, see she was fine, warn security to be on the lookout, and—

Something flashed in his vision. He squinted into the sun reflecting off the windshield. Two aircraft streaked low over the city.

Not aircraft—drones.

His pulse rattled like a snare drum. He stomped on the gas and accelerated, keeping an eye on the sky. Each drone carried an oblong canister beneath it with a spout dangling like a stinger.

Mechanical hornets.

He slid into the school's driveway, and his tires squealed as his Mustang leaned into the corner. The cabin filled with the stench of burning rubber. He shuffled the wheel, steering and counter-steering.

The mechanical buzzing of drones reverberated through the air. Nathan craned his neck to see through the windshield. The drones neared the school.

Two predators. Technological birds of prey. He must stop them from raining death onto the school. Amelia's school.

They flew toward the east wing where Ms. Batchelder's classroom was located. He glanced at the front doors. Why weren't they coming out? The school structure would afford them some protection from aerosolized chemicals, but once the drones pierced a window, air circulation would take care of the rest. Getting away from the building was their only hope.

He hugged the circular drive. His brakes grew mushy, and his engine roared. He skidded to a stop outside the school's entrance. Where was the security guard who usually stood guard? Was he helping students escape out the back door, or was he barricaded behind locked doors like the rest of them, waiting for the middle school to transform into a gas chamber?

Nathan's stomach tightened until it threatened to crush his organs. He unlatched his seatbelt and sprang from the vehicle in a movement perfected over years as a street cop. He bolted for the front door.

The drones buzzed down the building, their engines sounding like Weedwackers ready to lop off the heads of innocent children.

The drones simultaneously descended, dropping altitude fast. Did a single operator fly both? Thumping rotors filled the air. Nathan had no time to contact the administration. He had to stop them.

And he had to do it now.

He broke right and raced along the building to intercept the drone—a running back charging up the sideline. Faces of boys and girls pressed against classroom windows. Damn them for adhering to protocol and sheltering in place. Didn't they understand? Hadn't they watched the news? These drones would turn that school into a toxic wasteland.

Nathan sprinted past dozens of children. The drones dropped low over the lawn.

He brushed his blazer back and wrapped his fingers around the textured grip of his Glock. His thumb broke open the snap, and he drew with a fluid motion.

The drones slowed, transforming from airplanes to helicopters. As they closed, their details came into focus. These weren't civilian toys bought online but serious military grade weapons of war. Besides the bulbous tanks, each drone had metal rods with drums affixed to their hulls. Not tubes—gun barrels.

That's how they planned to pierce the school's outer shell. Were their projectiles packed with poison or meant to shatter the windows? Or were they designed to take out anyone who opposed them?

He silenced the alarm bells in his head and dismissed his fear. He'd give his life for his daughter. He'd risk it for any of the children inside.

Nathan waved at the drones to draw their attention. If they fired at him, at least they wouldn't be shooting at the school. Maybe not the best plan, but it didn't matter, because the drone operators ignored him.

The craft descended fifty feet over the grass and slipped along the building's façade, searching. He'd been right. They targeted Amelia's classroom.

Nathan stopped, his heart thundering from adrenaline and exertion. He raised his Glock and pressed his hands together to create a stable platform. His gun sights bobbed with each respiration. Decatur Elementary School lay under a mile from the capital in a dense urban environment. He couldn't miss. Any bullet that wasn't stopped by the drone's body would land in a heavily populated area and could kill an innocent civilian.

But he had no choice.

Both drones yawed and slowed to a hover.

He had to act.

Nathan aligned his front sight with the first drone. At fifty feet high and forty yards away, they looked like the postage-stamp-sized targets he'd shot at Quantico so many years ago. He dropped his index finger onto the trigger and took up the slack. Only a few pounds of pressure would discharge a round.

He stopped breathing, but his thumping heart made his sights float. He aimed at the drone's hull and focused on it until his target turned hazy in the background. He locked his arms, and his sights made tiny figure eights in the air.

He squeezed the trigger.

Bang.

The bullet smashed into the drone, sending pieces of black plastic fluttering into the air. Nathan recentered his sights. His pulse pounded in his neck. He pulled the trigger again. Another single shot.

His round nicked a rotor on the drone's starboard side. The rotor flopped around, and the drone turned in a tight circle. A wounded bird. The aircraft rose then dropped. It canted left, the turned right. It rotated faster, out of control.

If it crashed, would it release its toxic load? No time to worry about that.

Thud, thud, thud, thud . . .

The gun on the second drone barked to life with puffs of smoke. Rounds shattered glass on the first-floor classroom windows.

Amelia's classroom.

Nathan's throat clenched. He aimed at the drone and double-tapped. At least one round connected, and a piece of the fuselage broke off.

The drone slipped to starboard but continued firing.

Nathan tracked it as the first drone flashed in his peripheral vision and spun into the playground a hundred yards away. A cloud of maroon powder billowed into the air.

He'd worry about that later.

The second drone peppered the building with bullets, spraying wildly as its operator tried to control it. Nathan dropped his muzzle and aimed just below diving aircraft. He double-tapped again. Hunks of plastic splintered, but its gun kept firing.

Red smoke seeped out of its rear nozzle—a cloud of death.

Missing didn't matter anymore. Nathan opened up, and his bullets smashed into the drone. Hunks of metal flew off. The drone jerked, and its gun silenced as the craft rolled onto its side.

It dropped sideways in an uncontrolled dive. It exploded in a mangled pile twenty yards from the building.

A cherry cloud seeped out of the wreckage, and the toxic vapor danced on the wind.

Nathan held his breath and prayed it wouldn't drift into the shattered windows. The heavy vapor turned the dying grass bloodred.

Nathan bolted for the front entrance.

81

Nathan yanked on the school's glass door. Locked. He tried the next, but they'd secured it too. Instinct urged him to kick it in or shoot his way through it, but paternal fear drove those impulses. He took a breath then holstered and rapped his knuckles on the door.

Nothing.

He cupped his hands against the window and peered inside. A young security guard peeked out of the administrative office. He looked familiar, and he'd probably seen Nathan at school before, but his eye widened with terror.

Nathan took out his credentials and slapped his badge against the glass. "FBI. Open up."

The officer exited the office and approached Nathan, resting his hand on his gun. He had to be in his twenties, but he looked young enough to be a high school student. He fumbled with a dozen keys hanging off a chain attached to his belt before he found the right one. His wide eyes, pale skin, and twitchy movements indicated he balanced on the verge of panic.

He opened the door, and Nathan stepped inside. "Special Agent Nathan Burke, FBI. We're under a WMD attack, and we—"

"WMD?"

"The drones are down, but they dumped gas and powder all over the east lawn. Evacuate everyone to the north end of the school but keep them inside. The wind could blow the toxin anywhere."

The guard's eyes widened. "Toxin?"

"Some kind of aerosolized poison, probably carfentanil. Call 911 and report a HAZMAT situation, then get the kids going. Nobody approaches the school without Level A protection. Have them roll ambulances with plenty of naloxone. We may have injured kids inside."

"I don't understand."

"The gas in those drones is an opioid. One whiff and you'll go down."

The officer looked over Nathan's shoulder and out the front doors. He could barely hold himself together. Of all the emergencies he'd envisioned happening, this had probably never occurred to him. No way his training prepared him for a drone gas attack. His nametag read "Officer Jenkins."

"Jenkins, how many officers are on duty?"

Jenkins looked around and licked his lips.

Nathan lowered his face close. "Jenkins, you've got to focus."

Jenkins looked at him. "Just me."

Nathan would have asked for his first name to establish a closer bond, but he needed Jenkins to think of himself as an officer, not a person with vulnerabilities. He needed to be objective and professional. They both did.

"Get the principal on the PA and order the staff to shut every door and window and wedge towels or clothing under the doors."

"The policy's for them to barricade in place, but if there's gas, shouldn't we get them out and—"

"Nobody leaves. Not with that shit blowing in the air. Do it now."

Amelia.

Had Lily heeded his warning or followed protocol and stayed inside? Nathan started down the hallway.

"Where you going?"

"To find my daughter's classroom."

Nathan sprinted toward her classroom. He ripped off his jacket as he did and tied it around his head like a mask. It wouldn't be very effective, but something was better than nothing—and becoming a victim wouldn't help Amelia.

Nathan raced passes tiny blue lockers with three-digit combination locks then turned right past the auditorium. His footsteps echoed down empty hallways as he zipped passed closed classroom doors. Not a voice reached his ears, as if the building had been abandoned.

Eerie.

He veered down the long hallway that followed the east wing, his eyes locked on the teacher nameplates affixed beside each door.

There.

He stopped and tried the handle. Locked. He peered through the narrow vertical window. The classroom was empty.

Nathan's heart imploded. Where was Amelia? Had they retreated to a common room or escaped out the back? He turned to leave then hesitated. The room had been locked from the inside.

He pressed his face against the glass.

Nathan pounded on the door. "Ms. Batchelder? Lily?"

Her head popped up from behind her desk. She'd been hiding, but where were the children? Outside, red gas buffeted on the wind, twirling and wafting—a ballet of death.

Lily extricated herself from the desk, hurried across the room, and opened the door.

"Mr. Burke, thank God."

"Where's my daughter?" Panic seeped into his voice. He'd kept his cool during shootings and battles to the death, but a threat to Amelia amplified everything and made it personal.

The supply cubby in back opened, and Amelia pushed through the throng of children hiding inside.

"Daddy," she screamed as she ran to me.

He swept her into his arms. "Thank you, thank you, thank you," he muttered in prayer.

"What's happening?" Lily asked.

"Opioid gas attack. That poison is everywhere outside. Keep the kids in here and—"

Two white vans screeched into the driveway and skidded to a stop. Their doors opened and armed men climbed out wearing a mismatched HAZMAT gear and carrying long guns. Not cops—terrorists.

They headed for the school.

"Oh, my God," Lily said. "What are they . . . they're not . . . are they coming for the children?"

"Some of them," Nathan said. "They're here for politicians' families. They're searching for Maria and Teddy. And Amelia. They either want hostages, or they plan to murder them. Get the kids moving."

"Out the back?"

"If you go outside, you risk exposure. The gas is everywhere."

"They have guns."

"Take them into the basement and hide as best you can. Keep everyone quiet and wait for rescue."

Eight carbine-wielding terrorists moved across the driveway toward the school's front door. They didn't rush in their HAZMAT gear, and somehow, their deliberate movements seemed more menacing. They knew they'd have little resistance.

Did the men have photos of the students belonging to politicians, or did they plan to kill all the children? Terrorism sowed seeds of fear, and killing people's children did that better than anything.

A chill passed through him.

"Get the children into the basement," Nathan said. "Now."

He stepped into the hall and held his gun at the low ready. Lily escorted the children out of the room behind him, and he shielded them with his body. He should use the classroom doorframe for cover, but no man would hide behind cover while innocent children entered the fatal funnel.

The children whispered loudly in bursts of curiosity and fear as their little shoes clip-clopped on the tiled floor. A tug on his shirt from behind, and he glanced down. Amelia looked up at him.

"I'll wait with you, Daddy."

Nathan's heart ached. What bravery. He'd never been prouder of her. But she'd never been in more danger.

"Go with Ms. Batchelder," Nathan said. "Stick close to her."

"But, Daddy—"

"There's no time. Follow her into the basement and wait for me."

"You're not coming with us?"

"I have to deal with this."

Amelia's lower lip quivered, but she pivoted and scampered off after her classmates. Despite her worry, she trusted him to survive.

Let's hope she's right.

An image of Amelia and Reagan standing over his grave flashed in his mind. His core cooled. He would not make Amelia an orphan.

Nathan dialed 911.

"911, what's your emergency" the operator asked.

"This is FBI Special Agent Nathan Burke. We've got armed men storming the Stephen Decatur Elementary School. We need emergency response."

"Yes, sir, we're responding to the toxic gas report."

Officer Jenkins must have called it in, or a teacher watching from a window had decided to act.

"You don't understand," Nathan said. "There is a toxic cloud of something outside, probably carfentanil, but armed jihadists in HAZMAT gear are entering the school. I think they're targeting senators' children."

"Sir, how do you know these men are jihadists if they're wearing—"

"I don't have time for this," Nathan said. "Get a SWAT team here now."

"Sir, officers cannot approach a HAZMAT spill. They'll cordon off—"

"A school shooting requires a rapid response. Tell officers to make entry from the rear to avoid the powder on the front lawn."

"Sir, I, uh, you and the children must remain inside until the toxic materials are cleaned. Wait for—"

"You've got to be shitting me. Put out the call about the armed insurgents and let the officers do what they do best." Nathan hung up and pocketed his phone.

Lily opened a heavy fire door in the hall, and the children climbed downstairs to the lower level. Nathan watched the corner where the threat would materialize. The men should have reached the entrance already, and if they meant to kill indiscriminately, he'd intercept them—but not until Amelia and her high-profile classmates had concealed themselves downstairs.

He checked their progress. The last six children waited for their turn on the stairs. They edged forward.

Close enough.

Nathan moved down the corridor with his Glock at the high-ready position and his finger on the slide.

Crack, crack, crack.

Gunfire from the direction of the entryway.

Nathan exploded into a sprint.

82

Nathan sprinted down the hall, looking over his bobbing gun sights. He'd heard three rifle shots and then nothing. Poor Jenkins. If those bullets had been for the kid, he hadn't popped off a shot.

Sirens wailed in the distance. If the 911 operator had reported the armed men, officers would push their vehicles to the limit to reach the school. When criminals threatened children, cops put their lives on the line.

Patrol cars would arrive soon. The jihadists weren't dumb, and they'd understand that too. So why had the shooting stopped? Occupied classrooms filled the two hallways between the lobby and Nathan. Maybe they weren't killing indiscriminately. Hope filled his chest.

Amelia. He deflated. The killers were coming for Amelia and her friends.

Nathan slowed as he neared the main corridor. Rubber boots slapped the tile nearby. The swishing of HAZMAT suits grew louder.

Nathan knelt on one knee and extended his arms into an isosceles shooting stance. He bent at the waist and edged around the corner.

Terrorists in HAZMAT suits headed toward him. Five feet away, the closest man's eyes widened in surprise behind his foggy face mask.

Nathan dropped his finger to the trigger and punched his gun toward the man's chest. He fired three times.

The man jerked sideways and dropped his AK-47. The terrorists behind him broke left and right. They had training.

The hallway erupted with discharging weapons. Bullets ricocheted off the tile and gouged trails along the brick walls.

Nathan ducked back behind cover and sprayed bullets down the hallway to slow their advance.

He sprang to his feet and bolted toward the fire door leading to the basement. He pumped his knees high as he closed the sixty feet.

Shouts echoed behind him. The terrorists had been close to the corner. If they fired around it, they'd have him dead. Thirty yards was an easy shot with a carbine, even at a moving target, especially when they didn't mind what their bullets struck.

Nathan slowed and canted his body. He fired at the empty intersection with the other hallway. Suppressing fire might make them hesitate.

He dashed toward the fire door.

Crack.

A round smacked off the wall above him, sending chips of cement slicing through the air. A pain seared his eye and jammed it shut. Debris or shrapnel?

Nathan swung his barrel around. The shooter stood in the hall, exposed, and a second man stepped around the corner.

Nathan fired again and again.

The first man went down, and his carbine clanked against the tile. His compatriot dove back behind the wall as Nathan's slide locked back.

Empty.

He dropped his empty magazine and slammed in a full one—his last. He glanced down the hallway, another twenty yards to go—he'd never make it—and nowhere else to go except restrooms and four more classrooms, probably filled with cowering children. If he ran into any of those rooms, he'd end up shooting it out with a dozen children behind him.

Nightmare.

Nathan fired a single round at the corner then yanked open the fire door and jetted down the steps to the basement.

He jumped into a wide hallway with concrete walls illuminated by stark LED lights. Closed metal doors leading to janitorial closets, supply rooms, and other support functions lined the corridor leading toward the building's front. Nathan followed an orange stripe that ran down the center of the floor, then he stopped. Where would a sheltered elementary school teacher take a bunch of terrified children? Instinct honed from 70,000 years of running from predators would drive her away from the threat. And the bad guys had come in the front door.

He turned and headed down a short hall where double doors led into the workshop. He'd toured the space when he first scoped out the school for Amelia. If the kids hid in there, maybe they'd stay safe long enough for him to slip outside and come up behind the terrorists.

Nathan cranked the handle and shoved the door open. A little girl screamed. The children huddled behind a woodworking lathe, and Lily held out a hammer out like a sword. Nathan's urge to protect them filled him with resolve. He'd been born to protect people.

"They're coming," Nathan said.

Lily lowered the hammer, but her eyes remained frozen with fear. "We've got to escape." She pointed at the exit.

Nathan jogged to the door. Sunlight filtered in through a small window with reinforced metal. Outside, a riding lawn mower sat on a tiny patch of pavement, and the playground lay beyond it.

"It's dangerous," he said. "Could be contaminated."

A heavy door slammed open somewhere in the hallway, and boots thumped down the stairs. The terrorists had heard the stairwell door close, and they were coming.

The children stared at him, terrified.

Time to act.

Nathan looked from the closed double doors to the exit behind him. He could make a stand there. The police had to be minutes away, if they'd come at all. No matter how brave and well-intentioned the responding officers, the opioid spill posed a deadly threat to rescuers. If they tried to race into the building, they may end up collapsing on the lawn before getting inside.

But the back of the school should be clear—in theory.

He scanned the room. A pile of lumber was stacked four feet high in the corner. "They're hunting for Maria and Teddy, and maybe Amelia. Those kids will come with me, and you stay with everyone else. Duck behind that pile of wood and stay quiet."

"What'll you do?" Lily asked.

"We're making a run for it, and getting the kids they're targeting off of the X."

"We'll go with you."

"There's no way we'll make it with everyone, and they're not after you. If they wanted to shoot everyone, they'd be doing it now. Their actions confirm they're here for a purpose. "

"How will you get away?"

"We'll sneak out the back."

"They'll see you."

"Then at least we'll lead them away from the school. Maybe we can reach the responding police units before they catch us."

"But, Daddy," Amelia said, "what about the poison gas?"

He clasped her face in his hands. "We can't stay here. This is our chance to draw evil men out of the school. Don't you want to save everyone?"

Amelia bit her lip and nodded.

"Hide the kids now," Nathan told Lily.

He grabbed Amelia's hand and led the three children to the door. He inhaled and flung it open.

"Get ready to run."

83

Nathan had run low on ammunition, hope, and options, and if opioid gas tainted the yard, Nathan, Amelia, Maria, and Teddy would die. If they stayed in the school, they'd die. His Glock's last magazine of .40 ammo would be no match for at least eight ISIS killers carrying rifles. The terrorists were coming for the three children with him. They hunted the children of the political class and knew where to find them.

The kids only had Nathan to protect them.

He sniffed the air. Nothing. If the opioid gas was present, he'd collapse. He moved across the pavement outside the workshop with Amelia, Teddy, and Maria on his heels.

Nathan glanced both ways, but the service area lay in a shallow depression, concealing most of the east and west wings of the building. Dozens of sirens wailed from around the neighborhood.

Had the terrorists set a perimeter?

"Wait here," Nathan said.

The children looked at him wide-eyed. Teddy cried.

He climbed the slight incline with his Glock at the low, ready in case he tripped. The browning lawn behind the western wing was vacant. He spun and faced east, moving his gun in concert with his head. No one there either. He glanced up at the building, but the sky reflected off its windows. No sign of students, teachers, or terrorists.

"C'mon." He motioned for the kids to follow.

"Where?" Amelia asked.

The jihadists would reach the shop any minute, so they had to hurry, but moving across an open field would be suicide if the Phantoms spotted them.

"That way," he said, pointing east. "Stay close to the building in case they look out a window."

Nathan moved fast, hugging the wall, but he slowed and peeked into each window before passing them. The basement consisted mostly of storage and maintenance, but the Phantoms would search everything, hounding them. The children stayed close, like bear cubs following their mother. He wanted to scoop them into his hands, hug them and tell them everything would be all right, but even he didn't believe that.

Crack.

A bullet pierced the air. Nathan whirled around. A Phantom wearing a HAZMAT suit stood at the far corner of the west wing holding his carbine awkwardly.

Crack, crack.

"Run," Nathan yelled.

He hustled east, shielding the kids with his body. Bullets snapped past. Hitting a moving target at that distance wasn't easy, and the bulky HAZMAT suit made it harder, but the shots would summon every terrorist.

He turned and fired three rounds at the man. The shooter ducked—which was the point, because Nathan had no chance of hitting him.

He caught up with the kids as they reached the end of the building. He opened his mouth to tell them to wait before they raced around the corner, but a round sent a puff of dirt into the air at his feet. A bullet would eventually find its mark. He sprinted ahead and rounded the corner with his finger on the trigger.

No bad guys.

Now out of the line of sight, the children slowed around him, but more terrorists would arrive soon. He watched the opposite corner. The drones had crashed on that side, and if the wind blew the wrong way, they'd be in trouble.

"Where are we going?" Amelia asked.

"No more hiding. We need to escape."

Seventeenth Street peeked through a stand of trees. The police should be close. If he could get the kids to safety, he could lead officers back inside the building. When they saw him unaffected by the gas, they'd follow. Cops were brave.

"This way." He guided them into a small copse of maple trees. Soft moss squished under their feet, silencing their footfalls. He stopped at the curb across from the Congressional Cemetery. No cars, no pedestrians, nothing.

He stepped onto the pavement.

Blue and red lights flashed in the distance where the police blocked traffic in both directions. They stayed away, having learned their lesson from the emergency responders who'd fallen at the previous chemical attacks.

Nathan waved his arms to get their attention. What if they mistook him for a terrorist?

"Let's go meet the cops?" he said.

Gunfire erupted from behind them, and a fusillade of bullets snapped branches off trees. Six jihadists marched toward them, shooting as they moved.

They'd shred Nathan and the kids with lead before he could reach the police.

"Get into the cemetery and take cover."

84

Bullets thwacked into trees and stray rounds buzzed through the air above them. Nathan aimed in their direction to return fire, but his bullets wouldn't make it through the trees, so he lowered his Glock. He needed to conserve ammo.

"Zigzag," he said.

Nathan ushered the children toward the cemetery. Amelia and Maria needed little encouragement, zigging and zagging their way across the street. Teddy did his best to keep up, huffing and puffing—his face red and sweaty. Nathan kept himself between the kids and the shooters.

Their gunfire tapered off then stopped, their futility apparent, given the trees.

The children scampered across the pavement and up a grassy incline to five-foot-high brick wall that enclosed the historic cemetery.

Police waited behind patrol vehicles that blocked the intersection 300 yards away. The cops probably couldn't see what was happening without binoculars, but they certainly heard the gunfire. A school shooting with chemical warfare—a nightmare scenario.

Nathan grabbed Amelia under her arms and hoisted her up. She landed on her hands and knees atop the wall, like a cat. The girl's athleticism gave her a real advantage. Nathan hoisted Maria up, and she clutched the top as Amelia dropped into the cemetery. He tried to lift Teddy, but the dumpy kid weighed too much. Nathan interlaced his fingers.

"Step up."

Sweat streaked down Teddy's cheeks, and terror glazed his eyes. "It's too high."

"Move."

Teddy put his hands on Nathan's shoulders and stepped into the hand. Nathan strained, and his shoulder screamed. He bit his lip as sweat broke out on his forehead.

Teddy belly-flopped on top of the wall and gripped the brick as if he'd fall to his death.

Nathan glanced down the street. No response from the police. They must have been under orders to keep their distance. They'd come eventually—but would they arrive too late to save them?

Shadows moved from the school through the woods. The terrorists advanced. Once they cleared the wood line, they'd open up.

Nathan holstered and leapt onto the wall. He grasped the top and swung his leg over. Teddy struggled beside him. Nathan grabbed the kid's shirt and lowered him onto the grass.

Teddy toppled onto his butt. Amelia looked at him and shook her head. She had the same look in her eyes Reagan often gave Nathan.

Nathan jumped off the wall and landed hard beside Teddy. Gravestones, from tiny monuments to flat markers, covered the ground between bushes and trees. The cemetery stretched for five city blocks.

He peeked back over the wall. Three terrorists fanned out, two pointing up and down the road, while a third came straight for him. They'd shed their HAZMAT gear and moved nimbly, like predators. More shadows flickered behind them. Specters in the woods. He'd been right about the Phantoms wanting the senators' children—and Amelia. At least he'd drawn them away from the school.

"Here they come," Nathan said. "Let's go."

Nathan ducked as the first round smacked into the wall, sending pieces of mortar into the air. He hunched at the waist and corralled the kids around him.

Most of the gravestones in this section of the cemetery only stood waist high—not much concealment or cover—but a marble structure stood forty yards away.

"Head for the mausoleum," Nathan said.

"The what?" Teddy asked.

Nathan pointed. "The little brick house."

Teddy's forehead wrinkled, but he followed the girls across the lawn, past dozens of graves. The shooting stopped behind him, which meant the Phantoms were coming fast. Nathan kept his head beneath the rim of the wall and scuttled after the kids.

Halfway across, he looked back. A rifle appeared atop the wall, then a terrorist climbed after it.

They'd never make it to the mausoleum.

He had to give the kids time to get away. He stopped and faced their tormentors. He unsnapped his Glock.

The first man dropped onto the grass, and two more climbed the wall behind him. The man on the ground crouched and raised his rifle.

Nathan knelt and locked his elbows in an isosceles stance. He aimed at the man's chest—a long shot, but not impossible. He pulled the trigger. The Glock recoiled from the shot, and its slide locked back. Out of ammo.

"Dad?"

Nathan spun around. Amelia, Maria, and Teddy stood a few yards away and gawked at him. Why hadn't they kept going?

"Get behind cover," Nathan yelled.

A rifle shot echoed over the cemetery. Nathan yanked Amelia to the ground and shuffled behind an obelisk. Maria and Teddy ducked behind gravestones.

The sun cast long shadows, making it harder for the Phantoms to see them, but they'd all be dead before dark, unless they could hide until help arrived.

He peeked around the marker. Two terrorists moved to the sides, and the third came straight for him. More killers climbed the wall behind them.

Where were the police?

Amelia stared up at him with trembling lips, but she seemed more concerned about him than herself. Maybe she'd inherited his guardian gene or whatever evolutionary influence made him risk himself to save the weak.

"What do we do?" she asked.

"We'll dash stone to stone. Run past a few then crouch down, catch your breath, then sprint again. Stay low and move fast. You ready?"

She nodded.

The Phantoms closed the distance. He rolled onto the balls of his feet.

"Go."

85

Nathan sprinted through the cemetery behind Amelia, Maria, and Teddy as bullets winged off stones around them. The terrorists ran faster than the kids, and they drew close. They'd catch them soon.

Amelia and Maria reached the brick mausoleum with Teddy staggering behind. Nathan had been fleeing all day, and he tired of running. But he'd run out of ammunition, and the Phantoms outnumbered him. Shadows slid past stones on either side of them as the net closed. A figure slipped around a tree, twenty yards ahead. The Phantoms had circled them.

They were trapped.

The rotors of a police helicopter thumped overhead, and its spotlight illuminated the cemetery in the evening twilight. If only Nathan had reached the cemetery after dark, they could've hidden, or if they'd slipped out the back of the school before the lookout had spotted them, or . . . so many variables. He sighed. Like baseball, life was a game of inches.

Fuck these guys.

Nathan gathered the kids. He pointed to tall grave markers adorned with potted flowers. "Hide behind those stones, and don't come out, no matter what you hear."

Nathan knelt beside the black iron gate on the mausoleum. Dark figures moved through the surrounding stones, tightening the noose. He flicked open his blade and jammed it into the space between the lock and the brick. He applied pressure and pried the bolt back. The gate creaked open.

The louder the better.

Nathan pulled the gate open wide and looked inside. Three cement vaults lined the walls. If he opened one, maybe they could conceal themselves in—

A twig snapped nearby.

Nathan stepped to the corner of the mausoleum and pressed his back against the marble. Soft footfalls crunched the earth. The man knew his targets hid nearby, but he approached from the south and did not have an angle to see Nathan pry the door open.

The muzzle of an AK-47 poked out around the mausoleum only a foot away.

Rookie mistake.

Nathan grabbed the barrel with his left hand and yanked it toward him. The movement pulled the terrorist forward, exposing his head.

Nathan jabbed with his knife. The six-inch blade penetrated the skin over the man's temple and punctured his skull with a pop. The steel buried into his head as the man's momentum carried him forward. His feet stopped moving, and he toppled face first. Nathan held on to the barrel and his knife and rode him into the grass.

The man squirmed beneath him. A groan escaped his lips. Blood ran over Nathan's knuckles.

Nathan twisted the knife and plucked it out. The terrorist fell silent. He lay still.

Nathan wiped blood and brain matter on his leg and pocketed the knife.

A bullet ricocheted off the mausoleum as the shot thundered through the cemetery.

Nathan ducked and twisted the carbine out of the dead man's hands. He dove over his body and rolled behind a stone. The shot had been fired from near the school, but the Phantoms were close.

He mounted the stock in the hollow between his pectoral muscle and his shoulder. His thumb found the safety, but it was already disengaged. Nathan popped up from behind the stone.

A Phantom with an AR-15 stood twenty feet away and aimed at the mausoleum's open gate.

Nathan depressed the AK-47's trigger and held it to release a burst, but only a single round came out. A single-action weapon. He reset the trigger and fired again, but his first round had hit the man square in the chest, and he tumbled backward with a scream.

More men came from the west and north. Bullets stippled the earth around him and gouged chunks out of the gravestone.

He ducked behind it. They'd use their overwhelming firepower to close the distance. He had to flee, but he could leave the kids who were hiding somewhere close. He had to fight. For them.

The shooting stopped.

Nathan inhaled a breath. Possibly his last. He leaned around the stone, laid his sights over the closest man, and fired.

The man yelped and crumpled on the ground.

Nathan swung toward the next man and pulled the trigger.

Click.

The gun ran dry, and the sound of his hammer falling on an empty chamber filled the silence. They heard it too.

The nearest man peeked over a stone. He swept his rifle back and forth, then stood. He knew Nathan had no ammunition. They all did. The others stood too. They approached with their muzzles raised.

Looking down the barrel of a rifle raised the hair on Nathan's neck. Had the kids slipped away? Nathan glanced behind him. Maria and Teddy huddled together a few feet away. They seemed frozen with fear. Where was Amelia?

The men leered as they approached. They aimed their rifles at his chest.

Everything slowed down. Nathan had no options. He had to charge them. Maybe the surprise move would give the children enough time to escape. If they decided to flee. He was going to die. They all were.

Nathan exploded out of his crouch and sprinted toward the men.

Gunfire filled the night air.

The closest man jerked and stumbled as if punched. The head of the man beside him exploded like a smashed pumpkin. Others turned away from Nathan and toward the gunfire.

But too late.

They fell beneath the gunfire and lay still.

The acrid odor of gunpowder tingled his nose. Nathan gawked at the bodies of the men who'd been about to murder him. Had the police arrived?

A shadowy figure stepped out from behind a stone—the same the man who'd cut off the escape to the east and trapped them. He approached with an AK-47 mounted against his shoulder. He stepped into the light.

Hamid.

Nathan froze. He was unarmed, and his daughter and classmates hid nearby—all of them vulnerable and at the mercy of this monster.

But Hamid ignored him and walked over to the Phantoms' bodies. He stepped over them and then turned to Nathan. They locked eyes.

"Why did you do that?" Nathan asked.

Hamid opened his mouth. "I . . ." He shook his head. He bit his lip. "I have awakened from a dream. A nightmare."

"What are you saying?"

Hamid looked at the ground. "I was . . . wrong. What became of me? I'm sorry."

Rage filled Nathan. "You're sorry? You murdered innocent people. You killed women and children. You ruined lives. You—"

A shot rang out.

Hamid arched his back, and his face twisted in pain. He dropped his carbine and collapsed to his knees. He looked at Nathan, pleading. Sorrowful.

He fell face first onto the grass.

Behind him, a man wearing a blood-red taqiyah moved into the open.

86

Stabbing pain crackled through my chest and waves of agony flashed up and down my spine. It hurt, but I didn't care. I deserved to suffer. The brown grass smelled like paper, and the odor of dirt filled my lungs. I would die there, in a cemetery. How fitting.

What had I become? What had I done? How had my hatred consumed me? It had to be *Iblīs,* an evil spirit taking possession of me. How else could I have committed such acts?

But the Americans had taken my wife and child. They abandoned me. They forsake all Afghans, their allies, the people who trusted them. They deserved to feel the loss—a flicker of anger tingled my core. I pushed the darkness back into the depths where it belonged.

At least I saved the girl.

The world darkened. No sound reached my ears. This was it. The end.

I stood in a white field with a glowing, warm light at the end of a tunnel. How had I arrived there?

Farzana and Tara waited for me. Tara smiled. They held out their hands to me, beckoning.

I clasped their warm palms in mine, and they led me into the light.

87

The taqiyah-clad Phantom stared at Hamid and smirked, then he met Nathan's eyes. He looked . . . triumphant. He sidestepped over a body and moved to Hamid, keeping his eyes on Nathan. He looked down at Hamid and spat on his body.

"He was not a true believer," the man said in perfect English. "He never was. I saw his false piousness. Following him was a mistake. I knew it from the beginning."

In the distance, silhouettes glided through the cemetery. The police approached. If Nathan could stall, maybe they'd have a chance.

"Who are you?" Nathan asked.

"Allah's warrior, a servant of Mohammad."

"You killed your leader."

"I follow Allah."

"Your men are dead. It's over."

The man sneered, hatred contorting his face into an ugly fist. The monster inside him revealed itself. "It won't end until our caliphate controls the world, until all men prostrate themselves before Allah."

What consumed these men? They brought death and misery wherever they went. "This isn't the way," Nathan said. "Violence only invites destruction."

"I welcome it."

Metal clinked against something near the street, and the man noticed the approaching police. He turned back and set his jaw. He knew their time was up. He aimed his carbine at Nathan's chest.

"You will learn the error of your ways," he said. "It's time for you to meet Allah and answer for your devotion to a false God. Prepare to suffer eternally."

Nathan glanced at a dead jihadist crumpled against a headstone, twenty feet away. His weapon—an old hunting rifle—lay at his feet. Too far, but what choice did Nathan have? He looked down the barrel of the carbine and prepared to run.

Something flashed through Nathan's field of vision, and he flinched.

Thwack.

It struck the jihadist in the face, like a line drive. His body went limp, and the carbine dropped from his hands. He collapsed, and his head collided with a gravestone with a sickening *thunk*. The pieces of a shattered flowerpot lay near his head.

Nathan turned. Amelia stood beside an obelisk, breathing hard. Defiant. She glared at the unconscious man.

Nathan ran forward and knelt on the killer's back. He placed two fingers on his carotid artery. His pulse felt rapid and thready. Amelia hadn't killed him, but the man wouldn't get up.

The helicopter illuminated them as police approached.

Nathan moved to Hamid and check his pulse too. Nothing. He was gone.

Amelia stood beside him. "Is he . . . ?"

Nathan nodded. "You saved my life."

She nodded.

He pulled her into a tight embrace. "You could have been killed."

"You told me I needed to be brave and take chances to win."

"You're your father's daughter."

88

Bridget continued to improve, and her doctors found no indication of brain damage. All indications pointed to a full recovery. Nathan had called and visited several times already, and she seemed like herself. He padded down the hospital corridor with a lightness in his step he hadn't felt since Bridget collapsed inside the Wells Fargo Center.

He paused outside Room 102 and knocked on the door. "Bridget, you awake?"

"Howahya?" she called from inside.

Nathan pushed open the door and leaned in. "You decent?"

"I won't be decent until I take a sudsy bath at home with a box of wine and wash off this hospital grime. I haven't had a real night's sleep since they admitted me."

He crossed the room to her bed. A few days ago, her IV stand had looked like hanging ivy, but now, only a single bag of saline dripped into her arm.

She stared at a soap opera and dug under the covers. "Can't find the damn clicker."

"How do your tests look?"

"All my labs are back to normal. They're discharging me tomorrow."

Nathan sat on the end of her bed and sighed with relief. He hadn't realized how much he'd suppressed his worry. "You coming back to work soon?"

"Not for a while, but yeah, you're stuck with me."

"I'll come early and drive you home."

"That's sweet, but my *fathah* and brothers are still here."

"They didn't go back to Boston?"

Bridget smiled. "Said they weren't leaving without me."

"Looks like you mean more to them than their department."

Her eyes misted. "Those chowderheads."

"Let's talk tomorrow."

"You heading back to the grind?"

"Still wrapping up loose ends. We think most of the Phantoms are dead or in custody, but a few slipped through the cracks. Hamid had support here, and it'll take us time to locate everyone involved."

"You gotta catch a breather."

"I'll stop when they do. Call me if you need anything."

Nathan winked at her and let himself out. He shut the door behind him, then stopped. Meili and Rahimya walked up the hallway, chatting.

"I'm not sure I like you guys talking," Nathan said. "Your last conversation could have ended in my medical discharge."

"We discussed that in the elevator," Meili said. "I told her you'll get your shoulder checked while you're on admin leave."

"I don't appreciate—"

Rahimya held up her hand. "You proved you're able to do your job when you saved those kids. If you need another surgery or rehab, do it now, and I promise you won't lose your job."

His shoulder ached the moment he thought about it. Amazing how his mind masked the pain. He needed to get his shoulder fixed.

"Fair enough," he said.

"How's our girl?" Rahimya asked.

"They'll discharge her tomorrow."

Rahimya smiled. "I'll tell her to take her time coming back. She's been through the wringer."

"I briefed her on my source meeting in Taiwan," Meili said.

"Scary," Rahimya said.

Nathan's stomach knotted. Meili had been meeting a Chinese national in a Taipei warehouse when her cover officer spotted countersurveillance. That wasn't unusual, but two thugs defeated a lock and slipped into the building carrying handguns. Meili had aborted the meeting, and thanks to her meticulous prior planning, both her team and the source had escaped.

"Next time," Nathan said, "I'm coming with you."

"You have enough to do wrapping up loose ends with your Phantoms investigation. Imam Qadir is still on the loose."

Nathan frowned. "It's the same case. The Slayer's carfentanil originated in China."

"Chinese labs made it," Rahimya said, "but did their government have a hand in fueling terrorism?"

"They know exactly what they're doing," Meili said. "They use drugs as a tool of warfare, just like directed-energy weapons."

"We should charge them," Nathan said.

"With what?"

Anger bubbled in Nathan's chest. Their job was to protect the country, yet they continued to be reactive. "Terrorism. Drug trafficking. Murder. Take your pick."

"We don't have proof the manufacturers knew the drugs would be used as weapons. Charging them would be like arresting a gun manufacturer for a street robbery or a car dealer for a drunk driving fatality."

"The Chinese allow labs to spew poison," Meili said.

"We can't prove it, and we have less implicating the CCCP than the drug traffickers."

Meili scrunched her face. "Not yet, but I've talked to my ASAC—"

"Mark Dalton?" Rahimya asked.

"That's right. I can't get any operation targeting the Chinese approved. That's why I went to meet that new source. Our group has been relegated to intelligence collection"—she stared at the floor— "like before the Havana attacks."

Anger built inside Nathan. Why did so many decision makers in the US government run cover for China? Was it because they were bureaucrats unwilling to make unpopular decisions, or was a fear of confrontation pushing them to appease hostile global actors?

Or were they driven by something more sinister?

"I want to focus our investigation on the Chinese source," Nathan said. "As bad as this was, my gut tells me it's just the beginning of something bigger."

Meili cleared her throat. "Before I aborted my meeting, my source claimed the government orchestrated these attacks."

"Is he in a position to know that kind of information?" Rahimya asked.

Meili nodded. She hadn't told Rahimya that her source was a woman.

"That's still not compelling evidence," Rahimya said, "especially if you're talking about a case with serious geopolitical implications."

"We're just beginning," Nathan said. "Chinese involvement will come out."

"Our latest data dump from FinCen pointed to Qatar financing the shipments," Rahimya said. "They laundered money through offshore accounts, but it came from the Middle East."

"That doesn't mean the trail ends there," Nathan said. "Give me the green light to target China. Whether we find transnational criminal groups or government involvement, I believe they helped plan this."

Rahimya shook her head. Was she aware she did that? "I need you focused on the bad guys we know. Islamists seek a worldwide caliphate. China isn't interested in that vision. They have their hands full with a Uyghur insurgency."

"It's hard to mount an insurgency from inside camps," Meili said. "But it's academic. My ASAC has us reined in."

Nathan rubbed his temples. The FBI should thank Meili for risking her life to develop intelligence, not worrying about uncovering Chinese complicity. "I need to pull this thread."

"I require more to shift focus," Rahimya said.

At least Rahimya's heart was in the right place. She had the eyes of the media and the entire Bureau on the Phantoms, so her reluctance to expand the investigation made sense.

"What else did your source say?" Nathan asked.

"Not much before those armed thugs ended our interview, and HQ ordered us home. I need more time."

Rahimya sighed and stared at Nathan. "Let's shelve these conspiracy theories and focus on tracking down the operatives who slipped through the cracks."

"We'll catch those animals," Nathan said, unable to contain his anger. "Then we're going to mobilize every resource the federal government has and capture or kill every monster who orchestrated the attacks."

Rahimya put her hand on his arm. "I appreciate your passion. But address the immediate threat first."

"It's . . . I'm worried," he said. "The targets the Phantoms chose exposed our weaknesses as a free society. They showed the world that low-tech operations are difficult to defend."

"They're diabolical," Rahimya said.

"Or the Chinese provided strategic direction. What if they did more than provide the opioids? What if this was an extension of their attempts to cripple us and—"

"We can't prove that."

"Chinese intentions are clear."

"You're saying they used the Phantoms as a tool?"

"The Chinese government wants to bring America to its knees, yet the attacks spread more terror than actual damage."

"Meaning?"

"They could have targeted infrastructure, political institutions, and our economy."

Meili nodded. "Maybe using ISIS to deliver carfentanil gave them deniability, less chance of starting a shooting war with us."

"Maybe, or . . ."

"What?" Rahimya asked

"This was only the first phase. What if the Chinese used the Phantoms to test our response?"

"You're saying it's not over?"

"This may only be the opening salvo. I sense something bigger is looming."

Rahimya smirked. "You're always fun to chat with. I'd call you a conspiracy nut if you weren't right so often."

"Let's hope I'm wrong."

"I'm going to spend some time with Bridget," Rahimya said. "See you back at the office." She entered the hospital room.

Meili rested her head on his chest and hugged him.

"I needed that," he said.

"How are you doing?" Meili asked. "I know you won't admit it, but you've exhibited some serious PTSD signs."

Nathan smiled. "I admit I was on edge, but wiping out the Phantoms brought me back. I slept like a baby last night."

"You cried yourself to sleep and wet the bed?"

"Funny. A weight's lifted off me."

"You do seem better . . . somehow. How does another shootout cure PTSD?"

Nathan scratched his head. "I wondered that too, but identifying Zabihullah and stopping the killing helped me turn the corner. When people were dying around me and I couldn't prevent it, I felt useless, like I wasn't fulfilling my telos."

"Aristotle?"

"More than that."

She raised her eyebrows. "Tell me."

"I focused my energy on catching the terrorists, but what I really needed was to protect Amelia. I feared people dying at the hands of the Phantoms, but my real terror came from the thought of orphaning Amelia."

"She has Reagan."

"I mean, leaving her without a father. I amplified that fear by worrying about her being killed. When we fought off those men in the cemetery, I faced my worst fears and survived."

"But she almost died. You both did."

Nathan nodded. "I saved her, and then she saved me. When she defended herself, I realized she'd be able to protect herself one day."

"She has your genes."

"An asset . . . and a liability."

Meili wrapped him in an embrace and pressed her lips against his. She broke the kiss and smiled. "I vote for *asset.* You're a good man."

That warmed him, but the wound in his heart from her reluctance to get serious remained. "Good enough to move in with us?"

Meili chewed her lip and looked down.

Nathan held his breath.

She met his stare with warm eyes. "I can leave a few things at your place. How about we start with spending the night and take it from there?"

He inflated. "Let's head to my place and make up for lost time."

The China Gambit
Nathan Burke Thrillers #3

The nation is crumbling from within, and one agent is the last line of defense.

A sting operation in Tampa to capture the elusive Chinese operative known as "Leopard" ends in chaos, forcing FBI Agent Nathan Burke and his boss, Meili Chan, to pursue a volatile lead to Macau. There, in the maze of glittering casinos and dark corners of China's southern coast, an enigmatic intelligence source delivers a chilling revelation: the Ministry of State Security's Second Bureau has embedded itself in the very fabric of American society—compromising politics, law enforcement, and beyond.

The situation turns explosive when a presidential nominee is assassinated, plunging Washington into turmoil and setting the stage for an unprecedented political crisis. As the country teeters on the edge, Ming Zhao, the ruthless director of the Second Bureau, accelerates his campaign of disintegration warfare. His strategy is as bold as it is deadly—arming radicals with weaponized opioids and fueling chaos across the United States.

But Zhao's ambitions come with a lethal cost. His operatives close in, targeting everyone Nathan cares about. With assassins lurking at every turn and trust becoming a scarce commodity, Nathan uncovers the terrifying scope of a conspiracy years in the making. As the clock ticks down, every step forward brings new risks—not just to Nathan and Meili, but to the nation itself.

ACKNOWLEDGMENTS

Writers need people in their corner, and my wife, Cynthia Farahat Higgins, has always encouraged me. She is my biggest fan, and I write all my books for her.

My parents, Nadya and James Higgins, sparked my imagination by reading me stories every night. They fostered my love of books. They provided love and security, and they've never stopped supporting my work.

Writers need a literary community, and I've been blessed to know so many wonderful authors. Thanks to International Thriller Writers, Sisters in Crime (Chessie and New England chapters), The Virginia Writers Club, the Northern Virginia Writers Club, and The Royal Writers Secret Society.

My wife and I own Elaine's restaurant in Old Town Alexandria's Historic District, and we've turned it into a literary salon. As a way to give back to the writing community, we offer free space to writers for them to celebrate their work. I interview almost 100 authors per year, and I've learned something from all of them. I hope they all keep writing.

I'm fortunate to have found an amazing publisher who believes in my writing. Thanks to Andrew Watts, Amber Hudock, Julia Hastings, Mo Metlen and the entire team at Severn River Publishing.

ABOUT THE AUTHOR

Jeffrey James Higgins, author of the Nathan Burke Thrillers, is a retired supervisory special agent who writes thrillers, short stories, scripts, creative nonfiction, and essays. He has wrestled a suicide bomber, fought the Taliban in combat, and chased terrorists across five continents. He received the Attorney General's Award for Exceptional Heroism and the DEA Award of Valor. Jeffrey has been interviewed by CNN, National Geographic, and The New York Times. He's a #1 Amazon bestselling author and has won numerous literary awards, including the Claymore Award, PenCraft's Best Fiction Book of 2022, and a Reader's Favorite Gold Medal. Jeffrey is an active member of the Authors Guild, The Virginia Writers Club, International Thriller Writers, Sisters in Crime, and the Royal Writers Secret Society. His first three thrillers are *Furious, Unseen,* and *The Forever Game.*

Sign up for the reader list at
severnriverbooks.com

Printed in the United States
by Baker & Taylor Publisher Services